Honoré de Balzac

The Cat and Battledore and Other Tales

ISBN/EAN: 9783337072445

Printed in Europe, USA, Canada, Australia, Japan

Cover: Foto ©Andreas Hilbeck / pixelio.de

More available books at **www.hansebooks.com**

Honoré de Balzac

The Cat and Battledore and Other Tales

THE

CAT AND BATTLEDORE,

And Other Tales,

BY

HONORE DE BALZAC.

TRANSLATED INTO ENGLISH BY

PHILIP KENT, B.A.,

TRINITY COLLEGE, CAMBRIDGE; BARRISTER OF THE INNER TEMPLE.

▶◆●◀

CHICAGO:

BELFORDS, CLARKE & CO.

1879.

THE CAT AND BATTLEDORE.

(La Maison Du Chat Qui Pelote.)

DEDICATED TO MADEMOISELLE MARIE DE MONTHEAU.

In the middle of the Rue St. Denis almost at the corner of the Rue du Petit Lion, there formerly stood one of those precious houses which render it easy for the historian, with the aid of analogy, to reproduce old Paris. The menacing walls of the rickety old building seemed to have been spattered with hiero-glyphics, for hieroglyphics is the only word that the watchful idler could apply to the X's and V's traced upon the facade by the horizontal or diagonal pieces of wood whose course was marked in the whitewash by small parallel chinks. It was obvious that the passage of the lightest vehicle would cause every one of these beams to tremble in its socket. The vener-able building was surmounted by a triangular roof of a kind of which very soon not a single example will be left in Paris. This roof, stained by the inclemency of a Parisian atmosphere, overhung the street to a distance of three feet, as much for the purpose of protecting the doorstep from rain-water, as for afford-ing cover to the wall of an attic with its sill-less window. This last storey was built of planks nailed one upon the other, like scales ; in order, doubtless, not to over-weight the frail erec-tion.

On a rainy morning in the month of March, a young man carefully wrapped in his mantle, was stationed under the pent-house of a shop opposite to the old dwelling, which he was scrut-inizing with all the enthusiasm of an archæologist. In truth this relic of the bourgeoisie of the sixteenth century, supplied the observer with more than one problem for solution. Each storey had its peculiarity ; in the first there were four long

narrow windows, closely packed, and having their lower por-
tions filled with wooden squares with the object of producing
that treacherous light, by whose aid a skilful shopkeeper lends
to his articles the particular shade desired by his customers.
The young man seemed to entertain a profound contempt for
this very necessary part of the house; his eyes did not rest
there, even for a moment.   The windows of the second storey
—whose blinds were raised so as to display through their
large panes of Bohemian glass, the small curtains of red
muslin—did not excite in him any deeper interest.   His attention was particularly directed to the third storey, to some humble windows whose roughly finished wooden frames would have
deserved a place in the School of Arts and Manufactures, as a
sample of the earliest French joining.   These windows were
glazed with little panes, so green that, but for his excellent
sight, the young man could not have seen the calico curtains
with their blue squares which concealed from the eyes of the
profane the mysteries of the apartment.   At times our watcher,
wearied by his fruitless observation, or by the silence in which
the house and the whole neighborhood were buried, bent his
gaze upon the lower parts of the house.   An involuntary smile
then formed itself upon his lips, as the shop, with its amalga-
mation of ridiculous objects once more met his gaze.   A formidable piece of wood laid horizontally upon four pillars,
which seemed to be bowed by the weight of the decrepid
dwelling, had been retouched with as many coats of different
colors as the cheek of any old duchess with layers of rouge.
In the centre of this large beam, which was delicately carved,
was to be seen an old picture representing THE CAT.

It was this picture that excited the amusement of the
young man.   But we must admit that the cleverest of modern
painters could not invent so comical a caricature.   The ani-
mal held in one of its front paws a racket, as big as itself, and
was raising itself upon its hind paws, to take aim at an enormous ball thrown back to it by a gentleman in an embroidered

coat. Designs, color, accessories and all were treated in such a manner as to give rise to the idea that the artist's intention was to make game of shopkeeper and passer-by. Time, by changing the appearance of this primitive picture, had rendered it still more grotesque by introducing a certain vagueness which might distu:b the conscientious idler. Thus the spotted tail of the cat was so cut out that it might be taken for a looker-on ; so big, so lofty, and so thick were the tails of our ancestors' cats. To the right of this picture, on an azure field, which only in part concealed the rottenness of the wood, the passer-by beheld the word *Guillaume*, and to the left *Successeure du Sieur Chevrel.* Sun and rain had destroyed the greater part of the gilt, which had been parsimoniously applied to the letters of this inscription, in which the *u's* stood for *v's*, and the *v's* for *u's* according to the laws of our ancient orthography. Here, with a view to taking down the pride of those who believe that the world grows cleverer from day to day, and that the charlatanism of modern times is unrivalled, it is fitting to point out, that these signs, whose etymology seems strange to many a Parisian shopkeeper, are the inanimate representations of living presentations, by aid of which our cunning ancestors had succeeded in attracting customers to their houses. Thus the Spinning Sow, the Green Monkey, &c., were caged animals whose skill surprised the passer-by, while their education demonstrated the patience of the tradesman of the fifteenth century. Such curiosities enriched their fortunate owners more speedily than the Providences, the Good Faiths, the God's graces, and the decapitations of St. John the Baptist, which are still to be seen in the Rue St. Denis.

However, our young man was assuredly not standing there to admire the cat, which a moment's careful notice would grave in the memory. He also had his singularities. His mantle, folded like the drapery of an ancient statue, did not hide his well-made shoes, which were the more noticeable amid the mud of Paris, in that he wore white silk stockings, whose stains bore

witness to his impatience. It was evident that he had just
left some ball or wedding, for he held a pair of white gloves in
his hand, and the disordered curls of his black hair lay scattered
on his shoulders, and displayed the Caracalla cut rendered
fashionable by the school of the painter David, as well as by
that passion for Greek and Roman fashions which marked the
early years of this century.   In spite of the noise made by certain market-gardeners, who set their horses at a gallop in order
to reach the central market betimes, the busy street was
wrapped in that silence whose magic is known only to those
who have wandered through the deserted city at those hours,
when its clatter, for a moment stilled, begins again to break
forth, and is heard in the distance, like the great murmur of
the sea.   This strange young man must have been as much an
object of curiosity to the shop folks of the Chat qui-pelote, as
the Chat-qui-pelote was to him.   A cravat of dazzling whiteness rendered his anxious face paler than in reality it was. The
fire, now sombre, now sparkling, cast by his dark eyes, harmonized with the strange contours of his face, and with his large
and many-folded mouth that narrowed when he smiled.   His
forehead now wrinkled by some acute disappointment, was
stamped with some fatality.   Is not the forehead the most pro-
phetic part of the face ? When the forehead of the stranger
expressed passion, the furrows which it formed inspired a kind
of terror by their vigorous developement ; yet when restored to
that repose which was so readily disturbed, this forehead dif-
fused around it a luminous grace which lent a certain charm to
a face in which joy and sorrow, love, anger, and disdain shone
forth so contagiously that the coldest could not escape being
impressed by it.

The stranger was in such a fretful mood at the moment
when the attic window was hastily opened, that he did not perceive three gladsome faces pink and white—but commonplace
as the figure-heads of Commerce to be found on certain monuments.   These three faces, to which the dormer window formed

a sort of frame, recalled the chubby faces of the cherubs scattered among the clouds that surround the *Père éternel*. The apprentices inhaled the exhalations of the street in a manner which proved how heated and mephitic was the atmosphere of their attic. After having pointed out the curious sentinel, the apprentice who seemed the most jovial of the three, disappeared and came back holding in his hand an instrument, whose unbending metal has recently been replaced by supple leather; then every face assumed a mischievous expression as they watched the loiterer whom they sprinkled with a fine white spray, whose odor clearly showed that the three chins had just been shaved. Standing on tiptoe and ensconsed in the back part of their attic, in order to enjoy the vexation of their victim, the three assistants ceased to laugh, when they observed the careless contempt with which the young man shook his mantle, and the profound disdain depicted on the countenance which he raised to the empty window. At that moment a white and delicate hand raised the lower part of one of the rude windows of the third storey, by means of one of those slides the tourniquet of which frequently drops without a warning the heavy window which it should secure. Then was the passer rewarded for his lengthy watch. A young girl's face, as fresh as one of those white cups that emboss the bosom of the lake with flowers, appeared, crowned with a ruche of crumpled muslin that gave the head an air of admirable innocence. The neck and shoulders, though covered with some brown material, could yet be seen, thanks to some slight interstices produced by the slumberer's movements. There was no expression of constraint either in the ingenuous face or in the calm eyes immortalized by anticipation in the sublime productions of Raphael. There were to be seen the selfsame grace, the selfsame tranquility which have become proverbial. Charming was the contrast between the youthful cheek on which sleep had produced the appearance of overflowing life, and the antique massive window with its rough outlines and black sill.

Like those flowers **of the daytime** which the morning finds with
the still unfolded tunic which the chilly night has closed, the
only half-awakened girl cast her **blue eyes** upon **the** neighboring roofs and **on the sky ;** but, in obedience to **a** kind of habit
they sank to the sombre regions **of the street, and** there at once
encountered those **of her** adorer. **Doubtless her** vanity was
wounded at being **seen in such** unfashionable **garb. So** she
suddenly drew back, the well-worn tourniquet **yielded, the** window came down with that rapidity which has **gained for this**
primitive invention of our ancestors an odious name, and the
vision disappeared. To that young man the brightest of the
morning stars seemed **to have** been suddenly hidden by a
cloud.

While these little events **were in** progress **the** heavy inside
shutters which reinforced the fragile casement of the shop of
the *Chat-qui-pelote* have been removed as if by magic. **The**
old knockered door was folded **back upon the** interior **wall of**
the house by a servant, seemingly contemporary with the sign,
who with trembling hand fastened to the door the scrap of
square cloth on which was embroidered in yellow silk the name
Guillaume, Successeur de Chevrel. More **than one** passer-by
would have been puzzled to discover the nature of the business
carried on by M. Guillaume. It was barely possible to distin-
guish through the thick iron bars which protected the exterior
of the shop, the brown calico-covered parcels numerous as a
shoal of herrings. **Spite of** the apparent simplicity of this
Gothic front, M. **Guillaume** was of all Parisian linen-drapers
the one whose warehouses were ever the best supplied, whose
connections were most widely spread, while his commercial
integrity was beyond suspicion. If any of his compeers entered
into a government contract without having **the** requisite quan-
tity of cloth, he was always **ready** to deliver **it to** them, however great might be the number of pieces tendered for. The
wily merchant knew a thousand ways of securing for himself
the greatest share of profit without being **driven** like them to

cringe or offer rich bribes to powerful patrons. If his compeers could pay him only in sound but somewhat long-dated bills, he referred them to his notary as an accommodating person, and thus made a double profit, thanks to this expedient, which gave rise among the shopkeepers of the Rue St. Denis to the proverbial saying "God preserve you from the notary of M. Guillaume, " meaning a heavy discount.

The old shopkeeper was to be found, as if by miracle, at the door of his shop at the moment when the servant withdrew; he gazed upon the Rue St. Denis, the neighboring shops and the sky, like a man who disembarking at Havre sees France once more after a long voyage.

Having satisfied himself that all was as it had been when he went to bed, he at length perceived the sentinel stranger, who in his turn contemplated the patriarch of drapery much as Humboldt must have examined the first electric gymnote that he saw in America. M. Guillaume wore ample breeches of black velvet, stockings, and square-toed shoes with silver buckles. His slightly stooping figure was clothed with a square-lapped, square-tailed, square-collared coat of greenish cloth, whose large white metal buttons were somewhat tarnished by wear. His grey hairs were so scrupulously smoothed and combed, and flattened down upon his yellow skull, as to make it look like a field in furrows. His small green eyes, which looked as if they had been pierced with a gimlet, gleamed beneath two arches, on which a faint red mark supplied the place of brows. Care had traced upon his forehead straight furrows, numerous as the creases in his coat. His pale face spoke of patience, commercial prudence, and that species of cunning cupidity which business requires. At the period of which I am speaking those old families, wherein the manners and fashion of dress distinctive of their calling, were preserved as precious traditions, were more frequently to be met with than now-a-days. There they were, in the midst of modern civilization, like relics of an antediluvian age, discovered in a quarry by some Cuvier.

The head of the Guillaume family, was just one of these notable guardians of old customs. You would catch him regretting the provost of the shopkeepers, and whenever he spoke of a decision of the tribunal of commerce, he always called it the sentence of the consuls. The earliest riser, doubtless in accordance with those ancient customs, of his household, he was awaiting with firm foot the advent of his clerks, ready to scold them in case of their being late. Those young disciples of Mercury knew of nothing so much to be dreaded as the silent activity with which their chief examined their faces and their movements on Monday morning, with an eye to the discovery of proofs and traces of their escapades. But at the present moment the old draper was not paying any attention whatever to his young apprentices; he was busy in discovering the motive of the anxiety which the young man in the mantle and silk stockings displayed by gazing first at the sign and then into the depths of the shop.

It was now much lighter, and the desk with its iron grill and curtains of old green silk, the desk which held the ponderous books, mute oracles of the house, was now visible.— The too inquiring stranger seemed to covet that little spot, and thence to take a plan of a lateral dining-room lighted by a window in the ceiling and affording the family during meal-time a ready view of the slightest incidents which might take place at the door of the shop. So great a passion for his abode seemed suspicious to a shopkeeper who had undergone the Maximum of 1793. It therefore very naturally occurred to M: Guillaume that that sinister countenance boded an attack upon the strong box of the Chat-qui-pelote. After having discreetly enjoyed the mute duel which took place between his employer and the stranger, the eldest of the clerks, seeing the young man cast a furtive glance at the windows of the third storey, ventured to place himself on the floor of the shop beside M. Guillaume. Then taking two steps into the street, the clerk looked up, and fancied he saw Mademoiselle Augustine Guil.

laume hastily withdraw from the window. Not relishing the
perspicacity of his chief clerk, the draper cast a side-glance at
him, but all at once the mutual fears which the stranger's
presence aroused in the mind of the shopkeeper and the
enamored clerk were soothed. The stranger hailed a cab
which was driving to some neighboring stand, and quickly took
his seat with an air of deceptive indifference. His departure
was not without its calming effects upon the minds of the other
clerks, who were far from easy, when on coming downstairs
they found the victim of their practical joke still on the spot.

" Well, gentlemen, what do you mean by sticking there
with your arms folded?" said M. Guillaume to his three
neophytes. " Why formerly, by Jove, when I was clerk to M.
Chevrel I should have examined two pieces of cloth by this
time."

" The sun must have risen earlier then," said the second
clerk, on whom this duty devolved. The old shopkeeper
could not forbear from smiling.

Although two of these three young men who had been confided to his care by their fathers, who were wealthy manu-
facturers at Louviers and Sedan, had nothing to do but to ask
and have four thousand pounds as soon as they should be old
enough to start upon their own account, Guillaume deemed it
his duty to keep them under the ferule of an antique depotism
quite unknown in our day, in the gay shops of modern times,
whose clerks want to be rich at thirty. Guillaume made his
clerks work like slaves. Between the three of them they
sufficed for all the demands of a business which would have
tried the metal of ten of those assistants whose luxurious tastes
swell the columns of the budgets of to-day.

No noise disturbed the peace of the staid old house, in which
the hinges seemed to be always oiled, and every piece of furniture, even the most trifling, showed that admirable neatness
which bespeaks the severest order and economy. Often and
often had the wag amused himself by inscribing on the gruyère

which was left to the mercy of the clerks at luncheon, and which they made a joke of saving, the date of its original admission. This pleasentry and others of a similar character sometimes raised a smile upon the features of M. Guillaume's youngest daughter, the pretty maiden who had just disappeared from the gaze of the enchanted stranger. Although each of the apprentices, even the eldest, paid a handsome sum for board, not one of them would have been bold enough to remain at his patron's table when dessert made its appearance. When Madame Guillaume talked of dressing the salad, these poor young fellows shuddered as they thought of the parsimony displayed by her prudent hands in dispensing the oil. It would never have entered their heads to stay out all night without having given long beforehand a plausible excuse for such an irregularity. Every Sunday two of the clerks took it in turn to accompany the Guillaume family to mass at St. Leu and to vespers. Mademoiselle Virginie and Meadmoiselle Augustine, chastely attired in print, took each the arm of one of the clerks, and walked before under the penetrating eyes of their mother, who brought up the rear of this family procession, accompanied by her husband drilled into the duty of carrying two large prayer books bound in black morocco. The second clerk had no salary. As for the one whom twelve years of perseverance and discretion had instructed in the secrets of the establishment, he received 32l. a year as compensation for his labor. On certain family high days and holidays he received certain presents (whose value consisted in the fact that they came through Madame Guillaume's dry and wrinkled hand); thread purses stuffed with cotton to exhibit the open work designs, braces, or a pair of silk stockings of the thickest kind. At times, though rarely, this first minister was allowed to share the diversions of the family, either excursions to the country, or when, after months of expectation, it was decided to exercise the right of commanding some long-forgotten piece, which taking a box confers. As for the other clerks, the barrier of respect which formerly separated a master-draper from his apprentices was so firmly erected between them and the old shopkeeper, that it would have been easier for them to steal a piece of cloth, than to disturb that august etiquette. This reserve may appear ridiculous to-day; but for all that, these old-fashioned houses were schools of morality and integrity. The masters *adopted* their apprentices. A young man's linen was looked after, mended, sometimes renewed, by the mistress of the house. Did one of the apprentices fall ill? He became the object of a thoroughly maternal care. Was the illness dangerous? The master scattered his money about in fees to the most celebrated doctors; for he did not undertake to look after the morals and education only of the young folks. If one of them of honorable character, encountered some misfortune, these old tradespeople knew how to appreciate the intelligence which he had displayed, nor did they hesitate to entrust the happiness of their daughters to one to whom they had long entrusted their fortune. Guillaume was one of these men of the olden times, and if he was not free from their absurdities, he possessed all their good qualities. Accordingly Joseph Lebas, his chief clerk, a portionless orphan, was in his ideal scheme, the future husband of Virginie, his eldest daughter. But Joseph did not share the symmetrical notions of his patron, who would not, for an empire, have married his second daughter before the first. The unhappy clerk felt that his heart was entirely wrapped up in Mademoiselle Augustine, the younger daughter. In order to justify this passion, which had secretly acquired strength, we must penetrate a little deeper into the springs of the absolute government that ruled the establishment of the old draper.

Guillaume had two daughters. The eldest, Mademoiselle Virginie, was the exact portrait of her mother. Madam Guillaume, the daughter of M. Chevrel, used to sit so upright upon the bench behind her counter, that she had more than once heard some wags bet that she was empaled there. Her long thin face showed signs of boundless sanctimoniousness.

Ungraceful in person, unengaging in manner, Madame Guillaume habitually adorned her head, which had weathered sixty winters, with a cap of inflexible design and trimmed with weepers like that of a widow. She was known to the whole neighborhood as "the messenger nun." Her language was concise, and her gestures recalled the jerky movements of a telegraph. Her eye, clear as that of a cat, seemed to seek revenge from every one for its owner's ugliness. Madamoiselle Virginie, who, like her younger sister, had been brought up under the domestic rule of her mother, was now twenty-eight. Her youth softened the ungraceful caste of countenance which her resemblance to her mother sometimes lent to her features; but the maternal strictness had endowed her with two great qualities which might serve as a set-off against all defects; she was gentle and patient. Her sister, Mademoiselle Augustine, was barely eighteen; she bore no likeness either to father or mother. She was one of those girls who, from the absence of all physical bonds between them and their parents, support the old maids' sayings that children are the gift of God. Augustine was small, or better to describe her, little; and so full of simplicity and grace that a man of the world could find no fault in her except that her gestures, and sometimes her attitudes, were somewhat common, and that she was not perfectly free from constraint. Her still and silent features were suffused with that transient melancholy which seizes all young girls who lack strength to oppose a mother's will. The plainness of their dress always prevented the two sisters from satisfying the innate coquetry of woman, except by displaying a luxury of neatness which became them admirably and introduced an admirable harmony between them and the shining counters and the shelves, cleansed by the old servant from every particle of dust, and the antique simplicity of all their surroundings.

Forced by their mode of life to seek the elements of happiness in unremitting toil, Augustine and Virginie had never given cause for aught but satisfaction to their mother, who congratulated herself in secret on the perfection of her daughters' characters. It is easy to imagine the results of the education which they had received. Brought up to business, accustomed to hear nought but discussions and calculations sombrely commercial; grammar, book-keeping, Jewish history, and Rajou's history of France, their only studies; their only reading, books approved by their mother; the ideas of the sisters were somewhat narrow. They had a perfect knowledge of housekeeping, were familiar with the prices of goods, understood the difficulty of making a fortune, were economical, and held in high esteem the qualities which go to make a man of business. Notwithstanding their father's wealth, they could darn a stocking as well as make a wreath; their mother often talked about teaching them cookery, in order that they might know how to order a dinner and scold a cook *secundum artem.* Ignorant of the pleasures of the world, and observing how placidly the exemplary lives of their parents glided on, they very seldom cast a glance beyond the precincts of the old paternal house, which was their mother's universe. The whole future of their terrestrial pleasures consisted in the social gatherings to which their family fête-days gave rise. When the large drawing-room on the second-floor was about to receive Madame Roguin, a Mademoiselle Chevrel fifteen years younger than her cousin and who wore diamonds, young Rabourdin, under-secretary in the Financial Department, Monsieur César Birotteau a rich perfumer and his wife, who went by the name of Madame César, Monsieur Camusot, the wealthiest silk merchant in the Rue des Bourdonnais, his father-in-law Monsieur Cardot, two or three old bankers, and some ladies of spotless virtue; the preparations necessitated by the manner in which the plate, the Saxony porcelain, the candles and the crystals were packed up, introduced some diversion into the monotonous existence of these three women. They trotted about and became as excited as a parcel of nuns when they are about to receive their bishop. And then, when

B

in the evening they were all three worn out with dusting, rubbing, and unpacking, Madame Guillaume would say to the girls as they helped her to undress, "We have done nothing to-day, my children." It would sometimes happen upon these solemn occasions that "the messenger nun" would allow dancing, and confine the boston whist and backgammon parties to her bedroom. Such a concession was regarded as a most unlooked-for piece of happiness, and caused a joy not less than that of going to the two or three grand carnival balls to which M. Guillaume duly conducted his daughters. And then once a year the honest draper gave an entertainment for which he spared no expense. The persons invited, however wealthy and fashionable they might be, took care to be present; for the most important houses in the neighborhood had recourse to the large fortune, vast credit, and matured experience of M. Guillaume. But the two girls of the worthy tradesman did not derive so much advantage as might be supposed from the instruction which the world offers to the young. The meanness of the dresses which they wore at these festivals (which by the way were carried to the profit and loss account of the house) made them feel ashamed. They had no particular turn for dancing, and their mother's watchful eye precluded them from holding with their partners any conversation beyond yes and no. Then the law of the old sign of the Chat-qui-pelote compelled them to go home at eleven o'clock, the very moment when the ball and festive meetings begin to grow animated. Thus their diversions, seemingly in conformity with the fortune of their father, often became insipid through circumstances connected with the habits and principles of the establishment.

As to the routine of their daily existence, a single observation will describe it. Madame Guillaume required her daughters to be dressed very early in the morning, to put in an appearance at the same hour every day, and subjected their employments to a monastic regularity. Chance, however, had given to Augustine a mind sufficiently elevated to feel the emptiness of such an existence. Her blue eyes would at times be raised as if to interrogate the depths of the dark staircase, and the damp warerooms; after having sounded that cloistral silence, she seemed as it were to listen to the confused revelations of that passionate existence which places sentiments on a higher level than things. At such moments her face would flush, her listless hand would drop the muslin on the polished oaken counter, and soon her mother's voice, which retained its native harshness even in its mildest tones, would be heard exclaiming,—

"Augustine, what are you thinking about, my treasure?"

It may be that "Hippolyte Comte de Douglas" and "Le Comte de Commingues," two novels recently discovered by Augustine in the chest of drawers of a cook recently dismissed by Madame Guillaume had contributed to the development of the young girl, who had positively devoured them during the long nights of the preceding winter.

These manifestations of vague desire, the sweet voice, the jasmine skin and blue eyes of Augustine had then kindled in the heart of poor Lebas a passion as violent as it was respectful. Through a very intelligible caprice Augustine did not feel the slightest penchant for the orphan; perhaps because she was unconscious that he loved her. On the other hand, the long legs, chestnut hair, large hands, and vigorous frame of the chief clerk had found a secret admirer in Mademoiselle Virginie, who, spite of her portion of £6,000, was not sought by any one. Nothing could be more natural than these two cross-purpose passions born amid the silence of that obscure counter, just as the violets bloom in the deep woods. The mute and constant observation which through a violent desire for diversion amid that unceasing toil and that religious calm, chained the eyes of these young people upon one another, was certain sooner or later to excite love. To have a face constantly before our eyes leads us to trace in it the feelings of the heart, and ends by obliterating its defects.

"At the rate at which this man is travelling," said M. Guillaume to himself as he read the first decree whereby Napoleon anticipated the classes of conscripts, "our daughters will soon be going on their knees to a sweetheart."

And from that day forward, grieved to the heart to see his daughter fading, the old shopkeeper remembered that he had married Mademoiselle Chevrel when their relative position was very much like that of Joseph Lebas and Virginie. It would be a capital stroke of business to get his daughter married, and at the same time discharge a sacred debt by bestowing on an orphan the benefits which he himself had formerly received at the hands of his predecessors, under similar circumstances.

Joseph Lebas however was thirty-three years of age, and was turning over in his mind the difficulties which a disparity of fifteen years would place between Augustine and him. He was, moreover, too clear sighted not to guess the intention of M. Guillaume, and he was sufficiently well acquainted with his inexorable principles to know that the younger sister would never be allowed to marry until the elder was settled. Thus, then, the poor clerk whose heart was as noble as his legs were long, and his chest deep, suffered in silence.

Such was the condition of affairs in this small republic, which, while situated in the middle of the Rue St. Denis, bore a close resemblance to a chapel of ease of La Trappe.

But in order to give an exact account of the external situation of affairs as well as of the internal feelings, we must go back to some months before the opening scene of the story.

It was nightfall when a young man passing before the dimly-lighted shop of the Chat-qui-pelote, stood still for a moment to contemplate a picture which would have arrested the attention of any painter in the world. The shop, as yet unilluminated, formed a black foreground, behind which was to be seen the shopkeeper's dining-room, over which an astral lamp was flinging that yellow light which gives so much grace to pictures belonging to the Dutch school. The white table-linen, the plate and the cut glasses formed brilliant accessories to the scene, which was still further enhanced by the keen contrast of light and shade. The face of the father of the family, that of his wife, the countenances of the clerks, and the pure outlines of the features of Augustine, close to whom stood a strapping red-faced servant-girl, all these together formed a group so striking; the heads were so original, and each character was so frankly expressed on the features; while the peaceful, quiet, modest life of the family was so clearly to be gathered from the scene; that an artist accustomed to paint from nature might well experience a desperate desire to reproduce the chance-begotten picture.

The passenger whose gaze was thus arrested was a young painter who seven years before had gained the grand prize for painting.

He had just returned from Rome. His soul that had been fed on poetry, his eyes that had been satiated with Raphael and Michael Angelo, thirsted for genuine nature after his long sojourn in that land of pomp, over every part of which Art has thrown her majesty. False or not, such was his personal feeling on the subject. His heart that had been long abandoned to the torrent of Italy's impetuous passion, thirsted for one of those modest and retiring maidens which at Rome he had, unfortunately, found only upon canvas.

From the enthusiasm to which the natural group he gazed on gave rise in his excited breast, he passed by a natural transition to a profound admiration for the principal figure. Augustine seemed pensive and was not eating; owing to the situation of the lamp, whose light fell full upon her face, her whole bust seemed to move in a circle of flame, which brought out more fully the contours of her head and lighted it up in a manner almost supernatural. Involuntarily the artist compared her to an angel bethinking herself of the heaven from which she had been banished. A sensation almost unknown before— a limpid boiling passion deluged his bosom.

After remaining for a moment almost crushed beneath the weight of his ideas, he tore himself away from the scene of his enjoyment and went home—but not to eat and not to sleep. The next day he shut himself in his studio and there remained until he had deposited on canvas the main scene whose memory had well-nigh turned him into a fanatic. His happiness was imperfect so long as he was without a faithful portrait of his idol. Several times did he pass before the Chat-qui-pelote; once or twice he even had the hardihood to enter the shop in disguise in order to obtain a nearer view of the enchanting creature whom Madame Guillaume covered with her wing. During eight months, slave of his love and of his brushes, he remained invisible to his most intimate friends; the world, poetry, the drama, music and all his cherished habits, were forgotten.

One morning, Girodet broke through all the impediments to admission which artists know and can ellude, burst in on him and roused him with the question, "What are you going to exhibit?"

The artist seized his friend's hand, dragged him to the studio and uncovered a little easel picture and a portrait.

Girodet, after a slow but eager contemplation of the two masterpieces, threw his arms round his comrade's neck, and silently embraced him. His feelings could not be expressed, save, as he experienced them, from heart to heart.

"You are in love?" said Girodet.

They both knew that the finest portraits of Titian, Raphael, and Leonardo da Vinci were the offspring of excited feelings, which, under varying conditions, are the source of every kind of masterpiece. The young artist replied to the interrogation only by a movement of the head.

"Happy mortal, to be in love here after returning from Italy! I would not advise you," added the great painter, "to exhibit such works as these ; for, look you, these two pictures will not be understood. These true colors, this prodigious labor cannot as yet be appreciated ; the public are not accustomed to so much depth. The pictures which we paint, my good friend, are fire-screens and door-screens. Yes, let us rather write verses and translate the ancients, we shall reap more glory from that than from our miserable pictures."

In spite of this charitable advice the pictures were exhibited. The picture representing the interior created a revolution in painting. It gave rise to those pictures of " genre " which, to judge from the prodigious number of them imported into all our exhibitions, must, one would imagine, be produced by a purely mechanical process. As for the portrait, very few artists can have forgotten that living canvas to which the public, which is occasionally just, as a body, assigned the crown that Girodet himself had awarded. The two pictures were surrounded by an immense crowd. There was a death struggle to get to them, as the women say. Enterprising purchasers and aristocratic magnates covered the pictures with double Napoleons, but the artist resolutely refused to sell them or to make copies of them. He was offered an enormous sum for permission to engrave them, but the men of business were as unsuccessful as the amateurs had been.

Now, although this adventure engaged the attention of the world, it was not of a kind to penetrate to the little Thebais of the Rue St. Denis. Yet it so happened that the notary's wife, during a visit to Madame Guillaume, mentioned the exhibition in the presence of Augustine, of whom she was very fond, and explained to her its object. The chatter of Madame Roguin naturally inspired Augustine with the desire to see the pictures, and the boldness to ask her cousin in secret to take her to the Louvre. The cousin succeeded in the negotiation which she set on foot in order to obtain Madame Guillaume's consent to withdraw her young cousin from her melancholy toils for about two hours, and so the young girl made her way through the crowd and reached the prize picture. She trembled like a birch leaf when she recognized her own likeness. She was frightened, and looked round in order to find her way back to Madame Roguin, from whom she was seperated by a crowd of people. At that moment her frightened eyes encountered the excited face of the young painter. She at once recalled the features of a pedestrian whom in her curiosity she had often remarked, taking him for a new neighbor.

" You see what love has inspired me to do," whispered the artist to the timid creature, who was quite frightened at his words.

She summoned up a supernatural courage to pierce the crowd and rejoin her cousin, who was still busy trying to penetrate the mass of people, who kept her at a distance from the picture.

"You would be stifled if you got there," said Augustine. "Let us go."

But there are certain moments at the Exhibition when two women are not always at liberty to direct their steps in the galleries as they would. Madamoiselle Guillaume and her cousin were pushed to some little distance from the second picture by virtue of the irregular pressure of the crowd. As chance would have it, they found an easy access to the picture which fashion, for once in unison with the world of artists, had distinguished. The exclamation of surprise which escaped from the wife of the notary was lost among the hum and buzzing of the crowd ; but Augustine shed involuntary tears at sight of the marvelous scene. Then, actuated by an almost inexplicable sentiment, she placed her finger on her lips as she caught sight of the ecstatic face of the young artist within two feet of her. The stranger responded by a movement of the head and indicated that Madame Roguin was *de trop*, in order to show Augustine that she was understood. This pantomime was like a furnace to the young girl, who looked upon herself as a criminal at the idea that a compact had just been entered into between her and the artist. The stifling heat, the constant sight of the most brilliant costumes, and the stupefaction which Augustine experienced at the truth of the colours, the crowd of faces on canvas or alive, and the profusion of gilt frames, excited in the girl a species of intoxication which redoubled her apprehensions. She would perhaps have fainted, but that in spite of this chaos of sensations she felt in the depths of her heart a rising joy that gave fresh life to her whole frame. At the same time she believed that she was under the empire of that demon, of whose fearful snares she had heard from the thundering lips of the preacher. That moment was to her a moment of madness. She found herself escorted to the carriage of her aunt by the young painter, buoyant with happiness and love. An excitement altogether unknown, an intoxication which in some sort made her the prey of her natural feelings, led her to listen to the eloquent language of her heart, and several times she cast upon the young painter a glance in which was written all the emotion which she felt; never had the carnation of her cheek formed a more striking contrast with the whiteness of her skin. The artist then beheld her beauty in all its bloom, her modesty in all its glory. Augustine experienced a mingled sensation of joy and terror when she recognized that her presence was the source of the happiness of him whose name was on every lip and whose talent conferred immortality upon a transient image. She was beloved; there could be no doubt of that. When the artist was no longer in her presence, the simple words, "You see what love has inspired me to do," still found an echo in her heart, and its yet deeper palpitations seemed to her quite painful; so great were the unknown powers stirred within her by her now more ardent blood. She feigned a violent headache in order that she might avoid answering the questions of her cousin about the pictures; but when they got back to the house, Madame Roguin could not keep herself from speaking to Madame Guillaume of the celebrity which the Chat-qui-pelote had acquired, and Augustine trembled in every limb when she heard her mother announce her intention to go to the Exhibition to see her own house. The young girl renewed her complaints and was allowed to go to bed. " Yes, that is just what one gets by going to see these sights—headaches," said M. Guillaume ; " It is so very amusing to see on a piece of canvas what you can see every day in our street. Don't talk to me about your artists, they are just like your authors—starvation birds. Why the devil do they want to take my house and vilipend it in their pictures ? "

" It may lead to our selling a few more ells of cloth," said Joseph Lebas. But spite of this observation, art and thought were once again found guilty at the tribunal of commerce. It may well be supposed that such conversation as this did not greatly raise the hopes of Augustine, who, during the night resigned herself to her first love meditation. The events of the day were like a dream, which it pleased her to reproduce in thought. She underwent her apprenticeship to those fears, those hopes, and that remorse, to all those undulations of feeling, by which a heart so simple and so timid as hers must needs be swayed. What a void she now discovered in that dark dwelling ! what a treasure she discovered in her heart ! To be the wife of a man of talent, to share his glory ; what ravages must such a thought create in the heart of a child nurtured in the bosom of such a family ! What hopes did the idea awaken in a young woman who, educated as yet on vulgar principles, had nevertheless wished for a life of elegance. A ray of light had lighted up the prison, and all at once Augustine loved. In her case so many feelings were gratified at once that she succumbed without a single calculation. At the age of eighteen love throws its prism between the eyes of a young girl and the world. Without an inkling of the stern realities which result from the union of a loving woman with a man of imagination, she believed herself called upon to confer happiness on her artist, without perceiving any disparity between herself and him. To her the present was the whole future.

When, on the morrow, Augustine's father and mother returned from the Exhibition, their faces showed that they had sustained some disappointment. In the first place, the two pictures had been removed, and in the second, Madame Guillaume had lost her Cashmere shawl. When Augustine heard of the disappearance of the paintings, following her visit to the exhibition, she saw in it, that delicacy of sentiment which women always appreciate, even instinctively.

The morning on which, on his returning from a ball, Theodore de Sommervieux, for that was the name which renown had carried to Augustine's ear, was sprinkled by the clerks of the Chat-qui-pelote, as he waited for the appearance of his simple mistress, who certainly was unconscious of his presence, was the fourth occasion only, on which the two lovers had seen each other, since the scene which had taken place at the Exhibition. The obstacles which the *régime* of the Guillaume establishment opposed to the fiery temper of the artist, gave to his passion for Augustine a violence that may readily be imagined. How was it possible to accost a young girl seated at a counter between two such women as Virginie and Madame Guillaume? How could he correspond with her when her mother never left her? With that skill in creating imaginary troubles which every lover displays, Theodore made one of the clerks his rival, and made the others his accomplices. Could he deceive so many Arguses, he saw himself discovered by the severe eyes of the old shopkeeper and Madame Guillaume. Everywhere were barriers, everywhere despair. The very vehemence of the young painter's passion prevented him from hitting upon those ingenious expedients, which with prisoners as with lovers, seem to be the last effort of reason stirred by the savage thirst for liberty, or by the fire of love.

Theodore patrolled the neighborhood with the restlessness of a madman, as if motion might suggest devices. After

having thoroughly tortured his brain, it occurred to him to
bribe the blowsy servant.   Thus it happened that sundry
letters were exchanged at distant intervals during the fortnight
which followed the unlucky morning on which M. Guillaume
and Theodoré had examined each other with such minute
attention.

At the period at which our story has now arrived, the two
young people had agreed to see each other at a certain hour
every weekday, and on Sunday at St. Leu during mass and
vespers. Augustine had sent her beloved Theodore a list of the
relations and friends of the family ; andto these the young
painter tried to get introduced in order to engage, if possible,
in the interest of his love, one of these hearts to which money
and business were the be-all and the end-all, and a genuine
passion, a most monstrous, and a most unheard-of speculation.
For the rest, the habits of the inmates of the Chat-qui-pelote
had undergone no change.   If Augustine was preoccupied, if
in violation of all obedience to the law of the domestic charter,
she went up to her bedroom to establish, by means of a pot of
flowers, signals with her lover; if she sighed, if indeed she
thought, no one, not even her mother, noticed it.   This circumstance may cause some surprise to those who have seized
the pervading spirit of this house, where any idea tainted with
poetry must necessarily be in opposition to its inmates and its
furniture ; where no one could indulge in a gesture or a look
that were not seen and analyzed.   And yet nothing could be
more natural ; for the tranquil vessel which sailed the stormy
sea of the Exchange of Paris under the flag of the Chat-qui-
pelote, was at this time the prey of one of those gales which
from the periodicity of their return we may style equinoctial.
For the last five days the five men who constituted the crew,
Madame Guillaume and Mademoiselle Virginie, had been
engaged in that engrossing toil, which is called stock-taking.
Every package was turned over, and the measure of every
piece was taken, in order to ascertain the exact value of the

remnant. The ticket affixed to each parcel was carefully examined, in order to fix the date when the cloth was purchased. The exact price was determined. Ever on foot, with his ell-wand in his hand, M. Guillaume resembled a captain giving orders as to the conduct of the vessel. His shrill voice echoing through a loophole in interrogation of the deeps that lay beneath the hatchways of the lower shop, gave forth those barbarous commercial phrases which can only be expressed by enigmatic signs. " How much of H.N.Z. ? " " All gone." " What left of Q.X. ? " " Two ells." " What price ? " " Five five three " " Put all J.J., all M.P., and the residue of V.D.O. in three A. ; " and a thousand other phrases equally intelligible, rumbled over the counters, like the lines of some modern poem recited by the votaries of the Romantic School in order to keep alive their enthusiasm for one of their poets. In the evening Guillaume shut himself up with his chief clerk and his wife, paid accounts, carried them over, wrote to delinquents, and jotted up invoices. All three of them took part in the immense labor whose result contained in a simple sheet of foolscap—proved to the house of Guillaume that it was worth so much in cash, so much in goods, so much in drafts and bills ; that it did not owe a farthing ; that it was a creditor to the amoun of from four to eight thousand pounds ; that its capital had increased, and that its farms were to be increased, houses repaired, or rents doubled. Whence this obvious consequence—tha it was absolutely necessary to begin with redoubled ardour the task of piling crown on crown. Never did it occur to those brave ants to ask themselves the question —*Cui bono?*

Under cover of this annual commotion the happy Augustine escaped the scrutiny of her Arguses. At length one Saturday evening the stock-taking came to an end. The sum total of the credits showed a sufficient number of cyphers to induce M. Guillaume under the circumstances to suspend the severe restriction which reigned throughout the year—as to dessert.

The wily draper rubbed his hands and allowed his clerks to remain at table. Scarcely had each member of the crew finished his little glass of home-made liqueur when the roll of carriage-wheels was heard. The family was going to see Cinderella at the Variétés, while the two junior clerks received each a double crown piece, with permission to go where they liked, provided always that they were home by twelve o'clock.

In spite of this debauch, the old draper was busy at six o'clock next morning, shaving himself, incasing himself in his maroon-colored coat, from whose splendor he always derived the same amount of satisfaction, and fastening the golden buckles of his velvet breeches. At seven o'clock, while all was still silent throughout the house, he directed his steps to the little cabinet attached to his first floor shop. This cabinet was lighted by a window protected by strong iron bars, and looking on a little square court whose walls were so black that it looked like a well. The old tradesman opened with his own hand the iron-plated shutters which he knew so well, and raised one half of the glazed framework of the window. The chilly air of the court rushed in and cooled the heated atmosphere of the cabinet, which was redolent of that odor which is peculiar to offices. Upright he stood, with his hand resting on the greasy arm of a cane chair covered with morocco whose original color had disappeared. He seemed to hesitate about sitting down. As he looked at the bureau with its double desk, near which his wife's seat was placed in a little arch let into the wall, opposite to his own seat, his features softened. He looked at the numbered boxes, the bands, the utensils, the branding irons, and the cash box—objects of immemorial origin, and seemed to feel the shadowy presence of the deceased Chevrel. He pushed forward the very stool on which he used himself to sit in the presence of his departed patron. This tool, covered with black leather, and whose horsehair stuffing had long since been exposed though without actually escaping, he placed with trembling hand upon the very spot where his predecessor had placed it. Then with an agitation difficult to describe, he pulled the bell-rope which communicated with the bedhead of Joseph Lebas. When this decisive blow had been struck, the old man whose reminiscences were undoubtedly too overpowering, took up two or three bills of exchange which had been presented to him, and gazed at them, though without really seeing them, when Joseph Lebas suddenly appeared.

" Sit down there," said Guillaume, pointing to the stool.

As this was the first time that the old master-draper had ever made his clerk sit down in his presence, Joseph Lebas trembled.

" What do you think of these drafts ?" asked Guillaume.

" They won't be paid."

" Why ?"

" Oh, I heard that Etienne and Co. were paying in gold he day before yesterday "

" Ah, ah !" cried the draper ; " people must be very sick when they show their bile. Let us change the subject Joseph, the stock-taking is finished."

" Yes, sir, and the dividend is one of the best you ever had.'

" Don't use those newfangled words, say ' the product,' Joseph. Do you know, my lad, that it is in some measure to you that we owe these results ? which being so, I don't wish to pay you by salary any longer. Madame Guillaume has suggested to me the idea of offering you a share—there, Joseph ! Guillaume and Lebas won't sound badly as the name of a firm, will they ? We might add ' and company' to round the signature."

Tears stood in Joseph's eyes, but he made an effort to conceal them. " Ah, M. Guillaume ! what have I done to deserve such goodness ? I do only my duty. It was no slight matter fo you to take an interest in a poor orph—"

He began to brush the braid of his left sleeve with the right, and dared not look at the old man, who smiled at the thought that the modest youth, like himself in former days, required to be encouraged to render the explanation complete.

"But at the same time," resumed the father of Virginie, "you have no great title to this favor, Joseph. You are not so frank with me as I am with you." (At these words the clerk briskly raised his head.) "You know the secrets of the strong box. During the last two years I have told you nearly all my affairs. In short, I have concealed nothing from you. But as for you—you have a certain predilection, and have not said a single word to me about it." (Joseph Lebas blushed.) "Ah, ah!" cried Guillaume; "did you think you could deceive an old fox like me—me, who, to your knowledge, smelt the Lecocq failure?"

"What, sir," answered Joseph Lebas, examining his patron as carefully as his patron examined him, "you know whom I love?"

"I know all, you good-for-nothing fellow!" said the worthy and crafty tradesman, tweaking the end of Lebas' ear, "and I forgive you. I did just what you have done."

"And you will give her to me?"

"Yes, with a portion of £6000, and will leave you as much more, and we will embark upon fresh enterprises under a new firm. We will brew some more business yet, lad," cried the old shopkeeper, rising and flinging his arms about. "Look you, son-in-law, there is nothing like business. Those who want to know what pleasure one can find in it, are idiots. To be on the track of what is going on, to know how to take the lead on 'Change, to wait anxiously as if one were at the gaming-table, to see whether Étienne and Company turn bankrupt or not; to see a regiment of the imperial guard dressed in our cloth pass by, to trip up (in all honesty, be it understood) one's neighbor; to produce cheaper than others; to follow up a scheme from its first rough sketch—as it begins, grows, falters, and succeeds; to know, just like a minister of police, all the secret springs of commercial houses, in order not to take the wrong road, to keep one's feet when others go to wreck and ruin; to have correspondents in every manufacturing town:

isn't this a continual game, Joseph? That is what I call life. I shall die amid this bustle as old Chevrel did—but still taking things easily."

In the heat of the longest impromptu he had ever indulged in, Father Guillaume had scarcely looked at his clerk, who was shedding scalding tears, "Why, Joseph, my good lad, what is the matter?"

"Oh, I love her so dearly, M. Guillaume, that my heart fails me. I believe—"

"Well, my lad," said the tradesman, who was touched, "you are more lucky than you imagine, by Jove; for she loves you! I know it!" and he winked his small green eyes as he looked at his clerk.

"Mademoiselle Augustine, Mademoiselle Augustine!" cried Joseph Lebas, in his enthusiasm.

He was about to rush out of the cabinet, when he felt himself stopped by an arm of iron, and his astounded patron hastily placed him before him again.

"What has Augustine to do with this business?" asked Guillaume, in a voice which instantly froze the unfortunate Lebas.

"Is it not she . . . whom . . . I am in love with?" asked the stuttering clerk.

Guillaume, disconcerted at his own want of perspicacity, resumed his seat and placed his piriform head on his two hands, to reflect upon the strange position in which he found himself. Joseph Lebas, desperate and ashamed, remained upon his legs.

"Joseph," resumed the draper with frigid dignity, "I was talking to you about Virginie. Love cannot be commanded, I well know. I know your discretion, we will forget all that. I will never allow Augustine to marry before Virginie; your interest in the business will be ten per cent."

The clerk, inspired by love, with almost boundless courage and eloquence, clasped his hands, spoke up, and for a quarter of an hour discoursed with so much warmth and good feeling,

c

that the situation changed. If this had been a matter of business, the old trader would have had certain fixed rules to guide
him to a decision. But thrown as he was a thousand leagues
out of the domain of commerce, and afloat without compass
upon a sea of sentiment, he drifted irresolutely before an event
so original, as he termed it. Carried away by his fatherly
affection he spoke a little at random.

"What the devil, Joseph, you need not be told that I had
my two children at an interval of ten years. Mademoiselle
Chevrel was not handsome, but she has no reason to complain
of my conduct to her. Do as I did before you; give over
crying, and don't be stupid. What would you have? the
matter will perhaps be settled, there is always some way out
of a scrape. We men are not always like gingerbread to our
wives,—do you take me? Madame Guillaume is a little over-
religious, and—come my boy, give your arm to Augustine this
morning as you go to mass."

Such were the exclamations which Guillaume randomly
ejaculated. The conclusion with which they wound up threw
the enamoured youth into ecstasies. When he quitted the
smoky little cabinet, after having squeezed the hand of his
future father-in-law, and proclaimed with a little look of intelligence that all would turn out for the best, he was already plann-
ing a marriage between Mademoiselle Virginie and one of his
friends.

"What will Madame Guillaume think of it?" Such was
the idea that prodigiously tormented the worthy tradesman
when he found himself alone.

At breakfast Madame Guillaume and Virginie, whom the
draper had provisionally left in the dark as to his disappointment, looked very knowingly at Joseph Lebas, who displayed
grave embarrassment. The modesty of the clerk made a
favorable impression upon his mother-in-law. The matron
regained so much of her youthful gaiety that she smiled at M.
Guillaume, and indulged in some of those little pleasantries

which are so well established in these innocent households. She expressed a doubt about the relative heights of Virginie and Joseph, in order to get them to stand up together. This preliminary trifling produced some clouds upon the brow of the head of the family, and he even affected such a passion for decorum as to tell Augustine to take the chief clerk's arm as they went to St. Leu. Madame Guillaume, astonished at so much delicacy on the part of a man, honoured her husband with an approving nod. So the procession, so marshalled as to afford no ground for the mischevous interpretation of the neighbours, left the house.

"Don't you think, Mademoiselle Augustine," said the trembling clerk, "that the wife of a tradesman whose credit is staunch, of such a man as M. Guillaume for example, might allow herself a little more amusement than Madame Guillaume takes, might wear diamonds, keep a carriage? For my own part, if I married, I should like to take all the trouble on my own shoulders and see my wife enjoy herself. I should not put her in my counting-house. For, you see, in the cloth-trade, woman are not wanted as they were in former times. M. Guillaume was quite right to act as he did, and besides, it was his wife's desire. But it seems to me, that if a woman keeps her eye upon the book-keeping, the correspondence, the details of the business, the orders, and her own household affairs, that is all that could be expected. After seven o'clock, when the shop was closed, I, for my part, should amuse myself, go to the theatre, and see a little society. But you are not listening to me."

"Oh yes, I am, Mr. Joseph. What do you think of painting? is not that a good calling?"

"Yes, I know a house-painter in a large way of business—M. Lourdois, who has plenty of money."

Thus chattering the family reached the church of St. Leu.

There Madame Guillaume resumed her authority, and for the first time made Augustine sit beside her, while Virginie took the fourth seat beside **Lebas**.   During the sermon all went well between Augustine and Theodore, who, standing behind a pillar, prayed to his Madonna with **the utmost** fervour.   **But** at the **raising of the host, Madame Guillaume perceived, rather late in the day, that her daughter Augustine was holding her prayer-**book **upside down.   She was about to scold** her **vigorously,** when **lowering her veil, she took** her eyes **off her book, and began to gaze in** the direction affected by **her** daughter's eyes.

Aided by her spectacles she caught sight **of the** young artist, **whose mundane elegance seemed to** denote **him** some cavalry **captain on furlough, rather than a** tradesman of the district. **It is difficult to imagine the state of agitation into which Madame Guillaume was thrown by discovering this clandestine** love in Augustine's **heart.   She who flattered herself that** she had brought **her daughters up with the utmost propriety!** Her prudery **and** ignorance, led her **to magnify the danger. She** believed **her** daughter corrupted **to the very core.**

" Hold your book properly, **miss," she exclaimed in a low** tone, though **she was trembling with anger.   She** quickly snatched the **accusing** prayer-book **from her** daughter's hand **and** restored the letters **to their** natural **direction.**

" Don't make the mistake of raising **your eyes from** your **prayers," she** added, " otherwise you will **have** me **to deal** with. After mass your father and I will have **something to say to you."**

These words were like a thunderbolt **to poor** Augustine. **She felt herself fainting, but** between the **pain she** felt and **the fear of creating a scandal in the** church, **she found** courage **to con-**ceal her anguish.   **However,** it was easy **to** discern her **excite-**ment by the trembling of her prayer-book, and the tears which **she shed on each leaf she turned.**

From the indignant look **cast at him by** Madame Guillaume, **the** artist saw the perils that assailed **his** amour, and left the **church** with rage in his heart, and fired **with** the determination **to** dare everything.

" Go to your room, miss," said Madame Guillaume **to her**

daughter on their return to the house; "we will send for you; and take special care that you don't leave it."

The conference between husband and wife was so secret that not a jot of it transpired at first. Virginie, however, who had encouraged her sister by a thousand gentle suggestions, carried her *complaisance* so far as to steal to the door of her mother's bedroom, where the discussion was going on, in order to pick up some phrases. The first journey which she made from the third to the second storey, she heard her father exclaim,—

"Do you want to kill your child, then, madame?"

"My poor darling," said Virginie to her weeping sister, "papa is taking your part."

"And what do they mean to do to Theodore?" asked the simple creature.

The inquisitive Virginie then went down again. This time she stayed longer, and learned that Lebas was in love with Augustine. It was decreed that during this memorable day a house generally so calm should be a little hell. Monsieur Guillaume threw Lebas into despair by informing him of Augustine's love for a stranger. Lebas, who had instructed his friend to solicit the hand of Mademoiselle Virginie, thus saw all his castles in the air overthrown. Mademoiselle Virginie, overwhelmed at the news that Joseph Lebas had in a manner refused her, was seized with a headache. The dissension sown between the husband and wife by the explanation which had taken place between Monsieur and Madame Guillaume—the first occasion during their married life that had found them of different opinions—showed itself in a fashion truly terrible.

At length at four o'clock in the afternoon Augustine, pale, trembling, and red eyed, stood before her father and mother. Fortified by the address of her father, who had promised to listen to her in silence, she gathered a certain courage as she pronounced in presence of her parents the name of her dear

Theodore de Sommervieux, and cunningly emphasized its aristocratic particle. Yielding to the novel charm of speaking of her sentiments, she gained sufficient confidence to declare with an innocent firmness that she loved M. de Sommervieux, that she had written to him, and she added with tears in her eyes, "to sacrifice me to another would be to render me miserable."

"But, Augustine, you don't know what an artist is then," cried her mother in dismay.

"Madame Guillaume," said the old father, silencing his good lady,

"Augustine," he continued, "artists are, as a general rule, starvation birds. They are too extravagant to be other than ne'er-do-wells. The late M. Joseph Vernet, the late M. Lekain, and the late M. Noverre, were customers of mine. Oh, if you only knew what trick that M. Noverre, the Chevalier de St. Georges, and especially M. Phillidor, played poor dead daddy Chevrel. They are a droll set of fellows and no mistake They have all of them a way of talking—and manners—oh, as for your Monsieur de Sumer—Somm—"

"De Sommervieux, father."

"Well De Sommervieux then—he can never have made himself so agreeable to you as M le Chevalier de St. Georges was to me the day when I obtained a judgment of the consuls against him. Ah, they were people of quality in those days."

"Ah, but father, Monsieur Theodore is of noble blood, and he told me in one of his letters that he was rich, and that his father was called the Chevalier de St. Georges before the revolution."

At these words M Guillaume looked at his formidable better-half, who like a woman baulked of her will, beat the floor with her foot and maintained a frigid silence. She even averted her indignant gaze from Augustine, and seemed to leave all the responsibility of so grave a matter to M. Guillaume, since her warning was unheeded. Nevertheless, in spite of her seeming indifference, when she saw her husband making up his mind so easily on a matter out of the ordinary routine of business, she exclaimed,—

" Well, I must say that as regards your daughters, your weakness is—but—"

The noise of a carriage stopping at the door of the house, suddenly interrupted the lecture which the old shopkeeper was already dreading. In an instant Madame Roguin stood in the middle of the room, and looking at the three actors of this domestic scene, said with a patronizing air,—

" I know all that has happened, cousin." Madame Roguin had one fault ; she believed that the wife of a Parisian notary could play the part of a *petite-maîtresse.*

" I know all," she repeated, " and I am come to Noah's ark like the dove with the olive branch. I found that allegory in the ' Génie du Christianisme,' " said she, turning towards Madame Guillaume ; " the comparison ought to please you, cousin. Do you know," she added, smiling at Augustine, " that this Monsieur de Sommervieux is a charming man. This morning he presented me with my portrait painted in a masterly fashion. It is worth at least £240."

And so saying she tapped M. Guillaume's arm. The old tradesman pursed up his mouth in a manner peculiar to himself.

" I know M. de Sommervieux well," resumed *the dove.* " For the past fortnight he has attended my Soirées, of which he is the life. He has confided to me all his love difficulties and engaged me as his advocate. I learned this morning his admiration for Augustine, and he must have her. Oh, don't shake your head, cousin—but listen. They will make him a baron ; he has just been appointed a Chevalier of the Legion of Honor by the Emperor in person, at the Exhibition. Roguin is now his notary, and knows the position of his affairs. Well, M. de Sommervieux derives from good substantial acres nearly £500 a year. Are you aware that the father-in-law of a man like him may become a somebody; mayor of his arron-dissement, for example? Have you not seen M. Dupont made a count and senator of the empire on account of his having presented himself in his capacity of mayor to pay his respect to the Emperor on his entry into Vienna? Oh, the marriage will take place; for my part I adore the young fellow. His conduct towards Augustine is such as one meets with only in novels. Come, my darling, you will be happy and everybody will envy you. Why, the Duchess of Carogliano, who comes to my soirées, is fascinated with M. de Sommer-vieux. Some ill-natured people say that she only comes to my parties to meet *him*, as if a duchess of yesterday were out of place in the house of a Chevrel whose family can boast a hun-dred years of good *bourgeoisie*."

"Augustine," continued Madame Roguin after a little pause, "I have seen the portrait. In truth it is beautiful. Do you know that the Emperor wanted to see it? He said laughingly to the Vice-constable, that if there were many such women as that at his court while he had so many kings there, he would be pretty sure to keep Europe in perpetual peace. Isn't that flattering?" The storms which ushered in that day were des-tined to resemble those of nature in being followed by a calm. Madame Roguin brought into play so many seductions in her harangue, and touched at once so many strings in the dry bosoms of M. and Madame Guillaume, that she ended by find-ing one of which she made good use.

At this strange epoch of French history, bankers and men of business were more than ever infected with the wild craze of intermarrying with the aristocracy, and the generals of the empire turned the inclination to good account. M. Guillaume opposed with unusual strength the ill-starred mania. His cherished axioms were, that a woman, if she desired happiness, ought to marry a man in her own class; that one was sure to be punished sooner or later for trying to rise above one's sphere; that love stood the wear and tear of family life so badly that both parties, to have a chance of being happy, must possess very substantial qualities; that it was not well for either of the married couple to be more intelligent than the other, because the first requirement was a mutual understanding; if the husband talked Greek, while the wife spoke Latin, they ran the risk of dying of starvation. He had invented a sort of proverb on the subject. He compared marriages thus concluded to those old stuffs which were half silk and half wool; the silk always destroyed the wool in the long-run. So great, however, is the fund of vanity in the human heart, that the prudence of the pilot who steered the Chat-qui-pelote with such address yielded to the aggressive volubility of Madame Roguin. The rigid Madame Guillaume was the first to discover in her daughter's predilection reasons for departing from the principles which have been mentioned, and for permitting the visits of Monsieur de Sommervieux, whom, she internally resolved to subject to a searching scrutiny.

The old man of business went in quest of Joseph Lebas, and told him the position of affairs. At half-past six the dining-room on which the artist had conferred celebrity, united beneath its roof of glass, Madame and M. Rougin, the young painter and his charming Augustine, Joseph Lebas, who endured his good fortune with resignation, and Virginie, whose headache had disappeared. Monsieur and Madame Guillaume saw in perspective their children married and the destinies of the Chat-qui-pelote entrusted to skilful hands. Their contentment reached its acme when Theodore, at the dessert-table, presented them with the marvellous picture which they had been unable to see, and which represented the interior of the old shop that had given rise to so much happiness.

"It's very pretty," cried Guillaume. "Fancy offering £1,200 for that."

"Ah, it's because my weepers are in it," continued Madame Guillaume."

"And these unfolded stuffs," said Joseph Lebas; "one can almost feel them."

"Drapery always looks well in a picture," replied the painter. "We modern artists would be overjoyed if we could rival the perfection of antique drapery."

"Oh, if you go in for drapery, I am with you, my young friend. Since you have a respect for trade, we shall hit it off together; and why should people despise trade? The world sprang from trade since Adam sold Paradise for an apple. That wasn't a very good stroke of business though." And the old tradesman broke out into loud and unrestrained laughter, excited by the champagne which he circulated freely. The band which covered the eyes of the young artist was so thick, that he thought his parents, that were to be, quite agreeable. He did not disdain to move them by some lively sallies in perfectly good taste, and so made himself a general favorite. In the evening, when the company had left the drawing-room with its substantial furniture (to employ one of Guillaume's expressions), and while Madame Guillaume bustled about from table to mantelpiece and from chandelier to candlestick, hastily blowing out the waxlights, the worthy tradesman, who was always keen-sighted where business or money was in question, drew his daughter Augustine to his side, and taking her upon his knees, thus addressed her,—

"My dear child, you shall marry Sommervieux, since such is your desire. You have a right to risk your capital of happiness. But I am not to be caught by your £1,200 gained by spoiling good canvas; money earned so quickly goes as quickly. Didn't I hear the young madcap say this very evening that if money was round, it was made so, that it might roll. If money is round for spendthrifts, it is flat for the econonomical people who amass it. Now, child, this handsome spark of yours talks about letting you have carriages and jewels. He has money; if he chooses to spend it on you, *bene sit.* I have nothing to do with that; but as to what I give you, I don't want the crowns it has cost me so much trouble to get together, to be spent on carriages and trinkets. The man who spends too much is never rich. With the £6,000 that make your portion, you can't as yet buy the whole of Paris. You may some day receive a few thousands more; good. I will make you wait for them as long as possible. Well, I took your intended into a quiet corner, and the man who managed the Lecocq bankruptcy so skilfully did not experience much difficulty in getting an artist to consent to a marriage settlement protecting the wife's fortune. I will keep an eye upon the deed of settlement, to see that the money he proposes to settle on you is all right; come, my child, I hope soon to be a grandfather. I am already anxious to busy myself about my grandchildren; swear to me, then, here on the spot, never to sign any document relating to money without my advice, and that in case I go to join old father Chevrel too soon, you will consult young Lebas, your brother in-law; now promise me."

"Yes, father, I swear it."

At these words uttered in a gentle voice the old man kissed his daughter first on one cheek and then on the other. That night all the lovers slept almost as peacefully as M. and Madame Guillaume.

Some months after this memorable Sunday, the high altar at St. Leu witnessed two very different marriages. Augustine and Theodore presented themselves in all the glittering parade of happiness; their eyes overflowed with love; their toilettes were most elegant, while a dashing equipage awaited them. Virginie, accompanied by her family, came in a decent hackney carriage; and leaning on her father's arm and more simply attired, followed her younger sister like a shadow, necessary to complete the harmony of the picture. M. Guillaume had taken the utmost possible trouble to induce the clergy to marry Virginie before Augustine; but he had to undergo the mortification of seeing both the superior and inferior clergy address themselves in the first instance to the more elegant of the two brides. He

overheard some of the neighbors express marked approval of
the good sense of Mademoiselle Virginie, who was making, as
they said, the more solid marriage and remaining faithful to
the quarter, while they indulged in certain disparaging com-
ments, born of envy, upon Augustine, who was marrying an
artist and a nobleman. They added with a sort of horror, that
if the Guillaumes gave way to ambition, the drapery trade was
doomed. An old fan merchant, having remarked that that
spendthrift would very soon reduce Augustine to a bed of
straw, father Guillaume secretly congratulated himself on the
prudence which he had displayed in the provisions of the
marriage settlement.

In the evening after a sumptuous ball, followed by one of
those abundant suppers which in the present generation are
almost forgotten, M. and Madame Guillaume stayed at their
house in the Rue Colombier in which the marriage festivities
had been held ; M. and Madame Lebas returned in their hired
carriage to the old house in the Rue St. Denis, there to direct
the course of the good ship Chat-qui-pelote ; while the artist,
intoxicated with happiness, took his beloved Augustine in his
arms, and when their carriage reached the Rue des Trois
Frères, raised her quickly and carried her to a room which all
the arts had combined to embellish. The impetuous passion
with which Theodore was inspired continued for nearly one
whole rapid year, during which not the slightest cloud over-
shadowed the azure heaven under which they dwelt. With the
two lovers life had no burdens. Theodore surrounded each
passing day with incredible flourishes of happiness ; he took
pleasure in varying the transports of passion by that soft langour
of repose in which two souls are launched so far in ecstasy that
they seem to forget their bodily ties. The happy Augustine,
incapable of reflection, gave herself up to the rhythmical march
of her joy ; she did not feel that she did as much as was required of her by yielding entirely to the lawful and sanctified
love of marriage. In her artlessness and simplicity, moreover,

she was entirely ignorant of the coquetry of withholding her
favours and of the adroit caprices, whereby the young ladies of
high life secure an empire over their husbands.   She loved too
well, to indulge in calculations of the future, nor did it ever
enter her head that so delightful an existence could ever cease.
Happy then in being the source of all her husband's pleasures,
she believed that his inextinguishable love would ever be the
brightest of all her jewels, just as her devotion and obedience
would form an eternal attraction ; and moreover, the happiness
that waits on love had rendered her so radiant, that her beauty
inspired her with pride, and assured her of her continued power
to reign over a man so susceptible as M. de Sommervieux.
Thus her position as a wife taught her nothing but the mere
lessons of love. In the midst of her happiness she remained the
ignorant little girl who led an obscure existence in the
Rue St. Denis, and she did not think of acquiring the manners
the education, and the tone, of the world in which she was
called upon to live.   Her language being the language of love,
she displayed in the use of it a certain suppleness of intellect
and delicacy of expression, but then she was employing the
language which all women have in common, when plunged in
the passion which seems to be their element. If it came to
pass that Augustine gave vent to any ideas that jarred with
those of Theodore, the young artist laughed at them, as one
laughs at the first mistakes made by a foreigner, which nevertheless grow wearisome if he fails to correct them.   In spite of
such a fund of love, Sommervieux at the end of this all brief
and happy twelvemonth, felt the necessity of recurring to his
old labors and modes of life.   In addittion to this his wife was
enceinte. Thus he saw his friends once more.   During the
protracted sufferings of the year during which a young wife
suckles her first child, he worked, it is true, with ardor,
but he from time to time returned to seek some dis-
traction in society. The house which he most readily visited,
was that of the Duchess de Carigliano, who had at last suc-

ceeded in securing the celebrated artist as one of her habituès. When Augustine had regained her strength, and her son no longer needed the unremitting care which precludes a mother from entering into the gaieties of social life, Theodore had begun to desire that satisfaction which our self-love derives from appearing in society accompanied by a beautiful woman who is an object at once of envy and admiration. Augustine reaped a fresh harvest of pleasure in parading reception-room after reception-room, surrounded by the éclate conferred by her husband's fame, and in finding herself envied by other women. But this was the last ray shed by her married bliss. She began by wounding her husband's vanity, when, in spite of her fruitless efforts, she exposed her ignorance, the impropriety of her language, and the narrowness of her ideas. At the expiration of two years and a half the taming influence of the first transports of passion passed away; the character of De Sommervieux regained, as the satiety of lengthened possession set in, its original bent; and he returned to that course of life from which he had for a brief period deviated. Poetry, painting, the exquisite delights of the imagination, possess over elevated minds claims which no prescription can defeat. These claims of a powerful mind had not in Theodore's case been defeated during these two years. They had simply found fresh pasturage. When the fields of love were thoroughly explored, when, like some child, the artist had gathered roses and cornflowers with such avidity that his hands could hold no more, the scene changed. If he showed his wife the sketches of his most beautiful compositions, he would hear her exclaim just as her father Guillaume would have done, "That's very pretty."

This lukewarm admiration was not the result of internal convictions, but of faith *on word of love*. Augustine preferred one look to the most beautiful picture. The only sublime she recognized was that of the heart. In short, Theodore could not resist the proof of this cruel fact; his wife was not alive to poetry, she did not live in his world; she did not share his whims, his sudden inspirations, his joys and sorrows. Her food was on the solid earth of prosaic reality, while his head was in the skies. Ordinary minds cannot appreciate the constantly recurring sufferings of him, who, being united to another by the closest of all ties, is perpetually forced to trample down the most treasured flights of his fancy, and to annihilate the images which a magic power constrains him to create. In his case the torture is the more cruel in that the fundamental law of the feeling which he entertains towards his companion compels them to hide nothing from each other, and to share both the out-pour of the brain and of the heart. Not with impunity can we do violence to the dictates of nature; she is inexorable as fate, which indeed is a species of social nature.

Sommervieux sought refuge in the silence and the calm of his studio, while he nourished the hope, that the habit of living among artists might form his wife and develope in her those dormant germs of high intelligence which certain gifted spirits hold to be innate in every human being. But Augustine was too sincerely religious not to be alarmed at the tone assumed by artists. At the first dinner given by Theodore she heard a young painter say, with that childish levity which she could not discern, and which robs a joke of all its impiety, " Yes, madame, but your paradise is not more beautiful than the Transfiguration of Raphael, and yet I grew tired of looking at that ; " and thus it happened that Augustine encountered this witty society with a feeling of distrust which no one could fail to perceive. She prevented people from feeling themselves at their ease. Now artists suffering under such constraint are unmerciful; they resort either to flight or to ridicule. Madame Guillaume, among other absurdities in which she indulged, carried to a ridiculous extent the dignity which seemed to her the fitting appanage of a wife, and Augustine, often as she had laughed at it, could not entirely refrain from slightly imitating her mother's prudery. This exaggerated modesty, which

virtuous women do not always escape, gave rise to certain epigrams, in the shape of sketches, the gentle satire of which was
too much in accordance with the dictates of good taste to give
serious annoyance to De Sommervieux. Had they been far
more severe, they would have been merely reprisals inflicted on
him by his friends. But nothing could be more trivial to a
mind so susceptible to foreign impressions as Theodore's, and
thus a certain coolness gradually stole over him which could
not fail to grow. Connubial felicity is, as it were, situated on
the level but narrow summit of a hill, close to which lies a
steep and slippery decline, and the painter's passion was now
descending it. He deemed his wife incapable of appreciating
the moral considerations, which, in his own eyes, justified the
peculiarity of his conduct towards her, and held himself clear
of all blame in concealing from her, ideas which she could not
understand, and escapades which he held to be beyond the
cognizance of the tribunal of a bourgeois conscience. Augustine cloistered herself in calm and silent sorrow. These unex-
pressed feelings established between the husband and the wife
a veil which was doomed to grow thicker day by day. Augustine's husband was not wanting in politeness towards her; but
she could not observe without a shudder that he reserved for
the world those treasures of wit and grace which he formerly·
laid at her feet. She very soon began to give the most ominous
interpretation to those smart sayings as to the inconstancy of
men, in which society indulges. She did not give vent to any
reproaches, but the attitude which she assumed amounted to a
reproach.

Three years after marriage this pretty young woman, who
drove by so brilliant in her brilliant carriage, who was living in
an environment of glory and of wealth which made her an
object of envy to many thoughtless and undiscriminating persons, was a prey to violent grief. Her color faded; she reflected,
she compared; then she read by the light of misfortune the first
texts of experience. She resolved bravely to confine herself

within the circle of her duties, hoping that her generous conduct would sooner or later win back her husband's love. But
it was not so. When Sommervieux exhausted with labor left
his studio, Augustine did not manage to hide her work so
speedily, but that the painter could see that his wife was mend-
ing all the house-linen and her own, with all the minute attention of a good house-wife. She would produce generously and
without a murmur the money necessary to her husband's profusion ; but actuated by a desire to spare the fortune of her
dear Theodore, she exhibited a spirit of economy as regarded
herself and certain details of the domestic administration.
Such conduct is incompatible with the free and easy method
of artists, who, when their career terminates in ruin, have so
thoroughly enjoyed existence that they never inquire into the
cause of that ruin. It is useless to depict every shade of
degradation of colour as it invaded and finally involved in profound obscurity the brilliant tints of the honeymoon. One
evening the melancholy Augustine who, for some time past,
had heard her husband speaking in enthusiastic language of
the Duchess of Carigliano, received from a female friend certain mischievously charitable hints as to the nature of De
Sommervieux's attachment to that renowned coquette of the
imperial court. Augustine, who was only twenty-one and in
the full bloom of youth and beauty, found herself betrayed for
the sake of a woman of thirty-six. Feeling herself miserable in
the midst the world and its festivities, which were deserts to
her, the poor girl lost all consciousness of the admiration, and
the envy which she excited. Her face assumed a new expression. Melancholy shed upon her features the resignation and
the pallor of neglected love. The most seductive men did not
long delay to pay their court to her; but she remained solitary
and virtuous. Certain contemptuous phrases uttered by her
husband filled her with incredible despair. A sinister light
revealed to her the defective contact which, resulting from the
narrowness of her education, prevented the perfect union of her

D

mind with that of Theodore. She loved so well, that she
acquitted him and condemned herself. She wept tears of
blood; she discovered all too late that there are unequal mar_
riages in mind as well as in rank and manners. When she
reflected on the vernal ecstacies of her union, she measured
the extent of her vanished happiness and came to the conviction that so rich a harvest of love was equivalent to a whole
life, and could be purchased only by compensating misery.
Nevertheless she loved too sincerely to lose all hope; and so,
at the age of twenty-one, she began to educate herself and to
raise her imagination to a level worthy of that which she
admired so much. "If I am not a poet," she said to herself,
"I will at least understand poetry." And then putting forth
that force of will, that energy which all women possess when
they love, Madame de Sommervieux endeavored to change her
disposition, manners, and habits. But the only result of her vor-
acious reading and courageous application was that she became
less ignorant : nimble wit and graceful conversation are gifts of
nature, or else the fruit of training begun in the cradle. She
could appreciate music and enjoy it, but she could not sing
with taste. She could understand literature and the beauties
of poetry, but it was too late to fix them in her rebel memory.
She listened with pleasure to the chit-chat of the world, but
could not contribute to its brilliance. Her religious views and
the prejudices of her childhood clung to her and prevented the
complete emancipation of her intellect. In short, a foregone
conclusion to her disadvantage had stealthily established itself
in Theodore's mind, and she could not dislodge it. The
artist laughed at those who spoke the praises of his wife to him,
and his mockery was not without foundation; he was so much
an object of reverence to the young and interesting creature,
that she trembled when she was in his presence and when she
was alone with him. Embarrassed by her excessive anxiety to
give satisfaction, she felt her wit and learning swallowed up in
one overwhelming feeling. The very fidelity of Augustine dis-

pleased the faithless husband, who seemed to invite her to go astray by terming her chastity constitutional frigidity. It was in vain that Augustine put force upon herself to abdicate her reason, to bow to the whims and caprices of her husband, and sacrifice herself to the egotism of his vanity; she did not gather the fruit of her sacrifices. It might be that they had both allowed the moment favorable to a complete mutual understanding to glide away. On one particular day the over-sensitive heart of the young wife received one of those blows which so completely loosen the bonds of feeling that they seem to be broken. She shut herself up; but soon the fatal idea suggested itself, to go and seek consolation and counsel in the bosom of her family.

One morning, then, she directed her steps to the grotesque facade of the homely and silent house in which the days of her childhood had been spent. She sighed as she caught sight once more of the window, from which she had one day kissed her hand to him who was now surrounding her existence with glory and with sorrow. All was unchanged in the cave in which nevertheless the cloth trade was renewing its youth. Augustine's sister occupied her mother's seat at the old counter. The youthful mourner found her brother-in-law with his pen stuck behind his ear and so busy that he hardly listened to her. He was surrounded by the formidable symptoms of a general stock-taking, and begging to be excused, he left her to herself. Her sister received her with a coolness which betrayed a certain grudge; for in fact Augustine had never been to see her sister except when, elegantly dressed, she would leave her well appointed carriage to pay her a passing visit; so the wife of the prudent Lebas fancied that money was the real cause of this early call, and she accordingly endeavored to maintain a tone of reserve which more than once made Augustine smile. The wife of the artist perceived that, barring the weepers on the cap, her mother had found in Virginie a successor who preserved the old-standing reputation of the Chat-qui-pelote.

During lunch she noticed certain alterations in the household regulations which did honor to the good sense of Joseph Lebas; the clerks did not leave the table at dessert; they enjoyed freedom of speech; while the abundant fare spoke of affluence without luxury. The elegant young woman noticed the counterfoils of a box at the Théâtre Francais, where she remembered to have seen her sister from time to time. Madame Lebas wore upon her shoulders a Cashmere shawl whose magnificence bore witness to the generous attention bestowed on her by her husband. In short the worthy couple advanced with the age. A tender melancholy took possession of Augustine's mind as she observed during the two-thirds of the day which she spent at her sister's, the even happiness of the well assorted pair. It had no transports but then it had no storms. They had accepted life as a commercial enterprise, the leading principle of which was the due conduct of their business. Virginie had not found in her husband an ardent affection; so she set to work to create one. Joseph Lebas was led by imperceptible degrees, first to esteem and then to love his wife, and the time which elapsed ere the flower of happiness bloomed was a security for its permanence. Accordingly when the querulous Augustine explained her painful predicament, she had to endure a deluge of commonplaces suggested to her sister by the stock morality of the Rue St. Denis.

" The evil is done, wife," said Joseph Lebas, " our duty is to give our sister sound advice."

Then the skilful tradesman proceeded to a weighty analysis of the expedients which law and the usages of society afforded Augustine as means of extricating herself from the existing crisis. He ticked off, so to speak, the various considerations, and arranged them according to their weight, in categories; just as if he were dealing with goods of different qualities. Then he put them in the balance, weighed them, and wound up by demonstrating that it was incumbent on his sister to take decisive action. Now this did not accord with the affection which Augustine still entertained for her husband, and so when she heard Lebas talking of legal measures, that feeling awoke in all its strength.

She thanked her two friends and returned home, still more doubtful how to act than before she consulted them. Then she ventured to wend her way to the old-fashioned house in the Rue du Colombier, with a view to confiding her misfortunes to her father and mother; for she now resembled those desperate invalids who will try any prescription, and surrender themselves even to the nostrums of old women. The aged couple received their daughter with an effusive kindness which deeply affected her. Her visit formed a break in the monotony of their existence which was invaluable to them. For four years they had lived like mariners without a destination and without a compass. Seated in the chimney-corner they would chat to one another about the disasters of the *maximum*, their bygone purchases of cloth, their skilful avoidance of bankruptcies, and especially that celebrated Lecocq failure, which was father Guillaume's battle of Marengo. Then, having exhausted their old law-suits, they would recapitulate the totals of their most productive stock-takings, and narrate once more the old stories of the Quartier St. Denis. When two o'clock came daddy Guillaume would set out, just to catch a glimpse of the progress of affairs at the Chat-qui-pelote. As he made his way back he would stop at all the shops which had formerly been his rivals ; while the young proprietors would endeavour to involve the old tradesman in some risky discount transaction which, according to his inveterate habit he never positively declined. Two stout Normandy horses were dying of mesenteritis in the stable, for Madame Guillaume never used them, except when, as each Sunday came round, they dragged her to high mass at the parish church. Three times a week the worthy couple kept open house. Thanks to the influence of his son-in-law Sommervieux, father Guillaume had been appointed a member of the consulting committee for the clothing of the troops; and

since the elevation of her husband to that important government appointment, Madame Guillaume had made up her mind
to give entertainments, and her rooms were encumbered with
so many ornaments in gold and silver, and tasteless but expen-
sive furniture, that the least sumptuous apartment looked like
a chapel. Economy and prodigality seemed to be at feud with
one another in every detail of the establishment. One would
have said that M. Guillaume had been thinking of making a
profitable investment even in the purchase of a candlestick.

In the midst of this bazaar, whose fertility proved the leisure
of the worthy pair, De Sommervieux's famous picture held the
place of honour and afforded great consolation to M. and
Madame Guillaume, who twenty times in the course of the day
would turn their spectacled gaze to that delineation of the old
existence which had been so replete with activity and amusement for them. The aspect of the house and of the apartments,
redolent as they were of age and mediocrity, and the spectacle
presented by the two inmates who seemed, as it were, cast
upon a rock, far from the world and its vitilizing thoughts,
struck Augustine with surprise. She now saw the second part
of the tableux, the first part of which she had witnessed in the
dwelling of Joseph Lebas. Here was an existence busy yet
stationary—a life guided, like that of the beaver, by a mechanical instinct. Under the influence of this reflection she took a
sort of pride in her sorrows as she thought that they had their
source in eighteen months of happiness which were worth a
thousand such lives as that which she saw before her in all its
horrible emptiness. However, Augustine concealed the uncharitable thought and displayed for the benefit of her aged
parents, the novel charms of her intellect and the seductive
tenderness which love had taught her. Thus she disposed
them to lend a favourable ear to her matrimonial troubles. Old
people have a weakness for confidential communications of the
kind. Madame Guillaume wanted to learn the most trivial
details of the strange existence which was almost fabulous to

her. The travels of Baron de la Houtau, which she was always taking up without ever reading it through, contained nothing more unheard of, about the savages of Canada.

"What, child, do you mean to tell me that your husband shuts himself in with naked women? and are you simple enough to believe that he draws them?"

And with this ejaculation the grandmother laid her spectacles on a little work-table, shook her petticoats, and placed her folded hands on her knees, raised above their natural level by a foot-warmer, her favorite foot-stool.

"But, mother, all artists are obliged to have models."

"He took good care to say nothing to us about that, when he proposed. If I had known it, I would not have given a girl of mine to a man who pursues such a calling. Religion prohibits such dreadful practices. It's immoral. What time do you say he comes home?"

"Oh, one or two o'clock."

The old folks looked at one another in deep amazement.

"Then he gambles," said M. Guillaume. "In my day only gamblers stayed out so late."

Augustine made a slight grimace in repulse of this accusation.

"He must cause you to pass fearful nights sitting up for him," resumed Madame Guillaume. "But no, you go to bed, don't you? And when he has lost money the monster wakes you up."

"No, mother, on the contrary, he is often in excellent spirits. Very often when it is fine he asks me to get up and go with him to the parks.

"To the parks at that time in the morning? You must be very much cramped for space if he hasn't room enough in his bed-room and drawing-rooms, and must needs scamper about, —but it must be to make you catch cold that the villain asks you to join in such excursions; he wants to be rid of you, depend upon it. Did you ever hear of a married man in a snug business galloping about like a man-wolf?"

"But, mother, you don't understand that in order to develope his talents he requires excitement. He is very fond of scenes which—"

"Scenes—I'd show him some scenes, trust me," cried Madame Guillaume, interrupting her daughter. "How can you at all bear with a man like that? In the first place, I don't like his drinking nothing but water. It isn't wholesome. Then why does he dislike to see women eating? What a queer notion, why he must be mad. What you have told us about him is impossible. A man *can't* leave his house without saying a word to anybody, and stay away ten days. He tells you he has been at Dieppe to paint the sea. Do people ever paint the sea? Why he crams you with children's stories."

Augustine opened her mouth to defend her husband, but Madame Guillaume motioned her to hold her tongue with a gesture to which early habit lent authority, and then proceeded in a dry tone of voice,—

"Stop, don't talk to me about the man. He never set his foot inside a church except to look at you and to marry you. Irreligious people are capable of anything. Do you suppose that Guillaume ever took it into his head to hide anything from me, to go three days together without even opening his lips, and then begin to chatter like a one-eyed magpie?"

"My dear mother, you are too hard upon superior people. If their ideas resembled those of other people, we should have no talented people at all."

"Well, then, let men of talent keep to themselves, and live single. What? things are come to a pretty pass if a man of talent is to make his wife miserable because he is a man of talent. Talent! talent! I don't see much talent in perpetu-ally talking black and white, interrupting people, blowing one's own trumpet, never letting one know what to be at, compell-ing a woman to abstain from enjoying herself until my gentleman's spirits look up, and to be gloomy because he is gloomy.'

"But, mother, the peculiarity of imagination is—"

"What sort of imaginations are they, I should like to know," resumed Madame Guillaume, again interrupting her daughter. "There seem to be some fine ones indeed. What sort of a man is he who suddenly takes it into his head, without consulting a doctor, to eat nothing but vegetables? If he did it from religious motives, well and good; his abstinence must be of some use to him; but he has no more religion than a Huguenot. Did ever one hear of a man caring more, as he does, for horses than for his neighbor, getting his hair curled like a pagan, wrapping statutes in muslin, and closing shutters in the daytime to work by lamplight? No, really if he were not so flagrantly immoral, he ought to be sent to the Petite-Maison. Consult Monsieur Loraux, the vicar of St. Sulpice; take his advice upon the whole matter, and he will tell you that your husband's conduct is not that of a Christain."

"Oh, mother, can you believe—"

"Oh, yes, I do believe! You loved him and don't observe these things. But for my part I remember having met him in the Champs-Elysées very shortly after his marriage. He was on horseback. Well, at one time he would start off at full gallop, and then the next he would stop and go at a snail's pace; I said to myself then, 'That man wants judgment.'"

"Ah!" exclaimed M. Guillaume, rubbing his hands, "it was well I had your fortune settled to your separate use when I let you marry such a queer character."

When Augustine had the imprudence to relate the real grievences which she had against her husband, the two old folks was struck dumb with indignation. The word divorce soon fell from the lips of Madame Guillaume and aroused the retired old tradesman.

Spurred by the love which he entertained for his daughter as well as by the excitement which a legal process would impart to his endless life, father Guillaume spoke up. He assumed

the lead and conduct of the divorce suit, began almost to
plead it, offered his daughter to pay all the costs, to see the
judges, attorneys, and advocates, and to move heaven and
earth.

Madame de Sommervieux became alarmed, declined her
father's services, declared that she would not be separated from
her husband, even if she was rendered ten times more unhappy;
and said no more about her troubles. After being loaded by
her parents with all those little attentions and unspoken con-
solations by which the two old people vainly endeavored to
soothe the sorrows of her heart, Augustine withdrew, feeling
the impossibility of getting ordinary minds to form a just estimate of superior beings. She found that a woman must conceal
from every one, even from her parents, misfortunes for which
it is so difficult to enlist sympathy. The storms and troubles
of superior spheres can only be appreciated by the lofty spirits
which inhabit them. In every crisis we can be judged only by
our peers.

So poor Augustine found herself once more in the chilling
atmosphere of hope, abandoned to her own terrible reflections.

Study was nothing to her now, since it had failed to win
back her husband's heart. Initiated into the secrets of those
fiery souls, but not possessing their resources, she was condemned to share their pains without partaking of their pleasures.
She had contracted a distaste for the world, which seemed to
her mean and paltry in the presence of the grand catastro-
phes of passion. In short, her life was a failure.

One evening an idea flashed across her mind, and lighted
up as with some celestial ray, her sombre sorrows.

Such an idea could have commended itself only to a heart
so pure and virtuous as Augustine's. She made up her mind
to go to the Duchess of Carigliano, not to ask her to restore
her husband's heart, but to learn the artifices by which he had
been torn away from her; to excite in the haughty woman of
the world an interest in the mother of her lover's children; to

work upon her feelings and make her the accomplice of her future happiness, as she was then the instrument of her present misfortunes.

And so one day it came to pass that the timid Augustine, armed with supernatural courage, took her seat in her carriage at two o'clock in the afternoon, to make her way to the boudoir of the celebrated coquette, who was never visible at an earlier hour. Madame de Sommervieux was as yet unacquainted with the old fashioned sumptuous houses of the Faubourg St. Germain. As she traversed the majestic vestibules, the spacious staircases, the vast saloons adorned with flowers in the depth of winter, and furnished in that good taste which is peculiar to woman to whom opulence and habits of aristocratic distinction are familiar from the cradle, she felt a painful tightness at the heart. She was envious of the secrets of that elegance of which she had never had a notion. She breathed an atmosphere of grandeur which revealed the charm which that house exercised upon her husband. When she reached the private apartments of the duchess, the voluptuous arrangement of the furniture, of the drapery and the hangings filled her with jealousy and a feeling of despair. There, even disorder was graceful and luxury itself seemed inbued with a species of contempt for wealth. The perfumes that reigned in the mild atmosphere of the apartments gratified without irrating the sense of smell. The accessories of the chamber harmonized with the view of grassplat and evergreen that met the eye through the transparent windows. The whole aspect of the place was seductive, and yet there was no evidence of artifice throughout. The very spirit of the owner of these apartments could be traced in the drawing-room in which Augustine had to wait. She sought to gain some idea of the disposition of her rival from the scattered objects that lay before her; but there was something in the very disorder, there was something in the very symmetry, that was impenetrable to Augustine, something which was un-decypherable to her simplicity; all that she could perceive was that the duchess as a woman was a superior woman. And then there occurred to her this painful thought; "Ah me! can it be true that a fond and simple heart is not sufficient for an artist; must his strong mind be joined by way of counterpoise, to a female heart as potent as his own? Had I been educated as this siren was, our weapons would at least have been equal when the contest began."

"But I am not at home." Such were the few harsh words, which though uttered in a low voice in the adjoining room, Augustine overheard. They set her heart a-beating.

"But the lady is there," answered the lady's maid.

"You must have lost your wits. Show her in," replied the duchess in a voice which had now lost its harshness and assumed the soft accent of politeness. *Now* it was clear that she meant that what she said should be overheard.

Augustine stepped timidly forward and saw the duchess indolently reclining on a brown velvet ottoman at the end of the boudoir. The ottoman was placed in the centre of a sort of semicircle formed by soft folds of muslin which covered some yellow material. Ornaments of gilded bronze artistically arranged gave a heightened tone to this kind of dais, under which the duchess lay like some antique statue. The deep-coloured velvet brought into full play everything that could add to the effect. The subdued light, favorable to her beauty, seemed to be reflected rather than direct. A few choice flowers raised their scented blossoms from vases of the richest Sèvres. Just as this tableau met the eye of the astonished Augustine, she caught, so noiseless had been her approach, a glance cast by the enchantress. This glance seemed to say to a person, whom the artist's wife had not at first observed, "Don't go, you will see a pretty woman and render her visit less tiresome to me."

At the sight of Augustine the duchess rose and made her sit down beside her. Then with a charming smile she inquired,—

"To what am I indebted for this agreeable visit, madam?"

Why such duplicity? thought Augustine, who only answered with a bow.

Her silence was enforced. The young wife saw before her an observer of the scene who was entirely *de trop*. This person was the youngest, the most elegant, and the best built of all the colonels of the imperial army. His half-dress uniform set off to the utmost advantage the graces of his person.

His face which beemed with life and youth, and was already full of expression, derived further animation from the small moustaches turned up and drawn out into a point and black as jet; from the thick imperial, carefully combed whiskers, and the forest of black hair now considerably disarranged. He was playing with a whip and wore an air of ease and freedom which suited the self-satisfied aspect of his features and the neatness of his dress. The ribands attached to his buttenhole were negligently tied and he seemed much vainer of his handsome figure than of his courage. Augustine looked from the duchess to the colonel with a glance whose petition was thoroughly comprehended.

"Well, good bye, M. d'Aiglemont, we shall meet again at the Bois de Boulogne."

These words were uttered by the duceess as if they were the result of an understanding arrived at previously to Augustine's arrival; and they were accompanied by a threatening look which the young officer perhaps deserved, on account of his evident admiration for the modest flower of beauty who contrasted so well with the haughty duchess. The young fop bowed silently, turned on his heal, and walked gracefully out of the boudoir. At that moment, Augustine, who was watching her rival as she pursued with her eyes the dashing officer, detected in the glance a trace of that feeling whose fugitive expressions are known to every woman. She thought with the profoundest sorrow that her visit would be thrown away; the crafty duchess was to eager for homage to be merciful.

"Madame," said Augustine, in a broken voice, "the step

which I am now taking **in coming to you will** seem to you very
extraordinary; but the madness of despair ought to excuse
everything. "I now understand too well why Theodore prefers
your house to any other, and why your mind exercises so great
an influence over his.   Alas, I have only to look into my own
breast to discover reasons more than enough.   But, madame,
I adore my husband.   Two years of sorrow have not erased
his image from my heart, though he is lost to me.   In my
madness I have dared to entertain the idea of measuring myself with you, and I have come to see how I can triumph over
you.   Oh, madame!" exclaimed the young wife, eagerly seizing
the hand which her rival abandoned to her, " I shall never pray
to God for my own happiness with such fervor as I will entreat
Him for yours, if you will aid me to regain, I do not say the
love, but merely the friendship of Sommervieux.   My only
hope is in you.   Oh, tell me how you won his heart, and made
him forgetful of the first days of——"

At these words Augustine was forced to stop, choked with
the sobs which she could not restrain : ashamed of her weakness she hid her face in her handkerchief, which was soon
deluged with her tears.

"Why what a child you are, my little beauty," said the
duchess, for whom the novelty of the scene had a certain
charm, and who was touched in spite of herself by the homage
paid to her by perhaps the most spotless woman in Paris.   So
saying she took Augustine's handkerchief, and began to wipe
her eyes with it, accompanying the process with sundry
monosyllabic murmurs of graceful pity.   After a moment's
silence the coquette, imprisoning poor Augustine's pretty
hands in her own, which were specially remarkable for their
beauty and their power, said in a gentle and affectionate
tone,—

"My first advise to you is not to cry so; crying makes
people ugly.   You must make short work with troubles which
cause illness, for love cannot long survive a sick-bed.   True it

is that mèlancholy lends at first a certain engaging charm, but in the long-run it draws the features, and withers the most charming face; and then our tyrants are so vain that they want their poor slaves to be always gay."

"Ah, madame, I cannot control my feelings. How is it possible without experiencing a thousand deaths to see a face once radiant with love and joy, gloomy, pale, indifferent? Oh, I cannot command my feelings."

"So much the worse, my darling, but I believe I already know your whole story. In the first place make sure of this; if your husband has been faithless to you, *I* am not his accomplice. If I made it a point to have him at my receptions, it was, I freely admit, from mere vanity; he was famous and went nowhere. I like you already too well to give you a list of the follies he has been guilty of on my account. I will merely show you one of them, because it will perhaps help us to restore him to you, and to punish him for the audacity of his proceedings as far as I am concerned. If he went on he would compromise me. I know the world too well, my dear, to be willing to place myself at the mercy of a man of very great talent. To allow them to pay their addresses to us is very well, but as to marrying them, that is a mistake. We women may admire men of genius, enjoy them as we do a spectacle, but as for living with them; oh, never. Why 'tis like seeking amusement by looking at the machinery behind the stage of the opera, instead of sticking to one's box and enjoying the brilliant illusions. But in your case, my poor child, the mischief is done, is it not? Well, then, we must try to furnish you with weapons against tyranny."

"Oh, madame, before I came into this room and saw you, I already recognized certain artifices which I did not suspect."

"Well, come and see me occasionally and you will very soon have the secret of these trifles, which by the way are very important trifles. External objects are for fools, the full half of existence; and in that respect more than one man of talent is a fool in spite of all his art. But I will take on me to say, that you have never let Theodore know what a refusal is."

" How, madame, can one refuse anything to the man one loves ? "

" You innocent little creature, I could dote on you for your silliness. Learn this; the more we love the more should we endeavor to conceal the strength of our passion from the man we love. It is the one who loves most who is trampled on and, what is worse, deserted, sooner or later. He who would reign must—"

" What, madame, must one then dissimulate, calculate, become false, create for one's self an artificial character and maintain it? Oh, how can one live so? Can you . . .?"

She hesitated; the duchess smiled.

" My dear," resumed the great lady in a serious voice, " conjugal happiness has been at all times a speculation, a matter of business. If you persist in talking passion, when I am talking marriage, we shall very soon fail to understand each other. Listen to me," she continued with a confidential air. " I have been in a position to observe some of the most eminent men of this age. Those who have married, have, with few exceptions, married commonplace women. Well, those women governed them as the emperor governs us, and were; if not loved, at least respected by their husbands. I am sufficiently fond of secrets, especially of those which concern us women, to have taken a pleasure in finding the solution of this enigma. Well, my angel, these good women had the faculty of analyzing the characters of their husbands. Without being alarmed, like you, at the superiority of their husbands, they adroitly noticed in what qualities they were deficient; and whether it was that the wives possessed those qualities, or only pretended to possess them, they managed to make such a display of them in the eyes of their husbands that in the end they inspired respect. Lastly, remember that these minds which seem so lofty are all slightly infected with madness, of which we ought to know how to take advantage. By making up our minds to get the upperhand of them, by sticking to that one object and in the midst of all our actions, thoughts, and coquetries, keeping it steadily in view, we subdue these eminently capricious spirits; the very nobility of their ideas furnishes us with the means of influencing them."

"Oh, heavens," cried the young wife in terror. "This then is life. It's a combat."

"Yes, a combat in which you must be always threatening an attack," resumed the duchess with a laugh. Our power is altogether factitious. So we must never allow a man to des. pise us; to recover from such a fall one must resort to odious manœuvres. Come with me," she added. "I am going to give you the means of binding your husband."

She rose and laughingly conducted the young and innocent apprentice to the tricks of matrimony, through the mazes of her little palace. They reached a private staircase which led to the reception-rooms. As the duchess was turning the handle of the door, she stopped, looked at Augustine with an inimitable air of subtilty and grace, and said, "Look here, the Duke de Carigliano worships me; well, he dare not come in by this door without my permission. And he is a man who is accustomed to command thousands of soldiers. He can assail a battery, but in my presence—he is afraid."

Augustine sighed. They reached a splendid gallery, and there the duchess led the painter's wife to the portrait which Theodore had painted of Mademoiselle Guillaume. When Augustine caught sight of it she shrieked.

"I knew well it was no longer in my house," said she, "but —here !"

"My little darling, I merely demanded it in order to learn of what folly a man of genius may be guilty. Sooner or later I should have returned it to you, for I did not look forward to the pleasure of seeing the original here, before the copy. While we finish our chat, I will have it taken to your carriage. If, armed with this talisman you are not your husband's mistress for a hundred years, you are not a woman, and you will deserve your fate."

Augustine kissed the hand of the duchess, who pressed her to her heart, and embraced her with a tenderness all the more lively because she would be forgotten on the morrow. This scene would perhaps have destroyed for ever the candor and purity of Augustine, to whom the secrets revealed by the duchess might do as much harm as good; for the astute policy of the loftiest social sphere, did not commend itself to Augustine, any more than the narrow common sense of Joseph Lebas, or the stupid morality of Madame Guillaume. Strange result of the false positions into which we are thrown by the least blunders committed in life! Augustine was like some Alpine shepherd overtaken by an avalanche; if he hesitates or listens to the cries of his companions, he generally perishes. In these grand crises the heart is broken or is bronzed. Madame de Sommervieux went home in a fit of agitation which it would be difficult to describe. Her conversation with the Duchess of Carigliano awakened in her breast a thousand conflicting ideas. Like the sheep in the fable, full of boldness when the wolf is away, she harangued herself and traced out for herself admirable plans of conduct: she invented a thousand schemes of coquetry, she even addressed her husband, discovering, in his absence, all the resources of that genuine eloquence which never deserts women; and then as she thought of the clear and steady gaze of Theodore, she began to tremble, even in his absence.

When she asked whether her husband was at home her voice failed her. When she heard that he would not come back to dinner she felt an inexplicable sensation of delight. She resembled the criminal who appeals from his death sentence ; a delay, however brief, seems like a whole lifetime. She placed the portrait in her own room, and waited for her husband in all the agonies of hope. She felt so sure that this attempt of hers would be decisive of her whole future, that she trembled at every noise, even at the ticking of her time-piece, which seemed to add weight to her terrors by measuring them. She tried to while away the time by a thousand devices She took it into her head to dress herself just as she was dressed in the portrait. Then, conscious of the restlessness of her husband's disposition, she caused her room to be lighted up with unaccustomed brilliancy, feeling sure that in-quisitiveness would attract her husband to her chamber on his return. It was striking twelve when at the sound of the postilion's voice, the gate of the hotel flew open, and the artist's carriage rolled over the pavement of the silent court-yard.

"What is the meaning of this illumination?" asked Theodore in a gay tone, as he entered his wife's room.

Augustine adroitly seized the propitious moment, threw her arm round her husband's neck and pointed to the portrait. The artist stood motionless as a rock and turned his eyes now on Augustine, and now on the accusing toilette. The timid wife, half dead with fear, who was watching the changing, the awe-inspiring brow of her husband, saw its expressive lines mass by degrees like clouds. Then she fancied she could feel the blood freezing in her veins, as with flaring eye and deep and hollow voice he asked,—

"Where did you find that picture?"

"The Duchess de Carigliano restored it to me."

"Did you ask her for it?"

"I did not even know she had it."

The sweetness, nay the enchanting melody of the voice of such an angel, would have softened the heart of a cannibal, but not that of an artist suffering from the tortures of wounded vanity.

"That is an act well worthy of her," cried the painter in a

voice of thunder. "I will revenge myself," he added, striding
about the room. "She shall die disgraced for having done
this; I will paint her, yes, I will represent her in the character
of Messalina stealing by night from the palace of Claudius."

"Theodore !" exclaimed a dying voice.

"I will murder her."

"My friend."

"She is in love with that little cavalry colonel, because he is
a good horseman."

"Theodore."

"Oh, leave me," said the painter to his wife, in a voice
which resembled a roar.

It would be odious to describe the whole of this scene,
towards the end of which the intoxication of anger drove the
painter to language and gestures which an older woman than
Augustine would have attributed to phrenzy. About eight
o'clock the next morning, Madame Guillaume, breaking in
upon her daughter, found her pale, red-eyed, and with dis-
hevelled hair, holding in her hand a handkerchief drenched
with tears, and gazing at the fragments of a tattered dress and
a large gilt picture-frame that lay scattered on the floor.
Augustine, who was almost mad with grief, pointed to the
wreck with a gesture of despair.

"Ah, it may be a very serious loss," cried the old regent of
the Chat-qui-pelote. "It was certainly very like you; but I
have heard of a man on the boulevards who paints charming
portraits for 150 francs apiece."

"Oh, mother."

"My poor darling, you are quite right," answered Madame
Guillaume, who misinterpreted the meaning of the look which
her daughter cast at her. "Never mind, my child. No one
can love so tenderly as a mother. I can understand it all, my
darling; but come and tell me all your troubles, and I will
comfort you. Have I not told you already that the man is mad.

Your maid has told me some queer things about him. Why, he must be a regular monster."

Augustine placed her finger on her pale lips, as if to implore her mother to be silent for an instant. During that terrible night, misfortune had taught her that patient resignation, which seems, in the case of mothers and of women who love, to transcend the limits of human strength, and shows, perhaps, that there are certain chords in the female heart which God has denied to men.

An inscription on a tombstone in the cemetery of Montmartre shows that Madame de Sommervieux died at the age of twenty-seven. In the simple lines of that epitaph, a friend of the timid creature recognizes the last scene of a tragedy. On the solemn festival of the 2nd of November in each year, that friend, as he passes the recent gravestone, asks himself the question, whether the powerful embrace of genius does not require women of a robuster type than poor Augustine?

"It may be," such is his internal reflection, "that these humble and modest flowers of the valley, perish when they are transplanted to a too elevated region, the sphere of gathering tempests and of scorching suns."

THE VENDETTA.

(LA VENDETTA.)

DEDICATED TO PUTTINATI, SCULPTOR, OF MILAN.

TOWARDS the end of October in the year 1800, a foreigner accompanied by his wife and child arrived in front of the Tuileries, and planted himself for a considerable time near the *débris* of a house, then recently demolished, on the spot now occupied by the unfinished wing which was to connect the palace of Catharine de Medici with the Louvre of the Valois. There he remained with folded arms and bowed head, which he raised from time to time to look at the consular palace, and at his wife, who was seated near him on a stone. Although the female foreigner seemed to be confining her attention to the little girl of nine or ten, whose raven locks were as a plaything in her hands, she did not miss one of the looks which her companion directed to her. A single sentiment, other than love, united these two beings, and imparted the same uneasiness to their movements and their thoughts. Poverty is perhaps the most potent of all bonds. The foreigner had one of those large, massive, hair-abounding heads which are so often to be met with in the paintings of the Caracci. His jet-black locks were interspersed with a large number of white hairs. His features, though noble and lofty, were marred by an air of harshness. In spite of his strength and upright figure, he seemed to be over sixty. The style of his much-worn garments showed that he came from a foreign land. Although the once handsome, but now faded, features of the woman bespoke a profound melancholy, yet when her husband looked at her she forced a smile and assumed an heir of calmness. The young girl remained standing, though it was clear from the appearance of her youthful sun-burnt face that she was tired. Her features were of the Italian cast; she had large black eyes shaded by strongly arched brows, a certain native nobility and genuine grace. Not a few of those who passed this group were moved at the mere sight of these three persons, who made no effort to conceal a despair which was as profound as its expression was simple. But the source of this transient kindness, which characterizes the Parisian, was soon exhausted; for so soon as the stranger saw that the attention of some idler was attracted to himself, he looked upon him with so fierce an air that the boldest flâneur quickened his step as if he had trodden on a serpent. After having remained for a long time in a state of indecision, the tall stranger suddenly passed his hand across his forehead, chased from it, so to speak, the thoughts which had gathered it into furrows, and evidently made up his mind to some desperate step. Casting a penetrating glance at his wife and daughter, he drew a long poinard from his bosom, held it out to his companion, and said to her in Italian, "I am going to see whether the Bonapartes remember us." Then he walked with a slow, firm step towards the entrance of the palace, where he was, as was to be expected, stopped by a soldier of the consular guard, with whom he was prevented from having a long discussion; for, perceiving the old man's persistence, the sentinel pointed his bayonet at him by way of *ultimatum*. As chance would have it, the soldier upon guard was at that very moment relieved, and the corporal with great civility directed the foreigner to the spot where he would find the commandant of the station.

"Let Bonaparte know that Bartholoméo de Piombo wishes to speak to him," said the Italian to the captain on duty. It was all very well for the officer to represent to Bartholoméo that the first Consul was not to be seen unless a written request for an audience had been previously laid before him; the foreigner insisted that the soldier should carry the intimation to Bonaparte. The officer opposed him on the ground of the positive regulations, and formally declined to obey the order of this singular petitioner. Bartholoméo frowned, darted at the commandant a terrible look, and seemed to hold him responsible for the evils which might result from this refusal. Then, without another word, he folded his arms firmly across his chest and proceeded to take up his position under the portico, which serves for a communication between the court and the gardens of the Tuileries. Persons who have a strong desire for anything are almost always well backed by chance. At the moment when Bartholoméo de Piombo sat down on one of the railings near the entrance to the Tuileries, a carriage drove up, and set down Lucien Bonaparte, then minister of the interior.

"Ah, Lucien, it is very lucky for me that I met you," cried the stranger.

These words, uttered in a Corsican patois, arrested Lucien at the moment when he was driving under the arch; he looked at his compatriot and recognized him. At the first word that Bartholoméo whispered to him, he took the Corsican with him. Murat, Lannes, and Rapp were in the first Consul's closet. On the entrance of Lucien, followed by a man of so strange an appearance as Piombo's, the conversation ceased, Lucien took Napoleon's hand and led him into the embrasure of the window. After having exchanged a few words with his brother, the first Consul made a gesture with his hand, which Murat and Lannes obeyed by going away. Rapp pretended not to have observed it, in order that he might remain; but Bonaparte spoke to his aide-de-camp peremptorily, whereupon he sullenly left the room. The first Consul, who heard the footsteps of Rapp in the next room, went out suddenly and found him close to the wall which separated the closet from the anteroom.

"You are determined not to understand me, then?" said the first Consul. "I want to be alone with my compatriot."

"A Corsican," replied the aide-de-camp. "I distrust those people too much not to—"

The first Consul could not refrain from smiling, and gave his faithful officer a slight push on the shoulder.

"Well what have you come here for, my poor Bartholoméo?" said the first Consul to Piombo.

"To ask you for an asylum and for protection, if you are a true Corsican," answered Bartholomèo in a brusque tone.

"What misfortune has driven you from the country? you were the richest, the most—"

"I have killed all the Portas," said Piombo, in a deep voice and with a frown. The first Consul drew back two paces, as if astonished.

"Are you going to betray me?" cried Bartholoméo scowling at Bonaparte. "Do you know that there are still four Piombos in Corsica?"

Lucien grasped his compatriot's arm and shook it, then said sharply,—

"Are you come hither to threaten the Savior of France?"

Bonaparte made a sign to Lucien, who said no more; then looking at Poimbo he said,—

"Why did you kill the Portas?"

"We had struck up a friendship," he answered, "the Barbantis had reconciled us. On the morrow of the day on which we drowned our quarrels in a friendly cup, I left them, because I had business at Bastia. They remained at my house and set fire to my vineyard at Longuel; they killed my son Grégorio. But my wife and daughter, who had taken the sacrament that morning, and were under the special protection of the Virgin, escaped. When I returned I could not see my house; as I searched for it my feet were upon ashes. All at once I stumbled against the body of Grégorio which I recognized by the light of the moon. 'Ah, the Portas have struck this blow,' I said to myself. I went forthwith into the mâquis. I there collected certain men to whom I have been of service: do you understand me, Bonaparte? and we marched to the vineyard of the Portas. We reached it at five o'clock in the morning, and at seven they were all in the presence of God. Giacomo maintains that Elisa Vanni saved one child, the little Luigi, but I myself had tied him to his bed before I set fire to the house. I left the island with my wife and child without having been able to ascertain whether Luigi Porta still lived."

Bonaparte looked at Bartholoméo with curiosity but without surprise.

"How many were there of them?" asked Lucien.

"Seven," replied Piombo. "They persecuted you at one time," he added; but as these words caused no expression of hatred on the faces of the two brothers, Bartholoméo exclaimed with a sort of despairing accent, "Ah! you are no longer Corsicans; adieu! I protected you in days gone by," he added in a reproachful tone. "But for me, your mother would not have reached Marseilles," said he addressing Bonaparte, who was lost in thought, with his elbow leaning on the mantlepiece.

"In conscience, Piombo," replied Napoloen, "I cannot take you under my wing. I am become the chief of a great nation; I command the republic, and am bound to see that the laws are executed."

"Ah, ah," cried Bartholoméo.

"But I can shut my eyes," resumed Bonaparte. "The prejudice as to the Vendetta will for a long time obstruct the sovereignty of the laws in Corsica," he added, speaking to himself. "But it must be destroyed at any price."

Bonaparte was silent for a moment, and Lucien signalled to Piombo not to speak. The Corsican was already beginning to shake his head in a token of disapprobation.

"Remain in Paris," resumed the first Consul, addressing Bartholoméo, "we shall know nothing about it. I will procure a purchaser for your estates, so that you may in the first place have something to live upon. Then later on, after the lapse of some little time, we will think of you. But no more

Vendetta. There are no Màquis here. If you use the poniard here, you must not hope for pardon. Here the law protects the citizens, and people don't take the law into their own hands."

"He has become the chief of a singular country," replied Bartholoméo, taking Lucien's hand and squeezing it. "But you acknowledge me in misfortune. Now I am yours in life and to death, and you may dispose at your pleasure of all the Piombos."

As he said this the forehead of the Corsican grew smooth, and he looked around him with satisfaction.

"You are not badly lodged here," said he, smiling, as if he would like to live there. "And you are dressed all in red like a cardinal."

"It depends entirely on yourself to succeed and have a palace at Paris," said Bonaparte, examining his compatriot from head to foot. "It will happen to me more than once to look round me in search of a devoted friend in whom I can confide."

A sigh of joy escaped from the capacious chest of Piombo, who held out his hand to the first Consul, and said, "There is still something of the Corsican left in you!"

Bonaparte smiled and gazed in silence at the man who might be said to bring with him Bonaparte's native air, the air of that isle in which he had formerly been so miraculously saved from the hatred of the English party, of that isle which he was destined never to see again. He made a sign to his brother, who led Bartholoméo di Piombo away. Lucien anxiously inquired about the financial situation of the ancient protector of their family. Piombo took the minister of the interior up to a window, pointed out his wife and Ginevra, both seated on a heap of stones, and said,—

"We have come hither from Fontainebleau on foot, and haven't a farthing."

Lucien gave his purse to his compatriot, and advised him to

come the next day, in order to consult about the means of providing some support for his family. The value of all the property which Piombo owned in Corsica would scarcely enable him to live decently in Paris.

Fifteen years elapsed between the arrival of the Piombo family in Paris, and the following adventure; which, without the recital of the preceding events, would have been less intelligible.

Servin, one of our most distinguished artists, was the first to conceive the idea of opening a studio for young girls desirous of taking lessons in painting. He was a man of forty, of pure morals, entirely devoted to his art, and had made a love-match with the daughter of a general who had no fortune. At first, mothers conducted their daughters to the professor in person, but subsequently, when they came to know his high principles and appreciate the pains he took to deserve their confidence, contented themselves with sending them. It had been part of the painter's plan to accept as scholars none but such as belonged to wealthy or highly respectable families; so as to avoid any criticism as to the constituent elements of his studio. He even declined to receive young girls who wanted to become artists by profession, to whom it would have been necessary to give certain instruction, without which talent in painting is impossible. Gradually his prudence, the superiority of his method of initiating his pupils into the secrets of the art, the feeling of security arising from the character and morals of the artist, and the fact of his marriage, procured for him an excellent reputation in the drawing-rooms of Paris. When a young girl exhibited a desire to learn to paint or draw, and her mother wanted advice upon the subject, "Send her to Servin," was the answer made by every one. Hence Servin obtained in the matter of girl-teaching a specialty, as Herbault had for bonnets, Leroy for fashions, and Chevet for eatables. It was acknowledged that a young woman who had taken lessons from Servin could pronounce a conclusive opinion on the pictures at the

museum, paint a portrait in superior style, copy a picture, and
paint her picture of genre. Thus this artist supplied all the
requirements of the aristocracy. But notwithstanding the con-
nexions he had with the best families in Paris he was independent, he was a patriot, and maintained, no matter to whom
he was talking, that gay, witty, sometimes comical tone, and
that freedom of judgment which distinguishes painters.

He had extended his scrupulous precautions even to the
arrangement of the place in which his scholars studied. The
entrance to the attic which surmounted his dwelling had been
walled up. In order to reach that retreat, which had all the
sanctity of a harem, it was necessary to use a staircase which
had been erected in the interior of the house. The studio,
which occupied all the upper part of the house, was of those
enormous dimensions which always surprise the curious, who,
when they have climbed to a height of sixty feet from the
ground, expect to find the artist lodged in a rain-spout. This
species of gallery was profusely lighted by great windows fitted
with those large green blinds, by means of which artists regulate
the light. Caricatures, heads dashed off at a stroke, either in
color, or scratched with the point of a knife, crowded the
dark grey walls and proved that, allowing for the different manner of expressing it, girls, even of the highest class, have as
much folly in their composition as men can possibly have. A
little stove with its large flues, which described a hideous zig-
zag ere they reached the regions of the roof, was an inevitable
ornament of this studio. Around the walls ran a wooden shelf,
supporting plaster models, which lay scattered in confusion,
being for the most part covered with light dust. Here and
there, beneath this shelf, was to be seen hanging on a nail, a
head of Niobe in her pose of grief, a smiling Venus, a hand
thrust brusquely forward like that of a beggar asking for alms,
and sundry écorchés embrowned with smoke and looking like
limbs lately torn from their coffin. Paintings, sketches, mannikins, frames without pictures, and pictures without frames,

completed the studio-like character of this disorderly apartment —a character which consists in an extraordinary mixture of ornament and nakedness, of poverty and richness, of care and neglect. This immense place, in which everything seems insignificant, even man, is suggestive of the back of a stage; and is full of old clothes, gilded armor, fragments of various stuffs and machines; but there is something about it great as thought; genius and death are there, the Diana or the Apollo, close to a skull or a skeleton; beauty and disorder, romance and reality, rich colors in shadow, and, not unfrequently, a complete though mute and motionless drama. What a symbol of an artist's brain!

At the moment when this narrative begins, the brilliant July sun was lighting up the studio, and two rays of light shot through its whole length large transparent bands of gold, glittering with grains of dust. A dozen easels raised their pointed tops like ship-masts in a port. Several young girls with their various faces, attitudes, and dresses, gave life to the scene, while the green serges, so arranged as to suit the requirements of each easel, produced a number of contrasts and startling effects of clear-obscure. This group of girls was the prettiest picture in the studio. A fair young creature, very simply dressed, stood aloof from her companions and worked courageously as if forecasting misfortune. Not one of the girls looked at her or spoke to her; she was the prettiest, the most modest, and the poorest of them all.

Two principal groups, separated one from the other by a slight space, showed that there were two societies and two spirits even in this studio, where the differences of rank and fortune ought to have been forgotten. Sitting or standing, these young girls, surrounded by their color-boxes, playing with pencils or preparing them for use, handling their shining palettes, painting, laughing, singing, giving free play to their natural characters, and displaying their natural dispositions, constituted a spectacle not to be seen by men. Here a proud,

haughty, capricious girl, with raven locks and beautiful hands,
scattered carelessly her kindling glances; there, gay and heedless, with a smile upon her lips, stood a girl with chestnut hair
and white delicate hands, the true French maiden, frivolous,
unthinking, heedless of aught beyond the enjoyment of the
passing day.   There, again, was a girl, dreamy, melancholy,
with pallid face, and head bent like a drooping flower; while
her neighbor, on the other hand, was tall, indolent, inclined to
oriental habits, and had a long, dark, humid eye.   This one
spoke seldom, but pondered and cast stolen glances at the head
of Antinous.   In the midst of the girls, like the *jocoso* in a
Spanish play, stood a girl who was full of wit and epigrammatic
phrases, a girl who embraced all their movements at a single
glance, made them all laugh and was perpetually looking up
with a face too full of life not to be pretty.   This girl was the
leader of the first group, which consisted of the daughters of
bankers, notaries, and merchants, all rich, yet all subjected to
the intangible yet penetrating disdain lavished on them by the
other young girls who belonged to the aristocracy.   These
were governed by the daughter of an officer of the royal household, a little creature equally vain and foolish, who was proud
of being the daughter of a man who held an appointment at
court.   She wished to appear as if she grasped without any
effort the observations of her master, and seemed to work as a
matter of favor.   She used an eye-glass, always came late,
elaborately dressed, and entreated her companions to speak
low.   In this latter group might be seen exquisite figures and
faces full of distinction; but the girls of this group lacked simplicity.   Their postures were elegant, and their movements
graceful, but there was a want of frankness in their faces, and
it was easily seen that they belonged to a world in which politeness gains an early hold upon the character and the abuse of
social enjoyments kills the sentiments and developes egotism.
But amongst the whole assembly were to be found childlike
heads, maidens of exquisite purity, faces whose half-opened

mouths disclosed virgin teeth, while virgin smiles played upon the lips. Under this aspect the studio did not look like a seraglio, but like a group of angels seated on a cloud.

It was now noon, and Servin had not yet shown himself. For some days past he had spent the greater part of his time at a studio of his, situated elsewhere, in which he was finishing a picture for the Exhibition. All at once Mademoiselle Amélie Thirion, the leader of the aristocrats of this little assembly, held a long conversation with her next neighbor. Then there was a dead silence in the patrician group, while the bank section also was silent in surprise, and endeavored to guess the subject of such a conference. But the secret of the young ultras was soon divulged. Amélie rose, and taking up an easel which stood some paces from her, replaced it at a considerable distance from the noble group, near a rough partition which separated the studio from the dark closet containing the broken casts, the paintings rejected by the professor, and a supply of firewood, in winter. This action of Amélie's evoked a murmur of astonishment, which did not however deter her from completing the removal by hastily rolling alongside of the easel, the box of colors, stool, &c., including a picture by Prudhon which the tardy pupil was copying. After this *coup d'état*, if the party of the right set itself silently to work, that of the left entered into a long debate.

"What will Mademoiselle Piombo say to that?" inquired a young girl of Mathilde Roguin, the mischievous oracle of the first group.

"She is not a girl to talk," replied Mathilde; "but fifty years hence she will remember this insult as if it had been offered to her only the day before, and will find a cruel vengeance. She is a person with whom I should not like to have a feud."

"The prosecutions to which those young ladies are subjecting her is all the more unkind," said another young girl, "because Mademoiselle Ginevra was very sad the day before

7

yesterday; it was said that her father had tendered his resignation. So that this will be an addition to her misfortune; and
she was very good to those young ladies during the hundred
days. Did she ever say a single word to them that could
wound their feelings? On the contrary, she never mentioned
politics. But our ultras seem to be acting from jealousy,
rather than party-spirit."

"I feel inclined to go and get Mademoiselle Piombo's easel
and place it next to mine," said Mathilde Roguin. She rose
but sat down again as a thought occurred to her, which she
expressed in these words. "We cannot tell how a person of
Mademoiselle Ginevra's disposition might take our civility;
let us await the event."

"Eccola," said the black eyed girl languidly.

In fact the sound of the footsteps of a person coming up the
staircase was heard in the studio. The words "Here she is,"
passed from mouth to mouth, and then the profoundest silence
reigned throughout the room.

In order to explain the importance of the ostracism which
Amélie Thirion had carried into effect, it is necessary to add
that this scene took place towards the end of the month of July,
1815. The second return of the Bourbons had just disturbed many a friendship which had resisted the commotion
produced by the first restoration. At this moment the schism
between the different members of nearly every family caused
a revival of those lamentable scenes which soil the history of
every country during periods of civil or religious war.
Children, girls, old men, all felt the monarchical fever which
consumed the governing powers. Discord entered every dwelling and distrust stained with its sombre hues the most private
actions and conversations. Ginevra Piombo loved, nay, idolized Napoleon; how could she hate him? The emperor was
her father's fellow-countryman and benefactor. The Baron
de Piombo was one of those servants of Napoleon who co-oper-
ated most efficaciously in bringing about his return from the

island of Elba. The old Baron de Piombo, who was not only incapable of renouncing his political creed, but even anxious to confess it, remained at Paris in the midst of his foes. Ginevra Piombo, therefore, was the more liable to be included in the number of suspected persons, in that she made no secret of the chagrin which the second restoration caused her family. Perhaps the only tears which she had ever shed were extorted from her by the double news of Napoleon's captivity on the "Bellerophon" and the arrest of Labédoyère. The young women composing the patrician group belonged to the highest royalist families in Paris. It would be difficult to give an idea of the over excited feelings of the epoch, and of the horror in which the Bonapartists were held. Trifling and insignificant as the action of Amélie Thirion may now seem, it was then a very natural mode of expressing hatred. Ginevra Piombo, one of the earliest of Servin's pupils, had occupied the place, of which it was desired to deprive her, since her first introduction to the studio; the aristocratic group had gradually formed itself around her; to expel her from a place which in a certain sense belonged to her, was not only to offer her an insult, but to cause her a certain amount of actual trouble; for all artists have a preference for some particular spot to work in. But political dislike had perhaps little to do with the conduct of this small *côté droit* of the studio. Ginevra Piombo, as the cleverest of Servin's pupils, was the object of profound envy. The master professed an equal admiration for the talents and for the character of this favorite scholar, who served as the basis of all his comparisons. In short, though no explanation of the superiority which this young person possessed over all who surrounded her was forthcoming, she enjoyed in that little world a prestige similar to that which Bonaparte had with his soldiers. The aristocracy of the studio had for several days past plotted the downfall of this queen; but no one having as yet ventured to draw away from the Bonapartist, Mademoiselle Thirion had just taken a decisive step in order to make her companions the accomplices of her hate. Although Ginevra was sincerely loved by two or three of the royalists, who had nearly all been well schooled at home in the matter of politics, yet, with that tact which is peculiar to women, they deemed that they were bound to remain neutral in the strife. On Ginevra's arrival then, she was greeted with a profound silence. Of all the young girls who had up to that time frequented the studio of Servin, she was the most beautiful, the tallest, and the most finely formed. There was in her carriage a certain grace and nobility which commanded respect. Her face, which bore the imprint of intelligence, had a radiant look, so full was it of that animation which is peculiar to Corsicans, and not inconsistent with repose. Her long hair and black eyes and eyelashes betokened passion. Although the corners of the mouth were lightly touched, and her lips were somewhat too pronounced, there was stamped upon them that look of benevolence which the consciousness of strength gives to the strong. By a singular caprice of nature the charm of the countenance was, to a certain extent, destroyed by a marble forehead that was almost savage in its pride and eloquent of the morals of Corsica. *There* was to be seen the only bond which existed between her and her native land. Throughout the rest of her person the simplicity and ease of the belles of Lombardy exerted so much charm that it was impossible in her presence to cause her the least pain. So great was the attraction she exercised, that her father did not allow her to go to the studio without an attendant. The only defect of this truly poetical creature was the potency of a beauty so fully developed. She had declined all offers of marriage from love for her father and mother: she felt she was indispensable to them in their old age. Her taste for painting had taken the place of those passions to which women generally are subject.

"You are remarkably silent to-day, young ladies," she observed after having advanced a few steps among her companions. "Good-day, my little Laura," she added in a sweet caressing tone, as she drew near to a young girl who was painting at a distance from the others. "That head is very good, the flesh is a little too ruddy, but the whole is admirably drawn." Laura raised her head and looked at Ginevra affectionately; and the faces of the two girls glowed with the expression of a mutual regard. A faint smile played upon the lips of the Italian girl. She seemed to be in a reflective mood, and moved slowly towards her place, glancing listlessly at the drawings and paintings, and bidding good-day to each of the girls of the first-mentioned group, without observing the unwonted curiosity excited by her presence. She looked like a queen surrounded by her court. She took no heed of the deep silence which reigned among the patricians, and passed in front of their camp without uttering a single word. So great was her preoccupation, that she took her seat at her easel, opened her color-box, took up her brushes, put on her brown sleevelets, adjusted her apron, looked at her picture, and examined her palette without thinking, so to speak, of what she was doing. Every head in the plebeian group was turned towards her, while the eyes of the young ladies who formed the Thirion camp were directed, with less frankness, yet with equal fixity, to Ginevra.

"She does not notice the change at all," said Mademoiselle Roguin. But at that moment Ginevra threw off the meditative air which she had worn while contemplating her picture, and turned her head towards the group of aristocrats. She measured at a single glance the distance between it and herself, but said nothing. "She does not think that any insult was intended," said Mathilde. "She has neither blushed nor turned pale. How annoyed those young ladies will be if she finds her new place more to her liking than the old one." Then addressing Ginevra she exclaimed in a loud voice, "You are quite out of line there, mademoiselle." The Italian girl pretended not to hear. It may be that she really did not hear.

She rose abruptly, walked somewhat slowly by the partition which separated the dark closet from the studio, and appeared to be examining the window whence the light came, seeming to attach so much importance to it that she mounted upon a chair in order to raise the green serge which intercepted the light, a good deal higher. When upon a chair she was close to a slight chink in the partition, which was the real goal of her efforts ; for the look she cast through the chink can be compared only to that of a miser discovering the treasures of Aladdin. She then speedily descended, went back to her place, readjusted her picture, pretended to be dissatisfied with the light, drew a table near to the partition, placed a chair upon it, then mounting upon that scaffolding, looked through the chink once more. It was but a single glance she threw into the closet, then lighted by a *jour de souffrance* which had been opened in it. What she saw in the closet produced so lively an emotion that she trembled. " You will fall, Mademoiselle Ginevra," cried Laura.

All the young people looked at the adventurous girl, who was reeling. The fear that her companions would come up to her, gave her courage ; she regained her strength and equilibrium, and turning to Laura, and while swaying herself upon the chair, exclaimed in a voice of emotion, " Bah ! it is at least a little more solid than a throne." She then hurriedly removed the serge, got down, pushed the table and chair far away from the partition, returned to her easel, and made some further seeming efforts to obtain a suitable body of light. But she was not thinking about her picture ; her real object was to get close to the dark closet, by the door of which she fixed her place as she desired. Then she set herself to get her palette ready, maintaining all the while the strictest silence.

hus placed, she soon heard much more distinctly the gentle noise which on the previous evening had aroused her curiosity and led her youthful imagination through the vast field of conjecture. She readily recognized the strong, firm breathing of the sleeping man of whom she had caught a glimpse. Her curiosity was more than satisfied, but she found herself weighted with a grave responsibility. Through the chink she had caught sight of the imperial eagle, and the face of an officer of the guard, upon a dimly lighted folding-bed. All was now clear to her; Servin was hiding an outlaw. And now she began to fear that one of her companions would come to look at her picture and hear the respiration of the poor fellow or some too deep-drawn inspiration, such as that which had reached her ear during the last lesson. She came to the resolution to remain near the door, trusting to her skill to defeat the accidents of fate.

"It will be better that I should be here to guard against some sinister occurrence, than leave the poor prisoner at the mercy of some bit of negligence." So she thought; and the thought explains the indifference displayed by Ginevra when she found her easel removed. She was secretly overjoyed at the incident; since it had afforded her the opportunity of satisfying her curiosity in the most natural manner; and moreover she was at that moment too preoccupied to seek for the reason of the removal of her seat.

Nothing is more annoying to young girls, and indeed to any one, than to see a bit of spite, an insult, or a smart sting, fail of its effect by reason of the indifference manifested by its object. It would seem that our hatred of a foe gains depth in proportion to the height to which he rises above us. The conduct of Ginevra was an enigma to all her companions. Her friends and her enemies were equally surprised, for they gave her credit for every good quality except forgiveness of injuries. Although the events of her studio life had afforded few occasions for the display of that defect, the examples of vindictive feeling and of firmness which she had displayed, had not produced any the less effect on the minds of her companions. After many conjectures, Mademoiselle Roguin concluded by imputing the silence of the Italian girl to a magna-

nimity that was beyond all praise; and thereupon her retinue
inspired by her, entered into a scheme for humiliating the
aristocrats of the studio.   They achieved their object by means
of a volley of sarcasms which lowered the pride of the *côté
droit*.   The arrival of Madame Servin put an end to this contest of vanity.

Amélie Thirion, with that cunning which always accompanies malice, had observed, analyzed, and reflected on, the
prodigious preoccupation, which prevented Ginevra from over-
hearing the bitter but polite dispute of which she was the
object.   Thus the retaliation inflicted by Mademoiselle Roguin
and her companions had the fatal effect of inducing the young
ultras to inquire into the reason of Ginevra's silence; so that
the beautiful Italian became the centre to which every eye
was directed, and was closely watched both by her friends and
by her enemies.   It is extremely difficult to conceal even the
least emotion or the lightest feeling from fifteen young girls
full of curiosity and idleness, whose love of mischief and whose
intelligence are athirst for secrets to be discovered, and
intrigues to be worked out or defeated, while their skill in
putting a number of different interpretations upon a particular
gesture, glance, or word, infallably directs them to the right
one.   Accordingly the secret of Ginevra de Piombo was
speedily in great danger of being found out.   At that moment
the presence of Madame Servin produced a break in the representation of the drama, which was being silently carried on in
the depths of those young hearts; a drama whose sentiments,
ideas, and progress were expressed by means of phrases
which were almost allegorical, by mischievous glances, by gestures, even by silence, which is sometimes more intelligible than
language.

As soon as Madame Servin entered the studio, her eyes
sought the door near which Ginevra had taken up her position.
Under the existing circumstances that look was not forgotten.
If none of the pupils paid any attention to it at first, Made-

moiselle Thirion afterwards recalled it, and interpreted the mistrust, the fear, and the mystery which almost glared in the eyes of Madame Servin.

"Mesdemoiselles," said she, "Monsieur Servin cannot be here to-day."

Then she complimented the young ladies all round, and received from each of them a heap of those feminine caresses which lie as much in the voice and in the looks as in the actions. Governed by an uneasiness which she vainly endeavored to disguise, she soon came to where Ginevra was sitting.

The Italian girl and the painter's wife exchanged a friendly nod, but did not speak, while the one painted and the other looked on. The respiration of the soldier could easily be heard, but Madame Servin seemed not to hear it, and so great was her effort to dissimulate, that Ginevra was tempted to suspect her of voluntary deafness. The stranger, however, turned in his bed. The Italian looked fixedly at Madame Servin, who thereupon said to her without the slightest change of countenance, "Your copy is as beautiful as the original. If I had to choose between them, I should be puzzled." "Monsieur Servin has not taken his wife into his confidence in this matter," thought Ginevra, who replied to the young wife's observation with a smile of incredulity, and then began to warble one of her native conzonettas, in order to drown any noise which the prisoner might make.

It was so unusual to hear the studious Italian sing, that all the young girls looked at her in astonishment, and the circumstance was afterwards regarded as a proof of the charitable suppositions of hatred. Madame Servin soon went away, and the sitting came to an end without further incident. Ginevra allowed her companions to go away, while she herself seemed inclined for more work; but she unwittingly betrayed her anxiety to be alone; for as the pupils proceeded with their preparatians for departure, she eyed them with looks of ill-concealed impatience. Mademoiselle Thirion, who had in a few short hours become a cruel enemy of the girl who excelled her in everything, was guided by the instinct of hate to the conclusion, that beneath the assumed application of her rival, there lay a mystery.   She had several times been struck by the attentive manner in which Ginevra had disposed herself to listen for a noise which no one heard.   The last expression which she caught gleaming in the eyes of the Italian, was a ray of light to her.   She was the last of all the pupils to go away, and went down to Madame Servin's apartments, talked with her for a moment, then, pretending to have forgotten her bag, she quietly remounted the staircase, and saw Ginevra mounted on a hastily erected scaffolding, and so absorbed in her contemplation of the unknown soldier, as not to have heard the light steps of her companion.   It is true that, to use an expression of Sir Walter Scott's, Amélie walked as if she had been treading on eggs.   Having regained the door of the study, she coughed; Ginevra trembled, turned her head, saw her enemy, and blushed.   She then hastily let down the green serge, in order to disguise her real object; and having set her paint-box in order, left the studio.   She carried with her, graven on her memory, the image of a man's head as graceful as that of the Endymion, the *chef-d'œuvre* of Girodet which she had copied some days before.

"Outlaw so young a man !   Who can it be ?   For it is not Marshal Ney."   These two phrases are the expression, in their simplest form, of all the ideas which Ginevra turned over in her mind during the two following days.   The next day but one, in spite of the haste she made to be the first to reach the studio, she found there Mademoiselle Thirion, who had come in a carriage.   Ginevra and her enemy looked at each other for a long time, but their faces were impenetrable masks.   Amélie had seen the enchanting head of the stranger, but fortunately, and at the same time, unfortunately, the eagles and the uniform were not within the space which the chink enabled her to embrace. She was therefore lost in conjecture, when Servin suddenly arrived much earlier than usual.

"Mademoiselle Ginevra," said he, after having glanced round the studio, "why have you stationed yourself there? The light is bad, come nearer to these young ladies, and lower your curtain a little." Thereupon he sat down by Laura, whose labors deserved the most complaisant of his corrections.

"Well now," said he, "here is a head extremely well painted. You will be another Ginevra."

The master went from easel to easel, scolding, flattering, joking, and making himself, as usual, more formidable on account of his witticisms than his reprimands. The Italian girl had not obeyed the direction of the professor, and stuck to her post with the firm determination not to be driven from it. She took a scrap of paper, and began to make a rough sepia drawing of the head of the poor recluse. A work which is the fruit of passionate conception always has a certain peculiar stamp. The faculty of interpreting the production ot nature, or of the imagination in true colors, constitutes genius; passion often supplies its place. Thus in the situation in which Ginevra was placed, the intuition which she owed to the vivid impression made upon her memory, or perhaps necessity, that mother of great things, endowed her with supernatural talent. The officer's head was reproduced upon the paper, under the influence of an internal tremor which Ginevra ascribed to fear, though a physiologist would have regarded it as the fever ot inspiration. She cast from time to time a furtive glance at her companions, in order that she might be prepared to hide the water-color in case of any indiscretion on their part; but in spite of her sharp lookout, there was a moment in which it escaped her notice that her remorseless enemy's eye-glass hidden by a portfolio, was directed full upon the mysterious sketch. Mademoselle Thirion, who recognized the face of the outlaw, brusquely raised her head, and Ginevra concealed the scrap of paper.

"Why have you remained there in spite of my advice, mademoiselle?" asked the painter gravely.

The pupil hastily turned her easel in such a direction, that no one could see her sketch, then showing it to the painter she said with emotion, "Don't you agree with me, that this light is more favorable? Had I not better stay here?"

Servin turned pale. Since nothing escapes the piercing eye of hate, Mademoiselle Thirion made a third party, so to speak, in the emotions which agitated the master and pupil.

"You are right," said Servin; "but you will soon know more than I do," he added with a forced laugh. There was a pause during which the professor looked at the sketch of the officer's head.

"This is a *chef-d'œuvre* worthy of Salvator Rosa," cried he with the energy of an artist. At this exclamation all the young girls rose, and Mademoiselle Thirion rushed up with all the impetuosity of a tiger throwing itself upon its prey. At this very moment the outlaw, awakened by the noise, moved in his bed; whereupon Ginevra knocked down her stool, uttered a few incoherent phrases, and began to laugh; but she had folded up the portrait and thrown it into her portfolio before her formidable foe had time to catch sight of it. The easel was now surrounded. Servin pointed out in a loud voice the beauties of the copy on which his favorite pupil was engaged, and everybody was deceived by the stratagem—except Amélie. She, placing herself behind her companions, tried to open the portfolio in which she had seen the sketch put—Ginevra seized the portfolio, and placed it in front of her without a word. The two young girls then scrutinized each other in silence.

"Come, ladies, to your seats," said Servin. "If you want to know as much about painting as Mademoiselle de Piombo knows, you must not be constantly talking about balls and fashions, and fiddle-faddling as you do."

When all the young women had got back to their places, Servin sat down beside Ginevra.

" Was it not better that I, rather than another should have discovered this secret ?" said the Italian girl, speaking in a low tone.

" Yes," replied the painter. " You are a patriot ; but even if you were not, I should still have chosen you for my confident."

The master and pupil understood each other, and Ginevra no longer feared to ask,—

" Who is he ?"

" The intimate friend of Labédoyère, the man who, next to the unfortunate colonel, has contributed most to the junction of the seventh regiment with the grenadiers of the Island of Elba. He was commander of a squadron in the guard, and has just returned from Waterloo."

" Why did you not burn his uniform, and give him a suit of plain clothes ?" asked Ginevra sharply.

" They will bring me some this evening."

" You ought to have closed the studio for a few days."

" He is going away."

" He wants to die then ?" said the young girl. " Let him stay with you during the first stage of the commotions. Paris is still the only place in France where you can safely hide a man. Is he a friend of yours ?" she inquired.

" No ; he has no title to my protection other than his misfortunes. I will tell you how he was saddled upon me. My father-in-law, who had re-entered the service during this campaign, met this poor young fellow, and rescued him from the claws of those who arrested Labédoyère. He was mad enough to want to defend him !"

" Is it you who call him mad for that ?" asked Ginevra, staring at the painter, who was silent for a moment.

" My father-in-law is too closely watched to be able to keep any one at his house ; so he brought me this stranger by night, last week. I hoped to conceal him from every one by shutting him up in this corner, which is the only spot in the house where he can be in safety."

"If I can be of any use to you, employ me," said Ginevra. "I know Mashal Feltre."

"Well, we shall see," replied the painter.

This conversation was too prolonged to escape the observation of any of the girls. Servin left Ginevra, and paid a visit to each easel, giving such lengthy lessons that he was still upon the stairs when the clock struck the hour for the pupils' departure.

"You are forgetting your bag, Mademoiselle Thirion," cried the professor, running after the young girl, who descended to the trade of a spy, in order to gratify her hate.

The inquisitive pupil, assumed an air of surprise at her own stupidity, went back to look for her bag, but Servin's caution was to her another proof of the existence of a mystery, whose importance was beyond a doubt. She had already invented all that could possibly be, and might say, with the Abbé Bertot, "*Mon siége est fait.*" She ran noisily down the stairs and slammed the door which opened into Servin's apartments, so as to create the impression that she had gone away; but she stealthily reascended the stairs, and ensconced herself behind the door of the studio. When the painter and Ginevra thought they were alone, he tapped in a peculiar manner at the door of the attic. The door immediately turned on its rusty and creaking hinges, and the Italian girl beheld a tall, well-made young man, whose Imperial uniform stirred her heart. The officer's arm was in a sling, and the pallor of his features showed how keen had been his sufferings. When he saw a stranger he trembled. Amélie, who could not see anything, was afraid to remain any longer; but it was enough that she had heard the creaking of the door, so she stole noiselessly away.

"Fear nothing," said the painter to the officer; "this is the daughter of the emperor's most faithful friend, the Baron de Piombo."

The young soldier cast away all doubt as to the patriotism of Ginevra so soon as he had seen her.

"Are you wounded?" she inquired.

"Oh, it is nothing, mademoiselle; the wound is closing."

At that moment the harsh and penetrating voices of the newsmen, proclaiming, "This is the sentence of death pronounced—" reached the studio.

All three of them trembled; the soldier was the first to catch a name which blanched his face.

"Labédoyère!" he exclaimed, sinking on to the stool.

They looked at each other in silence. Beads of sweat oozed from the pale forehead of the young man. Seizing in one hand, with a gesture of despair, the black clusters of his hair, he rested his elbow on the edge of Ginevra's easel.

"After all," he exclaimed, drawing himself up briskly, "Labédoyère and I knew what we were doing. We knew the lot which awaited us after the triumph, and after the failure. He dies for the cause, and I am in hiding . . . ."

He rushed to the door of the studio, but Ginevra, more alert than he, had darted forward, and barred his path.

"Can you re-establish the emperor?" said she. "Do you think that you can raise the giant who was unable to stand upright himself?"

"What would you have me to do with myself?" said the outlaw, addressing the two friends whom chance had sent him. "I have not a single relation in the world. Laédoyère was my protector and my friend. I am now alone. To-morrow, perhaps, I shall be outlawed or condemned. I never had any fortune besides my pay; I employed my last crown in endeavoring to save Labédoyère from his fate and carry him off. Therefore death is a necessity for me; and when one is determined to die, one must sell one's head to the executioner as dearly as possible. I was thinking just now that the life of one honest man is quite as valuable as the lives of two traitors, and that a well-planted stab with a poniard may confer immortality."

This fit of despair frightened the painter and also Ginevra, who well understood the young man's frame of mind.

The Italian girl admired the beautiful head and the exquisite voice, whose sweet tones lost but little of their sweetness even under the influence of fury; and she forthwith proceeded to pour balm into all the wounds of the unhappy youth.

"Sir," said she, "as for your pecuniary distress, suffer me to offer you the gold which I have saved. My father is rich, I am his only child, he loves me, and I am quite sure that he will not blame me; don't scruple to accept my offer; our wealth is the emperor's gift; we do not possess one centime which is not the result of his munificence. Is it not a proof of gratitude to him, to render a service to one of his faithful soldiers? Take, then, this sum, with as little scruple as I feel in tendering it. It is only money," she added in a tone of contempt. "Now, as to friends, you will be sure to find some," as she said this she proudly raised her head, and her eyes gleamed with an unwonted light. "The head which will droop to-morrow under the fire of a dozen muskets saves yours," she pursued. "Wait until this storm be past, and you may go and seek service in some foreign army, if they do not forget you, or in the French service, if they do."

There is in the consolation that comes from a woman something maternal, foreseeing, and complete; but when words of peace and hope are spoken with that eloquence which proceeds from the heart, and especially when the benefactress is beautiful, it is difficult for a young man to resist. The colonel drew in love through every sense; a faint rose-tint colored his white cheeks, his eyes lost something of the melancholy which obscured them, and he said in peculiar tone of voice, "You are an angel of goodness, but—Labédoyère! Labédoyère!"

At that cry the three looked at each other in silence, and

understoon one another. They were no longer friends of only twenty minutes' standing, but of twenty years'.

" My good fellow," resumed Servin, " can you save him ? "

" I can avenge him."

Ginevre trembled. Although the stranger was handsome, it was not his appearance which had worked upon the young girl; the gentle pity which woman find in their hearts for those sorrows which are not ignoble, had stifled in Ginevra every other affection; but to hear the cry of vengeance, to find in this outlaw an Italian heart, devoted to Napoleon, Corsican generosity, this was too much for her. She therefore contemplated the officer with respectful emotion, which made a deep impression on his heart. This was the first time that any man had aroused in her so lively a feeling. She took a pleasure, as any other woman would have done, in establishing a harmony between the mind of the stranger and the distinguished beauty of his features and happily proportioned figure, which she admired as an artist. Led by chance curiosity to pity, and from pity to intense interest, she was proceeding from that interest to feelings so profound, that she deemed it dangerous to remain there any longer.

" Till to-morrow," she said, leaving behind her with the officer one of the sweetest of her smiles, by way of consolation.

When he saw that smile which threw, as it were, a new light upon the face of Ginevra, the stranger was, for a moment, oblivious of everything.

" To-morrow," he repeated sadly, "to-morrow, Labédoyère—"

Ginevra turned round, placed a finger on her lips, and looked at him as if she would say,—

" Be calm, be prudent."

Thereupon the young man cried, "O Dio, che non vorrei vivere dopo averla veduta" (O God, who would not desire to live after having seen her?)

The peculiar tone in which the words were pronounced made Ginevra tremble.

G

"Are you a Corsican?" she enquired, going back to him, while her heart fluttered with delight.

"I was born in Corsica," he replied, "but was taken to Genoa when I was very young; and as soon as I was old enough for military service, I enlisted."

The beauty of the stranger, the extraordinary charm inspired by his devotion to the emperor, his wound, his misfortunes, even his peril, all vanished from the mind of Ginevra, or rather all were blended in a single new and exquisite feeling. The outlaw was a child of Corsica; he spoke its cherished tongue! For a moment the young girl stood motionless, chained to the spot by a magical sensation; she had under her very eyes a living picture, to which chance and every human feeling combined, contributed their lively colors. At the invitation of Servin the soldier had sat down upon a sofa, and the artist had unfastened the scarf which supported the arm of his guest, and was engaged in baring it in order to dress the wound. Ginevra shuddered when she saw the long deep wound inflicted by a sword blade on the fore-arm of the youth, and uttered a wail. The stranger raised his head to look at her, and smiled There was something touching, something that went to the heart in the care with which Servin removed the lint and touched the wounded flesh; while the face of the patient, though pale and worn, showed pleasure rather than suffering as he looked at the young girl. An artist must needs admire this opposition of sentiments, and the contrasts produced by the white linen and naked arm with the red and blue uniform of the officer. At that moment the studio was somewhat dark, but a parting sunbeam shed its light upon the spot where the outlaw was seated, so that his fine pale face, black hair, and uniform were bathed in light. This simple effect, the superstitious Italian took as a lucky omen. Under this aspect the stranger looked like a heavenly messenger come to her with her native language on his lips, to place her under the charm of the memories of childhood, while her heart gave birth to a feeling as fresh and pure as her early days of innocence. For one brief moment she paused to reflect, as if buried deep in infinite thought; then blushing at having allowed her preoccupation to be seen, she exchanged one sweet, short glance with the outlaw, and fled with his image still before her.

The next day was not a lesson day. Ginevra came to the studio, and the prisoner was able to enjoy the society of his compatriot. Servin, who had a sketch to finish, allowed the recluse to be in the studio, and acted as Mentor to the two young people, who often talked to each other in the Corsican tongue. The poor soldier narrated his sufferings during the retreat from Moscow, for though then only nineteen, he had been present at the passage of the Beresina, he alone of all his regiment; for he had lost his comrades, the only persons who would interest themselves in an orphan. He described in fiery language the grand disaster of Waterloo. His voice was music to the Italian girl. Brought up in Corsican fashion, she knew not what it was to lie, and abandoned herself, with perfect freedom, to her feelings; she avowed them, or rather allowed them to be divined, without resorting to the artifices of the petty calculating coquetry of Parisian young ladies. During this day she frequently paused with her palette in one hand and her brush in the other, not dipping her brush into the colors, but keeping her eyes fixed upon the officer; thus with slightly parted lips would she listen, ever ready to give the picture that touch which she never gave. She was not surprised to see so tender an expression in the eyes of the young man, for she felt her own grow tender in spite of her wish to keep them severe and calm. Then she went on painting for hours together, without raising her head, because he was there, close by her, watching her paint. When first he came to sit beside her and watch her silently, she said to him in a tone of deep emotion and after a long pause, " It amuses you, then, to see people painting ?" On this day, too, she learned that his name was Luigi. Before they separated, it was agreed between them that if any important political event should happen, Ginevra should inform him of it by singing in a low voice certain Italian songs.

On the next day Mademoiselle Thirion informed all her companions, in the strictest confidence, that Ginevra de Piombo had for a lover a young man who came during lesson-time and took up his quarters in the dark closet in the studio.

"Do you," she said to Mademoiselle Roguin, "you who take her part, examine her closely, and you will see how she passes her time."

Ginevra, therefore, was subjected to a diabolical scrutiny. Her songs were listened to; her looks closely watched. At the moment when she fancied she was seen by no one, a dozen pairs of eyes were incessantly brought to bear upon her.

Thus forewarned, these young girls interpreted in their true sense the expressions which flitted across the bright face of the Italian girl, her warblings, and the attention which she devoted to the indistinct sounds which traversed the partition and were audible only to her. At the end of a week, only one of Servin's fifteen pupils had resisted the temptation to examine Louis through the chink in the partition. This one was Laura, who from an instinctive weakness still defended the beautiful Corsican girl. Mademoiselle Roguin tried to induce Laura to remain upon the staircase at the hour of departure, in order that she might have proof of the intimacy between Ginevra and the handsome young man, by taking them by surprise when they were together. But she refused to stoop to play the spy when she could not even plead curiosity, and so became the object of universal reprobation. Ere long the daughter of the officer of the king's chamber discovered that it was not at all fitting that she should go to the studio of a painter whose opinions were tinged with patriotism or Bonapartism, which at that epoch were one and the same thing. So she returned to Servin's no more. If Amélie forgot Ginevra, the evil seed which she had sown produced its fruit; for it gradually came to pass, that either by chance, or from a love of chattering, or through prudery, all the other young women informed their mothers of the strange things which were going on at the studio. One day Mathilde Roguin absented herself; the next lesson-day some other young lady was away, and at last, some three or four of the pupils who had lingered behind after the others had gone, returned no more. Ginevra and Laura, her little friend, were for two or three days the only inhabitants of the deserted studio. The Italian did not notice the alling away, nor even inquire into the cause of the absence of her companions. Since she had invented the means of communicating with Louis, she lived in the studio as in some delightful retreat, alone in the midst of a world, thinking of nothing except the officer and the dangers by which he was threatened. This young girl, although she was a sincere admirer of those noble characters who adhere to their political faith, urged Louis to submit himself promptly to the royal authority, in order that she might keep him in France and Louis was unwilling to submit, because he wished to remain in his hiding-place. If the passions are born and flourish only under the influence of romantic causes, never had so many circumstances concurred to unite two beings in a single sentiment. The friendship of Ginevra for Louis and of Louis for her, thus made more progress in a month, than an ordinary friendship makes in ten years of drawing-room intercourse. Is not adversity the touchstone of character? Thus Ginevra was easily enabled to appreciate Louis and to know him, and they soon felt a mutual esteem, one for the other. Ginevra, who was older than Louis, derived some pleasure from being courted by a young man so great and so much tried by fate, who united manly experience to all the graces of adolescence. Louis, on his part, felt an inexpressible delight in allowing himself to be apparently protected by a young woman of twenty-five. Was it not a proof of love? The combination of gentleness and pride, of force and weakness, in Ginevra's character, was

irresistibly attractive, and Louis was consequently completely
subjugated by her. In short, they already loved each other so
deeply that they had no need either to deny it or to confess it.

One day towards evening Ginevra heard the agreed signal.
Louis knocked a pin against the wood of the partition without
producing much more noise than a spider produces in attach-
ing its web. That was how he asked to be let out of his retreat
Ginevra glanced over the studio, failed to see little Laura, and
therefore replied to the signal. But when Louis opened the
door he saw the young pupil, and hastily retreated. Ginevra,
much surprised, looked round, saw Laura, and going up to her
easel said, "You stay very late, my darling. That head, nevertheless, seems to me to be finished. All you have to do is just
to add one little touch of light on the top of this tress of hair."

"It would be very good of you," said Laura with feeling,
"if you would correct my copy, so that I might have something
of yours to keep."

"I am quite willing," said Ginevra, who was sure that this
would be the best way to get rid of her. "I thought," she
added, while giving a light touch to the picture here and there,
"that you lived a long way from the studio?"

"Oh, Ginevra, I am going away, and for good," said the
young girl sadly

"You are going to leave Monsieur Servin?" asked the
Italian girl, without seeming to be affected by Laura's words,
as she would have been a month before.

"You have not observed then, Ginevra, that for some time
past there is no one here but you and I?"

"That is true," replied Ginevra, on whom the idea flashed
like a souvenir. "Are these young ladies ill then? are they
going to be married? or are their fathers all on duty at the
court?"

"They have all left Monsieur Servin's," replied Laura.

"And wherefore?"

"Because of you, Ginevra."

"Of me !" repeated the Corsican girl, rising with threatening brow, proud look, and flashing eyes.

"Oh, don't be angry, my dear Ginevra," cried Laura sadly, "but my mother wishes me also to leave the studio. All these young ladies have been saying that you were carrying on a love intrigue, that Monsieur Servin was countenancing your lover's remaining in the dark closet. I never believed these calumnies, and said nothing about them to my mother. Yesterday evening, Madame Roguin met my mother at a ball, and asked her whether she continued to send me here. When my mother said yes, Madame Roguin repeated the lies of these young ladies. My mother scolded me soundly ; she maintained that I must have known all that was going on, that I had, by keeping silence, betrayed the confidence which should exist between mother and daughter. Oh, my darling Ginevra, how grieved I am not to be able to be your companion still—I who took you for my model !"

"Oh, we shall meet again in society ; young girls marry," said Ginevra.

"When they are rich," replied Laura.

"Come and see me ; my father has money."

"Ginevra," resumed Laura, who was much affected, "Madame Roguin and my mother are coming here to-morrow to reproach Monsieur Servin ; at least let him know of it beforehand."

If a thunderbolt had fallen two feet from where Ginevra was standing, she could not have been more astonished than she was by this revelation.

"What business was it of theirs ?" she said naively.

"Everybody considered it very wrong. Mamma says that it is contrary to morality. . . ."

"And you, Laura, what do you think of it ?"

The young girl looked at Laura and their thoughts blended ; Laura, who could no longer refrain from tears, threw her arms round her friend's neck and kissed her. At that moment Servin arrived.

"Mademoiselle Genevra," said he enthusiastically, "I have finished my picture; it is now being varnished. But what is the matter with you? It would seem that all these young ladies are taking a holiday, or are in the country."

Laura dried her tears, bowed to Servin, and retired.

"The studio has been deserted for several days past," said Ginevra, "and the young ladies will return no more."

"Bah!"

"Oh, it is no laughing matter," said Genevra. "Listen to me, I am the unwilling cause of your loss of reputation."

The artist began to smile and interrupted his pupil.

"My reputation!" said he. "Why, in a few days my picture will be exhibited."

"The question does not concern your talent, but your morality," said the Italian. "These girls have circulated the story of Louis being shut up here, and have said that you winked at —our love."

"Well there is some truth in that, mademoiselle," replied the professor. "The mothers of these girls are impertinent prudes," he continued. "If they had come to me, all would have been explained. But, do you think that I trouble my head about the matter? Life is too short." And the painter snapped his fingers above his head. Louis, who had heard a part of this conversation, now joined them.

"You are about to lose all your pupils," he cried, "and I shall have been the cause of your ruin?"

The artist took the hands of Louis and Ginevra, and joined them, "you will marry each other, will you not, my children?" he asked with a touching benevolence. They both looked down, and their silence was their first confession of love. "Well," cried Servin, "you will be happy, will you not? Is there anything which can weigh in the balance against the happiness of two creatures such as you are?"

"I am rich," said Ginevra, "and you will allow me to indemnify you."

"Indemnify!" cried Servin. "Why, when it is known that I have been the victim of the calumnies of a set of fools, and that I was harboring an outlaw; why all the liberals in Paris will send me their daughters. I shall then, perhaps, be your debtor."

Louis grasped the hand of his protector without being able to utter a single word; but at length he said with much feeling, "I shall be indebted to you, then, for all my happiness."

"Be happy; I unite you," said the painter, with comic unction, as he laid his hands upon the heads of the two lovers.

This bit of fun on the part of the artist put an end to their serious feelings. They looked at each other and began to laugh. The Italian grasped the hand of Louis tightly; and with a simplicity of action worthy of the manners of her country. "Ah, my dear children," resumed Servin, "you appear to think that everything is as smooth as possible. Well, you are in error." The lovers looked at each other in astonishment.

"Take heart; I am the only person embarrassed by your little frolic. Madame Servin is a little strait-laced, and in truth I don't quite know how we shall square matters with her."

"Good God, I forgot," cried Ginevra. "To-morrow Madame Roguin and Laura's mother are coming here to—"

"I understand," interposed the painter.

"But you can set yourself right," resumed the young girl with a haughty movement of the head; "Monsieur Louis," said she turning towards him and looking at him knowingly, "must by this time have laid aside all antipathy to the king's government. Well," continued she, catching her lover's smile, "to-morrow morning I will send a petition to one of the most influential personages in the war department, a man who can refuse nothing to the daughter of the Baron de Piombo. We will obtain a tacit pardon for Monsieur Louis, the commandant, for *they* won't recognize your colonelcy. And you," she added, turning, to Servin, "can comfront the mothers of my charitable companions by telling them the truth."

"You are an angel," criedServin.

While this scene was going on in the studio, Ginevra's father and mother were growing uneasy at her prolonged absence.

"It is six o'clock, and Ginevra has not yet returned," cried Bartholoméo.

"She has never stayed out so late," replied Piombo's wife.

The two old folks looked at each other with no ordinary anxiety depicted on their faces. Too much excited to sit still, Bartholoméo rose and walked twice round the room, showing a good deal of activity for a man of seventy-seven. Thanks to his robust constitution, he was not much changed since the day of his arrival in Paris, and notwithstanding his height, he still bore himself erect. His large protuberant head, which could be easily seen through the thin white hair, gave a high idea of his character and firmness. His face, which was marked with deep furrows, had assumed a very well marked character and retained that pallid look which inspires veneration. The unnatural fire in his eyes, whose brows were not quite white, and which retained their terrible mobility, showed that he was still under the influence of impetuous passions. The whole head had an aspect of severity; but it was clear that Piombo had the right to be severe His benevolence and gentleness were scarcely known except to his wife and child.

While exercising his functions, or in the presence of a stranger, he never laid aside the majesty which age gave to his appearance; and his habit of knitting his thick brows, of contracting the wrinkles of his face, and of infusing into his looks a Napoleonic fixity, rendered his address quite freezing. During the course of his political existence, he was so generally feared that he was held to be very unsociable; but it is not difficult to explain the origin of this opinion. The life, the morals, and the fidelity of Piombo were a standing reproach to the greater numbers of courtiers. Notwithstanding the delicate missions which had been entrusted to his discretion, and would have been highly profitable to any one else, he possessed no fortune beyond an income of 30,000 francs from money invested in the public funds.

Any one who considers the low price of the funds under the empire, and Napoleon's generosity to those of his faithful servants who were not too proud to ask, will see at once that the Baron de Piombo was a man of the strictest integrity. As for his baron's plumage, *that* he owed to the necessity Napoleon experienced of conferring on Piombo a title when he was sent to a foreign court. Bartholoméo had always possessed a profound hatred for the traitors whom Napoleon summoned around him, hoping to gain them over by dint of victories. It is said that it was Piombo who took three steps to the door of the emperor's cabinet after advising him to get rid of three men in France, on the eve of the day on which Napoleon started for his admirable campaign of 1814. Since the second return of the Bourbons, Bartholoméo gave up wearing the insignia of the Legion of Honor. Never was there a finer specimen of those old republicans, incorruptible adherents of the emperor, who survived like animated ruins of the two most energetic governments that the world has known. If the Baron de Piombo were distasteful to certain courtiers, he had such men as Daru, Drouot, and Carnot for his friends. As for the other politicians, he troubled himself as little about them since Waterloo, as he did about the whiffs of smoke from his cigar.

Bartholoméo de Piombo had bought the old Hôtel de Portenduère, with the very moderate sum which the emperor's mother had given for his Corsican property. He made no alterations in it; for being almost always housed at the expense of the government, he only occupied this dwelling since the catastrophe of Fontainebleau. Like all simple-minded people of high probity, the baron and his wife made no provision for external display; they retained the old furniture of the hotel. The large, lofty, sombre, and naked rooms of this abode, the

immense mirrors in their old gilt frames now nearly black, and
the furniture of the time of Louis XIV. were in keeping with
the appearance of Piombo and his wife—persons worthy of
the olden times.   Under the empire and during the hundred
days, while in the exercise of largely remunerated functions,
the old Corsican had kept a large establishment, from a desire
to do honor to the post he occupied, rather than from a desire
to shine.   His existence and that of his wife were so frugal
and so quiet, that their moderate fortune supplied all their
wants.   To them their daughter, Ginevra, was worth all the
riches in the world.   So, when in May, 1814, the Baron de
Piombo resigned his office, sent away his servants, and closed
his stable door, Ginevra, who like her parents, was simple and
unpretending, did not feel the least regret.   Like all great
minds, she sought her luxury in the strength of her feelings, as
she sought for happiness in solitude and work.   Moreover, these
three persons loved each other too well to attach any value to
the mere frame-work of existence.   Often, and especially since
Napoleon's last most fearful fall, Bartholoméo and his wife
would pass delightful evenings in listening to Ginevra playing
on the piano, or hearing her sing.   They found an immense
source of pleasure in her company, in her lightest word ; they
followed her with their eyes with tender anxiety ; they could
hear her footstep in the court, however lightly it might fall.
Sometimes the three would, like lovers, be silent for hours
together, understanding better than any words could teach
them, the unspoken feelings of their hearts.   This deep feeling, which was the very life of the old people, inspired all
their thoughts.   They had not three existences, but one existence, which, like the flame of a fire, divided itself into three
tongues.   If the recollection of Napoleon's benefits, if the
politics of the hour, would sometimes prevail over the persistent affection of the old people, they could talk on those topics
without breaking the community of their ideas.   For did not
Ginevra share their political passions ?   What could be more

natural than the eagerness with which they took refuge in the heart of their only child. Up till that period the avocations of public life had absorbed the energy of the Baron de Piombo; but when he had resigned his appointments, he found it necessary to transfer his energy to the last sentiment that remained to him. Then, moreover, there was perhaps, apart from the ties which bind a father and mother to their daughter, a powerful reason for the fanaticism of their reciprocal passion; their love was not divided; Ginevra's whole heart belonged to her father, as her father's did to her. Hence the only imperfection in this triple existence; Ginevra's volitions were intense; she was vindictive and impetuous as Bartholoméo had been in youth. The Corsican took a pleasure in developing these savage feelings in his daughter's heart, just as a lion teaches its whelps to spring upon their prey. But since this apprenticeship to vengeance could not very well go on, except under her father's roof, Ginevra forgave her father nothing, and he was obliged to give way to her. Piombo regarded these childish quarrels as mere trifles; but none the less did they teach the child the habit of tyrannizing over her parents. In the midst of the tempests which Bartholoméo loved to arouse, a single affectionate word, a single look, would calm their irritated souls, and they were never so nearly kissing, as when they were actually threatening each other. For the last five years, however, Ginevra, who had become wiser than her father, persistently avoided scenes of this description. Her fidelity, her devotion, the love which reigned in all her thoughts, and her admirable good sense, had conquered her irritations, but at the same time one great evil had resulted from them; Ginevra lived with her mother and father on a footing of equality, which is always fatal. In order to complete our account of the changes which had affected these three persons since their arrival in Paris, we must add that Piombo and his wife, who were uneducated, had allowed Ginevra to study according to her own inclination. Guided only by her girlish fancies, she had learned something of every subject, then quitted it, adopting and abandoning each line of thought in turn, until painting had become her dominant passion. Had her mother been capable of directing her studies, of giving her instruction, and bringing into harmony the gifts of nature, she would have been perfect; her defects arose from the fatal education which the old Corsican had taken pleasure in giving her.

After the old man's heavy footstep had for some time made the floor creak beneath him, he rang the bell and a servant appeared.

"Go and meet Mademoiselle Ginevra," said the baron.

"I always regretted we had no carriage for her," said the baroness.

"She did not want to have one," said Piombo, looking at his wife, who, faithful to the rôle of obedience which she had played for forty years, looked down.

The baroness, who was now seventy, was tall, withered, pale and wrinkled, and bore a close resemblance to those old women whom Schnetz introduces into the Italian scenes of his pictures of genre. She was so accustomed to hold her tongue, that one might have taken her for another Mrs. Shandy; but from time to time a word, a look, a gesture, announced that she had retained her youthful vigor and freshness. Her dress—which was perfectly unstudied—was often deficient in good taste. Generally like some Valideh Sultan, she remained passive, buried in a large armchair, waiting for or watching her Ginevra, her pride and life. Her daughter's beauty, dress, and grace seemed to have become her own. All was well with her so long as Ginevra was happy. Her hair had turned white, and a few scattered locks showed themselves above her brow and wrinkled forehead, or strayed adown her hollow cheeks.

"Ginevra has been rather late every day for about the last fortnight," said the baroness.

"Jean won't go quick enough," said the impatient old man,

buttoning up his blue coat, snatching up his hat, which he fixed firmly on his head, then taking his cane and making off.

"You wont have far to go," said his wife. For in fact the great door had opened and closed, and the old mother heard Ginevra's footsteps in the court. Bartholoméo suddenly reappeared, carrying his daughter in triumph, while she was struggling in his arms. "Here she is, the Ginevra, the Ginevrettina, the Ginevrina, the Genevrola, the Ginevretta, the Ginevra bella."

"Father, you hurt me."

Ginevra was immediately set down with a kind of respect. She shook her head gracefully, in order to allay her mother's fears, and show her that her cry was a mere ruse. Thereupon the mother's pale wan face regained its natural hue, and assumed an air of gaiety. Piombo rubbed his hands most vigorously; a sure sign that he was pleased. He had contracted this habit at the court by seeing Napoleon, when he flew into a rage with any of his generals or ministers who had served him ill, or had been guilty of some fault. When once the muscles of his face relaxed, the least wrinkle in it bespoke benevolence.

At this moment the two old people presented an exact analogy to drooping plants restored to life by a little water after a long drought.

"To table, to table," exclaimed the baron, presenting his large hand to Ginevra, whom he called Signora Piombellina, another symptom of gaiety, which his daughter acknowledged with a smile.

"Ah, yes," said Piombo, when dinner was over, "do you know that your mother says that during the last month you have stayed much later than usual at the studio. It would seem that painting takes precedence of us."

"Oh, father. . . . ."

"No doubt Ginevra is preparing some surprise for us," said the mother."

"What, going to bring me one of your pictures?" said the Corsican, clapping his hands.

"Yes, I am very busy at the studio," she replied.

"What is the matter with you, Ginevra, you look pale?" said her mother.

"No!" cried the girl with a gesture of determination. "No, it shall not be said that Ginevra Piombo has told a lie, even once in her life!"

When Piombo and his wife heard this singular exclamation, they looked at their daughter with an air of astonishment.

"I am in love with a young man," she added in a voice of emotion.   Then, without venturing to look at her parents, she dropped her large eyelids as if to veil the lightning of her eyes.

"Is he a prince?" asked the father ironically, in a tone which made the mother and daughter tremble.

"No, father," she modestly replied; "it is a young man without fortune."

"He must be very handsome then."

"He is unfortunate."

"What is he?"

"He was a comrade of Labédoyère, was outlawed and without a refuge.   Servin concealed him, and . . ."

"Servin is an honest lad, and has acted well," cried Piombo. "But you, my daughter, are acting badly in loving another man more than your own father. . . ."

"I cannot help loving," said Ginevra gently.

"I was hoping," resumed her father, "that my Ginevra would be constant to me until my death; that my care and that of her mother would be the only care she would receive; that our affection would have encountered no rival affection in her heart, and that . . ."

"Did I ever reproach you on account of your fanaticism for Napoleon?" said Ginevra.   "Have you loved no one but me? Have you not been away for months together, as an ambassador? Have I not borne your absence bravely? Life has certain necessities which we must learn to submit to."

" Ginevra."

" No, you do not love me for my own sake, your reproaches show an insupportable egotism."

" You dare to accuse your father's love !" cried Piombo with flaming eyes.

" No, father, I will never accuse you," said Ginevra, with more gentleness than her trembling mother looked for. " You are right in your egotism, just as I am right in my love. Heaven be my witness, that never has daughter better fulfilled her duties towards her parents. I have never seen aught but happiness and love where others often have seen nothing but duties. For fifteen years I have never been from under your protecting wing, and it has been a very sweet pleasure to me to make your days pass happily. But am I ungrateful in yielding to the charm of loving, in desiring to have a husband to protect me when you are gone ?"

" Ah, you are reckoning with your father, Ginevra," pursued the old man in a sinister voice.

Then there ensued a frightful pause, during which no one dared to speak. At length Bartholoméo broke the silence by crying in a heartrending voice,—

"Oh, stay with us, stay with your old father. I could not bear to see you loving a man. You won't have to wait for your liberty long, Ginevra."

" But consider, father, that we shall not be parted, that there will be two to love you instead of one, and that you will know who the man is, in whose care you leave me, when you go. You will be doubly cherished, cherished by me and by him; by him who is one with me, and by me who am altogether one with him."

" Oh, Ginevra, Ginevra," cried the Corsican wringing his hands; "why did you not marry at the time when Napoleon

H

had accustomed me to the idea, and introduced to you dukes and counts?"

"They loved me according to order," said the girl. "Besides, I didn't want to leave you, and they would have taken me away with them."

"You do not want to leave us alone," said Piombo, "but to marry is to leave us alone. I know you, my daughter, you will love us no more. Elisa," added he, looking at his wife, who sat motionless and almost stunned, "we have no longer a daughter, she wants to marry!"

The old man sat down after having raised his hands in the air as if to invoke the Almighty; then overwhelmed with sorrow he remained with his head bent down.

Ginevra saw the agitation of her father, and the moderation of his anger broke her heart. She expected a crisis, fury; she had not armed her heart against her father's gentleness.

"Father," said she in a touching voice. "No, your Ginevra will never forsake you. But love her also a little for herself. Oh, if you only knew how *he* loves me! ah, he would not cause me any pain."

"Comparisons already!" cried Piombo, in a terrible tone, "no, I cannot endure this idea," he continued. "If he loved you as you deserve to be loved, he would kill me; and if he he loved you not, I would stab him."

The hands of Piombo were trembling, his lips were trembling, his whole body trembled, and his eyes darted lightnings. Ginevra only could sustain his glance, for then her own eyes kindled and the daughter was worthy of the father.

"Oh, to love you. Who is the man who is worthy of such a life?" he resumed. "To love you as a father loves, is to be already in Paradise. Who, then, is worthy to be your husband?"

"He is," said Ginevra, "he of whom I feel I am unworthy."

"He?" repeated Piombo mechanically. "Who is *he*?"

"He whom I love."

"Can he know you well enough yet to adore you?"

"But father," said Ginevra, beginning to feel impatient, "even if he did not love me, yet from the moment I love him—"

"You do love him then," cried Piombo. Ginevra gently bowed her head. "You love him then more than you love us?"

"The two feelings cannot be compared," she replied.

"The one is stronger than the other," said Piombo.

"I think so," said Ginevra.

"You shall not marry him," cried the Corsican in a voice which shook the windows of the room.

"I shall marry him," said Ginevra quietly.

"My God! my God!" cried the mother; "how will this quarrel end? Santa Virgina! interpose between them."

The baron, who was striding about the room, sat down; an icy severity over-shadowed his face; he looked fixedly at his daughter, and then said to her in a voice that was sweet and gentle,—

"Well, Ginevra, no, you will not marry him. Oh, do not say that you will; this evening, let me believe the contrary. Do you want to see your father on his knees and his white hairs bowing down before you,—I will kneel down."

"Ginevra Piombo has not been accustomed to promise and not to keep her word," she replied, "I am your daughter."

"She is right," said the baroness, "we were sent into the world to marry."

"So you encourage her in her disobedience," said the baron to his wife, who, struck by his expression, became still as a statue.

"To refuse to obey an unjust order is not disobedience," said Ginevra.

"It cannot be unjust, since it emanates from the mouth of your father, my daughter! Why do you judge me? Is not the repugnance which I feel a counsel from on high? I am, perhaps, preserving you from some misfortune."

"The misfortune would be if he did not love me."

"Always *him*."

"Yes, always; he is my life, my wealth, my thought. Even if I obeyed you, he would be ever in my thoughts. To forbid me to marry him is equivalent to my hating you."

"You love us no longer."

"Oh!" cried Ginevra shaking her head.

"Well then, forget him, remain faithful to us. After we— you understand."

"Father, do you wish to make me long for your death?" cried Ginevra.

"I shall live longer than you! children who do not honour their father and mother die soon," cried the father, driven to the last stage of exasperation.

"The more reason why I should marry quickly and be happy," said she.

Her coolness, the strength of her reasoning, completed Piombo's trouble. The blood rushed violently to his head; his face grew purple.

Ginevra shuddered; she flew, swift as a bird, on to her father's knees, put her arms round his neck, stroked his hair, and quite overcome exclaimed,—

"Oh yes, let me die first. I could not survive you, my father, dear father."

"Oh Ginevra, my mad Ginevra!" replied Piombo, all his anger disappearing under this caress, as ice melts in the rays of the sun.

"It was time for you to finish," said the baroness with emotion.

"Poor mother!"

"Ah, Ginevretta, my Ginevra bella!" and the father played

with his daughter as if she were a child of six years old. He took a pleasure in undoing the wavy tresses of her hair, in dancing her upon his knee.

There was a touch of madness in the expression of his affection.

His daughter soon began to scold while she embraced him, and jokingly tried to get him to consent that Louis should be introduced to her home; but jokingly also, the father refused. Then Ginevra sulked, returned, and sulked again. At the end of the evening she felt glad that she had familiarized her father's heart both with her love for Louis and with the idea of a not distant marriage. The next day she said no more about her love, went later to the studio, and returned from it early, was more affectionate in her manner to her father than she had ever been, and showed herself full of gratitude, as if to thank him for the consent which, by his silence, he seemed to give to her marriage. In the evening she treated them to a good deal of music, and often did she exclaim,—" It requires a man's voice for this nocturne."

She was an Italian girl; that is saying everything. One day after an interval of eight days her mother beckoned to her; she went up to her mother, who said to her in a low whisper, "I have persuaded your father to receive him."

"Oh, mother, you make me very happy!"

That day then Ginevra had the pleasure of returning to her father's dwelling, hanging on the arm of Louis. This was the second time that the poor officer had come out of his lurking-place. The urgent solicitations which Ginevra addressed to the Duc de Feltre, then minister of war, had been crowned with complete success. Louis had just been restored to the list of officers unattached. That was a very great step towards a brighter future. Since he had been informed by his young friend of all the difficulties which awaited him at the hands of the baron, the young commandant felt a fear, which he did not dare to confess, of not pleasing him. This man, who had borne adversity with so much fortitude, who was so brave upon the battle field, trembled at the thought of entering the drawing-room of the Piombos. Ginevra could feel him trembling and his emotion, whose basis was their mutual happiness, was to her a further proof of love.

"How pale you are," she said to him when they reached the door of the hotel.

"Oh, Ginevra, if it were only life that was at stake!"

Although Bartholoméo had been informed by his wife of the official presentation of Ginevra's lover, he did not rise to meet him, but remained in the armchair in which he was wont to sit. The severity of his brow was quite glacial.

"Father," said Ginevra, "I bring you a person whom you will, no doubt, be pleased to see. This is Monsieur Louis, a soldier who stood within four paces distance of the emperor, at the battle of Mont Saint-Jean."

The Baron de Piombo rose, looked furtively at Louis, and said to him in a sardonic voice, "You wear no decoration, sir?"

"I don't wear the riband of the Legion of Honor now;" Louis uttered these words timidly, and remained standing in a posture of humility.

Ginevra, wounded by her father's want of politeness, brought forward a chair. The officer's answer satisfied the old servant of Napoleon. Madame Piombo, perceiving that her husband's eyebrows were resuming their natural position, said, with a view to sustaining the conversation,—

"The gentleman's resemblance to Nina Porta is astonishing. Don't you think that he has quite the features of a Porta?"

"Nothing more natural," replied the young man, on whom the flaming eyes of Piombo were now fixed. "Nina was my sister."

"Are you Luigi Porta?" asked the old man.

"Yes."

Bartholoméo de Piombo rose, staggered, was forced to take hold of a chair to support himself, and looked at his wife. Elisa Piombo went up to him; then the two old people quitted the room arm in arm, leaving their daughter with a sort of horror. Luigi Porta looked at Ginevra in astonishment; she grew as white as a marble statue, and stood with her eyes fixed upon the door through which her father and mother had disappeared. This silence and this retreat were so solemn that the feeling of fear, perhaps for the first time entered the soldier's heart. Ginevra clasped her hands tightly together and exclaimed in a voice so broken by emotion as to be scarcely audible, except to the ear of a lover, " What misery in a single word ! "

" In the name of our love, what have I said ? " asked Luigi Porta.

" My father," she replied, " has never spoken of our deplorable history, and I was too young when we left Corsica, to know anything of the story."

" Are we in *vendetta* ? " asked Luigi, trembling.

"Yes; on questioning my mother I learned that the Portas had killèd my brothers and burnt our house. My father then massacred all your family. How did you escape, you whom, as he supposed at least, he bound to the posts of a bed, before setting fire to the house ? "

" I don't know," replied Luigi. " When six years old I was taken to Genoa, to the house of an old man named Colonna. I did not hear a single detail about my family. I only knew that I was an orphan and without fortune. This Colonna acted the part of a father to me, and I bore his name until the day when I entered the service. As I required documents to show who I was, old Colonna said, that I, powerless as I was, and scarcely better than a child, had enemies. He persuaded me to take the name of Luigi only, in order that I might escape them."

" Fly, fly, Luigi ! " cried Ginevra, " but no, I must go with

you. So long as you are in my father's house you have nothing
to fear. As soon as you quite it, you must beware ; you will
be exposed to danger after danger. My father has two Corsicans in his service, and if he does not try to take your life,
they will."

"And will this hatred exist between you and me, Ginevra?"

The young girl smiled sadly, and bowed her head. She
then quickly and proudly raised it, saying,—

"Oh, Luigi, pure and sincere indeed must be our feelings
to give me strength to walk in the path which I am about to
enter. But the question is a question of life-long happiness,
is it not?"

Luigi made no verbal answer, but smiled and pressed
Ginevra's hand. The young girl understood that it was only
genuine love which could abstain at such a moment from vulgar protestations. The calm and conscientious manner in
which Luigi expressed his feelings, in some sort announced
their force and their durability. The destiny of the lovers was
then sealed. Ginevra foresaw that there were fierce conflicts
to be sustained, but the idea of giving up Louis, an idea which
had perhaps floated through Ginevra's mind, completely vanished. His and his for ever, she suddenly and energetically
drew him out of the hotel, and did not leave him until he had
reached the house in which she had procured for him a
modest lodging.

When she got back to her father's house, that kind of serenity
which is born of a strong determination had stolen over her.
There was not in her manner any change that betokened uneasiness. There was no boldness, there was even much sweetness of expression, in the look which she gave her father and
mother, whom she found on the point of sitting down to
dinner. She saw her mother had been weeping; the redness
of her aged eyelids shook Ginevra's resolution for a moment,
but she concealed her emotion. Piombo seemed to be under
the dominion of a sorrow too deep and concentrated to be

expressed in common language.   The servants brought in dinner, but no one touched it.   A loathing for food is one of the symptoms of these grand crises of the heart.   They all three rose to leave the table without one word having been exchanged between them.   When Ginevra was seated between her father and mother in the vast, sombre and solemn drawing-room, Piombo would have spoken but his voice failed him.   He tried to walk, but found himself unable, so he sat down and rang the bell.

"Pietro," said he to the servant, "Light a fire, I am cold."

Ginevra trembled and looked at her father with anxiety. The struggle that was on the eve of taking place must be terrible, and her face was quite upset.   She knew the extent of the danger which threatened her, but she did not tremble; while the furative looks which Bartholoméo cast upon his daughter seemed to announce that he was at that moment afraid of that character whose violence was his own handiwork.   Between them no middle course was possible. Thus the certitude of the change which might take place in the feelings of father and daughter kindled an expression of terror on the face of the baroness.

"Ginevra, you love the enemy of your family," said Piombo at length, without venturing to look at his daughter.

"That is true," said she.

"You will have to choose between him and us.   Our Vendetta is a part of ourselves.   The person who does not espouse my revenge, is not a member of my family."

"My choice is made," replied Ginevra in a calm voice.

Bartholoméo was deceived by his daughter's tranquillity.

"Oh, my dear daughter," cried the old man, whose eyelids were wet with tears, the first—the only tears he shed in the course of his life.

"I will be his wife," said Ginevra abruptly.

Bartholoméo felt stunned; but recovering self-possesion he replied,—

"This marriage shall not take place so long as I am alive. I will never consent to it."

Ginevra was silent.

"But do you consider" said the baron, "that Luigi is the son of the man who killed your brothers?"

"He was only six years old when the crime was commited, and must be innocent of it," she replied.

"A Porta!" cried Bartholoméo.

"But" said the girl sharply, "have I ever shared this hatred? Did you educate me in the belief that a Porta was a monster? Could I suppose that one of them was left? Is it not natural that your Vendetta should succumb to my feelings?"

"A Porta!" said Piombo. "If his father had formerly found you in your bed, you would not be alive now. He would have put you to death a hundred times."

"That may be" she replied; "but his son has given me more than life. To look upon Luigi is a happiness, deprived of which I cannot live. Through Luigi I have come to know the world of feeling. I have perhaps seen faces more beautiful even than his, but none which has had such a charm for me. I have perhaps heard voices—but no, no, never have I heard voices more melodious: Luigi loves me, he shall be my husband."

"Never," said Piombo, "I would rather see you in your coffin, Ginevra."

Tho old Corsican rose and began striding about the apartment. Then scanned by pauses which showed his intense agitation, the following words fell from his lips:—

"You think, perhaps, that you will bend my will—undeceive yourself—I will not have a Porta for my son-in-law. That is my final determination. Don't let the subject be mentioned to me again—I am Bartholoméo de Piombo: do you hear, Ginevra?"

"Do you attach any mysterious meaning to those words?" asked Ginevra coldly.

"They mean that I have a dagger, and that I have no fear of human laws. We Corsicans go before God to justify ourselves."

"Well," said the girl, rising, "I am Ginevra de Piombo, and I declare that in six months I shall be the wife of Luigi Porta. You are a tyrant, father," she added, after a fearful pause.

Bartholoméo clenched his fists and struck the marble mantelpiece. "Ah, we are in Paris," he murmured.

Then he was silent, and crossing his arms and drooping his head upon his breast, he uttered not another word during the whole evening. Ginevra having given vent to her determination, assumed an air of imperturbable self-possession. She sat down to the piano, and sang, and played some exquisite pieces with a grace and feeling which showed perfect freedom of spirit; so gaining a triumph over her father, whose brow showed no signs of calming. The old man deeply felt this tacit insult, and reaped at that moment one of the bitter fruits of the education which he had given to his daughter. Respect is a barrier which affords equal protection to parents and to children. It saves the former from sorrow, and the latter from remorse.

On the next day Ginevra, when about to leave the house, at the hour at which she usually started for the studio, found the door of the hotel fastened against her. But, however, she very soon found a way of informing Luigi Porta of her father's severity. A lady's-maid, who could not read writing, conveyed to the young officer a letter from Ginevra. During five days the two lovers carried on a correspondence, thanks to those schemes which young people of twenty can always invent. Thus, father and daughter rarely spoke to each other. There lay at the bottom of either heart an element of hatred; they suffered, but they suffered proudly, and in silence. When

they found how strong were the bonds of affection which
united them, they tried to break them, but without success.
No tender reflection now lighted up the stern features of
Bartholoméo when he looked at his daughter. When the girl
looked at her father, there was a touch of fierceness in her
face, and reproach sat upon her innocent forehead. She indulged indeed in a train of happy thoughts, but at times
remorse would steal the brightness from her eye. It was not
difficult to guess that she could never tranquilly enjoy a felicity
which would cause her parents unhappiness. But alike in the
case of Bartholoméo and in that of his daughter, all the irresolution caused by the native goodness of their dispositions
was doomed to give way before their pride, before the rancor
peculiar to Corsicans. They both nursed their anger and shut
their eyes to the future. Perhaps also they both flattered
themselves that the one would give way to the other.

On Ginevra's birthday her mother bethought her to take
advantage of the memories associated with the day to bring
about a reconciliation between the father and daughter, whose
grave disunion filled her with despair. They were all three in
Bartholoméo's own room. Ginevra guessed her mother's intention from the hesitation visible in her features, and smiled
sadly. Just at that moment a servant announced the arrival of
two notaries, who were ushered in, accompanied by several
witnesses. Bartholoméo looked fixedly at the two men, whose
cold and formal faces were calculated to wound feelings so
passionate as those of the three principal actors in the scene.
The old man looked uneasily at his daughter, whose face wore
a smile of triumph, which made him suspect that some catastrophe was about to take place. But he assumed, after the
manner of the savage, a delusive passiveness, and looked at
the two notaries with calm curiosity. At the silent invitation
of the old man, the strangers sat down.

"I assume that I have the honor of addressing the Baron
de Piombo?" said the elder of the two notaries.

Bartholoméo bowed. The notary slightly moved his head, and looked at the young lady; his expression being that of a sheriff's officer arresting a debtor. He then pulled out his snuff-box, and taking from it a pinch of snuff administered it to his nose in little doses, while he conned the opening phrases of his address. Its delivery was accompanied by continual pauses, an oratorical device which we shall imperfectly represent by a dash.

"Sir," said he, "I am Monsieur Roguin, notary to this young lady your daughter; and we are here—my colleague and I—with a view to carrying out the intent of the law, and —to put an end to the differences which—it would appear— have arisen—between you and the young lady, your daughter —on the subject of—her—marriage with Monsieur Luigi Porta."

It is probable that this period, which was most pedantically delivered, seemed to Maître Roguin too fine to be immediately understood; so he stopped and looked at Bartholoméo with an expression peculiar to men of business, an expression which is a mean between servility and familiarity. From their habit of feigning an interest in the persons whom they address, the features of notaries contract a grimace, which they put on and off, as they do their pallium of office. This mask of benevolence, which is obviously purely mechanical, so irritated Bartholoméo that he had to summon up all his self-control to resist the temptation of throwing Roguin out of the window. An angry expression stole over his furrowed face, and induced the notary to say to himself, "I am producing an effect."

"But," resumed he in hurried accents, "but, Monsieur le Baron, in cases of this description, it is our duty to be essentially mediatory at the outset,—I beg you will be good enough to listen to me.—It is evident that Mademoiselle Ginevra Piombo—attains on this very day—the age at which it is sufficient, merely to go through the prescribed formal demands, before proceeding forthwith to the celebration of her marriage

--in spite of the absence of her parents' consent : now—it is
customary among families—which enjoy a certain amount of
social consideration—which belong to society, in fact—which
possess a certain dignity—which deem it important, in short,
not to let the public into the secret of their dissensions—and
which, moreover, do not desire to injure themselves by stamp-
ing with disapprobation, the future of a young couple—(for
that is to injure oneself)—it is customary, I say—among these
honorable families—not to permit such formal records to sub-
sist—records which remain—which are monuments of a divi-
sion which—in the long-run comes to an end. From the
moment—sir, when a young woman has recourse to these
formal demands—she gives proof of an intention too decided
for her father, and—her mother (he added, turning towards
the baroness) to hope to see her follow their advice. Paternal
opposition being therefore of no effect—from this fact—in the
first place—and being also invalidated by the law, it is clear
that a prudent man, after having addressed a final remonstrance
to his child, accords her liberty to . . . ."

Monsieur Roguin stopped short when he perceived that he
might go on speaking for two hours in that strain, without
getting any answer ; and he experienced, moreover, a peculiar
sensation from the look of the man whom he was endeavoring
to persuade. An extraordinary revolution had taken place in
the countenance of Bartholoméo. The contraction of all the
muscles of the face gave him an appearance of cruelty altogether undefinable, and he looked at the notary with the look
of a tiger. The baroness remained mute and passive. Ginevra
waited calm and resolute ; she knew that the voice of the
notary was more powerful than her own, and thereupon she
seemed determined to keep silent. At the moment when
Roguin ceased to speak, the scene became so terrible that the
unknown witnesses trembled ; never, perhaps, had they experienced a similar silence. The notaries looked at each other

as if in search of counsel one from the other, then rose and went to the window together.

" Did you ever meet clients framed in this fashion ?" asked Roguin of his comrade.

" There is nothing to be done with them," replied the younger notary. " If I were in your place, I would confine myself to reading the documents. The old man does not seem to me to be an amusing character; he is passionate, and you will gain nothing by attempting to debate with him."

Monsieur Roguin then read a stamped document containing a written statement which had been prepared in advance, and coldly asked Bartholoméo what his answer to it was.

" There are then, in France, laws which take away a father's authority ?" asked the Corsican.

" Sir," said Roguin in his honied accents.

" Which tear a daughter away from her father ?"

" Sir," said the notary.

" Which rob an old man of his last consolation ?"

" Sir, your daughter does not belong to you, except . . . ."

" Which kill him ?"

" Sir, permit me."

There is nothing more frightful than the self-possession and the precise arguments of a notary, when intruded into the passionate scenes in which he is called upon to interpose. The faces which Piombo saw before him seemed to him to have come straight from hell; his cool and concentrated anger knew no bounds, from the moment when the calm and almost musical voice of his little opponent uttered that fatal *permit*.

He sprang forward, and seizing a long poinard suspended on a nail above the chimney-piece, rushed towards his daughter. The younger of the two notaries and one of the witnesses threw themselves between him and Ginevra; but Bartholoméo roughly overthrew the two mediators, while his inflamed features and flashing eyes seemed more terrible than the glittering dagger. When Ginevra found herself face to face with her father, she looked at him fixedly with an air of triumph, slowly approached him, and went upon her knees.

"No! no! I cannot," said he, casting the weapon so forcibly from him that it buried itself deeply in the floor.

"Well then, be merciful, be merciful," said the girl. "You hesitate to kill me, and yet you refuse to let me live. Oh, father, never did I love you so well as now. Give me then Luigi. Upon my knees I ask your consent. A daughter may humble herself before her father. Give me Luigi, or I die."

The violent emotion which choked her, prevented her from proceeding; she lost her voice, her convulsive struggles clearly showed that she was between life and death. Bartholoméo repulsed his daughter harshly.

"Away," he cried, "Luigi Porta's wife cannot be a Piombo. I have no daughter now. I lack strength to curse you, but I cast you off; you have no father now. My Ginevra Piombo is buried—there," he cried in deep tones, while he pressed his hands tightly to his heart. "Away with you, then, miserable being," he added, after a moment's pause. "Away, and never appear before me again." Then he took Ginevra's arm, and led her quietly out of the house.

"Luigi," cried Ginevra, as she entered the humble lodging of the officer, "my Luigi, we have no fortune but our love."

"Then we are richer than all the kings on earth," said Luigi.

"My father and mother have abandoned me," said she with profound melancholy.

"I will love you for them."

"We shall be very happy then?" cried she, with a gaiety that had something fearful in it.

"Yes, and for ever," replied he, straining her to his heart.

On the morrow of the day on which Ginevra left her father's house, she went to Madame Servin, and begged that lady to afford her shelter and protection, until the interval required by the law before her marriage with Luigi could take place, had elapsed. Then began her apprenticeship to those sorrows which the world scatters in the path of those who violate its usages. Madame Servin, in her grave annoyance at the injury inflicted on her husband through Ginevra's adventure, received the fugitive very coldly, and told her in language of circum-spect politeness that she must not count upon her support.

Too proud to insist, but astonished at a selfishness that was new to her, the young Corsican girl took some apartments in a furnished lodging-house near to the house in which Luigi was staying. The son of the Portas passed every day at the feet of his intended bride; his youthful love and high-toned lan-guage dissipated the clouds which a father's disapproval had piled upon the brow of his banished daughter. So beautiful a picture of the future did Luigi draw, that Ginevra learned at length to smile, though she could not forget the rigor of her parents.

One morning the servant of the house brought Ginevra several trunks containing various stuffs, linen, and a heap of things necessary to a young woman beginning house-keeping. She recognized in this consignment the thoughtful kindness of a mother; for on turning over these presents she found a purse in which the baroness had put the sum belonging to her daughter, and also her own savings. Accompanying the money there was a letter in which the mother conjured her daughter to abandon the fatal scheme of marriage if there was yet time. She had been obliged (so ran the letter) to adopt most unheard-of precautions in order to convey that slight assistance to Ginevra. She entreated her daughter not to accuse her of harshness, if in future she left her to her fate; she feared she could aid her no further, gave her a mother's blessing, and expressed a hope that Ginevra might find happinesss in that fatal marriage, if she persisted in it, and assured her that she thought of nothing but her dear daughter. Here several words of the letter had been effaced by tears.

"O my mother!" exclaimed Ginevra, quite softened. She felt a desire to throw herself at her mother's knees, to see her

I

and breathe the beneficent atmosphere of her father's house. She was just rushing out when Luigi entered, and at sight of him her filial affection gave way, her tears dried, and she did not feel strong enough to forsake this lad, who was so unfortunate and so loving. To be the only hope of a noble being, to love him, and to leave him—such a sacrifice is an act of treason of which young hearts are quite incapable. Ginevra had the generosity to bury her sorrow in the depths of her soul.

At length the wedding day arrived; Ginevra found herself alone. Luigi had taken advantage of the time she spent in dressing herself, to go and find the necessary witnesses to the signature of the marriage contract. These witnesses were two worthy people. One of them, a former quarter-master of the hussars, had, while in the army, contracted such obligations to Luigi as can never be erased from the mind of an honest man. He was now a coach-master, and possessed several hackney carriages. The second witness, a master builder, was the owner of the house in which the newly-married couple were to reside. Each of the witnesses got a friend to accompany him, and then the four men went with Luigi to fetch the bride. Being little accustomed to the conventionalities of social life, and deeming the service, which they were about to render Luigi, a very simple one, these worthy folks had dressed themselves decently, but not in holiday attire; so that they did not present the gay appearance of a wedding-party. Ginevra dressed herself very simply, that her attire might be in conformity with her fortune; nevertheless, there was something so noble and so imposing in her beauty, that at sight of her the compliments which the witnesses felt it their bounden duty to address to her, died upon their lips; they saluted her respectfully, and she bowed in return; they confined themselves to looking at her in silent admiration; joy can have free play only among persons who feel that they are equals.

Thus, as chance would have it, all the surroundings of the

betrothed were sad and sombre; there was nothing to reflect their happiness. The church and the mayor's house were not far from the hotel.

The two Corsicans, followed by the four witnesses required by law, determined to set out on foot; so that this grand scene in the drama of social life was deprived of all pomp and circumstance. The wedding party found in the court of the mairie a crowd of carriages, showing that there was a large gathering of visitors within. They went upstairs, and reached a very large hall, in which the couples who were to be made happy on that day were very impatiently awaiting the arrival of the mayor of the district. Ginevra sat down near to Luigi at the end of a long bench, while their witnesses remained standing for lack of seats. Two brides ostentatiously arrayed in white, covered with ribands, lace, and pearls, and crowned with wreaths of orange flowers, whose satin buds glistened beneath the veils, were there, surrounded by their joyous relatives, and accompanied by their mothers, whom they looked at with a glance of contentment mingled with fear.

Every eye reflected their happiness, and every face seemed to shower blessings upon them. Fathers, witnesses, brothers, and sisters went and came like a swarm of bees, rejoicing in a transient sunbeam. Every one seemed to understand the value of that fugitive moment of existence, in which the heart finds itself between two sets of hopes—the aspirations of the past, and the promises of the future. At this sight, Ginevra felt her heart swell and pressed the arm of Luigi, who darted one glance at her. A tear stole to the eye of the young Corsican, for then he understood more fully than ever all that his Ginevra was sacrificing for him. That precious tear drove from the young girl's memory the isolation in which she found herself. Love poured its precious rays upon the two lovers, who under its influence saw nothing but each other in all that tumult; there, in that crowd, they were, as they would be in

life, alone.   Their witnesses, indifferent to the ceremony,
quietly discussed their own affairs.

"Oats are very dear," said the quarter-master to the mason.

"They are not yet so dear as plaster, proportionately," replied the builder, and they took a turn in the hall.

"What a lot of time is wasted here!" said the mason, re-
placing in his pocket a huge silver watch.

Luigi and Ginevra were sitting so close together that they
seemed only one and the same person.   Surely a poet would
have admired these two heads, brought together by the same
sentiment, and flushed with the same color; melancholy and
mute in the presence of two noisy wedding-parties, of four
boisterous families, decked with sparkling diamonds and with
flowers, and gay with transient gaiety.   All the joy which these
bustling and gorgeous groups displayed in their dress and
bearing, Luigi and Ginevra kept buried in the depths of their
hearts.   On the one hand was the coarse tumult of pleasure;
on the other the delicate silence of joyful hearts: earth and
heaven.   But the tremulous Ginevra could not entirely lay
aside the weakness of the woman. · With the superstition of an
Italian she saw a presage in this contrast, and thus a feeling of
terror, as unconquerable as her love, lurked in the bottom of
her heart.   All at once an official, dressed in the city livery,
threw open a folding door; silence was called, and his voice
rang out almost like a shriek as he summoned Monsieur
Luigi da Porta and Mademoiselle Ginevra de Piombo.   It
was an embarrassing moment for the two lovers.   The celebrity
of the name Piombo attracted attention; the spectators looked
about them expecting to see a sumptuous wedding-party.
Ginevra rose, took Luigi's arm, and, followed by the witnesses,
moved forward with a firm step, while her haughty air overawed the crowd.   A murmur of surprise which gradually
swelled, a general clatter of tongues, rose to remind Ginevra that
the world would hold her to account for the absence of her

parents. It seemed that she was pursued by her father's malediction.

"Wait for the respective families," said the mayor to the clerk, who was hastily reading the documents.

"The father and mother protest," replied the secretary phlegmatically.

"What, on both sides?" pursued the mayor.

"The husband is an orphan."

"Where are the witnesses?"

"Here," said the secretary, pointing to the four men, who, mute and motionless and with folded arms, resembled four statues.

"But if there is a protest?" said the mayor.

"The forms of respect have been complied with according to law," replied the clerk rising to hand over to the mayor the documents annexed to the marriage contract.

There was something dishonoring in this bureaucratic colloquy, which, in a very few words, summed up a complete history. The mutual hate of the Portas and Piombos, terrific passions were thus inscribed upon the pages of a public registrar as the annals of a nation are engraved upon a tombstone in a few lines, often indeed in a single word:—Robespierre, Napoleon. Ginevra shuddered. As the dove in its flight across the waters found no rest but the ark for the sole of her foot, so Ginevra could find no refuge for her eyes save the eyes of Luigi; for all around her was cold and sad. The mayor's look was stern and reproachful, while his clerk examined the two lovers with malevolent curiosity. Nothing could less resemble a fête. Like every other circumstance of life when stripped of its accessories, the situation was simple in itself, but vast and complicated to the eye of thought. After sundry interrogations to which the pair replied, after some words had been muttered by the mayor, and the signatures placed upon the registrar, Luigi and Ginevra were united. Then the young Corsicans, whose union presented all the romance which genius has consecrated in Romeo and Juliet, passed between two hedges of gay relatives who had no connexion with them, and were almost angry at the delay occasioned by that melancholy marriage. When the young girl found herself in the court of the mairie, under the open sky, a sigh escaped from her bosom.

"Oh, will a whole life of love and tender care suffice to repay the courage and affection of my Ginevra?" said Luigi.

These words, accompanied by tears of happiness, banished all remembrance of suffering from Ginevra's mind, for she *had* suffered by appearing in the face of the world to claim that happiness which her family refused to sanction.

"Why should people interfere with you and me?" she asked, with a simplicity of feeling which enchanted Luigi.

Pleasure lightened the hearts of the husband and wife. They saw neither earth nor sky, nor houses, but flew as with wings towards the church. At length they reached a small and obscure chapel, and before a simple altar an old priest celebrated their union. There, as at the mairie, they were surrounded by two weddings, which persecuted them with their display. The church, crammed with friends and relations, echoed with the noise produced by the carriages, the vergers, the beadles, and the priests. Altars blazed in full ecclesiastic pomp, fresh-looking wreaths of orange flowers adorned the statues of the Virgin. Everywhere were flowers, incense, sparkling lights, and velvet cushions trimmed with gold. God himself seemed to be a party to this pleasure of a day. At that stage of the ceremony, when that symbol of eternal union, that yoke of white satin which is so soft, so brilliant, and so light for some, so leaden to the greater number, should have been held above the heads of Luigi and Ginevra, the priests looked round in vain for the youths who generally perform the glad office. Two of the witnesses supplied their place. The clergyman delivered a hurried address to the young couple, about the perils of life and the duties which they should some day impress on the minds of their children ; and while dwelling on the topic he insinuated a reproach about the absence of Ginevra's parents. Then, having set the lovers in the presence of God, as the mayor had set them in the presence of the law, he finished the mass and left them.

"God bless them," said Vergniaud to the mason when they reached the church porch. "Never were two creatures better fitted for one another. The parents of this girl are dotards. I know no braver soldier than Colonel Louis. If every one had behaved as he did, *the other* would be still upon the throne."

The soldier's benediction, the only one which they had received that day, shed balm upon Ginevra's heart.

They separated with a hearty shake of the hand, and Luigi thanked his landlord cordially.

"Good-bye, my brave comrade," said Luigi to the quarter-master, "I thank you."

"Entirely at your service, colonel , heart, and body, horses and carriages, all I have is at your service."

"How he loves you," said Ginevra.

Luigi lost no time in taking his bride to the house which they were to inhabit. They soon reached their modest apart-ments, and there, when the door was closed behind them, Luigi took his wife in his arms, and exclaimed, "My Ginevra, for now you are mine ; here is the real festivity ; here all will wear smiles for us."

Together they went through the three rooms which com-posed their home. The anteroom was dining-room and drawing-room in one. On the right was a bed-room, and on the left a large study, which Luigi had arranged for the use of his dear wife. It contained easels, colour-boxes, casts, models, mannikins, in short all the implements of an artist.

"That is where I shall work then," said Ginevra, with an expression of childlike simplicity. She gazed for a long time at

the hangings and the furniture, turning from time to time to
Luigi to thank him ; for there was a kind of magnificence in
this little retreat. There was a book case containing Ginevra's favorite books, and at the bottom of the room there was
a piano.

Ginevra sat down upon a sofa, drew Luigi to her, and
squeezing his hand, said in a caressing tone, " You have good
taste."

" Your words make me very happy," said he.

" But let us look at everything," said Ginevra, from whom
Luigi had concealed the ornamental preparations he had introduced into their retreat.

Then they went into the nuptial chamber, fresh and white
like a virgin

" Don't let us stay here," said Luigi, laughing.

"Oh, but I must see everything !" and the imperious Ginevra
looked at every article of furniture with the inquisitive attention of
an antiquary examining a medal. She felt the silks and scrutinized everything with the artless contentment of a young bride
spreading out the riches of her trousseau.

" We are ruining ourselves at starting," she said, half gladly,
half sorrowfully.

" That is true ; all the arrears of my pay are here," replied
Luigi ; " I sold them to a good fellow named Gigonnet."

" Why ?" inquired Ginevra, in a reproachful tone, which betrayed a secret satisfaction. "Do you think I would be less
happy in an attic? But all this is very pretty and it is ours,"
she resumed.

Luigi gazed at her so enthusiastically that she looked down
and said to him,—

" Let us go and see the rest."

In the attics above these three rooms there was a study for
Luigi, a kitchen, a servant's room. Genevra was quite satisfied
with her little domain, though the only view it commanded
was the large blank wall of an neighboring house, and the

court which lighted it was sombre.   The hearts of the two
lovers were so glad, hope made the future so bright for them
that they could see none but enchanting images in their myste.
rious asylum. They were buried in that vast house, and lost in
the wilderness of Paris, like two pearls in their bed of shell in
the bosom of the deep, deep ocean.   To others such a dwelling would have been a prison, to them it was a paradise.

The first days of their union were given up to love.   It was
more than they could do to set themselves to work at once:
they could not resist the enchantment of their passion.

Luigi would lie for hours together at the feet of his bride,
adoring the color of her hair, the shape of her forehead, the
exquisite casing of the eyes, the purity and whiteness of the
arches beneath which they gently rolled, sweetly expressing the
happiness of contented love.

Ginevra would play with the hair of her Luigi, and never tire
of contemplating " la beltà folgorante," to use her own expression, of the young man, and the elegance of his features. She
was enchanted with the nobleness of his manners ; he with the
grace of hers.   Like children, they toyed with trifles ; those
trifles always carried them back to their love ; and they only
abandoned their gambols to fall back into the reverie of the
far niente.   An air sung by Ginevra brought before them again
the delightful gradations of their love.   Then uniting their
steps, as they had united their hearts, they wandered through
the fields and still found their love in all things—in the flowers,
in the sky, and in the burning colors of the setting sun. They
read it even in the capricious clouds which encountered in mid
air.   One day was never like another ; as time flowed on their
love increased in strength because it was true love.   They
had tested each other in a few days, and had instinctively re
cognized that their hearts belonged to that class whose inexhaustible wealth seems to give promise of new joys in the future.
Theirs was love in all its simplicity, with its interminable chit-
chat, its half-finished phrases, its long silences, its fierce out-

bursts, its oriental rest. Luigi and Ginevra had learned love in all its vast variety; for love is vast and various like the ocean, which viewed superficially or in haste, is accused of monotony by vulgar minds; while certain privileged beings might spend a whole lifetime in admiring it, and ceaselessly discover in it changing phenomena to enchant them.

The day, however arrived when prudence intruded, to drag the young couple from their Eden. They found that they must work in order to live. Ginevra, who possessed a peculiar talent for imitating old pictures, set to work to produce copies, and acquired a connection among the picture dealers. Luigi on his part was active in trying to obtain employment; but it was very difficult for a young officer, whose only acquirements were a thorough knowledge of military manœuvres, to find any-thing to do in Paris.

At last, one day, when weary of his fruitless exertions, and desperate at heart at finding that the burden of their existence fell entirely upon Ginevra, he bethought him to try and turn his penmanship, which was very good, to some account. With that perseverance of which his wife had set him an example, he went to the attorneys, the notaries, and the advocates of Paris to ask them for work. The frankness of his bearing, and the position in which he was placed, told greatly in his favor, and he obtained so many commissions, that he was obliged to get some young men to help him. Gradually he set up a whole-sale copying business, the profits of which, together with the amount produced by Ginevra's pictures, set the young couple at their ease—an ease which made them proud, as being the result of their own industry. That was the brightest period of their life.

Occupation and the joys of love made the days pass rapidly. In the evening after a good day's work, they came together joyfully in Ginevra's sanctum. Music indemnified them for their toils. The features of the young wife were never clouded with melancholy; never did she allow herself to utter a complaint. She always managed to appear in the presence of her husband with a smile upon her lips and with beaming eyes. Both of them nurtured a dominant idea which would have enabled them to find pleasure in the rudest toils; Ginevra would tell herself that she was working for Luigi, and Luigi would tell himself that he was working for Ginevra. It would indeed occasionally happen that the young wife, during her husband's absence, would think of the perfect happiness which she would have enjoyed, if that life of love had been passed in the presence of her father and mother. At such times she would fall into the deepest dejection, under the potent influence of remorse; sombre pictures would pass, like shadows, before her imagination; she would see her old father in his solitude, or her mother weeping in the evening and hiding her tears from the inexorable Piombo; those two white and serious heads would suddenly rise before her, and it seemed to her that she would never see them more, save by the fantastic light of memory. That idea haunted her like a presentiment. She celebrated the anniversary of their marriage by giving her husband a portrait, which he had often wanted—the portrait of ..is Ginevra. Never had the young artist composed anything so remarkable. Setting aside the perfection of the likeness, her striking beauty, the purity of her feelings, and the happiness of love were there almost magically depicted. The master-piece was inaugurated. And then they passed another year in the lap of affluence. The story of their lives might be written in three words, "they were happy." No event happened to them of sufficient importance to be noticed.

In the early part of the winter of the year 1819 the picture-dealers advised Ginevra to produce something else than copies, since competition prevented them from being sold to advantage. Madame Porta then saw that she had made a mistake in not practising the painting of pictures of genre, by which she might have made a name. She now took to painting portraits; but she had to contend against a crowd of artists poorer even

than herself. However, inasmuch as Luigi and Ginevra had
laid by some money, they did not despair of the future. At
the end of the winter of that same year Luigi worked incessantly. He also had to contend against competition; the
price paid for engrossing had fallen so much that he could no
longer employ any assistants, and found himself obliged to
work harder for the same amount of money. His wife had
produced several pictures of considerable merit; but the dealers
would hardly buy the paintings even of renowned artists. Ginevra offered them for the merest trifles, yet could not sell
them.

The situation of the young couple was somewhat appalling;
their hearts, it is true, were bathed in happiness; love showered
its treasures upon them; but poverty raised its skeleton head
in the midst of this harvest of pleasure, and they concealed
their anxieties from one another.

When Ginevra felt ready to burst into tears at the sight of
Luigi's sufferings, she heaped caresses on him; and Luigi also,
while black sorrow nestled at his heart, exhibited to Ginevra
the tenderest affection. They sought compensation for their
sufferings in the exaltation of their sentiments and their words,
their joys, and their amusements were tinged with a kind of
phrenzy. They dreaded the future. What feeling is there
which can be compared in strength to a passion which must
cease to-morrow under the cold hand of death or want?
When they talked about their penury, they felt impelled to
deceive each other, and were equally eager to grasp even the
slenderest hope.

One night Ginevra, after feeling about in vain, missed Luigi
from her side. A faint light reflected upon the dark wall of
the little court led her to the conclusion that her husband had
begun to work at night. (In fact, Luigi waited till his wife was
asleep, and then went upstairs to his study.) Four o'clock
struck; Ginevra lay down again and pretended to be asleep.
Luigi returned sleepy and overcome with fatigue, and Ginevra

gazed upon the beautiful face and saw that toil **and care** had already imprinted upon it some wrinkles.

"It is on my account that he spends his nights writing," she said tearfully. But a thought occurred to her which dried her tears. She resolved to imitate Luigi. That very day she went to a rich dealer in engravings, and owing to a letter of introduction given to her by Elie Magus, one of the dealers who bought her pictures, she obtained an order for coloring engravings. In the daytime she painted, and looked to the affairs of the household : then, when night came, she colored engravings. So that these two beings who loved each other so dearly, only entered the nuptial bed in order to quit it. Both pretended to be asleep, and so, from sheer devotion, deceived each other. One night Luigi, succumbing to the kind of fever set up by the toil which was beginning to be too much for him, opened the window of his study to breathe the pure morning air and relieve his pain ; when, looking down, he perceived the light thrown upon the wall by Ginevra's lamp. The unhappy man guessed everything, went downstairs, and treading softly, caught his wife in the middle of her studio, coloring engravings.

"Oh, Ginevra," he cried.

She started convulsively upon her seat, and blushed.

"How could I sleep while you were exhausting yourself with fatigue ?" said she.

"Yes, but I only have the right to work like this."

"Can I remain idle,", replied the young wife, as her eyes filled with tears, "when I know that every morsel of bread I eat costs us perhaps a drop of your blood ? I should die if I did not unite my efforts to yours. Ought not all things to be in common between us, pleasure as well as pain ?"

"She is cold," cried Luigi in despair, "fasten your shawl more over your breast, my Ginevra; the night is cold and damp."

They placed themselves before the window, the young wife

rested her head upon the bosom of her beloved, who held her
by the waist, and thus the two looked up in profound silence
at the sky, which was slowly brightening with the coming day.
Grey clouds sped lightly by, one after the other, and the east
grew lighter and lighter.

"Look," said Ginevra, "it is a presage; we shall be happy."

"Yes, in heaven," replied Luigi, with a bitter smile.
"O Ginevra, you who deserved all the treasures of the
earth—"

"I have your heart," she said joyously.

"Ah, I do not complain," resumed Luigi, straining her
tightly to his heart, and covering with kisses the delicate face
which was beginning to lose the freshness of youth, but whose
expression was so sweet and gentle that he could never look at
it without feeling consoled.

"How silent it is," said Ginevra. "My friend, I find a
great pleasure in sitting up. The majesty of the night is
truly contagious; it awes and it inspires; there is an indescribable potency in the thought 'everything slumbers, and I am
awake.'"

"O my Ginevra, not to-day for the first time have I discovered the delicate grace of your heart. But see, the sun is rising.
Come and sleep."

"I will," she said, "but not alone. I suffered much on
the night when I discovered that my Luigi sat up without me."

The courage with which these two young people fought
against misfortune was, for a time, not without its reward: but
that event which is generally considered the crowning felicity
of married life was doomed to be fatal to them. Ginevra had
a son, who, to borrow a popular expression, was as "lovely as
the day." The maternal feeling doubles the strength of a
young woman. Luigi borrowed money in order to provide for
the expenses of Ginevra's confinement. Just at first, therefore, she did not experience all the uneasiness of her situation,
and the husband and wife gave themselves up to the delights

of rearing a child. It was their last pleasure. At first the two Corsicans, like two swimmers uniting their efforts to swim against a stream, struggled bravely; but at times they gave way to an apathy resembling those fits of sleep which are the harbingers of death. They soon found themselves compelled to sell their jewels. Poverty suddenly showed herself, not hideous, but simply clad, and almost easy to be borne. There was nothing fearful in her voice; she did not bring in her train despair, and rags, and spectres; but she did banish the recollection and destroy the habits of affluence; she wore the springs of pride. Then came want in all its horrors, want, reckless of its tatters, want that treads under foot every human feeling.

Seven or eight months after the birth of little Bartholoméo, it would have been difficult to recognize in the mother who was suckling that sickly child, the original of the admirable portrait which was now the only ornament of the bare room. Without fire during that severe winter, Ginevra saw the graceful outlines of her face slowly disappearing; her cheeks grew white as porcelain, her eyes paled as if the sources of life were drying up within her. Seeing her child thin and discoloured, Ginevra suffered only from its infant misery, while Luigi had not even courage enough to smile at his boy.

" I have been all over Paris," said he, in a hollow voice. " I know no one, and how can I beg from strangers ? Vergniaud the grazier, my old Egyptian comrade, is implicated in a conspiracy; he has been thrown into prison, and besides, he has already lent me all he could spare. As for our landlord, he has not asked for any rent for a year."

" But we are not in want of anything," replied Ginevra gently, with assumed calmness.

" Every day that comes round brings some fresh difficulty," pursued Luigi with terror. Luigi took all Ginevra's pictures, the portrait, several pieces of furniture with which the household could still dispense, and sold the whole lot for the merest

trifle. The sum which he obtained for it prolonged for a brief
period the death-struggles of the household.

In these days of misfortune, Ginevra displayed the sublimity
of her character, and the extent of her resignation ; she supported the attacks of sorrow with stoicism.   Her energetic
mind sustained her against every evil, she worked with an
unfailing hand by the side of her dying boy, performed the
duties of the household with miraculous activity, and was equal
to every emergency.   She was happy, even now, when she saw
upon Luigi's lips a smile of astonishment at the sight of the
neatness which pervaded the one room in which they had
taken refuge.

"My friend, I have kept a bit of bread for you," said
Ginevra one night when he came back worn out with fatigue.

"And you ?"

"I have dined, dear Luigi, I don't want anything."

And the sweet expression of her face invited him more than
her words did, to accept the nourishment of which she was
robbing herself.   Luigi gave her one of those despairing kisses
which in 1793 friends used to give one another as they mounted
the scaffold together.   At such critical moments the hearts of
two beings are entirely laid bare to each other.   Accordingly
the miserable Luigi understanding at once that his wife was
fasting, caught the excitement which was devouring her, shuddered, and, under the pretence of having some pressing piece
of business on hand, went out; for he would rather have
taken the most subtle poison than escape death by eating the
last morsel of bread to be found at home.   He went forth
and walked about Paris among the most brilliant carriages, in
the midst of that insolent luxury which everywhere stares one
in the face.   He passed quickly by the shops of the morey-
changers with their piles of glittering gold; and at length
determined to sell himself, to offer himself as a substitute for
military service, hoping that that sacrifice would save Ginevra,
and that during his absence she might be restored to the

good graces of Bartholoméo. He therefore went to find one of those men who carry on the white slave-trade, and experienced a certain kind of pleasure in recognizing in him a foreign officer of the imperial guard.

"I have eaten nothing for two days," he said, in a slow and feeble voice. "My wife is dying of hunger, and does not utter a single complaint; she would smile in dying, I believe. I entreat you, comrade," he added with a bitter laugh, "to buy me in advance; I am strong, I am no longer in the service, and I . . . ."

The officer gave Luigi a sum on account of that which he undertook to procure for him. The wretched man gave vent to a convulsive laugh when he grasped a handful of gold. He ran with all his might towards his house, panting, and at times exclaiming, "O my Ginevra, Ginevra." Night was falling when he reached home. He entered quite quietly, fearing to cause too much excitement to his wife, whom he had left in a feeble state. The last rays of the setting sun penetrating the window were shedding their dying light upon the face of Ginevra, who was sitting in a chair asleep, holding her child to her bosom.

"Awake, my soul," said he, not noticing the posture of the child, who at that moment looked unnaturally bright.

Hearing that voice, the poor mother opened her eyes, encountered Luigi's look, and smiled; but Luigi uttered a cry of terror. He hardly recognized his half-mad wife, but with a gesture of savage energy showed her the gold. Ginevra began to laugh mechanically, and all at once cried in a fearful voice, "Louis, the child is cold." She looked at her boy and fainted; the little Bartholoméo was dead. Luigi raised his wife in his arms, and without taking the child, which she was clasping with incomprehensible strength, from her arms, laid her on the bed; then he went out and called for help.

"O my God," said he to the landlord, whom he met upon

J

the staircase. "I have gold, and my child is famished to death. My wife is dying—help us."

He returned in a desperate condition to his wife, and left the honest mason and several of the neighbors, to collect all that was needful to succor a misery until then unknown to them, so carefully had the two Corsicans, actuated by a feeling of pride, concealed it. Luigi had thrown his gold upon the floor, and was kneeling at the foot of the bed on which his wife was lying.

"Father, take care of my child, which bears your name," cried Ginevra in her delirium.

"O my angel, calm yourself," said Luigi, embracing her. "There are happy days in store for us."

That voice, and that embrace somewhat tranquilized her.

"O my Louis," she resumed, looking at him with close attention, "listen well to what I am going to say. I feel that I am dying; my death was to be expected; I suffered too much; and then a happiness like mine must be paid for. Yes, my Louis, console yourself, I have been so happy that if I were to begin life again I would accept our destiny. Ah! I am a bad mother, I regret you more than I regret my child. My child!" she added in deeper tone; her tears fell from her dying eyes, and she suddenly pressed the corpse which she had not been able to revive.

"Give my hair to my father in remembrance of his Ginevra. Tell him that I never accused him." Her head sank upon her husband's arm.

"No, you cannot die," cried Luigi; "the doctor is coming; we have bread. Your father will restore you to his favor. Prosperity has dawned for us. Remain with us, angel of beauty."

But the fond and loving heart was growing cold. Ginevra instinctively turned her eyes towards him whom she adored, although she was now no longer conscious of anything. Confused images flitted before her mind, which was just losing all recollection of earth. She knew that Luigi was there, for she clasped his icy hand, even more and more tightly still; it seemed as if she were trying to cling to a precipice over which she felt herself falling.

"My friend," she said at last, "you are cold: I will warm you."

She would have placed her husband's hand upon her heart, but she died. Two doctors, a priest, and some neighbors came in at that moment, bringing all that was needed to succor the husband and wife, and assuage their despair. These strangers created a good deal of noise at first, but when they had entered, a fearful silence reigned throughout the room.

While this scene was taking place, Bartholoméo and his wife were seated in their old fashioned arm-chairs, one on either side of the vast fireplace, whose blazing coals warmed the immense drawing-room of their hotel. The timepiece marked the hour of midnight. For a long time past the old couple had grown wakeful. At that moment they were silent, like two old people fallen into second childhood, who see all, yet notice nothing. The deserted room, so full of memories for them, was dimly lighted by a single lamp whose flame was almost extinct. But for the flickering flame of the hearth, they would have been in complete darkness. One of their friends had just left them, and the chair upon which he had sat during his visit stood between the two Corsicans. Piombo had already more than once looked at that chair—and these looks, pregnant with ideas, followed each other like so many twinges of remorse; for the empty chair was Ginevra's. Elisa Piombo was watching the expressions which chased each other across the pale features of her husband. Although she was accustomed to guess his feelings, from the changing revolutions in his face, these were by turns so menacing and so melancholy, that she could not read that incomprehensible mind.

Was Bartholoméo giving way under the potent memories aroused by that chair? Was he shocked to see that, for the first time since his daughter's departure, it had been used by a stranger? Had the hour of his clemency, that hour so vainly looked for until then, struck at last?

Such were the reflections which succeeded each other in the mind of Elisa Piombo. For a moment her husband's face assumed so terrible an aspect, that she trembled at having employed so simple an expedient to give rise to an opportunity of speaking of Ginevra. At that moment the north-east wind drove the snow-flakes so violently against the shutters, that the two old people could hear the light sound. Ginevra's mother bowed her head, in order to conceal her tears from her husband. All at once a sigh issued from the old man's breast, his wife looked at him, and he broke down; she ventured for the second time during three years to speak to him of his daughter.

"If Ginevra should be cold," she said gently. Piombo shuddered. "She is hungry perhaps," continued the old woman. The Corsican let fall a tear. "She has a child and cannot suckle it, her milk has dried up," continued the mother rapidly, in the accents of despair.

"Let her come! let her come!" cried Piombo. "Oh, my darling child! you have conquered me."

The mother rose as if to go and seek her child. At that moment the door flew noisily open, and a man whose face had nothing human in it stood suddenly before them.

"*Dead!* Our two families were fated to exterminate each other, for that is all that remains of her," said he, laying Ginevra's long black hair upon the table.

The two old people shudered as if they had felt a thunder-stroke, and lost sight of Luigi.

"He spares us a gun-shot, for he is dead!" said Bartholoméo slowly, looking on-the ground.

THE PURSE.

(LA BOURSE)

TO SOFKA.

HAVE you not remarked, mademoiselle, that the painters and
sculptors of the middle ages, in placing two faces in adoration
by the side of a beautiful saint, have never failed to impress
upon them a filial resemblance to her. When you see your
name among those which are dear to me, and under the protection of which I place my works, call to mind this touching
harmony, and you will find in this dedication, not so much an
act of homage, as the expression of the fraternal affection which
your humble servant De Balzac, has sworn to you.

"There is, for those minds which open freely, a delightful
hour which succeeds the moment when the night has not yet
fallen, though the day is no more. Twilight then sheds its
soft hues and strange effects on every object, and encourages
a reverie that vaguely mingles with the play of light and shade.
The silence which almost almost always reigns at this instant
renders it more particularly dear to artists, who meditate, place
themselves at some distance from the picture at which they can
no longer labor, and criticize it ; saturating themselves with its
subject, whose hidden meaning then stands revealed to the
inner eye of genius. He who has not dwelt in silent thought
beside a friend during this hour of poetic dreams, will find it
hard to understand its unspeakable delights. Under cover of
clear-obscure, the material artifices employed by the artist to
produce the appearance of reality entirely disappear. If the
work in hand be a picture, the persons depicted in it seem to
speak and walk : the shadow becomes shadow and the daylight
is daylight, the flesh lives, the eyes move, the blood courses

through the veins, and the stuffs shine. The imagination aids the naturalness of each detail, and suffers only the beauties of the work to be seen. At this hour illusion reigns despotically; perhaps it rises when the sun sets. (Is not illusion an intellectual night, which we people with dreams?) At this hour illusion unfolds its wings, carries the mind away to an ideal world—a world fertile in voluptuous fancies, and in which the artist forgets the world of reality,—yesterday, to-morrow, the future, everything, even his privations, good as well as evil.

At this magic hour, a young painter of great promise, who loved art for its own sake, was mounted on the double ladder which he used in painting a large and lofty picture, which he had almost finished. There, as he blamed and praised his own work with the utmost impartiality, and abandoned himself to the current of his thoughts, he lost himself in one of those reveries which enchant, enlarge, flatter and console the heart. His reverie must have been a long one. Night came on. Whether it were that he tried to come down from the ladder or made some unguarded movement in the belief that he was standing on the floor (the result prevented him from exactly remembering how the accident occurred), he fell, his head came into contact with a stool, he lost all consciousness, and remained motionless for a period the duration of which was unknown to him. He was aroused by a gentle voice from the kind of swoon in which he had been buried. When he opened his eyes, a glimpse of vivid light made him close them again promptly; but through the mist which enveloped his senses he heard the chit-chat of two women, and could feel two young and timid hands supporting his head. He soon recovered his senses, and could see by the light of one of those old lamps, called double ventilating lamps, a young girl's head, the most exquisite that he had ever beheld—one of those heads which are often regarded as a mere painter's whim. This head, however, realized the beau-ideal which every artist imagines, and which is the source of his talent. The face of this young stranger belonged, so to speak, to the fine and delicate type of the school of Prudhon, and possessed also that poetical air which Girodet gave to his fantastic figures. The freshness of the temples, the regularity of the eye-brows, the purity af the outlines, the marks of maidenhood so clearly imprinted upon every feature of the face, made the young girl a perfect creature. Her figure was slender and supple; her limbs delicate. Her dress, which was neat and simple, did not bespeak either riches or poverty. On recovering his self-possession, the painter expressed his admiration by a look of surprise, and muttered some confused acknowledgments. He found that his forehead was being pressed by a handkerchief, and recognized, in spite of the smell peculiar to studios, the powerful scent of ether, which had, no doubt, been used to recover him from his swoon. Then at length he noticed an old woman, who resembled the *marquise* of the *ancien régime*. She was holding a lamp, and giving directions to the younger stranger.

"Sir," replied the young girl to one of the enquiries made by the artist, while still under the influence of the disorder which the fall had introduced into his ideas, "my mother and I heard the noise which you made in falling upon the floor, and fancied we heard a groan. The silence that followed the noise of the fall alarmed us, and we came up in a hurry. Finding the key in the door, we fortunately took the liberty of coming in, and found you lying motionless upon the floor. My mother went to look for something to make a bandage with, and to bring you round. You have hurt your forehead, there; can you feel it?"

"Yes now I can," replied the artist.

"Oh! it wont be anything serious," pursued the old mother. "Luckily your head fell upon that mannikin."

"I feel infinitely better," replied the painter. "All I want now is a vehicle to take me home. The porteress will go and get one for me."

He wanted to express his thanks to the two strangers, but a

every phrase he uttered the elder lady cut him short with the
words,—

"Take care, sir, to apply some leeches or to get yoursel
bled to-morrow; drink a few cups of vulnerary, and take care
of yourself; falls are very dangerous things."

The young girl looked furtively at the painter and at the
pictures in the studio. Her face and her glances showed no
thing that was not becoming; her curiosity looked like abstraction, and her eyes seemed to express that interest which women
take, with graceful spontaneity, in all our misfortunes. The
two strangers seemed to forget the painter's works in the presence of the suffering painter. When he had set their minds
at rest with regard to his condition, they left the room, looking
at him the while with a solicitude that was quite free from
being either pronounced or familiar. They did not harass
him with questions or seek to inspire him with a desire to
become acquainted with them. Their interest was perfectly
natural, and in good taste. Their noble and simple bearing
at first produced but little impression upon the painter, but
afterwards, when he recalled all the circumstances of the accident, he was very much struck by their behavior.

When they had reached the floor which lay beneath that on
which the studio was situated, the old lady quietly said,—
" Adelaide, you left the door open."

"In order to hasten to my assistance," said the young
painter, with a grateful smile.

" Why, mother, you yourself ran down immediately," replied
the young girl, blushing.

" Would you like us to go down with you," said the mother
to the artist, "the staircase is very dark."

"No thank you, madame, I am much better now."

" Keep a good hold on the balustrade."

The two women remained upon the landing in order to light
the young man while they listened to his footsteps.

In order that the reader may understand all the raciness of

this little drama and the surprises which it presented to the painter, we must add that it was only a few days since that he had fixed his studio in the upper story of this house, which was situated in the obscurest, and therefore the muddiest, part of the Rue de Suresnes, almost in front of the Madeleine and only a few steps from his lodgings, which were in the Rue des Champs Elysées. The renown which his talent had procured for him, had made him one of the most highly esteemed artists in France, so that he was now leaving want behind him, and was enjoying, to use his own expression, his last struggles with poverty. Instead of going to work in one of those studios which are to be found near the barriers, and whose moderate rents were proportioned to his former modest earnings, he had gratified his daily recurring desire to avoid a long journey, and the loss of that time which had now become more valuable to him than ever.

No one in the world would have inspired so much interest as Hippolyte Schinner if he would have consented to make himself known; but he did not lightly expose the secrets of his existence. He was the idol of a poor mother, who had educated him by the endurance of stern privation. Mademoiselle Schinner, the daughter of an Alsatian farmer, had never been married. Her tender heart had formerly been cruelly wounded by a wealthy man who did not pretend to any great delicacy in love matters. On the day when, a young girl in all the brightness of her beauty, and all the pride of life, she gained, at the expense of her heart and all her beautiful illusions, that disenchantment which comes to us so slowly, yet all too soon (for we put off as long as possible our belief in misfortune, so that it always seems to have arrived too quickly), on that very day she went through a century of reflection, and took refuge in religion and in resignation. She refused the alms of the man who had deceived her, renounced the world, and made her shame her glory. She gave herself up entirely to maternal love, demanding from it all its delights in exchange

for those social pleasures to which she was bidding adieu. She
supported herself by work, laying up for herself a treasure in
her boy.   And so at length the day and hour arrived when he
repaid her for all the long and lingering sacrifices of her indigence.

At the last exhibition her son had received the cross of the
Legion of Honor.   The newspapers which pronounced unani-
mously in favor of the unknown genius, were still ringing with
sincere praise.   The artists themselves hailed Schinner as a
master, and the dealers covered his pictures with gold pieces.
At twenty-five, Hippolyte Schinner, who had inherited his
mother's woman's heart, had come to understand his position
in the world better than he ever did.   In his desire to afford
his mother those enjoyments which society had withheld from
her for so many years, he lived for her ; hoping that, by dint of
his fame and fortune, he might some day see her happy, rich,
respected, and the centre of a circle of celebrated men.   With
that view Schinner had chosen his friends from among the most
honorable and distinguished men.   Fastidious in the selection
of his acquaintances, he wished still further to raise a position
which his talent had already rendered so high.   The toil to
which he had been doomed from youth, by forcing him to remain in solitude—that mother of lofty thoughts—had preserved
in him those beautiful beliefs which gild life's earliest years.
His youthful mind was no stranger to any of the thousand
delicacies which render a young man a being *cui generis*, a
being whose heart teems with felicities, poetic dreams and
virgin hopes, which, however feeble in the eyes of world-worn
people, are still profound from their simplicity   Nature had
endowed him with those gentle and polished manners which
go direct to the heart, and win even those who do not understand them.   He was well formed.   His voice, that seemed to
come from the heart, inspired the hearts of others with noble
feelings, and there was a certain candor in its accents which
bespoke genuine modesty.   Those who saw him felt themselves

drawn towards him by some moral attraction which has fortunately escaped the analysis of men of science, who would resolve it into some phenomenon of galvanism, or into the play of some fluid or other, and would formulate our feelings by given proportions of oxygen and of electricity.

These details will perhaps explain to persons of a bold disposition, and to men who are overburdened with a sense of propriety, why Hippolyte Schinner did not take advantage of the absence of the porter (who had gone to the end of the Rue de la Madeleine in search of a coach) to cross-examine the porteress about the two strangers who had displayed so much kindness of heart on his behalf.

But although he, for his part, made answer yes and no simply, to the inquiries, (very natural under the circumstances,) which the woman addressed to him as to his accident, and the kind intervention of the fourth-floor lodgers, he could not prevent her yielding to the porters' instinct ; and accordingly she began to talk to him about the two strangers, in a strain colored by her peculiar politics and the subterraneous opinions of the porter's lodge.

"Ah !" she said, "it was Mademoiselle Lessigneur and her mother beyond a doubt; they have lived there for four years. We don't yet know what these two ladies do. In the morning, but only till twelve o'clock, an old charwoman, who is half deaf and as dumb as a wall, comes to do for them. In the evening two or three old gentlemen who are decorated like you, sir, and one of whom has a carriage and servants, and they say he has 60,000 francs a year, come to visit them, and often stay very late.

"Moreover, they are very nice lodgers, like yourself, sir, and economical,—why, they live upon nothing—as soon as ever a letter arrives they pay the postage; it's very funny, sir, the mother has not the same name as her daughter. Ah, when they go to the Tuileries, mademoiselle is very nicely dressed, and she never goes out without being followed by young men;

but she shuts the door in their faces, and she is quite right, the landlord would not allow . . ."

But here the carriage drove up. Hippolyte did not stay to hear any more, but went home. His mother, to whom he related what had happened, dressed the wound again, and would not let him go to his studio next day. A consultation having been held, various prescriptions were ordered, and Hippolyte remained at home for three days. During this seclusion his unemployed imagination brought before him vividly and in fragments the details of the scene which had followed his swoon. The profile of the young girl stood out clearly against the darkness of his mind's eye; he saw again the wan features of the mother, or felt once more the hands of Adelaide. A gesture which, when just seen, had made but little impression on him, but whose exquisite grace was thrown by memory into bold relief, reappeared before his mind. Then a particular posture, or the tones of a melodious voice, embellished by memory's distance, came back quite suddenly, like objects which, when plunged into the depths of the water, return to the surface.

Thus, on the day on which he was able to resume his labors, he went back to his studio very early. But the visit which he had, incontestably, the right to pay to his neighbors, was the real cause of his eagerness; he had already forgotten the pictures which he had begun. At the moment when a passion bursts from its swaddling clothes, it finds inexplicable sources of delight, which those who have loved will understand. Thus, certain persons will know why the painter mounted the staircase leading to the fourth story so slowly, and will be in the secret of the rapid pulsations of his heart at the moment when he caught sight of the brown door of the modest apartments inhabited by Mademoiselle Leseigneur. This girl, who did not bear her mother's name, had aroused a thousand sympathetic feelings in the young painter; he wished to trace between her and himself certain similarities of position, and

invested her with the misfortunes of his own origin.   While at
his work Hippolyte yielded himself up readily to dreams of
love, and made a good deal of noise in order to compel the
two ladies to think of him, just as he was thinking of Mademoiselle Leseigneur. He remained till late in his studio, dined
there, and then towards seven o'clock went down to call upon
his neighbors.

No painter of manners has ventured to introduce us into
the really curious interiors of certain Parisian existences, into
the secrets of those dwellings which pour forth such new and
elegant toilettes and gaily attired women, who, in all outward
seeming rich, exhibit throughout their abodes the symptoms of
a precarious fortune.

If my picture be in this respect too freely drawn, if the
reader finds my account tedious, let him not find fault with the
description, which forms an integral part of the story, so to
speak ; since the aspect of the apartments occupied by his two
neighbors had a great influence upon the feelings and the
hopes of Hippolyte Schinner.

The house belonged to one of those landlords who have a
pre-existing and a profound horror of repairs and decorations;
one of those men who look upon their position of Parisian
landlords as a calling. In the long chain of moral species,
these people occupy a middle position between the miser and
the usurer. Optimists by reflection, they are all devoted to
the *status quo* of Austria. If you talk to them about altering
a cupboard or a door, or of opening the most necessary venti-
lator, their eyes flash, their bile begins to work, and they rear
like frightened horses. Has the wind blown down some of
their chimney-pots ? they fall ill and cut off their visit to the
Gymnase, or the Porte Saint-Martin, on account of the repairs.
Hippolyte, who on account of some decorations which he
wanted carried out in his studio, had been present at the
gratuitous representation of a comic scene by M. Molineux,
was not surprised at the thick black hues, the greasy tints, the

blotches, and other disagreeable accessories which adorned the
woodwork of the apartments. Such stigmata of poverty,
moreover, are not altogether wanting in poetic charm to the
eye of an artist.

Mademoiselle Leseigneur herself came to open the door.
When she recognized the young painter, she bowed to him,
and at the same moment, with truly Parisian dexterity and
that presence of mind which pride confers, she turned to close
the door of a glazed partition, through which Hippolyte might
have caught a glimpse of some linen hanging on lines stretched
over fuel-saving stoves; of an old folding bed, the charcoal,
coal, irons, filter, crockeryware, and all the utensils peculiar to
small establishments. Muslin curtains, extremely neat, carefully concealed this *capharnaum* (such is the familiar name for
laboratories of this description), which, moreover, was dimly
lighted by windows looking into the neighboring court. With
the rapid all-embracing glance of an artist, Hippolyte saw at
once the uses to which this first room, thus cut in two, was
devoted; its furniture and its whole character and condition. The more honored portion, which served at the same
time as an ante-room, and a dining-room, was hung with an
old rose-colored paper, with a velvet border, which had doubtless been manufactured by Reveillon. The holes and stains
in it had been carefully concealed with wafers. Prints representing the battles of Alexander, by Lebrun, hung in their
worn frames symmetrically upon the walls. In the middle of
the room was an old-fashioned table of solid mahogany worn
at the edges. A small stove, whose straight unjointed flue
could scarcely be seen, stood before the hearth, which was
blocked up by a chest of drawers. The chairs, in strange
contrast with the rest of the room, showed some traces of
former splendor; they were of carved mahogany, but the red
morocco of the seats, the gilded nails and bindings, showed
scars as numerous as those of the old sergeants of the Imperial Guard. The room formed a museum of certain objects

that are to be met with only in amphibious establishments of this kind, nameless objects that are neither articles of luxury nor of poverty, but share the character of both.   Among other curiosities, Hippolyte observed a magnificently mounted tele-scope hanging over the little greenish glass which adorned the chimney-piece.   To match this queer bit of furniture, there stood between the fireplace and the partition, a wretched side-board, painted to look like mahogany, the most difficult of all woods to imitate.   But the red and slippery floor, the misera-ble little carpets placed in front of the chairs, the furniture, all exhibited that shining neatness which perpetual rubbing and dusting give to old-fashioned bits of furniture ; conferring on them a false lustre, and giving prominence to their defects, antiquity, and long service.

An indefinable odor, the result of the exhalations of the *capharnaum*, mixed with the vapor of the dining-room, and of the staircase, pervaded the apartments, although the window was open, and the air of the street shook the muslin curtains, which were carefully drawn so as to hide the embrasure on which previous lodgers had stamped their presence by divers incrustations— species of domestic fresco.

Adelaide made haste to open the door of the second room, into which she ushered the artist with a certain amount of pleasure.   Hippolyte, who had formerly seen in his mother's home the same signs of penury, observed them here with that keenness of impression which characterizes the first acquisi-tions of our memory, and entered more readily than any one else could have done into the details of this existence.   But the excellent young man, when he recognized the objects which had surrounded him in childhood's days, felt no contempt for this hidden poverty, and no pride in the luxury which he had won for his mother.

" Well, sir. I hope you have quite got over the effects of your fall," said the old mother, rising from an old-fashioned

easy chair at the corner of the fireplace, and giving him an
arm-chair.

"Yes, madame, and I am come to thank you for the kind
care you both bestowed upon me, and especially mademoiselle,
who heard me fall." As Hippolyte uttered this phrase, redolent of that admirable stupidity which the first agitations
arising from true love give rise to, he looked at the young girl.
Adelaide was lighting the double-ventilating lamp in order,
doubtless, that she might put out of sight a candle stuck in a
large flat-bottomed copper candlestick and festooned with
some salient flutings, the result of an unusual amount of
running. She made a slight bow, took the candlestick into
the anteroom, and returned to place the lamp upon the mantelpiece. Then she sat down beside her mother, a little in the
rear of the artist, in order that she might have a good look at
him, while all the time she seemed to be busily studying the
début of the lamp, whose light, arrested by the moisture of a
dirty glass, flickered as it struggled with a black and ill-
trimmed wick. Catching sight of the large mirror upon the
mantel-shelf, Hippolyte speedily fixed his eyes upon it in order
to admire Adelaide. The girl's little manœuvre, therefore,
served only to embarrass them both.

While Hippolyte chatted with Madame Leseigneur, for so
he ventured to christen her, he examined the room—not point-
edly but furtively. The Egyptian faces of the iron firedogs,
barely peeped through the cinders which encumbered the grate,
in which two brands were trying to effect a junction in front of
a sham log made of fire-clay, and buried as carefully as a
miser's hoard. The old Aubusson carpet, much darned, faded,
and thread-bare as a pensioner's coat, was not large enough to
cover the whole floor, the chill of which made itself sensible to
the feet. The walls were decorated with a reddish paper, representing a lampass material with yellow figures. In the
middle of the wall opposite to the windows the painter saw a
chink and the cracks in the paper produced by the double

doors of an alcove which doubtless formed the sleeping quarters of Madame Leseigneur, and was insufficiently concealed
by a sofa placed in front of it. Fronting the fireplace, and
over a mahogany commode whose ornamentation was not
wanting either in richness or good taste, there hung the portrait
of an officer of high rank. The light was not good enough to
enable the painter to see the portrait distinctly, but from what
he could see he thought that the execrable daub must be a
production of some Chinese artist. The red silk curtains and
the red and yellow chair-covers of this room " contrived a
double debt to pay," were alike discolored. On the marble
top of the commode was placed a valuable malachite tray,
with a dozen coffee cups magnificently painted,—of Sèvres
workmanship beyond a doubt. Upon the mantel-shelf stood
the inevitable *Empire* timepiece representing a warrior driving
a four-horsed chariot, with the figures of the twelve hours,
arranged upon the spokes of the wheel. The wax candles in
the candelabra were yellow with smoke, and at each end of the
chimney-piece, there was a porcelain vase crowned with artificial flowers full of dust and adorned with moss.

Hippolyte observed in the middle of the room a card-table
ready for use, and some packs of new cards. To the eye of
an observer there was something depressing in the sight of
this penury, tricked out like an old woman who wants her face
to lie. The spectacle presented was such as to induce any
man of sense to propose to himself off-hand this dilemma :—
" Either these two women are integrity personified, or they
lead a life of intrigue and gambling." But on looking at
Adelaide a young man so pure as Hippolyte Schinner was
bound to credit them with the most perfect innocence and to
ascribe the incongruities presented by the room to the most
honorable causes.

" My girl," said the elder lady to the younger, " make up a
little more fire, and give me my shawl."

Adelaide went into the drawing-room, in which no doubt the

K

slept, and returned bringing her mother a cashmere shawl
which, when new, must have been very valuable, for the designs were of Indian workmanship; but old, faded, and full of
darns, it was in keeping with the furniture. Madame Leseigneur wrapped herself up in it very artistically and with all the
skill of an old woman who wanted to be taken at her word.

The young girl ran lightly to the *capharnaum*, and reappeared
with a handful of small pieces of wood, which she courageously
threw upon the sinking fire. It would be very difficult to
transcribe the conversation which took place between these
three people. Guided by that tact which the experience of
early troubles rarely fails to confer, Hippolyte did not venture
to indulge in the slightest remark relating to the position of his
neighbors; having under his eyes the symptoms of a penury
so thinly veiled. The most ordinary question would have
been indiscreet and could only be conceded to old-established
friendship. Yet at the same time the artist was deeply
absorbed by this poverty in disguise; it wrung his generous
heart; but knowing that every kind of pity, even the most
amiable, may be offensive, he felt ill at ease on account of the
discordance between his thoughts and language. The two
ladies began by talking about painting, for women well understand the embarrassment that underlies a first visit. They
perhaps feel it; and the character of their intellect supplies
them with a thousand resources for putting an end to it. By
questioning the young man about the material processes of
his art and about his studies, Adelaide and her mother contrived to embolden him to talk. The indefinable trifles of
which their friendly conversation consisted induced Hippolyte
quite naturally, to give vent to remarks and reflections which
displayed the nature of his moral sentiments and the tone of
his mind. Grief had prematurely withered the old lady's
face, which had no doubt once been beautiful, though now
all that remained to her were the striking features, the outlines
in one word the skeleton, of a countenance which displayed,

as a whole, great refinement of intellect and much grace in
the play of the eye. There in the play of the eye,
could be traced the expression peculiar to the ladies of
the old French Court, an expression which cannot be
defined. Those fine and subtle features might just as well
be taken to denote bad sentiments and suggest the existence
of female craft and cunning carried to a high pitch of perver-
sity, as to indicate the delicacy of a lofty spirit. In fact the
face of a woman embarrasses the ordinary observer, because
the difference between candor and duplicity, between the
genius of intrigue and the genius of right feeling, cannot there
be traced. He who is gifted with penetrating vision divines
those subtle shades of difference arising from the less or
greater curvature of a line, the less or greater depth of a
dimple, the less or greater prominence of a projecting feature.
The correct appreciation of such diagnostics is entirely within
the province of intuition, which only can discover what all are
concerned to hide. The physiognomy of the old lady resembled the room which she occupied in this respect—that it
seemed equally hard to discover whether beneath this penury
lurked vice or strict integrity as to find out whether Adelaide's
mother was an old coquette accustomed to weigh, to calculate,
and barter everything, or a loving woman full of noble and
amiable qualities. But at Schinner's time of life the heart's
first impulse is to believe in the existence of good, and accordingly as he looked at the noble, almost disdainful, forehead of
Adelaide, and beheld her eyes that were so full of mind and
thought, he inhaled, so to speak, the suave and modest scent
of virtue. In the midst of their talk he seized the opportunity
of speaking of portraits in general, so as to acquire the right
of examining the hideous pastil, all the tints of which had
faded, while the greater part of the color had come bodily
away.

"You prize that painting, doubtless, on account of the

likeness, ladies, for the drawing itself is horrible?" he said,
looking at Adelaide.

"It was taken at Calcutta, in a great hurry," replied the
mother with emotion.

She gazed at the ill-favored sketch with that entire self-
abandonment to which the memories of by-gone happiness give
rise when they awake and bathe the heart as with some beneficent dew, to the refreshing influences of which we delight to
give way; but there was also in the expression of the old
lady's face, the face of an enduring sorrow. So at least did
the artist interpret the attitude and countenance of his neighbor. He thereupon went up to her and took a seat beside
her. "Madame," he said, "a little time longer and the colors
of this pastil will have completely disappeared. The portrait
will then exist only in your memory; where you will behold a
face that is dear to you, others will not see anything at all.
Will you permit me to transfer this likeness to canvas, where it
will be more securely fixed than on this paper. Grant me, on
the score of our neighborhood, the pleasure of rendering you
this service. There are hours during which an artist loves to
repose from his compositions by undertaking works of a less
elevated character; it will therefore be a diversion to me to
reproduce this head."

The old lady trembled as she heard these words, and Adelaide cast at the painter one of those concentrated glances
which seem like an emanation from the soul. Hippolyte
wanted to be connected with his two neighbors by some link,
and to acquire the right to take a share in their existence. His
offer being addressed to the liveliest affections of the heart,
was the only one which it was possible for him to make; it
satisfied his artist pride, and was in no way humiliating to the
two ladies. Madame Leseigneur accepted his offer without
expressing any enthusiasm or regret, but with the feeling of
noble hearts who know the strength of the bonds created by

such obligations, and whose acceptance of them is therefore a magnificent eulogy—a proof of esteem.

"It seems to me," said the artist, "that the uniform is that of a naval officer."

"Yes," said the old lady, "it is the uniform of the captain of a ship. My husband, Mons. de Rouville, died in Batavia from the result of a wound received during an engagement with an English vessel which fell in with him on the coast of Asia. His vessel was a frigate of fifty-six guns, while the *Revenge* was a ship carrying ninety-six. The combat was very unequal, but he defended himself so bravely that the fight lasted till midnight, and he was able to get away. When I returned to France, Bonaparte was not yet paramount, and they refused me a pension. When latterly I applied for it again, the minister harshly told me that if the Baron de Rouville had *emigrated* I should not have lost him, and that he would be a rear-admiral; and finally his Excellency wound up by opposing my claim with some law about forfeitures. I only took the step, urged to it by my friends, for poor Adelaide's sake. I always felt a sort of repugnance to making a sorrow which robs a woman of her voice and strength, the ground of an appeal for alms. I don't like this setting of a money value upon blood that has been irreparably spilled."

"Mother, this is a subject which always makes you ill." When Adelaide had said these words, Madame Leseigneur de Rouville bowed her head and was silent.

"I thought, sir," said the young lady to Hippolyte, "that an artist's work was as a rule very quiet?"

At this question Hippolyte blushed, remembering the noise he had made. Adelaide did not pursue the subject, and saved him the trouble of telling some fib, by suddenly rising as she heard the noise of a carriage stopping at the door. She went into her own room, whence she returned carrying in her hand two large candlesticks furnished with wax candles which had already done duty. These she speedily lighted, and then·

without waiting for the tinkle of the bell, she opened the door
of the anteroom, in which she left the lamp. The sound of a
kiss given and returned went straight to the very heart of Hippolyte; but the young man's impatience to see who it was that
treated Adelaide with such familiarity was not quickly satisfied.
The new arrivals had a whispered conversation with Adelaide,
which he thought very protracted. At length, Mademoiselle
de Rouville reappeared, followed by two men whose dress,
faces, and general appearance a whole history in themselves.
The first, who was about sixty years of age, wore one
of those coats which were invented, I believe, for Louis XVIII.,
who was then upon the throne; a kind of coat which offered a
solution of the most difficult of all vestmental problems, that
ought to have immortalized the tailor who discovered it. This
genius understood for certain the art of transitions, which was
the very spirit and essence of that epoch of political mobility.
Is it not a very rare merit to be able to gauge the era in which
we live? This coat, which the young men of this age may
take for a fable, was neither a civil nor a military coat, and
could pass in turn for a military or a civil coat. The flaps of
the two hind tails were ornamented with embroidered *fleurs-
de-lys*. The gilt buttons were also stamped with *fleurs-de-lys*.
Upon the shoulders were two empty loops, awaiting their useless epaulettes. These two traces of martiality stood there like
a petition without a countersign. In the case of this old man
the button-hole of this coat of royal blue blossomed with several
ribands. It was clear that he always kept his three-cornered
hat, with its golden string, in his hand; for the snowy *ailes de
pigeon* of his powdered hair showed not a trace of the pressure
of a hat. He did not *look* more than fifty, and seemed to
enjoy robust health. While his physiognomy exhibited the
frank and loyal character of the old *émigrés*, it also bespoke the
light and easy morals, the gay amours, and the levity of those
musketeers who were formerly so renowned in the *fasti* of
gallantry. His gestures, his gait, and his manners all an-

nounced that he did not want to be cured either of his royal-
ism, or of his religion, or of his amours.

A truly fantastic figure it was which followed this pretentious
Voltigeur de Louis Σ . I. (for such was the nickname given by
the Bonapartists to these noble relics of the monarchy.) But
fairly to paint this second figure it should be made the principal object of the picture in which it is but an accessory.
Imagine, then, a dry and wiry figure, dressed like that which
has been first described, but being only its reflection, its shadow
if you will. While the coat of the former was new, that of the
latter was old and shabby. The powder in the hair of the
second seemed less white, the gold of his lilies was less bright,
his epaulette loops were more drooping and more shrivelled:
his intellect was less keen, and his age more advanced than
that of the other. In short he realized the saying of Rivarol
about Champcenetz :—" He is my moonshine." He was but
the other's double—a poor pale double, for there existed between them all the difference that there is between the first and
the last proof of an engraving. This mute old fellow was a
mystery to the painter, and a mystery he always remained. The
chevalier (for he was a chevalier) did not speak to any one and
no one spoke to him. Was he a friend, a poor relation, a man
who stuck to the old gallant as a humble companion sticks to
an old woman?

Was he something between the dog, the parrot, and the
friend? Had he saved the fortune, or merely the life of his
benefactor? Was he the trim of a second Captain Toby? Not
only at the Baronne de Rouville's but elsewhere also he excited
curiosity without ever satisfying it. Who, living under the
Restoration, could possibly recall the attachment which before
the Revolution bound this chevalier to his friend's wife, who
had now been in her grave for twenty years?

The personage who seemed the more recent of these two
relics advanced gallantly towards the Baronne de Rouville,
kissed her hand. and sat down by her side. The other bowed

and placed himself near to his type at a distance represented
by the width of two chairs. Adelaide went and leaned her
elbows upon the back of the armchair occupied by the old
gentleman, unconsciously imitating the posture which Guérin
in his celebrated picture has given to the sister of Dido. Although the familiarity of the old gentleman was that of a father,
the liberties which he took seemed for the moment to displease
the young lady.

"What, are you sulky with me?" said he.

Thereupon, he looked at Schinner with one of those oblique
glances full of subtilty and insight which may be called diplomatic glances. Its expression showed the prudent uneasiness,
the polished curiosity, of well-bred people who at sight of a
stranger seem to put the question, "Is he one of us?"

"This is our neighbor," said the old lady, pointing to Hippolyte. "The gentleman is a celebrated painter, whose name
you must know in spite of your indifference in matters of art."

The gentleman observed his old friend's roguish omission of
the name, and bowed to the young man.

"Certainly," he said, "I heard the gentleman's pictures
much talked about at the last exhibition. Talent has glorious
privileges, sir," he added, looking at the red riband of the
artist. "The distinction which we purchase at the cost of our
blood and long service, you obtain while still young; but all
kinds of distinction are sisters," he continued, placing his hands
upon his cross of St. Louis.

Hippolyte murmured a few words of thanks and again became silent, confining himself to admiring with growing enthusiasm the beautiful girlish head, which had bewitched him. He
was very soon buried in this contemplation, and thought no
more about the extreme poverty of the household. To him
the face of Adelaide stood out in an atmosphere of light. He
gave brief answers to the questions addressed to him, which he
fortunately heard, thanks to a singular faculty of the mind,
which enables us at times to divide the current of our thoughts.

Has it not happened to every one of us to remain plunged in some sad or pleasurable meditation, to listen to its voice within ourselves, and at the same time, attend to a conversation or a reading? Admirable duality! how often does it enable us patiently to endure the bore!

Hope, fruitful and smiling, filled Hippolyte with a thousand thoughts of happiness, and he no longer cared to take notice of any of his surroundings. He was a child full of delight, and it seemed to him disgraceful to analyze pleasure.

After the lapse of a certain time, he perceived that the old lady and her daughter were playing cards with the old gentleman.

As for the satellite of the latter, he, faithful to his character of shadow, was standing behind his friend watching his game, and relying to the mute inquiries of the card-player by little grimaces of approval, which reflected the questioning movements of the other's face.

"Du Halga, I always lose," said the gentleman.

"You discard badly," replied the Baronne de Rouville.

"Why for the last three months I have not been able to win a single game from you," he continued.

"Have you the aces, Monsieur le Comte?" asked the old lady.

"Yes, that is another for me to mark," he said.

"Shall I be your counsellor?" asked Adelaide.

"No, no, keep opposite to me. Zounds! it would be too hard to lose my money, *and* the sight of your face."

At last the match came to an end. The gentleman took out his purse, and throwing two louis upon the cloth somewhat ill-temperedly, exclaimed,—

"Forty francs, as true as gold. And, what the deuce! It's eleven o'clock."

"It's eleven o'clock," repeated the mute looking at the artist.

The young man hearing this phrase a little more distinctly

than all the others, came to the conclusion it was time to go.
Returning, therefore, to this lower world of vulgar ideas, he
stumbled on some commonplaces for the sake of saying something, bowed to the baroness, her daughter, the two strangers,
and quitted the apartments under the influence of the maiden
joys of genuine love; nor did he seek to analyze the little
events of the evening.

The next day the young artist felt the keenest possible desire
to see Adelaide again. If he had listened to the voice of
passion he would have invaded his neighbors at six o'clock in
the mórning, as soon as he reached his studio. He had, however, still sufficient reason left to wait till the afternoon. But
so soon as he thought he could in decency present himself
before Madame de Rouville, he went down, and while his
heart beat loudly, rang the bell. The door was opened by
Mademoiselle Leseigneur, and Hippolyte, blushing like a
young girl, timidly asked for the portrait of the Baron de
Rouville.

"Oh, come in," said Adelaide, who no doubt had heard
him coming down from his studio.

Bashful and out of countenance, so stupid with happiness
that he knew not what to say, the artist followed her. To see
Adelaide, to hear the rustle of her dress after having spent the
livelong morning in wishing to be near her, after having risen
from his seat a hundred times saying, "now I am going down,"
and then not going down; this to him was life, and life so
abounding that such sensations long protracted would have
worn his very soul. The heart possesses the singular power of
giving an extraordinary value to the merest trifles. What a joy
it is for a traveller to gather a blade of grass, an unfamiliar leaf,
if he has risked his life in pursuit of them. Thus it is with
love's trifles. The old lady was not in the reception-room.
When the young girl found herself alone with the painter, she
brought forward a chair in order to reach the portrait, but
finding that she could not unhook it without placing her foot

upon the commode, she turned to Hippolyte, and blushing said to him, "I am not tall enough. Will you take it down?"

It was a feeling of modesty, traceable in the expression of her features and in the tones of her voice, that was the real motive of her request; and the young man, understanding this, threw her one of those intelligent looks which are love's sweetest language. Seeing that the artist had guessed her feelings, Adelaide dropped her eyes proudly, in a manner the secret of which only maidens possess. Finding not a word to say for himself and feeling almost intimidated, the artist took the picture down, examined it carefully, setting it in a proper light near the window, and went away, simply saying to Mademoiselle Leseigneur, "I will return it to you soon."

During this brief moment both of them felt one of those keen emotions whose effects upon the mind may be compared to the effects produced by a stone thrown into a lake. The sweetest reflections spring up and succeed one another, indefinable, numerous, vague, agitating the heart, just as the rippling circles, starting from the spot where the stone was thrown in, long continue to furrow the surface of the water.

Armed with the portrait, Hippolyte returned to his studio. His easel had already been fitted with a canvas, his palette charged with colors, his brushes cleansed, and the place and light in which he was to work, fixed. So until dinner-time he labored away at the portrait with that ardor which artists devote to their whims. That very evening he returned to the Baroness de Rouville's and remained there from nine o'clock until eleven. Barring the different topics of conversation, this evening bore a close resemblance to the preceding. The two old gentlemen came at the same time, the same match at piquet took place, the same phrases fell from the lips of the players, the sum lost by Adelaide's friend was about as large as that which he had lost the night before. Only Hippolyte, who had gained a little confidence, ventured to chat with the young lady.

Thus eight days glided away. Meanwhile the feelings of the artist and Adelaide underwent those slow and exquisite transformations whereby two hearts are brought into complete unison. Thus day by day the look with which Adelaide greeted her friend became more intimate, more confiding, more gay and frank. Her voice and manners became more affectionate and familiar. They laughed and talked, communicated their thoughts to each other, and spoke about themselves with all the simplicity of two children who have contrived in the space of a single day to know each other as if they had been acquainted for three years. Schinner wanted to learn piquet. Being quite ignorant of the game, he naturally committed blunder after blunder, and, like the old gentleman, lost nearly every match. Without having yet told their love, the two young people knew that they belonged to each other. Hippolyte took a delight in exercising his power over the timid girl. Many were the concessions made by Adelaide, who in her timidity and devotion was the dupe of those mock fits of coldness which the least skilful lover and the most simple-minded young girl will plan and constantly employ, just as spoiled children abuse the power with which a mother's love invests them. Accordingly all familiarity between the old count and Adelaide promptly ceased. The young girl correctly interpreted the melancholy fits of the young painter, the thoughts that underlay his knitted brow and breathed in the brusque accent of the few words he uttered when the old gentleman freely kissed Adelaide on neck or hand. She, on her part, too, soon began to ask her lover for a strict account of his slightest actions; she was so uneasy, so unhappy, when Hippolyte did not come to see them, and scolded him so soundly when he absented himself, that he was obliged to give up seeing his friends and relinquished general society altogether. Adelaide betrayed the jealously which is innate in woman, on finding that sometimes after leaving Madame de Rouville's at eleven o'clock the artist would pay visits elsewhere and saunter through the gayest drawing-rooms in Paris. She told him that a life of that kind was injurious to the health; then, with that intense earnestness which gains so much power from the voice, the gestures and the look of the beloved one, she maintained that "a man who was obliged to squander on several woman at once, his leisure time and the graces of his intellect could not be the object of a very strong affection."

Thus the artist was led, as much by the despotism of passion as by the instances of a loving girl, to confine his existence to the small apartment where everthing was to his mind. In short, never was love more ardent or more pure. The faith and delicacy, which existed equally between them, nurtured their mutual passion, without the aid of those sacrifices by which many persons seek to prove to each other their affection. There existed between them a constant interchange of feelings so sweet that they did not know which of the two gave or received the most. A spontaneous inclination rendered the union of their hearts always very close. The progress of this genuine affection was so rapid that two months after the accident to which the artist owed the happiness of knowing Adelaide, their lives had become one life. From early morning the young girl hearing some one walking overhead could say to herself, "There he is." When Hippolyte went home to dine at his mother's he never failed to look in and say "How do you do" to his neighbors, and in the evening he would come at the accustomed hour with all a lover's punctuality; so that no woman, not even the most tyrannical and the most ambitious in the matters of love, could have brought the slightest reproach against the young painter. Thus Adelaide experienced the unmixed and boundless happiness of seeing the complete realization of that ideal which at her time of life it is so natural to dream of. The old gentleman did not come so often, the jealous Hippolyte had supplanted him in the evening at the green table and in his constant losses.

Yet in the midst of his happiness he was beset by one im-

portunate idea, when he bethought him of the unfortunate
circumstances of Madame de Rouville, for he had acquired
more than one proof of her distress. Several times already
he had said to himself on his way home, "What, twenty francs
every evening?" and he did not dare to avow even to himself
the odious suspicion.

It took him two months to paint the likeness, and when it
was finished, varnished, and framed, he considered it one
of his best works. Madame de Rouville had said nothing
further to him about it. Was this carelessness or pride? The
artist did not care to fathom the motives of her silence. He
entered gaily into a little plot with Adelaide, to put the
portrait in its place while Madame de Rouville should be away.
So one day during her mother's customary walk at the Tuileries,
Adelaide went up alone for the first time to Hippolyte's studio,
under pretence of seeing the portrait in the favorable light in
which it had been painted. She stood there mute and motionless, lost in a delightful reverie wherein all the feelings of a
woman blended in one—for are they not all summed up in
boundless admiration for the man she loves? When the
artist, uneasy at her silence, bent down to look at the young
girl, she held out her hand to him without being able to utter
a single word, but two tears fell from her eyes. Hippolyte
seized her hand, and for a moment they looked at each other
in silence, both wishing, but fearing, to confess their love. The
artist held Adelaide's hand in both of his, and the equal warmth
and equal movement told the lovers that their hearts beat with
an equal force. Overcome with emotion the young girl drew
herself gently away from Hippolyte and said with a look of
simplicity, " You will make my mother very happy."

" Only your mother?" he inquired.

" Oh, as for me, I am too happy already."

The artist bent his head and was silent, alarmed at the violence of the feelings which Adelaide's tone had awakened in
his heart. Fully understanding the danger of the situation,

they went down and put the portrait in its place. That day
Hippolyte dined for the first time with the baroness, who, in the
fullness of her heart, and bathed in tears, wanted to embrace
him.

In the evening the old *émigré*, the ancient comrade of Baron
de Rouville, paid his two friends a visit, to inform them that he
had just been appointed a vice admiral. His land voyages
across Germany and Russia had been reckoned as naval cam-
paigns. When he caught sight of the portrait he cordially
grasped the hand of the painter, and exclaimed, " Upon my
honor, although my old carcase is hardly worth the trouble of
perpetuating, I would gladly give 500 pistoles for so close a
likeness of myself as this is of my old friend Rouville."

At this suggestion the baroness looked at her old friend and
smiled, while her face showed signs of rising gratitude. Hippolyte fancied that the old man's intention was to offer him
the price of the two portraits in paying for his own ; not only
his artist's pride, but his jealousy also, was aroused by this reflection, and replied, " Sir, if I painted portraits I should not
have painted that."

The admiral bit his lips and sat down at the card-table The
artist remained near Adelaide, who suggested six games at
piquet which he accepted. While he was playing he noticed
in Madame Rouville an eagerness over the game which surprised him. Never had the old baroness exhibited so earnest a
desire to to win, nor so keen a pleasure in handling the gentleman's gold. During the evening Hippolyte's happiness was
invaded by suspicions of evil which caused him much uneasiness. Did Madame de Rouville live by gambling? Perhaps
she was playing at that moment, with a view to the payment of
some debt, or spurred by some pressing need. Her rent might
be unpaid, perhaps. The old man seemed sharp enough not
to allow himself to be robbed of his money. What, then, was
the inducement which drew him, rich as he was, to that abode
of poverty? Why had he, who had formerly been so free with

Adelaide, abandoned the footing of familiarity on which he had
stood, and which was perhaps his right ?

These involuntary reflections impelled him to scrutinize the
old man and the baroness, whose knowing look and certain side-
long glances which she cast at Adelaide and himself disturbed
him. " Can they be deceiving me ? " Such was Hippolyte's last,
horrible, withering thought, which had precisely enough hold
upon him to torture him. He resolved to remain, after the
two old men had gone, in order to confirm or dissipate his suspicions. On taking out his purse to pay Adelaide, he was
so carried away by his harrowing thoughts, that he put it down
upon the table, and fell into a brief reverie. Then, ashamed
of being silent, he rose, replied to some commonplace inquiry
from Madame Rouville, and went close to her, in order that he
might more closely examine her aged features, while he talked.
When he left, he was under the influence of a thousand conflicting ideas. After he had descended a few of the steps he
went back for the purse which he had forgotten.

" I left my purse with you," he said to the young girl.

" No," she replied, blushing.

" I certainly thought it was there," said he, pointing to the
card table.

Ashamed for Adelaide's sake, and that of the baroness, at
not seeing it, he looked at them with a stupified look which
made them laugh, turned pale, and then, tapping his waistcoat,
resumed, " I am mistaken, no doubt I have it."

In one end of the purse there had been fifteen louis, and in
the other some small change. The theft was so flagrant,
and was repudiated with such effrontery, that Hippolyte had no
further doubts as to the morality of his neighbors. He stood
still upon the staircase, then descended it with difficulty ; his
legs trembled, he felt giddy, sweated, shivered, and found himself unable to walk ; so completely was he overcome by the fearful emotion caused by the overthrow of all his hopes. From
that moment his memory brought back to him a crowd of ob-

servations, trifling in appearance, but corroborative of his frightful suspicions, and decisive of the character and mode of life of these two women, since they established the reality o this last incident.

Had they, then, awaited the completion of the portrait, before stealing the purse? As the result of a conspiracy the robbery seemed more odious still. The artist remembered to his sorrow, that for the last two or three evenings Adelaide had seemed to examine with all a young girl's inquisitiveness, the network of worn silk, while she was, probably, ascertaining how much the purse contained ; and that she had indulged in some jokes, to all appearance perfectly innocent, but whose real object was, no doubt, to cover her look-out for the moment when the sum should be large enough to be worth stealing.

"The old admiral," thought Hippolyte, "has perhaps some excellent reasons for not marrying Adelaide, and so the baroness thought she would try to inveigle—"

But at this hypothesis he stopped short without even finishing his thought, which was destroyed by one very just reflection :

"If the baroness wanted me to marry her daughter, they would not have robbed me." Then in order that he might retain his illusions and the love which had become so firmly rooted in his heart, he looked to chance for a favorable interpretation. "My purse may have fallen on the floor," he argued with himself; "it may have stuck on my armchair. Perhaps I have it on me, I am so absent-minded." Then he rummaged his pockets with feverish movements ; but the accursed purse was not forthcoming. Then his cruel memory brought back to him, from time to time, the fatal truth. He distinctly saw his purse lying on the cloth ; but though he no longer doubted that the robbery had been commited, he now framed excuses for Adelaide, saying that one ought not to condemn the unfortunate so hastily. There must be some secret explanation of this deed, which was, in outward seeming, so

L

degrading.   He could not bear to think that that proud and
noble countenance was—a lie.   But, now the poverty-stricken
apartments appeared before him, shorn of all the poetry of that
love which beautifies everything.   Faded and squalid they rose
before him, and he regarded them as the outward covering of
an inner life that was ignoble, idle, vicious.   For are not our
feelings written on the things by which we are surrounded?

The next morning he rose without having slept.   Sorrow of
heart, that serious moral malady, had made rapid progress in
him.   To lose a joy that has formed the subject of our dreams,
to renounce a whole future, is anguish more accute than that
caused by the destruction of happiness, however great, that
has been actually enjoyed; for is not hope better than recollection?   The reflections which suddenly arise out of such
ruin are like a shoreless sea; we may for a time swim upon its
bosom, but in the end our love must drown and perish.   And
it is a fearful death; for the feelings are the brightest portion
of our existence.   This partial death produces in certain organ-
izations. whether they be strong or delicate, fearful havoc, the
offspring of disenchantment, of defeated hope and cheated passion.   Thus was it with the young artist.   Early in the morning
he went out to take a walk under the fresh foliage of the gardens
of the Tuileries.   There, engrossed in thought and oblivious of
all the world contained, he stumbled on one of his most intimate friends, an old comrade at school and in the studio, with
whom he had lived on a footing of more than fraternal affection.

"Why, Hippolyte, what is the matter with you?" said his
friend, Francois Souched, a young sculptor, who had just gained the grand prize, and was on the wing for Italy.

"I am most unhappy," said Hippolyte gravely.

"It can only be a love-affair that can cause you any trouble.
As for money, fame, and social esteem—you have them all."

Thereupon the confidences gradually commenced, and the
artist confessed his passion.   As soon as he began to talk about

the Rue de Suresnes, and of a young woman who lived upon a fourth storey, Souchet gaily exclaimed,—

"Stop one moment; you are speaking of a little girl whom I go to the church of the Assumption every morning to see, and to whom I am making advances. Why, my dear fellow, we all know her. Her mother is a baroness. Do you believe in baronesses who live upon fourth storeys? Brrr— Why you are a man of the golden age. We see the old mother here, in this walk, every day; why she has a face and a way of carrying herself that betray everything. What, haven't you discovered what she is, from the way in which she carries her bag?"

The two friends walked together for a long time, and several young men, who knew Souchet or Schinner, joined them. The sculptor, who attached no great importance to his friend's adventure, related it to the rest.

"Our friend also," said he, "has seen the little girl."

Then there followed observations, laughter, harmless jokes, full of the gaiety habitual to artists, which inflicted terrible agonies upon Hippolyte. A certain ingrained modesty rendered him ill at ease when he saw his heart's secret thus lightly treated, his passion torn to rags and tatters, and an unknown girl, whose life appeared so modest, subjected to judgments, true or false, pronounced with so much indifference.

"But, my dear friend," said Souchett, "have you seen the baroness's shawl?"

"Have you followed the little girl when she trots to the Assumption in the morning?" asked Joseph Bridau, a young tyro from the studio of Gros.

"Yes, the mother possesses, among other virtues, a certain grey dress, which I regard as typical," said Bixiou, the caricaturist.

"Listen to me, Hippolyte," pursued the sculptor, "come here about four o'clock and analyze the walk of the mother and daughter a little. If, after that, you retain any doubts

why, we shall never make anything of you ; you will be capa
ble of marrying the daughter of your porteress."

Torn by the most conflicting feelings, the painter quitted his
friends.   It seemed to him that Adelaide and her mother
must be above such accusations, and he felt remorse in the
depths of his heart for having had any doubts about the purity
of this young girl, who was so beautiful and simple.   He went
to his studio, passed the door of the rooms where Adelaide
was, and felt in his heart a pang such as no man can fail to
understand.   He loved Mademoiselle de Rouville so passionately, that in spite of the stolen purse he adored her still.   His
love was that of the Chevalier des Grieux, admiring and
purifying his mistress even when she was in the van that was
carrying the abandoned women to jail.   " Why should not my
love make her the purest of women ?   Why leave her to vice
and evil without extending to her a friendly hand ?"   Such a
mission pleased him.   Love turns everything to its own
account.   Nothing is so seductive to a young man as to play
the part of good genius to a woman.

There is a vague romance about such an enterprise which
suits exalted minds.   Is it not the most unlimited devotion in
its highest and most graceful form ?   Is there not a certain
grandeur in the thought that one loves so well as to love even
under circumstances which kill the love of others ?   Hippolyte
sat down in his studio and looked at his picture without doing
anything to it.   He saw the figures in it only through the
tears which stood in his eyes ; then with his brush still in his
hand, he went up to the picture as if to tone down one of its
tints, but did not touch it.   Night came and found him still in
the same attitude.

Roused from his reverie by the increasing darkness, he went
down stairs, met the old admiral on the staircase, darted one
sombre glance at him, and rushed away.   It had been his
intention to pay his neighbors a visit, but the sight of Ade-
ide's protector froze his heart and banished his resolution.

He asked himself, for the hundredth time, what motive could induce the succersful old *roué*, who had an income of 80,000 francs, to visit this fourth floor lodging, where he lost about forty francs every evening. He believed he knew the motive. The next day and the succeeding days, Hippolyte plunged into work, in the endeavor to combat his passion by the seductive strength of ideas and the fire of conception. He half succeeded. Study comforted him, but it could not drown the recollection of so many happy hours passed by the side of Adelaide. One evening, on leaving his studio, he saw the door of the ladies' lodging half open. Some one was standing in the embrasure of the window. The arrangement of the door and staircase was such that the painter could not pass without seeing Adelaide. He bowed to her distantly, and cast at her a glance of complete indifference; but judging of the young girl's sufferings by his own, he felt an internal tremor as he thought of the bitterness which that look and that cold greeting might infuse into a loving heart. To crown the sweetest festivals that ever made the happiness of two pure hearts, with eight days of neglect and with the deepest and most thorough scorn—was not that a hideous *dénouement!* Perhaps the purse had been recovered; perhaps every evening Adelaide had been looking for her friend's arrival. This very natural and simple thought filled the lover with fresh remorse. He asked himself whether the proofs of attachment which the young girl had afforded him, and their enchanting little talks, instinct with the love which had bewitched him, did not at least demand that he should make some inquiry and give a chance for some justification. Ashamed of having resisted for a whole week the wishes of his heart, and looking on himself as almost a criminal for having combatted them, he went that very evening to Madame Rouville's. At sight of the young girl's pale thin face, all his suspicions and evil thoughts took flight.

"Good God, what is the matter with you?" he asked, after having paid his respects to the baroness.

Adelaide made no reply, but looked at him with a melancholy, wan, dejected look, which pained him.

"You have doubtless been very hard at work," said the old lady; "you are changed. We are the cause of your seclusion. That portrait has thrown you back with some pictures of importance to your reputation."

Hippolyte was glad to find so good an excuse for his want of attention.

"Yes," he said, "I have been very busy, but I have suffered—"

At these words Adelaide raised her head and looked at her lover. Her anxious eyes had no reproach in them.

"You must have supposed, then, that we were very indifferent as to your good or evil fortune," said the old lady.

"I was wrong," he continued. "But nevertheless, there are troubles which we cannot confide to any one, not even to friends of older standing than I have the honor to possess in you."

"The sincerity and strength of friendship cannot be gauged by the duration of time. I have seen very old friends bestow not a tear upon each other's misfortunes," said the baroness nodding her head.

"But what is the matter with you?" said the young man, addressing himself to Adelaide.

"Oh, nothing," replied the baroness, "Adelaide has sat up for several nights in order to finish a bit of feminine handicraft, and would not listen to me when I told her that a day sooner or later was of little consequence . . . ."

Hippolyte did not listen any further. As he looked at those two calm and noble faces, he blushed at his suspicions, and attributed the loss of his purse to some unknown chance. That evening was delightful to him and perhaps also to her.

There are certain secrets which young hearts understand so
well!

Adelaide guessed what was passing in Hippolyte's mind.

Without wishing to avow his fault, the artist recognized it;
he returned to his mistress more loving, more affectionate
than before, and thus endeavored to purchase an unspoken
pardon.

Adelaide now experienced joy so perfect and so sweet that
it did not seem too dearly bought by all the misfortune which
had so cruelly disturbed her mind. But this concord of their
hearts, this magic unison, was nevertheless disturbed by a few
words from the Baroness de Rouville.

"Are we going to have our little card-party?" said she,
"for my old Kergarouët is relentless."

This phrase reawakened all the young painter's fears. He
colored as he looked at Adelaide's mother, but he saw nothing
in her features save an expression of frank good-nature; there
was no *arrière-pensée* to destroy its charm, no trace of bad
faith in its intelligence; the mischief that played in it was a
gentle mischief, there was not a trace of remorse to disturb its
calm.

He proceeded to take his seat at the table. Adelaide resolved to share his luck, pretending that he did not understand
piquet, and required a partner. While the game went on
Madame de Rouville and her daughter exchanged signs of
intelligence which caused Hippolyte all the more uneasiness in
that he was winning; but at the end of the match a final stroke
made the lovers debtors to the baroness. The artist had no
sooner removed his hands from the table in order to search in
his pocket for some silver, than he saw before him a purse
which Adelaide had slipped there unperceived. The poor girl
was holding the old purse in her hand, and for the sake of
keeping her countenance, was looking in it for some money to
pay her mother with. All the blood in Hippolyte's body rushed

to his heart so swiftly that he almost fainted. The new purse which had been substituted for the old one, and contained his fifteen louis was worked with gold beads. Rings, tassels, and all bore witness to the good taste of Adelaide, who had doubtlessly exhausted her pocket-money in buying the ornaments which decked her pretty piece of work. It was impossible to express with greater subtlety the feeling that the gift of the portrait could be acknowledged only by some token of regard. When Hippolyte, overwhelmed with joy, turned his eyes towards Adelaide and the baroness, he saw them trembling with delight, and rejoicing in their amiable fraud. He considered himself petty, mean, and stupid; he could have wished to punish himself, to tear his heart out. Tears rushed to his eyes; impelled by some irresistable force, he rose, he took Adelaide in his arms, strained her to his heart, and snatched a kiss from her: then, with all an artist's straightforwardness, he turned to the baroness, and exclaimed, "I claim her from you for my wife."

Adelaide looked at the painter half-indignantly, and Madame de Rouville, somewhat astonished, was seeking for a reply, when the scene was interrupted by the ringing of the bell. The old vice-admiral appeared, followed by his *shadow* and Madame Schinner. Having guessed the origin of the grief which her son vainly attempted to conceal from her, Hippolyte's mother had gathered, from some of her friends, certain information about Adelaide. Justly alarmed at the calumnies which, unknown to the Comte de Kergarouët, attached to the young lady, Madame Schinner learned the count's name from the porteress, and went and told him what she had heard. He, in his wrath, would have liked "to cut the scoundrels' ears off," as he phrased it. Fired by his indignation, the admiral had told Madame Schinner the secret of his voluntary losses at the card-table—the pride of the baroness leaving him no other than his ingenious method of helping her.

When Madame Schinner had paid her respects to the

baroness, the latter, looking at the Comte de Kergarouët, the Chevalier du Halga (the former friend of the late Comtesse de Kargarouët), Hippolyte, and Adelaide, said with that grace which has its source in a good heart, "It seems that we are quite a family party this evening."

THE BALL AT SCEAUX.

(LE BAL DE SCEAUX.)

TO HENRI DE BALZAC.
HIS BROTHER, HONORÉ.

The Count de Fontaine, the head of one of the most ancient
families of Le Poitou, had devoted himself to the cause of the
Bourbons with intelligence and courage during the war which
the inhabitants of La Vendée carried on against the Republic.
After having escaped all the dangers which threatened the
royalist leaders during that stormy period of contemporary
history, he used jokingly to say, " I am one of those who were
killed upon the steps of the throne."

This witticism was not without some foundation in fact, in
the case of a man who had been left for dead on the bloody
field of Quatre-Chemins.

Although the faithful Vendean had been ruined by the con-
fiscations which took place, he continually refused the lucrative
posts offered to him by the Emperor Napoleon. Staunch in
his aristocratic convictions, he had blindly followed the maxims
of his creed in the choice of a mate. In spite of the seductions to which he was exposed by a wealthy parvenu of the
revolution, who set a high value on an alliance with him, the
Count de Fontaine married a De Kergaroüt, a young lady
without fortune, but belonging to one of the best families in
Brittany. When overtaken by the revolution, Monsieur de
Fontaine had a numerous family. Although it did not accord
with the ideas of this generous nobleman to solicit favors, he
yielded to his wife's desires, left his estate, (the rents of which
were hardly sufficient to supply the wants of his children) and
came to Paris. Grieved at the avidity with which his ancient

comrades hunted after the posts and dignities at the disposal
of the constitutional government, he was on the point of return
ing to his estate, when he received an official communication
from a well-known minister, announcing his nomination to the
grade of camp-marshal, in pursuance of the ordinance which
gave permission to the officers of the catholic armies to reckon
the first twenty years of the reign of Louis XVIII. as years of
service.   Some days later the Vendean also received, without
any solicitation on his part, and *officially*, the cross of the order
of the Legion of Honor and the cross of St. Louis.

Shaken in his resolution by these successive marks of favor,
for which he considered himself indebted to the memory of
his sovereign, he no longer confined himself to conducting his
family, as he had been wont to do, Sunday after Sunday, to
the Salle des Maréchaux at the Tuileries, to cry *Vive le Roi* as
the princes went to chapel; he requested the favor of a private
audience.   This audience, which was very readily obtained,
had nothing *private* about it whatever.   The royal reception-
room was crammed with old servitors, whose powdered heads,
seen from a certain elevation, locked like a carpet of snow.
There the nobleman renewed his acquaintance with some of
his old companions, who received him somewhat coldly; but
the princes were *adorable*, to use the enthusiastic expression
which escaped him when the most gracious of his masters, who,
the count imagined, knew him only by name, came up and
shook him by the hand, calling him the purest of the Ven-
deans. .

In spite of this ovation, however, it did not occur to any of
these august personages to ask him for an account of his losses,
or of the money which he had so generously poured into the
coffers of the catholic army.   He discovered, somewhat late,
that he had fought at his own expense.   Towards the conclusion of the evening, he thought he might venture to make a
witty allusion to the condition of his finances, which was very
similar to that of many another nobleman.   His Majesty began

to laugh very heartily, for he took a pleasure in any well-turned phrase, but he nevertheless replied by one of those royal pleasantries whose mildness is more formidable than an angry reprimand. One of the most intimate confidants of the king very soon drew near to the calculating Vendean, and in a well-turned and polished phrase, gave him to understand, that it was premature for him to come to a reckoning with his masters; that accounts of much older standing were under consideration, accounts which would doubtless furnish matter for a history of the revolution. The count beat a prudent retreat from the venerable group, which described a respectful semi-circle in front of the august family; then, after having, not without some difficulty, disengaged his sword from the attenuated shanks among which it was entangled, he crossed the court of the Tuileries on foot and regained the hackney-coach which he had left upon the quay. Endowed with that stubborn spirit which characterizes the old nobility, who still retain a recollection of the League and the Barricades, he complained to himself in the hackney-coach loudly, and in a manner that might have compromised him, about the change that had taken place at court. "Formerly," said he to himself, "every one used to speak freely about his little private affairs to the king; noblemen did not hesitate to ask him for favors and for money, and now to-day there is a difficulty in obtaining repayment of sums disbursed in the king's service. Zounds! the cross of St. Louis and the rank of camp-marshal are not worth the three hundred thousand francs which I put down in good hard cash in the royal service. I shall speak to the king to his face in his own apartment."

The scene that had taken place cooled the zeal of M. de Fontaine all the more, in that his applications for an audience always remained unanswered. He saw, moreover, the upstarts of the empire obtaining some of those posts which under the ancient monarchy had been set apart for the best families.

"All is lost," said he one morning. "It is clear that the

king was never anything but a revolutionist. If it were not
for the king's brother, who does not throw over old customs,
and consoles his faithful servants, I know not into what hands
the sceptre of France might pass, if this *régime* should continue.
Their damned constitutional system is the worst of all forms
of government, and will never suit France. Louis XVIII. and
M. Beugnot spoiled everything at Saint Ouen."

The count abandoned himself to despair and prepared to
return to his estate, with the noble determination to waive all
claim to indemnity. Just at that time the events of March 20,
1815, showed that a fresh storm was brewing, which threatened
to engulf the legitimate sovereign and his defenders. Monsieur
de Fontaine acted like those generous people who will not send
away a servant while it rains. He mortgaged his property to
follow the routed monarchy, without knowing whether this
partaking in the emigration would be more propitious to him
than his former self-sacrifice. But since he had noticed that
the companions of the sovereign's exile were held in more favor
than the brave men who had formerly protested against the
establishment of the Republic with arms in their hands, it may
be that M. de Fontaine hoped to find his sojourn in a foreign
land more profitable than active and dangerous service at
home. The calculations of the courtier were not like those
idle enterprises which on paper promise superb results, and
ruin those who attempt the execution of them. He therefore
was, in the witty language of the most brilliant and most skilful
of our diplomatists, one of the five hundred faithful servants
who shared the exile of the Court at Ghent, and one of the fifty
thousand who returned from it During this short absence o
royalty, M. de Fontaine had the good fortune to be employed
by Louis XVIII., and found more than one opportunity for
affording the king proofs of great political integrity and sincere
attachment. One evening when the monarch had nothing
better to do, he called to mind the *bon-mot* which Monsieur de
Fontaine had indulged in at the Tuileries. The old Vendean

did not permit so favorable an opportunity to remain unimproved, and told his story with so much wit that the king, whose memory was most tenacious, called it to mind as occasion served. The august man of letters observed the happy turn to certain memoranda, the editing which had been entrusted to the discreet nobleman. This little merit caused Monsieur de Fontaine to be engraved in the king's memory as one of the most loyal servants of the crown. On the second return of the Bourbons, the count was one of the envoys extraordinary who were commissioned to travel through the departments, and summarily judge the fomentors of the rebellion; but he exercised his terrible powers with moderation. As soon as this temporary jurisdiction had come to an end, the grand provost took his seat among the Councillors of State, was elected deputy, spoke little, listened a great deal, and considerably altered his political views. Certain circumstances, of which biography knows nothing, made him so intimate with the king, that on one day, on seeing him come in, the crafty monarch called out to him, "Friend Fontaine, I shall not take it into my head to make you a director-general or a minister. Both you and I, if we were government clerks, should lose our places on account of our opinions."

"It may be said in favor of representative government, that it saves us the trouble formerly imposed on us of dismissing in person our secretaries of state. Our council is a regular hotel to which public opinion very often sends strange travellers; but nevertheless we shall always be able to find a place for our faithful servants." This ironical exordium was followed by an ordinance giving to M. de Fontaine an office attached to the crown demesne extraordinary. In consequence of the intelligent attention with which he listened to the sarcasms of his royal friend, his name was found on his Majesty's lips whenever a commission was to be appointed the members of which were to be well paid. He had the good sense to say nothing about the favor with which the king regarded him, and man-

aged to cultivate it by the piquant manner in which, during the
course of one of those familiar chats in which Louis XVIII.
took as much delight as in well-turned notes, he related the
political anecdotes and, if the expression may be allowed to
pass, the cancans, diplomatic or parliamentary, which, at that
time, were so rife.   It is well known that the details of his
governmentability, a word adopted by the august jeerer, afforded
him infinite amusement.   Thanks to the good sense, the intelligence, and the skill of Monsieur de Fontaine, every member
of his numerous family, no matter how young, ended as the
count jocularly expressed it to his master, by settling himself
on the leaves of the budget like a silk-worm.   Thus the eldest
son, through the king's favor, obtained an eminent position
among the permanent judges ; the second, who was a simple
captain before the Restoration, obtained a company immediately after his return from Ghent.   Then, under cover of the
excitement of the year 1815, during which regulations were set
at nought, he was appointed to the Royal Guard, then again to
the Body Guard, and ultimately found himself, after the affair
of the Trocadéro, a lieutenant-general with a command in the
Guard.   The youngest son, who was originally appointed sub-
prefect, very shortly became Master of the Requests and director of a municipal administration of the city of Paris, a post
in which he was not exposed to the tempests which affected
the legislature.   These quiet favors, which were as secret as
those conferred upon the count himself, were showered down
unperceived.   Although the father and his three sons had, each
of them enough sinecures to produce a revenue almost as considerable as that of a director-general, their political emolu-
ments excited the envy of no one.   In these early days of the
constitutional system, few persons had accurate notions about
the peaceful regions of the budget, in which skillful favorites
managed to find equivalents for the Abbeys which had been
swept away.   Monsieur de Fontaine, who used formerly to
boast that he had not read the *Charte*, and displayed so much

indignation at the greed of the courtiers, hastened to prove to his august master that he understood as well as that master, the spirit and the resources of representative government. However, notwithstanding the stability of the careers in which his three sons had been launched, and the pecuniary advantages arising from the simultaneous tenure of four offices, M. de Fontaine's family was too numerous to allow him to re-establish his fortune with promptitude and ease. His three sons were rich in prospects, in favor, and in ability; but he had three daughters, and he was afraid of wearying the king's bounty. He determined only to mention one of these virgins, eager to kindle the hymeneal torch. The king had too much good taste to leave his work half done; and the marriage of the eldest daughter with a receiver-general, De Baudry, was brought about by one of those royal phrases which cost nothing .nd are worth millions. One evening when the monarch was a little sulky, he learned, with a smile, of the existence of another Demoiselle de Fontaine. Her he matched with a young magistrate, of middle-class origin, it is true, but rich and very clever. The king also made him a baron. When during the next year the Vendean mentioned the name of Mademoiselle Emilie de Fontaine, the king replied in his squeaky little voice,—

" Amicus Plato sed magis amica natio."

Then some days afterwards he treated his *Friend Fontaine* to a very mild quatrain, which he called an epigram, wherein he joked M. de Fontaine about his three daughters so skilfully brought forward in the form of a *Trinity*. If we are to listen to the chronicle, it would seem that the monarch had sought the point of his joke in the *unity* of the three divine persons.

" If the king would condescend to convert his epigram into an epithalam?" said the count, endeavoring to turn the freak to his own advantage.

" If I can see the rhyme, I don't see the reason of what you

M

say," answered the king brusquely; for he did not relish the joke about his poetry, lenient as it was.

From that day forward his intercourse with M. de Fontaine was not so agreeable as it had been. Kings like contradiction better than is generally supposed. Like the youngest child of almost every family, Emilie de Fontaine was a Benjamin whom everybody spoiled. The king's coldness, therefore, caused the count all the more concern because there never was a marriage more difficult to bring about than that of this petted daughter. In order to understand all these difficulties we must enter the precincts of the splendid mansion in which the commissioner was lodged at the expense of the Civil List. Emilie had passed her childhood on the De Fontaine estate, in the enjoyment of that abundance which suffices to render youth happy There her slightest wishes were law to her sister and brothers, to her mother and father. All her relatives doated on her. She reached years of discretion at the very moment when fortune was showering its favors upon her family, so that the enchantment of her existence continued. The luxury of Paris seemed to her quite as natural as that provincial affluence which had conferred enjoyment on her childhood. Just as her will had never been thwarted during her infancy, when she wanted to follow her joyous inspirations, so she still found others give way to her, when at the age of fourteen she was launched into the whirlpool of society. Having been thus gradually introduced to the pleasures which wealth affords, she found the elegant toilette, the gilded saloon, the well-appointed carriage, as necessary to her as the compliments, more or less sincere, of the flatterer, and the fêtes and frivolities of court life. Like most spoiled children, she tyranized over those who loved her, and kept her seductions for the indifferent. Her defects grew with her growth, and the time soon came when her parents were to reap the fruits of her fatal education. At the age of nineteen Émilie de Fontaine had not yet made choice among the many young men whom the policy of M. de

Fontaine brought to his entertainments. Although she was so young, she was as completely self-composed as a woman can be. Her loveliness was so remarkable, that for her to appear in a drawing room was to reign there; but, like kings, she had no friends, for she found herself in all places the object of a complaisance before which, perhaps, even a better disposition than hers would have given way. No man, not even an old one, had courage enough to contradict the opinions of a young girl, one look from whom was sufficient to rekindle passion in the coldest heart. Having been educated with a care that had not been bestowed upon her sisters, she could paint fairly, she spoke Italian and English, she played upon the piano admirably; and then her voice, trained by the best masters, had a certain timbre which made her singing irresistibly seductive. She was so quick, and so well read in every branch of literature, that she might well, in the words of Mascarille, induce one to suppose that people of quality know everything when they come into the world. She could readily talk about the Italian and the Flemish school of painting, the middle ages and the renaissance; rapidly pronounce judgment upon an ancient or a modern book, and bring to light with cruel grace, the shortcomings of a work. The simplest of her phrases was received by the idolatrous crowd like a fetfa of the sultan by the Turks. Thus, while she dazzled superficial people, her natural tact enabled her to discover those who were not superficial, and for them she was so full of coquetry, that aided by this seductive charm, she managed to escape their criticism.

Beneath this alluring varnish lay a reckless heart, a conviction (shared by many young girls) that no one occupied a sufficiently lofty sphere, to be able to comprehend her mental superiority, and a pride based as much upon her birth as on her beauty. Pending the absence of that potent passion which sooner or later seizes on the heart of woman, she found scope for her youthful ardor in an extravagant love for social distinctions, and she exhibited the most profound contempt for *roturiers.* Very impertinent in her manner to the new nobility, she devoted all her exertions to ensuring her parents' equality among the most illustrious families of the Faubourg St. Germain.

These views had not escaped the observant eye of Monsieur de Fontaine, who had more than once since the marriage of his eldest daughter groaned over the sarcasms and witticisms of Émilie. Consistent people will doubtless be surprised to see the old Vendean conferring his eldest daughter on a receiver-general, who certainly was the owner of sundry old seigniorial domains, but whose name was not preceded by that particle which distinguished so many of the defenders of the monarchy; while the second daughter had been married to a judge too recently *baronified*, to make the people forget the fact that his father had sold firewood. This noteworthy alteration in the ideas of a nobleman at the moment when he was attaining his sixtieth year, an epoch at which men rarely change their convictions, was not due merely to his lamentable sojourn in the modern Babylon, where in the long-run all provincials lose their angularities; the new political conscience of Monsieur de Fontaine was rather the result of the councils and friendship of the king. That royal philosopher had taken a pleasure in converting the Vendean to the ideas demanded by the progress of the nineteenth century, and the renovation of the monarchy. Louis XVIII. wanted to fuse parties, just as Napoleon had fused both men and things. The legitimate monarch, who was perhaps as intelligent as his rival, acted in a different direction. The last of the Bourbons was as anxious to satisfy the people and the imperialists, as the first of the Napoleons was to surround himself with the leaders of the aristocracy, and to endow the church. As the confidant of the monarch's thoughts, the councillor of state had gradually become one of the most influential and wisest chiefs of that moderate party which, in the name of the national interests, ardently desired the fusion of opinions. He preached the costly principles of constitutional government, and backed with all his might

the play of that political see-saw, which enabled his master in the
midst of political excitement to govern France. Perhaps M. de
Fontaine hoped to gain a peerage through one of those gusts of
wind which overtook the legislature, and whose strange results
used in those days to surprise the oldest politicians. One o:
his most stubborn principles was his non-recognition of any
nobility in France, except the peers,—the only class whose
families had any privileges.

"A nobility without privileges," he would say, "is a handle
without a .ool." Being as far removed from the party of La-
fayette, as from that of La Bourdonnaye, he entered with
ardor upon that general reconciliation out of which was to
arise a new era and a brilliant destiny for France. He sought
to convince the families who frequented his reception-rooms,
and among whom he visited, that the chances offered by the
army and the civil service would thenceforward be but small. He
urged mothers to place their sons in independent professions
and industrial pursuits, giving them to understand that military offices and the higher grades in the government departments
would ere long be reserved, most constitutionally of course, for
the younger sons of peers.

In his view, the people had obtained their full share of government appointments through their elective Assembly, and
the judicial and financial posts, which he said would always
be, as they had hitherto been, the appanage of the chiefs of
the people.

These new ideas of the head of the De Fontaine family,
and the prudent marriages which, in the case of his two elder
daughters, had resulted from the change, had met with strong
opposition at the domestic hearth. The Countess de Fontaine
remained faithful to the old beliefs which a woman who was
connected through her mother with the Rohans, could not
recant. But though she had for a time resisted the fortune
and happiness of her two elder daughters, she yielded to those
private considerations which husband and wife confide to each

other at night when their heads are resting on the same pillow.
Monsieur de Fontaine coolly demonstrated to his wife by the
most accurate calculations, that their residence in Paris. the
necessity of giving entertainments, the splendor of his establishment—a set-off against the hardships which they had so
bravely shared in the depths of La Vendée—together with the
expenses incurred on behalf of their sons, exhausted almost
the whole of their revenues, and that therefore it behoved
them to embrace as a heaven-sent favor the opportunity which
offered itself of getting their daughters so advantageously
settled.   Would they not sooner or later enjoy an income of
60,000, 80,000 or 100,000 francs? Such advantageous matches
were not to be met with every day for portionless girls. And
then, it was high time for them to think of saving, in order to
increase the De Fontaine estate, and reconstruct the ancient
territorial fortune of the family. The countess yielded, as any
mother in her position would (though perhaps with better
grace) have yielded to arguments so persuasive; but she
declared that at least her youngest daughter Émilie should find
a husband, calculated to gratify the pride which she had unfortunately helped to develope in her youthful breast.

Thus, those events which should have shed joy over this
family, introduced into it a slight leaven of discord. The
receiver-general and the young judge were exposed to a cere-
monious frigidity, set up by the countess and her daughter
Émilie. But their etiquette furnished them yet wider scope
for the exercise of their domestic tyranny. The lieutenant-
general married Mademoiselle Mongenod, the daughter of a
wealthy banker; the president very wisely married a young
lady, whose father had amassed, as a salt merchant, a fortune
of two or three millions. Lastly, the third brother exhibited
his fidelity to his plebian doctrines, by taking to wife Mademoiselle Grostête, the only daughter of the receiver-general of
Bourges. But the three sisters-in-law and the two brothers-in-
law derived so much pleasure and personal advantage from

remaining in the lofty circles of political power, and the society of the Faubourg St. Germain, that they all agreed to form a little court around the haughty Émilie. This pact between interest and pride, however, was not so well cemented, but that the young sovereign occasionally provoked a revolution in her miniature state. Scenes, not indeed transgressing the limits of good taste, tended to keep up among all the members of that powerful family an ironical mood, which, without interrupting the tone of friendship assumed in public, did sometimes degenerate at home into feelings decidedly uncharitable. Thus, the wife of the lieutenant-general, now a baroness, considered herself quite as noble as a Kergarouët, and maintained that a good four thousand a year gave her the right to be as impertinent as her sister-in-law, Émilie, to whom she would sometimes express an ironical hope that she would make a good match, telling her that the daughter of such and such a peer had just married plain Mr. So and-so. The wife of the Vicomte de Fontaine took pleasure in eclipsing Émilie by the luxurious elegance of her dress, furniture, and carriages. The ironical manner in which the sisters-in-law and the two brothers-in-law sometimes received the pretensions set up by Mademoiselle de Fontaine, threw her into fits of anger, which the production of a shower of epigrams could scarcely calm. When the chief of the family experienced a certain abatement in the covert and precarious friendship of the monarch, it caused him all the more apprehension, because, goaded by the ironical challenges of her sisters-in-law, Émilie had at that crisis fixed her hopes higher than ever.

While affairs were in this condition, and the little family strife was at its worst, the king, into whose good graces M. de Fontaine thought himself on the point of being restored, was attacked by the illness which was destined to carry him off. The wary politician, who knew so well how to steer his bark amid the tempest, very shortly died.

Sure of the favor of the succeeding monarch the Count de

Fontaine exerted himself to the utmost to gather round his
youngest daughter the pick of marriageable young men.
Those who have tried the solution of that difficult problem—
the establishment of a proud and capricious girl, will perhaps
understand the trouble which the poor Vendean took. If he
could accomplish the task to the satisfaction of his pet daughter, he would then have achieved a fitting termination of the
career which he had been pursuing at Paris for the last ten
years.

In respect of the manner in which his family had fastened
itself upon the revenues of the various departments of the
government it might be compared to the house of Austria,
which threatened through its alliances to invade the whole of
Europe.   Accordingly, the old Vendean went on courageously
presenting aspirant after aspirant, so dear to him was the
happiness of his daughter.   But nothing could be more
comical than the way in which the impertinent girl pronounced
sentence upon, and appraised the merits of her admirers. One
would have thought that, like one of the princesses whom we read
of in the Arabian Nights, she was rich and handsome enough to
have the right of selection from among all the princes in the
world.   To every suitor she raised an absurd objection followed by an objection yet more absurd.   The legs of one were
too lanky; another was knock-kneed; this one was near-
sighted; that one was named Durand; a third was lame, while
nearly all were too fat.   Livelier, gayer, more charming than
ever, after having rejected two or three applicants, she plunged
into the gaieties and balls of the season, scrutinizing with her
piercing eyes the celebrities of the day, and delighting in pro-
voking the offers which she invariably refused.   Nature had
bestowed upon her in profusion the gifts essential to the part
of Célimène.   Tall and exquisitely formed, Émilie de Fontaine
could be imposing or playful, as she pleased.   Her neck, which
was rather long, enabled her to assume delightful attitudes of
scorn and of impertinence.   She had formed a fertile repertory

of those airs *de tête* and those feminine gestures which give
such fatal or such favorable emphasis to a broken phrase or to
a smile. Beautiful black eyes, thick and well-arched eye-
brows, conferred upon her features an expression which
coquetry and the looking-glass taught her to heighten or to
moderate by the steadiness or the tenderness of her glance, by
the fixing or gentle flexure of the lips, by the coldness or
the graces of her smile. If Émilie wanted to win the heart of
any one, there was a certain melody in her pure voice ; but
she could also endow it with a sort of abrupt clearness when
she desired to paralyze the tongue of some prudent swain.
Her pale face and alabaster forehead resembled the limpid bosom
of a lake which now ripples in the breeze and now resumes its
glad serenity as the wind subsides. Several young men who had
suffered from her disdain, accused her of stage-play, but she
revenged herself by inspiring the calumniator with a desire
to win her favor and then subjecting him without mercy to all
the contempt which her coquetry could suggest. Among all
the fashionable girls of the day, none understood better than
she did how to assume a supercilious air when accosted by a
man of talent, or how to display that insulting politeness which
makes inferiors of our equals, or how to deluge with impertinence all who attempted to place themselves on a level with
herself. Wherever she appeared she seemed to be receiving
homage rather than compliments, and even in the presence of
a princess her bearing and her airs would have converted the
arm-chair in which she was seated into the throne of an
empress.

Monsieur de Fontaine discovered all too late how wrong was
the direction given to the education of his favorite daughter by
the affection of the entire family. The homage of the world—
for which the young woman who receives it has afterwards to
pay full dearly—had still further developed Émilie's pride and
augmented her self-confidence. The general deference had
fostered the growth of that egotism which is natural to spoiled

children who, like kings, make toys of all who approach them. At this moment the grace of youth and the charms of her accomplishments cast a thick veil over her defects—defects which are all the more odious in a woman, because it is only through love and self-sacrifice that she can hope to please. Since nothing escapes the eye of a good father, M. de Fontaine often endeavored to expound to his daughter the principal pages of the enigmatic book of life. Vain enterprise! Again and again he had had cause to mourn over the capricious indocility and the ironical prudence of his daughter; so that he at last abandoned the difficult task of correcting a sinister disposition, and confined himself to offering, from time to time, his gentle and benevolent advice. But he had the mortification to see his most affectionate words gliding from his daughter's heart, as if it had been made of marble. The eyes of a father are so long sealed that it required some experience ere M. de Fontaine perceived the condescension which his daughter mingled with her rare caresses. She was like a little child which seems to say to her mother, "Make haste and kiss me, and let me go and play." In short, Émilie condescended to be affectionate to her parents. But at times, in accordance with one of those sudden whims which seem inexplicable in girls, she shut herself up and would allow herself to be seen but rarely. She would complain that she had to share the affections of her parents with everybody; and grew jealous of everyone, even of her sisters and brothers. Then, after having been at great pains to surround herself with a dessert, the flighty girl would blame nature itself for her factitious solitude and self-inflicted sorrows. Armed with her twenty years' experience, she accused fate, because in her ignorance of the fact that the principle of all happiness lies in ourselves, she sought it in the externalities of existence. She would have gone to the end of the world to escape such marriages as her sisters had contracted, and yet her heart was beset with frightful envy at seeing them well and happily married. In fact she sometimes created in the mind of her mother (who was equally with M. de Fontaine the victim of her singularities) an impression that there was a grain of madness in her composition. But this aberration was easily explainable. Nothing is more common than this secret pride nurtured in the hearts of young women of the upper classes whom nature has endowed with great beauty. They are almost all persuaded that their mothers, having reached the age of forty or fifty, can no longer enter into their feelings nor understand their whims. They fancy that most mothers, being jealous of their daughters, want to dress them in their own fashion, with the premeditated design of outshining them and robbing them of the admiration which is their due. Hence secret tears and mute rebellion against this fancied maternal despotism. In the midst of these griefs, which though founded on an imaginary basis, become real enough, such girls harbor the additional mania of composing a scheme of existence for themselves, and casting a brilliant horoscope. Their magic consists in taking dreams for realities. They secretly resolve in their protracted meditations, to withhold their hands and hearts from the man who does not possess certain advantages. They produce an imaginary type, to which, come what may, the future husband must conform. After some practical experience of life, when they have indulged those serious reflections which years bring in their train, the bright hues of their ideal image fade away, under the influence of the world, with its prosaic routine. Then, one fine day they wake up, and find themselves in the full stream of existence, and are quite surprised at being happy, without the nuptial poetry of their dreams. In accordance with such poetry, Mademoiselle Émilie de Fontaine had, in her fragile wisdom, laid down a programme to which the successful aspirant to her hand must conform. Hence her disdain and hence her sarcasms.

"He must be,"—thus she reasoned with herself,—"not merely young and of the highest birth, but a peer, or the eldest son of a peer. I could not endure to see my arms upon a carriage-door, not surrounded by the flowing folds of an azure mantle, and not to share with princes the privilege of driving through the grand avenue of the Champs Élysées, during the Long-champs meetings. Moreover, my father maintains, that the day is coming, when a peerage will be the highest dignity in France. I should like my husband to be a soldier, reserving to myself the right to call on him to retire; and he must be decorated, so that arms will be presented as we pass."

These uncommon distinctions would go for nothing if this imaginary being were not extremely amiable, handsome, and clever, and above all—*if he were not slim.* Slimness, that corporal grace, however transient it may be, especially under a representative government, was a *sine quâ non.* Mademoiselle de Fontaine had a certain ideal measure which served as a model. The young man who did not at the first glance conform to the required condition, was not even favored with a second look.

"Oh! my God! how fat that gentleman is!" was with her the expression of sovereign contempt.

According to her, people endowed with an honest corpulence, were incapable of feeling; they must be bad husbands, and altogether unfit for civilized society. Though plumpness was looked upon as a beauty in eastern climes, it seemed to her a misfortune for women; in a man it was a crime.

These paradoxical opinions produced, thanks to the liveliness with which they were enunciated, a certain amount of amusement.

But, nevertheless, the Count de Fontaine felt that the pretensions of his daughter, the absurdity of which would very soon attract the attention of certain ladies, who were as clearsighted as they were malicious, would end by rendering those pretensions fatally ridiculous. He was afraid lest the peculiar notions of his daughter should degenerate in pronounced bad taste. He was afraid that an unpitying world might be already slily laughing at a person who remained so long upon the stage, without any dénouement to the piece which she was acting. Several of the actors, annoyed at having been rejected, seemed to be waiting for any slight disaster, which would enable them to revenge themselves; while the idle and the unconcerned began to grow weary. Admiration is always exhausting to human nature. The old Vendean knew, as well as any one, that, difficult as is the art of selecting the right moment for appearing on the stage of the world or of the court, for entering a drawing-room or a theatre, it is still more difficult to leave them in the nick of time. And accordingly, during the first winter that followed the accession of Charles X., he, in conjunction with his three sons and his sons-in-law, redoubled his efforts to attract to his receptions the most eligible men to be found in Paris, and among the deputies of the departments. The brilliance of his entertainments, the splendor of his dining-room, and his dinners, redolent of truffles, rivalled those celebrated banquets whereby the ministers of the period secured the votes of their parliamentary troops.

The worthy deputy was thereupon singled out, as one of the most potent corruptors of legislative integrity in that illustrious Chamber, which seemed to be dying of indigestion.

It was a strange result of his endeavors to get his daughter married, that he should preserve his popularity at court. Perhaps he found it secretly advantageous to sell his truffles twice. This accusation, which had its origin among certain Liberal carpers, who compensated the dearth of their adherents in the house by the abundance of their speeches, did not stick. The conduct of the Poitou nobleman was, for the most part, so upright and honorable, that he altogether escaped those epigrams which the malicious journals of the epoch hurled at the 300 voters of the centre, the ministers, the cooks, the directors-general, the princes of the fork, and the official defenders, who supported the Villèle administration. At the conclusion of this campaign, during which M. de Fontaine had several times taken the whole of his troops into action, he thought that his collection of admirers would not on this occasion be a mere optical illusion for his daughter, and that it was high time for her to come to a decision.

He derived a certain amount of internal satisfaction from the due fulfilment of his duty as a father; and besides, after having brought into play every resource, he hoped that among the many hearts laid at the feet of the capricious Émelie there might be found at least one whom she might have favored.

Feeling that he could not repeat such an effort, and weary of his daughter's conduct, he determined to have a consultation with her one morning towards the end of Lent, when the sitting of the House was not of a nature imperatively to demand his vote. While his valet was artistically designing upon his yellow cranium the delta of powder which, in conjunction with the pendant *ailes de pigeon*, formed his venerable head gear, Émilie's father, not without a secret tremor, requested his old *valet de chambre* to go and ask the haughty damsel to pay a visit to the head of the family.

"Joseph," said the old nobleman, when his head-gear was adjusted, "take away this napkin, draw the curtains, arrange the armchairs, shake the chimney-cloth, and put it on straight, and then dust the room. Now, just open the window, and let us have a little fresh air.

The count multiplied his orders and made Joseph quite out of breath. Joseph, who guessed his master's motive, restored some neatness to the room, which was naturally the most neglected in the house, and succeeded in producing a certain amount of order among the heaps of accounts, boxes, books, and other furniture of this sanctuary, in which the affairs of the royal demesnes were transacted. When Joseph had succeeded in introducing some order into this chaos, and had brought to the front, just as if he had been dressing the window of a fashionable shop, whatever would make the best show, and was calculated to produce, by means of its tints, a sort of bureaucratic poetry, he stopped in the midst of the maze of papers piled up in certain places, even on the carpet, gave a little nod of self-approval, and left the room.

The unhappy sinecurist by no means shared the satisfaction of his servant. Before taking his seat in his large arm-chair, he looked around him with an air of distrust, examined his dressing-gown with a hostile eye, swept away some particles of snuff, carefully wiped his nose, arranged the shovel and the tongs, stirred the fire, pulled up the heels of his slippers, threw back his little pigtail. which had assumed a horizontal position between the collar of his waistcoat and that of his dressing-gown, and caused it to resume its perpendicular position; then he gave a touch of the broom to the cinders of a hearth which afforded strong evidence of the inveteracy of his catarrh. In short, the old man did not sit down until he had glanced his eye for the last time over his study, in the hope that there was nothing to give rise to the very comical and impertinent remarks with which his daughter was wont to reply to his sage advice. On this occasion he did not want to compromise his paternal dignity. He gingerly took a pinch of snuff, and cleared his throat two or three times, as if he were about to demand, when he heard the light footstep of his daughter, who came in humming an air from "Il Barbiere."

"Good morning, father. What do you want me for so early?"

Having uttered these words as if they were the refrain of the air which she was singing, she kissed the count, not with that familiar fondness which makes the filial sentiment so sweet, but with the careless levity of a mistress who is sure that, do what she will, she will please.

"My dear child," said M. de Fontaine gravely, "I have sent for you in order to talk with you very seriously about your future. The necessity in which you are now placed of making such choice of a husband as may ensure your permanent happiness—"

"My dear father," said Émilie, interrupting her father in her most endearing tones, "it seems to me that the armistice, entered into between you and me in regard to my admirers, has not yet expired."

"Émilie, let us, from this day forth, cease to joke about so important a matter. For some time past, my dear child, those who truly love you have united their efforts to secure you a proper establishment, and you would be guilty of ingratitude were you to receive with levity the proofs of good-will which, not only I, but others also, shower upon you."

On hearing these words the young lady looked with an eye of mischievous investigation at the furniture of her father's study; she then selected the particular armchair which seemed to have least frequently afforded a seat to those who came to solicit her father's favors, placed it on the other side of the fireplace, so that she might face her father, assumed an attitude so grave, that it was impossible to avoid seeing therein certain traces of irony, and crossed her arms over the rich trimming of a tippet *à la neige*, whose numerous frills of tulle were thus mercilessly crumpled. After having cast a laughing side-glance at her old father's anxious countenance, she spoke. 'I never heard you say, father, that the government delivered its oracles in a dressing-gown. But, no matter," added she, "the people must not be critical. Let me hear what are your projects of law and official communications."

"I might not always be in a position to make you any, you young madcap. Listen Émilie. It is not my intention any longer to run the risk of injuring my reputation, which is a part of my childrens' fortune, by recruiting the regiment of partners whom it is your good pleasure to put to flight every spring. You have already been the cause of several dangerous misunderstandings with certain families. I hope that to-day you more fully understand the difficulties of your own position and of ours. You are twenty-two years of age, and you ought to have been married nearly three years ago. Your brothers and

your two sisters have all formed wealthy and happy unions.
But, my child, the expenditure which those unions have involved
and the style in which we are living on your account, have made
such a hole in our income, that it is as much as I can do to
give you a portion of a hundred thousand francs. From to-day
I want to study the future of your mother, who ought not to be
sacrificed to her children. If I should die, Émilie, Madame
de Fontaine ought not to be left to the tender mercies of any
one. She ought to continue to enjoy the affluence by which I
have recompensed, all too late, her devotion in my early misfortunes. You see, my child, that the insignificance of your
portion bears no sort of proportion to your ideas of grandeur.
Even that portion will be a sacrifice which I have not made for
any of my other children; but they have generously agreed
never to taunt you with the advantage which we are about to-
confer on a child too well beloved."

"In *their* position," said Émile, shaking her head ironically.

"My daughter, never try thus to depreciate those who love
you. Learn that it is only the poor who are generous. The
rich have always excellent reasons for not abandoning twenty
thousand francs to a relative. Now, don't sulk, my child, and
let us talk rationally. Among the young fellows who are looking out for a wife have you not noticed M. de Manerville?"

"Oh, he says *zeu* instead of *jeu*; he is always looking at his
feet because he considers them small; and he looks at himself
in the glass. Besides, he is fair, and I don't like fair men."

"Well, then, there is Monsieur de Beaudenord?"

"He is not a nobleman; he is badly built and thickset; I
grant you he is dark. The two gentlemen ought to come to
an agreement to unite their resources. The former ought to
give his figure and his name to the second, who might keep
his own hair, and then—perhaps—"

"What have you got to say against M. de Rastignac?"

"Madame de Nucingen has converted him into a banker."

"And our relation the Viscount de Portenduère?"

N

"A lad who dances badly, and besides has no fortune.
And then, father, none of them has a title. I should like to
be at least .. countess, like my mother."

"Then you have not seen any one this winter whom . . ."

"No father."

"Then what is it that you want?"

"The son of a peer."

"Daughter, you are mad," said M. de Fontaine, rising.

But all at once he looked upwards and seemed to imbibe a
fresh dose of resignation, from some religious reflection. Then,
looking at his child with a look of fatherly kindness, which
produced some effect upon her, he took her hand, pressed it,
and said tenderly, "I call God to witness, you poor deluded
creature, I have conscientiously fulfilled my duties towards
you; conscientiously, did I say? lovingly, Émilie. Yes, God
knows that I have this winter introduced you to more than
one honest man, whose capacity, morals, and disposition were
known to me, and all of them seemed good enough for you.
My child, my task is accomplished. From to day you are the
arbiter of your own destiny. I am both glad and sorry at
the same time, to find myself acquitted of the heaviest of all a
father's duties. I do not know whether you will hear much
longer a voice which unfortunately has never been severe, but
remember that the happiness of married life depends less upon
brilliant qualities and wealth, than on mutual esteem. Such
happiness is, from its very nature, modest and retiring. Now,
my child, my consent is given beforehand to the son-in-law
whom you present to me; but if you should be unhappy,
remember that you will have no right to blame your father.
I will not refuse to act in the matter, and to assist you, provided only that your choice be serious and definitive. I will
not compromise a second time the respect which is due to my
grey hairs."

The affection displayed by her father, and the solemn tone
of his pathetic harangue, made a keen impression on Made-

moiselle de Fontaine, but she concealed the depth of her feelings, seated herself on the knees of he count, who had sat
down still trembling with emotion, and lavished on him her
tenderest caresses, cajoling him so gracefully, that the old
man's forehead grew calm again. When Émilie thought that
her father had sufficiently recovered from his painful excitement, she said to him in a low tone,—

"I must thank you father for your delicate attention; you
had your room put in order for the reception of your darling
daughter. Perhaps you did not know that you would find her
so foolish and rebellious. But, father, is it then so difficult to
marry a peer of France? Ah, at all events, you won't refuse
me your advice."

"No, poor child, no, and I will call out to you more
than once—'Beware.' Consider, then, that the peerage is too
new a spring in our *governmentability*, as the late king used to
say, for peers to possess large fortunes. Those who are rich
wish to become still more so. The most opulent of all the
members of our peerage has not half the income of the poorest
member of the English House of Lords. Thus, the peers of
France will look out for wealthy heiresses for their sons, no
matter where they may spring from. This necessity for making wealthy marriages will last for more than two centuries.
It is just possible that by looking about for the lucky chance
which you desire, a search which may cost you the best years
of your life, your beauty (for a good many men marry for love
in this age) your beauty, I say, may bring about a miracle.
When experience is covered by so blooming a face as yours,
one may look for miracles. Do you not, in the first place,
posssess the gift of discovering worth by the greater or smaller
bulk of the human body? That is no slight accomplishment.
And therefore, it is needless for me to point out to a person so
wise as yourself, all the difficulties of the undertaking. I am certain that you will never credit a stranger with good sense because
his face is prepossessing, or with high moral qualities because he

has a good figure; and, finally, I quite agree with you in thinking that all peers' sons ought to have an air of their own and characteristic manners. Although now-a-days there are no distinctive symbols of rank, these young men will perhaps possess for you a *je ne sais quoi*, which will reveal them to your observation. Besides you keep your heart in check just like a good horseman, who is sure to keep his charger from stumbling. My daughter, I wish you good luck."

" You are laughing at me, father. But I declare to you that I would sooner go and die in Mademoiselle de Condé's convent, than not be the wife of a peer of France."

She escapsd from her father's arms, and proud of being her own mistress, she went away singing the air " *Cara non dubaitre*," from the " Matrimonio Segreto."

It happened that that day was a birthday in the family. At dessert, Madam Planat, Émilie's elder sister, the wife of the receiver-general, talked loud enough to be overheard, of a young American, the owner of an immense fortune, who had fallen desperately in love with Émilie, and had made her a brilliant offer.

" He is a banker, I believe," said Émilie carelessly. I don't like people connected with finance."

" But Émilie," said the Baron de Villaine, the husband of Émilie's second sister, you like the magistracy just as little, so that if you reject untitled landowners, from what class will you choose your husband ?"

" Especially taking into consideration your theory of thinness," added the lieutenant-general.

" I know what will suit me," replied the young girl.

" My sister requires a good name, a handsome young man, with a career before him, and an income of a hundred thousand francs."

" Monsieur de Marsay, for example," said the Baroness de Fontaine.

" I know, my dear sister," replied Émilie, " that I shall not make one of those foolish matches of which I have seen so many. But to avoid these matrimonial discussions, I declare, that I shall consider those who speak to me of marriage as the enemies of my peace of mind."

An uncle of Émilie, an old vice-admiral of seventy, whose fortune had just received an accession of 800*l.* a year in consequence of the law of indemnity, who was in a position to speak stern truths to his grand-niece, and was extremely fond of her, now interposed with a view to destroying the bitterness of the conversation. "Don't tease my poor Émilie. Don't you see that she is waiting until the Duc de Bordeaux comes of age."

The old man's joke was received with general laughter, while Émilie retorted,—

"Take care that I don't marry you, you old lunatic;" but the last words were fortunately drowned amid the noise.

"My children," said Madame de Fontaine, in order to tone down this impertinence. "Émilie, like all the rest of you, will consult no one but her mother."

"Oh, indeed," said Mademoiselle de Fontaine, with great distinctness, "in a matter which only concerns myself, I shall only consult myself."

Every eye was directed to the head of the family. Every one seems curious to see what course he would adopt in order to maintain his dignity; for not only was the aged Vendean held in high esteem by the world at large, but, more fortunate in this respect than many fathers, he was appreciated by his family, all the members of which had recognized the solid qualities which had enabled him to make the fortunes of those who were related to him. Accordingly, he was surrounded by that profound respect which English families and certain aristocratic houses on the continent entertain for the representative of the genealogical tree. There was a profound silence, and the eyes of the assembled guests travelled from the proud and pouting face of the spoiled child, to the stern faces of M. and Madame de Fontaine.

"I have left my daughter Émilie the mistress of her own lot," was the answer which the Count de Fontaine uttered in his deepest tones.

Thereupon the relatives aud guests looked at Mademoiselle de Fontaine with a look in which curiosity was blended with pity. The language of the count seemed to indicate that paternal kindness had been exhausted in the struggle with a disposition known by the family to be incorrigible. The sons-in-law murmured, and the brothers launched at their better halves, sarcastic smiles. From that moment no one took any further interest in the marriage of the haughty girl. Her old uncle, in his character as an old sailor, was the only person who dared to encounter her broadsides, and endure her whims, and was always ready to return shot for shot.

When the fine weather had set in and the budget had been voted, the De Fontaine family, a genuine model of the great parliamentary houses on the other side of the Channel, which have a footing in every ministry, and ten votes in the Commons, flew like a nest of birds to the lovely sites of Aulnay, Antony, and Châtenay. The opulent receiver-general had recently purchased in those regions, a country house as a residence for his wife, who remained at Paris only during the session. Although the beautiful Émilie despised plebians, she did not carry her feeling so far as to disdain the advantages of a fortune amassed by middle-class industry. She, therefore, accompanied her sister to her sumptuous villa, not so much from affection for those members of her family who took refuge in it, as because the rules of good society imperiously demand that every woman who has even the slenderest self respect, should leave Paris during summer. The verdant plains of Sceaux admirably fulfilled the conditions imposed by society, and by the duties of public life.

Since it is very doubtful whether the fame of the Bal de

Sceaux has ever passed beyond the limits of the department of the Seine, we must enter into some details about this hebdomadal festival, which from its importance at the time we are speaking of, threatened to become an institution. The environs of the little town of Sceaux enjoy a reputation arising from their sites, which are considered charming. It may be that they are after all extremely common-place, and owe their celebrity merely to the stupidity of the good citizens of Paris, who, when they emerge from the gulfs of freestone in which they are buried, would be inclined to admire the plains of La Beauce. But since the poetic shades of Aulnay, the hills of Antony, and the valley of La Bièvre are inhabited by certain travelled artists, by foreigners, who are very hard to please, and by a number of pretty women, who are not wanting in good taste, it is probable that the Parisians are right. But Sceaux possesses, for the Parisian, another attraction not less potent. In the middle of a garden commanding delightful views, is to be found an immense rotunda open on every side, but crowned with a dome of great lightness and extent, and supported by pillars. This rustic dais forms the covering of a dancing-saloon. It rarely happens that even the most starched gentle folks of the neighborhood do not once or twice during the season pay a visit to this palace of the rustic Terpsichore—either in glittering cavalcades, or in those light and elegant vehicles which sprinkle with dust the philosophic foot passenger. The hope of seeing some women of the upper ranks, and of being seen by them; the hope, less frequently betrayed, of meeting some young peasant girls (who are as cunning as judges), draws to the bal de Sceaux, on Sunday, swarms of attorneys' clerks, of the disciples of Æsculapius, and of those young fellows whose fair skins and fresh complexions are preserved by the damp atmosphere of the back-shops of Paris. Accordingly a goodly number of bourgeois marriages have been planned to the sounds of the orchestra, which occupies the centre of this circular saloon. If the roof could only speak, how many love stories it could tell !

This interesting medley conferred upon the bal de Sceaux, at that time, a keener interest than the other two or three balls in the environs of Paris excited ; and moreover, its rotunda, the beauty of the site, and the attractions of the garden, gave it an incontestable superiority over its rivals. Émilie was the first to exhibit a desire to go and " do the vulgar," at this gay ball of the arrondissement. She expected to derive immense enjoyment from finding herself in the midst of such a gathering. Her wish to wander among such a crowd created some astonishment ; but then is not the incognito one of the greatest pleasures of the great? Mademoiselle de Fontaine found amusement in picturing to herself all these citizen figures ; she imagined herself leaving in many a bourgeois breast the recollection of an enchanting dance or smile, laughed beforehand at the women who prided themselves on their dancing, and prepared her crayons for the scenes with which she expected to enrich the pages of her satirical album. Sunday did not come round quickly enough to suit her impatience. The good company from the Planat villa set out on foot, so as not to betray the rank of the party who were about to honor the ball with their presence. They had dined early, and the most beautiful evening of that month of May favored the aristocratic escapade. Mademoiselle de Fontaine was quite surprised to find, under the roof of the rotunda, certain quadrille parties composed of persons who seemed to be of good social position. She saw, it is true, here and there, some young men, who seemed to have spent a month's savings for the sake of shining for a day and she observed several couples whose frank enjoyment did not at all savor of matrimony ; but instead of reaping a harvest she had to glean. It surprised her to see that pleasure dressed in muslin was very like pleasure dressed in satin, and that the bourgeoisie danced as gracefully as the aristocracy, and in some cases even better. Most of the dresses were simple and worn with ease. Those who, in this assemblage, represented the suzerains of the territory, that is to say, the peasants, confined themselves to their corners, with wonderful politeness.

Even Mademoiselle de Fontaine had to devote a certain amount of study to the divers elements of which the meeting was composed, before she could discover any subject for ridicule. But she had neither time to devote to her malicious criticism, nor leisure to listen to many of those striking conversations which the caricaturist hails with so much delight. In this vast field the haughty creature suddenly discovered a flower (the metaphor is seasonable) whose splendor and whose colors acted upon her imagination with all the charm of novelty. It frequently happens to us, that we look at a dress, a wall, a piece of white paper, with so much abstraction, that we do not at once perceive some stain or some shining points which, subsequently, suddenly strike the eye, as if they had appeared only at the moment when we are first conscious of them. By a sort of moral phenomenon, very similar to that which I have mentioned, Mademoiselle de Fontaine suddenly recognized, in a certain young man, the type of that exterior perfection of which she had dreamed so long. Mademoiselle de Fontaine had seated herself on one of the rude chairs which defined the necessary boundaries of the saloon, at the end of the group formed by her family, so as to be able to follow the inclination of the moment by getting up and advancing as she pleased; for she acted in regard to the living tableaux, and the groups presented to her notice in the hall, just as she would have done at an exhibition at the museum. She fixed her eye-glasses on a person only two yards distant, and made remarks, just as if she was criticizing or praising a painted head, or a picture of genre.

Her eye, after having wandered over the vast animated picture, was all at once attracted by the face of which I spoke, which looked as if it had been purposely stuck in a corner of the canvas, in the very best light, as a figure out of all propor-

tion with the rest. The stranger, who seemed absorbed and
solitary, was leaning lightly against one of the columns which
support the roof, his arms were folded, and his head drooped,
as if he had been placed there to have his portrait taken. But
the attitude, though full of elegance and pride, was perfectly
free from affectation. There was not the faintest gesture to
indicate that, like Alexander, Lord Byron, and other great men,
he was presenting the three-quarter face and slightly bending
his head, solely for the purpose of attracting attention. His
steady gaze in following the movements of a lady who was
dancing, bore traces of some deep feeling. His elegant and
easy figure recalled the proportions of the Apollo. His beautiful black hair curled naturally upon his lofty forehead. At a
single glance Mademoiselle de Fontaine perceived the fineness
of his linen, the newness of his kid gloves, which had evidently
come from the best maker, and his small feet, neatly shod with
a boot of Irish leather. He did not wear any of those mean
trinkets of which the old fops of the National Guard and the
Lovelaces of the counter are so fond, but a black riband, to
which his eye-glass was attached, hung over his well-shaped
waistcoat. The exacting Émilie had never seen a man's eyes
shaded by lashes so long and strongly curved. Love and
melancholy breathed in the face, with its olive-hued and
masculine compelxion. The mouth seemed ever ready to
smile, and raise the corners of the eloquent lips; but this
tendency, far from suggesting gaiety, seemed rather to betray
a graceful sadness. There was too much promise in the head,
and distinction in the bearing, to call forth the expression
"What a fine man," or "What a good-looking man." You
wanted to know him. The most perspicacious observer would
at sight of the stranger, have been induced to regard him as a
man of talent, attracted to the village *fête* by some powerful
motive.

Such a mass of reflections did not cost Émilie more than a
moment's attention, in the course of which this privileged

being, thus subjected to a severe analysis, became the object of a secret admiration. She did not say to herself " He must be a peer of France," but " Oh, if he is only noble, and he cannot fail to be." She did not finish her thought, but rose at once, and, followed by her brother the lieutenant-general, went towards the column, pretending to be watching the gay quadrilles, though by an optical device familiar to woman, she did not miss a single movement of the young man, whom she was approaching. The stranger politely drew back, in order to make room for the two new comers, and took up his position against another pillar. Émilie, who was as much annoyed by the stranger's politeness as she would have been by an act of rudeness, began to talk to her brother in a voice much louder than the canons of good taste permitted ; she assumed certain *airs de tête*, and gesticulated and laughed immoderately, less to amuse her brother than to attract the attention of the imperturbable Unknown. But all her little artifices failed. Then Mademoiselle de Fontaine followed the direction of the young man's eyes, and perceived the cause of his indifference.

In the midst of the quadrille, immediately in front of her, there was dancing a pale young woman, who resembled those Scottish goddesses introduced by Girodet into his grand composition, Ossian receiving the warriors of France. Émilie thought that she recognized in the young dancer an illustrious lady, who had lately taken up her abode in a neighboring district. Her companion was a youth of fifteen, whose red hands, nankeen breeches, blue coat, and white shoes, showed that her passion for dancing prevented her from being fastidious in the matter of partners. Her movements showed no trace of her apparent weakness, but a slight flush was already visible in her pale cheeks and her complexion was beginning to grow more lively. Mademoiselle de Fontaine drew near to the quadrille party, in order to examine the strange lady as she returned to her place, while her *vis à vis* executed the same figure. But the Unknown came up, and bending over the pretty dancer, said in a voice at once gentle and commanding, "Clara, my child, don't dance any more," words which were distinctly overheard by the inquisitive Émilie. Clara pouted a little, bowed her head in token of obedience, and then smiled. After the termination of the quadrille, the young man showed all the attention of a lover in covering the young girl's shoulders with a Cashmere shawl, and placing her in a position where she would be sheltered from the wind. Then, soon afterwards, Mademoiselle de Fontaine, seeing them quit their seats, and walk round the enclosure, as people do when about to depart, contrived to follow them, under the pretence of admiring the various views from the garden. Her brother lent himself, with a mischievous good humor, to the vagaries of the somewhat devious march. Émilie then caught sight of the handsome couple, getting into an elegant Tilbury, which had been left under the care of a liveried and mounted servant. Just at the moment when the young man, having taken his seat, was adjusting the reins, Émilie first encountered from him one of those careless glances which one directs at a large crowd, and then she had the slight satisfaction of seeing him look back twice; an example which the young lady followed. Was it through jealousy?

"I presume that you have now seen enough of the garden, and that we can go back to the ball," said her brother.

"I am quite willing," she replied. "Do you think that she is a young relative of Lady Dudley?"

"Lady Dudley may have a young relative staying with her; but certainly not a young female relative!" said the Baron de Fontaine.

The next day Mademoiselle de Fontaine displayed an inclination for a ride. She gradually accustomed her old uncle and her brothers to accompany her in sundry morning rides, which, she said, were very conducive to her health. She exhibited a marked predilection for the vicinity of the village inhabited by Lady Dudley. But in spite of her cavalry manœuvres, she did not catch sight of the stranger again so speedily as the glad research, to which she abandoned herself, induced her to hope. She returned on several occasions to the Bal de Sceaux without meeting there the young Englishman, who had fallen from heaven to tyrannize over and adorn her dreams.

Although nothing spurs the rising passion of a young girl so much as an obstacle, there came a moment, nevertheless, when Émilie de Fontaine, almost despairing of the success of an enterprise, whose eccentricity will give some idea of the hardihood of her character, was on the point of giving up her strange and clandestine pursuit.

She might, indeed, have wandered for a long time around the village of Châtenay without again seeing her Unknown; for the youthful Clara, since such was the name which Mademoiselle de Fontaine had overheard, was not an Englishwoman, and the supposed stranger did not inhabit the flowery and perfumed groves of Châtenay.

One evening Émilie, having gone out for a ride with her uncle, to whom the gout had granted, during the fine weather, a considerable cessation of hostilities, met Lady Dudley. Seated in the open carriage, by the side of the illustrious foreigner, was Monsieur de Vandenesse. Émilie recognized the handsome pair, and her suspicions were dissolved, as a dream dissolves,—in a moment.

Vexed, as any woman who had been foiled, would be, she turned rein so rapidly that her old uncle had the greatest possible difficulty in following her; so great was the speed to which she had urged her pony.

"It would seem that I have grown too old to understand these brains of twenty," said the old sailor to himself, as he put his horse to a gallop, "or perhaps the young folks of to-day are not like what they used to be. But what can be the matter with my niece? now she is walking her pony as quietly as a gendarme patroling the streets of Paris. One would think that she wants to **beset** that worthy bourgeois, who looks to me like an author dreaming over his verses, for he seems to have an album in his hand. On my word, I am a great dolt. Isn't it the young man we are in search of?"

As this thought struck him, the old sailor checked his horse's pace, in order to place himself noiselessly at his niece's side. The vice-admiral had been guilty of too many peccadilloes in in 1771 and the following years, a period in our annals when gallantry was in vogue, not to perceive at a glance that Émilie had by the greatest chance, met the stranger of the Bal de Sceaux.

In spite of the veil which old age had spread over his grey eyes, the Count de Kergaroüet could recognize signs of unusual excitement in his niece, notwithstanding the immobility of feature which she endeavored to assume.

The penetrating eyes of the young lady were fixed in a kind of stupor upon the stranger, who was walking quietly before her.

"Just so," said the sailor to himself, "she will follow him, like a pirate after a merchantman. And when she has lost sight of him, she will be in a state of despair at not knowing who and what her lover is, and whether he is a marquis or a shopkeeper. Truly, young folks ought always to have an old periwig like me at their elbows."

He all at once, and without any warning, urged on his horse so as to make his niece's start off also, and then rode so quickly between her and the young pedestrian, that the latter was forced to take refuge on the sloping turf which bordered the road. Checking his horse suddenly, the count cried out,—

"Couldn't you have got out of the way?"

"Excuse me, sir," replied the stranger. "I did not know that it was for *me* to apologize to *you*, for your having very nearly knocked me down."

"Well, let's drop the subject, my friend," replied the sailor, in a voice whose sneering tone was positively insulting.

At the same time the count raised his whip as if to lash his horse, and touching the shoulder of his interlocutor said,—

"The liberal bourgeois is a reasoner, and every reasoner should be prudent !"

The young fellow mounted the slope when he heard this sarcasm ; then crossing his arms, he replied in feeling tones,—

" I cannot think, when I look at your white hair, that you still find amusement in picking quarrels . . . ."

"White hair," cried the sailor, interrupting him, "you lie in your throat, it is only grey."

A dispute thus commenced, waxed so warm in a few seconds that the younger adversary forgot the tone of moderation which he had constrained himself to preserve.   At the moment when the Count de Kergaroüet saw his niece approaching them, and exhibiting every symptom of lively apprehension, he gave his name to his antagonist, asking him to say nothing in the presence of the young lady, who was under his escort.   The stranger could not repress a smile, and gave his card to the old sailor, telling him at the same time that he was living in a country-house at Chevreuse, which he pointed out and then made off.

"You very nearly injured that poor péquin, niece," said the count, hastening to meet Emilie.   "Have you forgotten how to manage your horse?   You leave me stuck there to compromise my dignity in an endeavor to cover your follies ; whereas, had you remained, a single glance from you, or one of those pretty speeches which you can make so well when you are not impertinent, would have set everything right, even had you broken his arm."

"Why, my dear uncle, it was your horse, not mine, that caused the accident.   I really believe that you have lost the art of riding, you are no longer so good a horseman as you were last year.   But instead of discussing trifles—"

"Trifles, by Jingo ! you call it a trifle for a fellow to be insolent to your uncle?"

" Ought we not to go and find out whether the young man is hurt? He is limping. uncle, see there !"

" No, no! he is running. Ah, I gave him a rough lecture !"

" Ah, uncle, that is you all over !"

" Nay, nay, niece," said the count. stopping Émilie's horse by laying hold of the bridle. "I don't see the necessity of making advances to some shopkeeper, who ought to deem himself only too fortunate in having been knocked down by a charming young lady, or by the commander of 'La Belle Poule.'"

" Why do you take him to be a roturier, my dear uncle? It seems to me that he has very distinguished manners."

" Oh, everybody has good manners, now-a-days, niece."

" No, uncle, *everybody* has *not* the air and manner which the habit of frequenting good society confers, and I would gladly make a bet with you, that this young fellow is a man of family."

" You have not had much time to examine him."

" But this is not the first time I have seen him."

" No, nor the first time that you have tried to find him !" replied the admiral, laughing.

Émilie blushed ; her uncle enjoyed leaving her for some time to her embarrassment, and then said to her,—

" Émilie, you know that I love you as much as if you were my own child, just because you are the only one of the family who possesses that legitimate pride which high birth confers. Who the deuce, my dear grandniece, would have thought that good principles would become so rare? Well, I want to be your confidant. Now, I see, my darling, that this young gentleman is not quite an object of indifference to you. But, they would have the laugh of us in the family if we set sail under an unworthy flag ; you know what that means ; therefore let me assist you, niece. Let us keep our own counsel, and I promise to produce him in the midst of your assemblies."

" *When*, uncle ?"

" To-morrow."

" But, dear uncle, I am not to be fettered in any way ?"

'Not at all; and you may bombard him, set fire to him, and turn him adrift like an old carack, if such be your good pleasure. He won't be the first that you have served so, eh ?"

" You *are* kind, uncle !"

As soon as the count reached home he put on his spectacles, quietly drew the card from his pocket, and read " Maximilien Longueville, Rue du Sentier."

" Set your mind at rest, my dear niece," said he to Émilie, " you may harpoon him in all tranquillity of mind ; he belongs to one of our historic families, and if he be not a peer of France he will infallibly become one."

" How do you know all that ? "

" Ah, that is my secret."

" You know his name then."

The count silently inclined his grey head, which bore no faint resemblance to the trunk of some old oak, around which a few leaves, withered by autumnal frosts, are fluttering. At this signal, Émilie began to exert the ever-budding power of her coquetry. Experienced in the art of cajoling the old sailor, she showered upon him the most childlike caresses and the tenderest words ; she even went so far as to kiss him, in order to extort from him the revelation of so weighty a secret. The old man, who passed his existance in getting his niece to act scenes of this description, and very often rewarded her with the price of a dress, or by giving up his box at the opera for her use, took a delight on this peculiar occasion in being entreated, and especially kissed. But, as he protracted his enjoyment too long, Émilie grew angry, changed her caresses for sarcasms, and sulked. Then conquered by her curiosity, she returned to the attack. The diplomatic sailor extracted from his niece a solemn promise, to be for the future more reserved, more docile and less headstrong; to spend less, and above all to tell him everything. This treaty having been concluded and sealed with a kiss imprinted on Émilie's white forehead, he led he

o

to a corner of the drawing-room, set her on his knee, placed
his two thumbs upon the card so as to hide it, and then letter by
letter, disclosed the name of Longueville, obstinately refusing
to let her see anything more. This circumstance intensified
the secret feeling of Mademoiselle de Fontaine, who, during a
large portion of the night, conjured up the brightest pictures of
those dreams, on which her aspirations had been fed. At last,
thanks to that chance which she had often prayed for, Émilie
now saw something very different from a mere chimera at the root
of the imaginary riches with which she gilded her matrimonial
future. Like all young women who are ignorant of the dangers that wait on love and marriage, she grew enthusiastic
over the treacherous externals of marriage and of love. Or, in
other words, her passion sprang up as all these fancies of early
youth do spring—sweet, cruel errors which exercise so sinister
an influence on such young girls as are inexperienced enough to
assume the whole burden of providing for their future happiness.

The next morning, before Émilie was awake, her uncle had
made an excursion to Chevreuse. Finding the young man
whom, on the preceding evening, he had so persistently insult-
ed, standing in the court of an elegant villa, he accosted him
with the affectionate politeness characteristic of the gentlemen
of the old French court.

"Well, my dear sir, who would have ventured to tell me that
at the age of seventy-three I should involve myself in a duel
with the son, or perhaps the grandson of one of my best friends?
I am a vice-admiral, sir, and that is equivalent to telling you that
I think as little of a duel as I do of smoking a cigar. In my
time, two young fellows could never strike up an intimacy without having first seen the color of each other's blood. But,
zounds, yesterday, in my capacity of an old sailor, I had taken
a little too much rum on board and ran foul of you. There is
my hand; I would rather receive a hundred rebuffs from a
Longueville, than cause his family the slightest grief."

Whatever coolness the young man constrained himself to

throw into his bearing towards the Count de Kergaroüet, he could not long withstand the frank good nature of his manner, and suffered the old man to shake him by the hand.

"You were just going for a ride," said the count. "Don't let me interfere with you. But, unless your arrangements are made, come with me and dine at the Planat Lodge to-day. My nephew, the Count de Fontaine, is a man whom it is essential to know. Ah, I intend to indemnify you for my rudeness, by introducing you to five of the prettiest women in Paris. Yes, yes, young man, your brow unknits itself now. I am fond of young men, and I like to see them happy. Their happiness recalls to me the joyous hours of my early days, when there were plenty of love affairs as well as duels. We were gay in those times. Now-a-days you philosophize and take everything seriously, as if there had been no such thing as a fiftcenth or sixteenth century."

"But, sir, are we not right? The sixteenth century gave only religious liberty to Europe, and the nineteenth will give it political lib—"

"Oh, don't let us talk politics. I am a blockhead of an *ultra*, look you. But I don't want to prevent young folks from being revolutionists, so long as they leave the king at liberty to disperse their mobs."

When they had gone a little farther, and the count and his youthful companion were in the middle of the wood, the sailor singled out a young birch-tree, pulled his horse up, and took out one of his pistols : the ball lodged in the centre of the tree, which was fifteen paces distant.

"You see, my dear fellow, that I do not fear a duel," said he, looking at M. Longueville with comic gravity.

"Nor I either," replied the latter, who cocking his pistol promptly, and taking aim at the hole made by the count's bullet, lodged his own close to it.

"Now that is what I call well a trained youth," said the sailor with a kind of enthusiasm.

During his ride with the young man, whom he already look-ed on as his nephew, he found a thousand opportunities for in-terrogating him about all those trifles, perfect familiarity with which constituted, according to his particular code, an accom-plished gentleman.

"Are you in debt?" he inquired, after many questions.

"No sir."

"What, do you mean to say you pay all your tradesmen?"

"Punctually, sir; otherwise we should lose all credit and forfeit all respect."

"But at least you have several mistresses? Ah—you blush, my friend. Manners have greatly changed. With these ideas of legal order, Kantism, and liberty, youth has been spoiled. You have no Guimard, no Duthé, no creditors, and are quite ignorant of heraldry. Why, my young friend, you are not *educated !* Look you he who does not sow his wild oats in spring, sows them in winter. If I am now, at the age of seventy, in receipt of an income of 80,000 francs, it is because I spent the capital which would produce it—when I was thirty—oh, with my wife in all honor and good faith. Your imperfections, however, shall not deter me from presenting you at Planat Lodge. Bear in mind that you have promised me to come thither, and I shall look forward to seeing you there."

"What a funny little old man," said young Longueville to himself. "He is brisk and gay; but for all his efforts to ap-pear such a jolly good fellow, I shall not place too much confi-dence in him."

The next day, at about four o'clock, when the company were scattered, some in the drawing-room, and some in the billiard-room, a servant announced to the inmates of Planat Lodge, "Monsieur de Longueville."

At the name of the favorite of the old Count de Kergaroüet, every one, even the billiard-player who ran the risk of losing a hazard, rushed forward, as much with a view to studying the face of Mademoiselle de Fontaine, as to forming an opinion of the human phœnix who had obtained "honorable mention" at the expense of so many competitors. A dress as elegant as it was simple, manners full of ease, polished habits, ~ sweet voice that possessed a timbre which reached the heart-strings and caused them to vibrate, all combined to win for Monsieur Longueville the good will of the whole family. He seemed no stranger to the luxury which reigned in the abode of the pompous receiver-general. Although he talked like a man of the world, it was obvious to every one that he had received the most brilliant training, and that his acquirements were as solid as they were extensive. In a light discussion about naval architecture, which was started by the old sailor, Longueville hit upon the right words so readily that one of the ladies pointed out that he seemed to have been educated at the École Polytechnique.

"I consider, madame," replied he, that one may regard it as an honorable distinction to have been there."

In spite of much pressing, he politely but firmly opposed their wish to keep him to dinner, and put a stop to the observations of the ladies by saying, that he was a Hippocrates of a young sister, whose delicate health required great attention.

" You are, no doubt, a doctor?" inquired one of Émilie's sisters-in-law, ironically.

"The gentleman has just left the École Polytechnique," replied Mademoiselle de Fontaine graciously. (Her face had assumed its richest tints when she learned that the young girl she had seen at the ball was M. Longueville's sister.)

" But, my dear, it is possible to be a doctor, and yet to have been at the École Polytechnique; is is not sir?"

"There is no obstacle whatever, madame," replied the young man.

Every eye was directed at Émilie, who, at those words, looked at the engaging stranger with a sort of uneasy curiosity. She breathed more freely when he added, not without a smile, " have not the honor, madame, to be a doctor, and have even

declined to enter the service of roads and bridges, in order to
preserve my independence."

"And you did well," said the count. "But how could you
consider it an honor to be a doctor?" added the noble Breton.
"Oh, my young friend, for a man like you—"

"Monsieur le comte, I have an infinite respect for every
profession which has a useful end in view."

"Oh, we are quite agreed; you respect such professions
much in the same way as a young man respects a dowager."

The visit of M. Longueville was neither too long nor too
short. He withdrew at the moment when he perceived that
he had created a favorable impression upon every one, and
that every one's curiosity was awakened about him.

"He's a knowing fellow," said the count on returning to the
drawing-room after showing him to the door.

Mademoiselle de Fontaine, who alone was in the secret of
this visit, had dressed herself with such tasteful care as might
have attracted the notice of the young man; but she had to
undergo the slight mortification of observing that he did not
devote to her so much attention as she thought she deserved.
Her family were very much surprised at her reticence. As a
rule, Émilie displayed on behalf of a new comer her coquetry,
her witty chit-chat, and the inexhaustible eloquence of her looks
and attitudes. Whether it were that the melodious accents
and bewitching manners of the young man had acted as a
charm upon her, that she was seriously in love, and that that
feeling had worked a change in her, or not,—her bearing was
now entirely free from affectation. In her simplicity and
naturalness she was sure to appear more beautiful than before.
Some of her sisters and an old lady who was a friend of the
family saw in her conduct a refinement of coquetry. They
supposed that, deeming the young man a worthy mate for her,
Émilie intended, perhaps, to unfold her excellences gradually,
in order to dazzle him all at once, at the moment when she
should have won his heart. Every member of the family was

anxious to know what the capricious girl thought of the
stranger; but when, during dinner, they all amused themselves
by endowing M. Longueville with some new quality, each pretending to be the first to have discovered it, Mademoiselle de
Fontaine was for some time silent. A gentle sarcasm from her
uncle suddenly aroused her from her apathy. She said, in a
very epigrammatic fashion, that this celestial perfection must
needs cover some grave defect, and that she would take good
care not to form at the first glance an opinion of a man so
skilful. "Those who thus please everybody please no one,"
she added, "and the worst of all defects is to be free from
all." Like all young women when they love, Émilie nourished
the hope that she would be able to hide her feeling in the
bottom of her heart, by deceiving the Arguses by whom she
was surrounded; but at the expiration of a fortnight, not a single
member of that numerous family was uninitiated in the little
domestic secret. At the third visit paid by M. Longueville,
Émilie was convinced that she was in great measure the source
of it. This discovery caused her a pleasure so intoxicating,
that she was astonished at it when she reflected on it. It
wounded her pride. Accustomed as she was to make herself the
centre of the world, she was now compelled to acknowledge the
existence of a force which dragged her out of herself; she tried to
rebel, but she could not dismiss from her heart the enchanting
image of the young man. Then came many an anxious thought.
Two of M. de Longueville's qualities, his unlooked-for modesty
and his discretion, were very fatal to the general curiosity. He
never talked of himself or his pursuits, or his family.

The adroit innuendoes with which Émilie interspersed her
conversation, and the traps she laid in order to extract from
the young man some personal details, he evaded and avoided
with all the skill of a diplomatist who wants to conceal his
policy. If she talked about pictures, M. Longueville answered
her in the language of a connoisseur. If she played, the young
man showed without conceit that he was no mean performer

on the piano.   One evening he charmed the whole company by
uniting his voice with Émilie's in one of the fine duets of Cima-
rosa ; but when they tried to find out whether he was a professional musician, he joked upon the subject with so good a grace,
that he made it impossible for these ladies, who had had so
much experience in the art of probing the feelings, to discover to
what sphere of society he belonged.   No matter what hardihood the old uncle displayed in throwing the grappling-irons
upon this vessel, Longueville adroitly stole away, so as to preserve the charm of mystery ; and it was all the more easy for
him to maintain the character of "The handsome stranger"
at Planat Lodge, inasmuch as *there* inquisitiveness never
exceeded the limit of politeness.   Émilie, who was tortured by
this reserve, hoped to be more successful with the sister than
with the brother, in regard to confidences of that kind.
Backed by her uncle, who understood tactics of this sort, as
well as he did the art of seamanship, Émilie endeavored to
bring upon the stage the character, as yet silent, of Mademoiselle Clara Longueville.   The company at the lodge soon
manifested the strongest desire to become acquainted with so
amiable a person, and to contribute to her amusement.   A
dance was proposed and accepted.   The ladies did not entirely
despair of getting a young girl of sixteen to talk.

In spite, however, of such little clouds, created by curiosity
and massed by suspicion, a brilliant ray penetrated the heart
of Mademoiselle de Fontaine, who found great delight in existence by connecting it with a being other than herself.   She
began to understand social relations.

Whether it be that happiness improves us, or whether it were
that Émilie was too much engaged to torment others, she
became less caustic, more indulgent, and more gentle.   The
alteration in her character delighted her wondering relatives.
Perchance, after all, her egotism was being metamorphosed into
love.   To await the arrival of her retiring and unacknowledged
admirer, was a profound delight.   Without a single word of

passion having been breathed between them, Emilie knew that
she was loved ; and great was her pleasure in skilfully inducing
the young man to exhibit the treasures of that knowledge
which proved its own variety. She remarked that she also was
the object of careful observation, and thereupon she tried to
overcome all the defects which her training had allowed to
grow up in her. Was not this a first homage offered to love,
and a cruel reproach addressed by herself to herself? She
wished to please and charm ; she loved and was idolized. Her
family, knowing that her pride was an ample protection,
allowed her sufficient freedom to enable her to taste those little
childish joys, which gave so much charm and so much strength
to early love. Often did the young man and Mademoiselle de
Fontaine tread alone, but for each other's company, the alleys
of the park in which nature was decked by art, like a woman
dressed for a ball. Often did they hold together those aimless
and featureless conversations whose emptiest, idlest phrases are
precisely those which contain the greatest amount of hidden
feeling. Often did they admire, in each other's company, the
setting sun, with its rich tints. They gathered daisies only to
tear them to pieces, and sang the most passionate duets
together, employing the notes of Pergolese or Rossini
as faithful interpreters for the expression of their secret
thoughts.

The ball-day came ; Clara Longueville and her brother,
whom the footman would persist in decorating with the particle
which indicates nobility, were the heroes of the occasion. For
the first time in her life, Mademoiselle de Fontaine witnessed
the triumph of a young lady with delight. She showered upon
Clara in all sincerity those graceful endearments and minute
attentions which women do not generally bestow upon one another, except for the purpose of exciting the jealousy of men.
Émilie had an object in view ; she wanted to elicit secrets
unawarês. But, as being a girl, Mademoiselle Longueville
showed more deftness and ingenuity than her brother ; for she

was discreet without even seeming to be so, and managed to exclude the subjects of material interests from the conversation, while at the same time she invested it with so great a a charm, that Mademoiselle de Fontaine conceived a kind of envy of her, and surnamed her *the siren*. Whereas Émilie had intended to make Clara chatter, it was Clara who subjected *her* to an interrogatory. She wanted to judge Clara and Clara judged her. She was often vexed with herself for having permitted her character to leak out through certain answers mischievously extorted from her by Clara, whose air of candor and of modesty dissipated every suspicion of design.

On one occasion, Émilie could not hide her annoyance at having allowed herself to be provoked by Clara into a sally against rotouriers.

" Mademoiselle," said that charming creature, " I have heard Maximilien talk about you so much that from love for him, I felt the strongest desire to know you ; but is not a desire to know you a desire to love you ? "

" My dear Clara, I was afraid I should displease you in talk. ing thus of those who are not of noble birth."

"Oh ! make your mind easy. At the present day, discussions of this sort are perfectly objectless. As for me they do not affect me ; I am out of the question."

However arrogant this reply might be, it caused Mademoiselle de Fontaine the profoundest pleasure ; for, like all persons who are under the influence of passion, she interpreted it as oracles are interpreted, that is, in the sense which suited her inclinations ; and she rejoined the dancers more joyous than ever as she looked at Longueville, whose style and elegance perhaps surpassed those of her ideal type. She experienced an additional satisfaction when she reflected that he was of noble birth ; her dark eyes glittered, and she danced with all the pleasure which a women feels when she is dancing in the presence of the one she loves. Never did the lovers understand each other better than at that moment, and several times did they feel their fingers tingling and trembling as the exigencies of the quadrille brought them into contact.

Thus did early autumn overtake this handsome couple, surrounded by country fêtes and country diversions, allowing themselves to float on the stream of the sweetest feeling which life can offer, and heightening it by a thousand trifling details, which may be left to the imagination of the reader; for in certain points all love affairs are alike. Each studied the other as much as it is possible for two lovers to study one another.

"Well, never did a flirtation so speedily resolve itself into a marriage of inclination," said the old uncle, who kept his eye upon the young people as closely as a naturalist examines an insect under the microscope.

The expression frightened M. and Madame de Fontaine. The old Vendean ceased to be so indifferent in the matter of his daughter's marriage, as he had formerly promised to be. He went to Paris in search of information, and came back without obtaining any. Uneasy at the mystery, and not yet knowing what might be the result of the inquiry which he had begged a man of business in Paris to set on foot as to the Longueville family, he deemed it his duty to warn his daughter to conduct herself prudently. Her father's observation was received with an assumed obedience, that was full of irony.

"At least, my dear Émilie, if you love him, don't confess it to him."

"Father, it is true that I love him, but I will not tell him so until you give me leave to do so."

"But, Émilie, consider that as yet you know nothing of his family or his position in life.

"If I am ignorant, it is my wish to be so. But, father, you wanted to see me married; you left me at liberty to make my choice; it is made irrevocably; what more is needful?"

"You must learn, my dear child, whether the man of your choice is the son of a peer of France," replied the venerable nobleman, ironically.

Émilie was silent for a moment, but shortly raised her head, looked at her father, and said to him somewhat anxiously, " Are the Longuevilles then— ?"

" —Extinct in the person of the old Duc de Rostein-Limbourg, who perished on the scaffold in 1793. He was the last scion of the last younger branch."

" But father, there are some very good families which have sprung from bastards. The history of France swarms with princes who bore the bend sinister on their shield."

" Your ideas are greatly changed," said the old gentleman, smiling."

The morrow was the last day that the De Fontaine family were to pass at Planat Lodge. Émilie, who had been not a little disturbed by her father's intimation, awaited with keen impatience the hour at which young Longueville was wont to arrive, in order to get an explanation from him. She went out after dinner for a solitary walk in the park, directing her steps to the grove of confidences, whither she knew the impetuous young man would go to look for her. As she went she debated in her mind upon the best method of surprising so important a secret without compromising herself—no easy matter. Up to the present moment, no open avowal had sanctioned the feeling which bound her to this stranger. She had, like Maximilien, savored in secret the sweetness of first love ; but they were both equally proud, and it seemed that both of them were afraid to own their feelings.

Maximilien Longueville, whom Clara had inspired with some suspicions as to Émilie's disposition, which were not without foundation, had been, by turns, carried away by the violence of a young man's passion. and held back by a desire to know and test the woman to whom he was about to entrust his happiness. His love had not precluded him from observing that Émilie was under the influence of prejudices which spoiled her youthful nature; but he wanted to learn whether she loved him, before trying to fight against them ; for he was as reluctant to risk the fate of his love as that of his existence. He had accordingly maintained a silence which his looks, his attitude, and his slightest action belied. On the other hand, the pride, so natural to a girl, and which was enhanced in the case of Mademoiselle de Fontaine by the stupid vanity excited by her birth and beauty, prevented her from going half-way to meet a declaration, which her growing love sometimes impelled her to court. Thus, the two lovers had instinctively comprehended their position, without exactly explaining their secret motives to themselves. There are moments in life when the vague has a charm for youthful minds. From the very fact of their having both too long put off speaking, they both seemed to be making a cruel sport of their delay. The one seemed to be trying to discover whether he was loved, from the effort which an avowal would cost his haughty mistress, while the other hoped that every moment would see the rupture of a too respectful silence.

Seated on a rustic bench, Émilie was reflecting on the events which had occurred during these three months, that had been so full of enchantment. Her father's suspicions were the last apprehensions that could assail her; she even despatched them by two or three of such reflections as might occur to an inexperienced girl, and which seemed to her decisive. Above all, she came to the conclusion that it was impossible she could be deceived. She had failed throughout the season to discover in Maximilien a single gesture, or a single word, which indicated a plebeian origin or plebeian occupations. Better still, his mode of discussing a subject bespoke a man who was occupied with the highest interests of the country. "Moreover," she argued with herself, "a professional man, a financier, or a merchant, would not have had leisure to spend the whole season in paying his addresses to me, in the midst of the woods and fields, as lavish of his time as a nobleman who has before him a long lifetime void of occupation." She was yielding herself to the current of a

meditation much more interesting to her than these preliminary thoughts, when a slight rustling of the foliage informed
her that for some little time Maximilien had been looking at
her, admiringly without doubt.

"Do you know that it is very ill-bred to.take young ladies
by surprise like that?" she asked, smiling.

"Especially when they are engrossed by their secrets," replied Maximilien craftily.

"Why should I not have my secrets? You certainly have
yours."

"You really were thinking of your secrets then?" said Maximilien, with a laugh.

"No, I was thinking of yours. I know my own."

"But, perhaps," said the young man slowly, as he seized
the arm of Mademoiselle de Fontaine, and drew it through
his own, "perhaps my secrets are yours, and yours mine."

After walking a short distance, they found themselves under
a clump of trees, which the rays of the setting sun were
covering with a cloud of brownish red. Nature's magic invested the passing moment with a sort of solemnity. The life
and freedom of the young man's movements, and still more
the agitation of his overflowing heart, whose quick pulsations
spoke to the arm of Émilie, threw her into a state of excitement, which was all the more eloquent, because it was called
forth only by the simplest and most innocent accidents. The
reserve by which the young ladies of the great world are
habitually surrounded, gives an incredible strength to their
explosions of feeling, which is one of the greatest dangers to
which they are exposed, when they meet with a passionate
lover. Never had the eyes of Émilie and Maximilien said so
many things which the lips dare not utter. A prey to this
intoxication, they readily forgot the frail conventions of pride
and the frigid considerations of distrust. The only form of
expression they could find at first, was.a pressure of the hand,
which served as an interpretation of their joyous thoughts.

"I have one question to put to you," said Mademoiselle de Fontaine, trembling, and with a voice full of emotion, after the long silence, and after they had taken a few slow steps forward; but I beg you to consider, that it is in some sort forced upon me, by the very strange position in which I am placed with regard to my family."

A pause that was terrible to Émilie succeeded these words, which she had uttered with something approaching a stammer. During the time occupied by this pause, this proud young woman did not dare to encounter the ardent gaze of the man she loved, for she had a secret consciousness of the baseness of the ensuing words, as she added, "Are you of noble birth?"

When these last words had been uttered, she could have wished herself at the bottom of a lake.

"Mademoiselle," said Longueville gravely, as his altered countenance assumed an air of severe dignity, "I promise you that I will give a direct answer to that question, when you have replied with sincerity to that which I am about to put to you." He dropped the arm of the young girl, who suddenly felt herself alone in the world, and said to her, "What is your object in questioning me as to my birth?" Émilie remained cold, mute, and motionless.

"Mademoiselle," resumed Maximilien, "let us proceed no farther unless we understand each other—_I love you_," he added in a deep and tender voice. "Well, then," he continued, with a glad look when he had heard the exclamation of delight which the young girl could not repress, "_why_ do you ask me whether I am of noble birth?"

"Would he talk like that unless he were?" said an inward voice, which Émilie believed, issued from the depths of her heart. Thereupon she graciously raised her head, seemed to find new life in the young man's look, and held out her arm to nim, as if to form a fresh alliance.

" You thought that I attached great importance to dignities?"
she asked, with mischievous subtilty.

" I have no titles to offer to my wife," he replied, with an
air half gay, half serious. " But if I take her from a high
position, and from among those whose father's wealth has
made luxury and the pleasures of opulence habitual to them, I
know the duty which my choice imposes on me.   Love gives
all," he added gaily, " but only to lovers,—as to married folks,
they need something more than the dome of heaven and the
carpets of the meadows.

" He is rich," thought she.   " As to titles, perhaps he wants
to try me.   He has been told that I am wedded to nobility,
and that I will not marry any one but a peer of France.   My
impertinent sisters have played me that trick."

" I assure you, sir," she said aloud, " that I have had most
exaggerated views of life and of the world; but now " (this
was said intentionally, and as she spoke she looked at him in
a manner that might well have driven him mad) " *now* I know
where it is that a woman must look for real wealth."

" I wish to believe that you are speaking from the heart,"
replied he with gentle gravity.   But this winter, my dear
Émilie, in less than two months perhaps, I shall have reason
to be proud of the offers that I can make you—if you care for
the pleasures of affluence.   That is the only secret which I
shall bury *there*," said he pointing to his heart, " for upon its
success depends my happiness, I dare not say *ours*."

" Oh, say so, say so."

Amid the sweetest talk they returned with slow steps to rejoin
the company in the drawing-room.   Never had Mademoiselle
de Fontaine found her lover more agreable or more witty.
His well-shaped form and engaging manners seemed to her
more charming than ever, after the conversation, which seemed
in some sort to secure her the possession of a heart which any
woman might covet.   The lovers sang an Italian duet together
with so much enthusiasm that the assembled company

applauded them. Their farewell assumed a conversational aspect, beneath which they concealed their happiness. In short, that day acted as a chain, which bound Émilie more closely still to the fortunes of the stranger. The force and dignity which he had displayed in the scene, during which they had revealed their feelings to each other, had perhaps imposed upon Mademoiselle de Fontaine that respect for her lover without which there is no such thing as genuine love.

When she was left alone with her father in the drawing-room, the venerable Vendean went up to her, took her kindly by the hand, and asked her whether she had gathered any information which threw light upon the fortune and family of M. Longueville.

"Yes, dear father," she replied. "I am happier than I could ever wish to be. In short, Monsieur de Longueville is he only man whom I should wish to wed."

"That's well, Émilie," replied the count. "I know what remains for me to do."

"Is it possible that you know of any impediment?" asked Émilie, with unfeigned anxiety.

"My dear child this young man is altogether unknown, but unless he be a dishonest man, he is, the moment that you love him as dear to me as a son."

"A dishonest man?" continued Émilie. "I am quite easy upon that score. My uncle, who introduced him to us, can answer for him. Tell me, dear uncle, has he been a freebooter, a pirate, or a corsair?"

"I knew well that it would come to this," cried the old sailor, waking up.

He looked around the drawing-room, but his neice had disappeared like a St. Elmo's fire, to employ his habitual expression.

"Well, uncle," resumed M. de Fontaine, "how could you conceal from us all that you knew about this youth? Our

P

anxiety could not have escaped your notice. Is M. de Long-ueville a man of family?"

"I don't know him from Adam or Eve," exclaimed the Comte de Kergaroüet. "Confiding in the tact of that little madcap, I brought her her Saint-Preux, by a manœuvre which I understand. I know that the lad is an excellent shot with the pistol, is a good sportsman, and plays billiards, chess, and backgammon to perfection, while he fences and rides like the late Chevalier de Saint Georges. He has the devil's own knowledge of all that appertains to our vineyards. He can calculate like Barême, and is a good hand at drawing, dancing, and singing. Why, what the deuce is the matter with you folks? If that doesn't make a perfect gentleman, show me a bourgeois who can do all that; find me a man who lives as much like a gentleman as he does. Does he follow any occupation? Does he compromise his dignity by going to an office, by bowing and scraping to the upstarts whom you call directors-general? He holds his head up—he is a man. But, moreover, I have just recovered in my waiscoat pocket, the card which he gave me, when he thought that I wanted to cut his throat for him, poor simpleton? (The young men of to-day are not very sharp.) See, here it is."

"Rue de Sentier, number five," said M. de Fontaine, trying to recall, amidst all the information which he had obtained, something which might have reference to the young stranger. "What the deuce does that mean? Messieurs Palma, Wer-brust, et Compagnie, whose principal trade is wholesale dealings in muslin. calico, and prints, carry on business at that address. Good; I have it, Longueville the deputy, has an interest in their firm. Yes; but the only son of Longueville I know of, is thirty-two, and does not in any way resemble our Longueville; he is going to give that son 50,000 livres a year, in order that he may marry the daughter of a minister; for like every one else he wants to be made a peer. I have never heard him mention this Maximilien Then, has he a daughter?

Who is this Clara? Moreover, more than one adventurer may call himself Longueville. But the house of Palma, Werbrust, & Co., has been half ruined by some speculation in Mexico, or the Indies. I will clear this matter up."

" You are soliloquizing, for all the world, as if you were on the stage, and you seem to reckon me a mere cypher," said the old sailor suddenly. "You don't seem to be aware that if he is a gentleman, I have more than one bag under my hatchways to make up for the want of his fortune."

" For that matter, if he be a son of Longueville's, he is in no want of money," said M. de Fontaine, shaking his head from right to left, " but his father has not yet bought his snob-wash. Before the revolution he was an attorney, and as for the ' de ' which since the Restoration he has placed before his name, he has as much right to that as to the one half of his fortune."

" Pooh, pooh! happy are they whose fathers have been hanged," cried the old sailor gaily.

Three or four days after this memorable day, on one of those beautiful mornings in the month of November, when the Parisians see their bulevards cleansed by the refreshing cold of a first frost, Mademoiselle de Fontaine, arrayed in a new set of furs, which she wished to render fashionable, had gone out with two of her sisters-in-law, at whom she had formerly aimed the larger portion of her epigrams. The three women had been induced to undertake this drive through Paris, far less by their desire to try a very elegant new carriage, and to wear the dresses which were to give the tone to the winter fashions, than by their desire to look at a tippet which one of their friends had noticed in a grand linen-draper's shop at the corner of the Rue de la Paix. When the three ladies had entered the shop, Madame de Fontaine (the baroness), pulled Émilie's sleeve, and pointing to her Maximilien Longueville, who was seated at the counter, and was giving, with truly merchantile grace change for a piece of gold to the forewoman of the establishment, with whom he seemed to be holding a consultation.

"The handsome **stranger**" held in **his** hand certain samples which left no doubt **as to the nature** of his honorable calling. Unbeknown **to all**, Émilie **was seized with an icy** shudder. Thanks, however, to the *savoir-vivre* which **good** society confers, she completely concealed **the** rage **which devoured** her heart, **and said to her** sister, with a richness **of accent and intonation** which might have aroused the **envy of the most** celebrated actress of the age,—

"I knew it." She then drew **near to the** counter, Longueville raised **his head, put the samples** into **his** pocket with inimitable **coolness, bowed to Mademoiselle de** Fontaine, and, drawing **near to her, cast at her a** searching glance.

"Mademoiselle," said he to the forewoman, who looked at him with an uneasy air, "I **will send and** settle the account; such **is the wish of the firm.** But stay," said he in a whisper to **the young woman, giving her a bank** note for a thousand rancs, "take this ; it is a private **matter between ourselves.**"

"—You will pardon me, mademoiselle," said, he turning to Émilie, "you will **have the goodness to** excuse the tyranny which business exercises over us."

It seems to me, sir, that it is **a matter of supreme** indifference to me," responded Mademoiselle de Fontaine, looking at him with a hardihood and an appearance of sarcastic indifference, which **might well** create the **impression** that she had **never seen him** before.

"Are you in earnest?" asked Maximilien, in a broken voice

Émilie **turned her back** to him **with** incredible insolence The few words **which** had passed between them had escap her two inquisitive sisters-in-law. **When the** three ladies ha secured the tippet and reseated **themselves** in the carriag Émilie, who occupied **the** front **seat,** could not help casting one last all embracing look into the depths of the odious shop, and there saw Maximilien, in the attitude of a man who was superior to the misfortune which had so suddenly overtaken him. Their eyes met and exchanged two implacable glances.

Each of them hoped to inflict a cruel wound upon the heart of the loved one. In an instant they found themselves as far removed from one another as if one of them had been in China, and the other in Greenland. Has not vanity a breath that withers all it meets? Distracted by the most violent conflict which can possibly agitate the breast of a young woman,' Mademoiselle de Fontaine reaped at that moment the most abundant harvest of sorrow that prejudice and littleness ever sowed in human soul. Her face, that had been so smooth and fresh, was now streaked with yellow stripes and patches of red, while at times the white of her cheeks would suddenly turn green. Hoping to hide her sufferings from her sisters, she would point out to them some ridiculous passenger, or some absurd dress, and laugh. But the laugh was convulsive. She felt more deeply wounded by the silent compassion of her sisters, than she would have been by the epigrams by which they might have taken their revenge. She exercised all her ingenuity in endeavoring to draw them into a discussion, in which she sought to give vent to her anger, by insane parodies; seeking to overwhelm tradesmen with biting insults, and epigrams in very bad taste. When she reached home, she was attacked by a fever, which seemed at first to be of a dangerous type; but at the end of a month, she was restored to her prayerful family, through the tender care of her parents and her physician. Every one hoped that this lesson would be severe enough to soften Émilie's disposition; but she gradually resumed her old habits, and once more dashed out into the world. She maintained that there was no disgrace in having been deceived. She would say that if, like her father, she had any influence in the House, she would propose a law providing that merchants, especially calico-merchants, should be branded on the forehead, like the sheep of Le Berri, to the third generation. She wished that only noblemen had the privilege of wearing those old fashioned French costumes, which so well became the courtiers of Louis Quinze. To hear her, it was perhaps a misfortune for the monarchy that there was no visible distinction between a shopkeeper and a peer of France. A thousand other witticisms, easy to be gusssed, followed one another in quick succession, when some unforeseen accident set her upon the topic. But those who loved Émilie could discern through her satire a tinge of melancholy It was clear that Maximilien Longueville still reigned in the depths of her inexplicable heart. Sometimes she became gentle, as during the fugitive season which witnessed the birth of her passion; and sometimes also she grew insupportable. Every one forgave the inequalities of temper, which had their origin in sufferings that were at the same time secret and well known. The Count de Kergaroüet obtained some slight influence over her, thanks to increased liberality, a species of consolation which rarely fails to have some effect upon the fair youthful denizens of Paris. The first ball that Mademoiselle de Fontaine went to after her recovery was that of the Neapolitian ambassador. Just as she was taking up her position in the most brilliant quadrille set, she saw within a few paces of her, Longueville, who slightly nodded to her partner.

" Is that young man one of your friends?" she inquired of her cavalier, with an air of scorn.

" Only my brother," he replied.

Émilie could not refrain from shuddering.

" Ah," continued her partner in an enthusiastic tone of voice, " he is indeed the finest fellow in the world . . . ."

" Do you know what my name is?" interposed Émilie with emphasis.

" No, mademoiselle. It is, I confess, a crime to have forgotten a name that is on every lip; nay, I ought to say in every heart; but I have a valid excuse; I am only just returned from Germany. My ambassador, who is at Paris on leave of absence, sent me here this evening to act as chaperon to his amiable wife, whom you may see yonder in a corner."

"A regular tragic mask," said Émilie, when she had scrutinized the ambassadress.

"That, however, is her ball-room countenance," replied the young man, laughing. "It is my bounden duty to ask her to dance; and accordingly I wanted some compensation."

At this compliment Mademoiselle de Fontaine bowed.

"I was very much surprised," continued the talkative attaché, "to find my brother here. On my arrival from Vienna, I learned that the poor boy was ill in bed, and I fully reckoned on seeing him before coming to the ball; but politics do not always allow us to have such a thing as family affection. The *padrona della casa* prevented me from going up to see poor Maximilien."

"Your brother is not engaged in the diplomatic service, as you are?" asked Émilie.

"No," said the attaché, sighing, "he sacrificed himself on my account. He and my sister Clara have relinquished their share of my father's fortune, in order that he might create an entail in my favor. My father, like all those who vote for ministers, dreams of a peerage. He has a promise to that effect," he added in an undertone. "Having got together a certain amount of capital, my brother became a partner in some banking establishment, and I know that he has just engaged in some speculation in Brazil, which may make him a millionaire. You see me quite rejoiced at having contributed, through my diplomatic relations, to his success. I am even now impatiently waiting for a despatch from the Brazilian legation, which will be of a description to make him unknit his brow. What do you think of him?"

"But your brother's face does not appear to me to be that of a man who is engaged in money-making."

The young diplomatist cast one searching glance upon the seemingly untroubled face of his partner.

"What," he exclaimed with a smile, "young ladies then can read love thoughts also beneath dumb foreheads?"

"Is your brother in love?" she inquired, with a gesture indicative of curiosity.

"Yes; my sister Clara, of whom he takes a mother's care, wrote to tell me that he had fallen in love with a very pretty person this summer; but since then I have had no news about his love affairs. Would you believe that the poor boy used to get up at five o'clock in the morning, and go and do his business, in order that he might reach the country-house of his young lady at four in the afternoon? the consequence being that he ruined a beautiful blood horse, which I had sent him. Forgive my chatter, mademoiselle; I am just come from Germany. For the last year I have not heard French correctly spoken. I have been weaned from French and surfeited with German faces to such an extent, that in my patriotic enthusiasm I believe I could talk to the figures on a Parisian candlestick. Then again if I chatter away with a freedom which is very unbecoming in a diplomatist, the fault is yours, mademoiselle. For, was it not you who pointed out my brother? When he is the subject of conversation, I am inexhaustible; I should like to be able to tell the whole world how good and generous he is. The amount involved was no less than 100,000 francs a year, which is the value of the Longueville estate!"

If Mademoiselle de Fontaine obtained these important revelations, she owed them in part to the skill she displayed in interrogating her confiding partner, from the moment when she found that he was the brother of the lover whom she had spurned.

"And could you see your brother selling muslin and calico without feeling some annoyance?" asked Émilie, after finishing the third figure of the quadrille.

"How did you know that?" asked the diplomatist. "Like all the young diplomatists of my acquaintance, I have already, thank God, acquired the art of saying only what I wish to say, even while indulging in a torrent of words."

"It was you who told me, I assure you."

Monsieur de Longueville looked at Mademoiselle de Fontaine with an astonishment that was full of perspicacity. A suspicion entered his mind. He interrogated the eyes, first of his brother, then of his partner, guessed everything, pressed his hands together, raised his eyes to the ceiling, began to laugh, and said,—

"I am no better than a fool. You are the prettiest woman in the room; my brother looks at you sideways, dances in spite of his fever, and you pretend not to see him. Make him a happy man" said he as he led her back to her old uncle. "I shall not be jealous of him; but I shall always tremble a little when I call you my sister."

The two lovers however were destined to be inexorable towards each other. At about two o'clock in the morning a light supper was served, in an immense gallery, in which the tables were arranged as they are in restaurants, so as to leave persons in the same set at liberty to foregather if they chose. By one of those strokes of chance which are continually happening to lovers, Mademoiselle de Fontaine found herself at a table adjoining that at which the most distinguished members of the party were assembled. Maximilien was one of the group. Émilie, who lent an attentive ear to the talk that was going on among her neighbors, overheard one of those conversations which are so easily established between young women and young men possessing the graces and the bearing of Maximilien Longueville. The interlocutress of the young banker was a Neapolitan duchess, whose eyes darted lightnings and whose white skin shone like satin. The intimacy which young Longueville pretended to exist between him and this lady wounded Madamoiselle de Fontaine all the more, inasmuch as she had just bestowed upon her lover twenty times as much regard as she had formerly entertained for him.

"Yes, monsieur, in my country true love shrinks from no sacrifice whatever," said the duchess, smirking.

"You are more passionate than French women are," said

Maximilien, whose kindling glance fell full upon Émilie; "they are all vanity."

"Monsieur," said the young girl sharply, "is it not an unworthy action to traduce your country? Self-abnegation belongs to all countries alike."

"Do you think, mademoiselle," pursued the Italian lady with a sardonic smile, "that a Parisian woman is capable of following her lover wherever he may go?"

"Oh, let us not misunderstand each other, madame. We would go to the desert, to live there in a tent, but we don't go and sit in a shop."

She wound up her opinion with a gesture of disdain.

Thus the influence upon Émilie of her fatal bringing-up destroyed for the second time her budding happiness, and marred her career. The seeming coldness of Maximilien, and a woman's smile, had extorted from her one of those sarcasms, whose treacherous delights were ever leading her astray.

"Mademoiselle," said Longueville to her in a low voice, under cover of the noise made by the ladies in quitting the tables, "no one will form more ardent wishes for your happiness than I shall; allow me to give you that assurance, in bidding you farewell. In a few days I shall start for Italy."

"With a duchess, doubtless?"

"No, mademoiselle; but with a mortal malady, perhaps."

"Isn't that a mere fancy?" inquired Émilie, with an uneasy look.

"Not so," said he. "There are some wounds which never heal."

"You will not start," said the imperious young damsel, with a smile.

"Yes I shall," said Maximilien seriously.

"You will find me married on your return, I give you warning," said she coquettishly.

"I hope I may."

" The coxcomb," said Émilie, "He revenges himself cruelly enough."

Fifteen days afterwards Maximilien Longueville and his sister Clara set out for the warm and poetical climes of lovely Italy, leaving Mademoiselle de Fontaine a prey to the most violent regret. The young attaché embraced his brother's quarrel and contrived to visit Émilie's disdain with a striking retribution, by publicly announcing the grounds of the rupture between the two lovers. He repaid with usury to his partner at the ball, the sarcasms which she had formerly hurled at Maximilien, and often drew a smile from more than one minister, as he described the fair enemy of counters, the Amazon who preached a crusade against bankers, the young lady whose love had evaporated at the sight of half a foot of muslin. The Comte de Fontaine was obliged to use his influence in procuring for Auguste Longueville a mission to Russia, in order to withdraw his daughter from the ridicule which that young and formidable persecutor poured upon her in such abundance. Shortly afterwards the ministry, being compelled to raise a levy of peers, in order to strengthen the aristocratic vote, which was falling off in the upper chamber, under the influence of the oratory of an illustrious writer, made Monsieur *Guiraudin* de Longueville a peer of France and a viscount. Monsieur de Fontaine likewise obtained a peerage, a reward due not only to his name, which was missing from the hereditary chamber, but also to his fidelity during the evil days of the monarchy.

About this time Émilie, who was now of age, indulged, no doubt, in some serious reflections on life, for she evidently changed her tone and manners. Instead of exerting herself to say unpleasant things to her uncle, she showered upon him the most affectionate attentions, brought him his crutch with a perseverance which excited the laughter of the wags; gave him her arm to lean on, rode in his carriage with him, and accompanied him whenever he went out. She persuaded him that she even liked the smell of his pipe, and read to him his dear

Quotidienne in the midst of the puffs of tobacco smoke, which
the mischevious sailor designedly blew towards her. She
studied piquet in order to be a match for the old count, and,
to crown all, this most whimsical of young women listened
patiently to the periodic recitals of the combat of the " Belle
Poule," of the manœuvrings of the " Ville de Paris," of the
first expedition of M. de Suffren, and of the battle of Aboukir.
Although the old sailor had often said that he knew his lati-
tude and longitude too well to allow himself to be captured by
a young corvette, the *salons* of Paris one fine morning heard of
the marriage of Mademoiselle de Fontaine and the Comte de
Kergaroüet. The young countess gave splendid entertainments,
in order to drown reflection ; but she doubtlessly felt a sense of
emptiness at the bottom of the whirl of gaiety. Luxury did
but imperfectly conceal the void and unhappiness of her suffering heart ; and her handsome face, in spite of the outbursts of
fictitious gaiety, generally betrayed a mute meloncholy. Émilie
seemed, moreover, to be full of attention and regard for her
aged husband, who would often say, as he went off to his own
private room in the evening, to the sound of a gay orchestra,
" I don't seem to be the same man. Must I needs wait till I
was seventy-two to embark as pilot on board the Belle-Émilie,
after twenty years in the galleys of matrimony? " The conduct
of the countess was marked by so much austerity, that the most
quick-sighted criticism had nothing to lay hold of. The on-
lookers came to the conclusion that the count had reserved the
right of disposing of his fortune, in order to bind his wife more
closely to him,—a supposition that was insulting both to the
uncle and to the niece. The attitude of the husband and wife
was, moreover, so judiciously planned, that the young men, who
were most interersted in discovering the secrets of the house
hold, could not find out whether the old count treated his wife
as a husband or as a father. He was frequently heard to re
mark that he had picked up his niece as a woman who had been
shipwrecked, and that formerly he had never presumed upon

his hospitality when he happened to save an enemy from the fury of the tempest. Although the countess aspired to reign in Paris, and endeavored to march abreast with the Duchesses de Maufrigneuse and de Chaulieu, the Marchionesses d'Espard and d'Aiglemont, the Countesses Féraud, de Montcornet, de Restaud, Madame de Camps, and Mademoiselle des Touches, she gave no encouragement to the passion of the young Viscomte de Portenduère, who made her his idol.

Two years after her marriage, in one of the antique drawing-rooms of the Faubourg St. Germain, where her character was regarded with admiration, and deemed worthy of the olden time, Émilie heard the servant announce, "Monsieur le Vicomte de Longueville."

In the corner of the drawing-room in which she was seated, playing piquet with the Bishop of Persepolis, her emotion could not attract the attention of any one, but, on turning her head, she witnessed the arrival of her former admirer, in all the éclat of his youth. The death of his father, and that of his elder brother, who had succumbed to the inclement climate of St. Petersburg, had devolved upon the head of Maximilien the hereditary plumes of the cap of a peer. His fortune was on a par with his attainments and his worth. The very day before, his youthful and impetuous eloquence had enlightened the Assembly. At this moment, he appeared before the sorrowing countess, unmarried and adorned with all those advantages which she had formerly required from her ideal type. Every mother with marriageable daughters was making seductive advances to a young man who was endowed with those good qualities, for which those who admired his graceful bearing gave him credit. But Émilie knew better than any one, that the Vicomte de Longueville possessed that firmness of character, in which prudent women perceive a guarantee for happiness. She cast her eyes upon the admiral, who, according to his own familiar phrase, seemed likely to stick to his ship for a long time, and cursed the errors of her childhood.

At that moment the Bishop of Persepolis said to her with his episcopal grace, "Fair lady, you have discarded the king of hearts, and I have won. But do not regr your money: I keep it for my little schools."

A DOUBLE FAMILY.

(UNE DOUBLE FAMILLE.)

TO MADAME LA COMTESSE LOUISE DE TURHEIM,
AS A TOKEN OF REMEMBRANCE AND
AFFECTIONATE RESPECT.

THE Rue du Tourniquet St. Jean, formerly one of the darkest and most tortuous streets in the old quarter which surrounds the Hôtel de Ville, wound itself along by the side of the small gardens of the prefecture of Paris, and terminated in the Rue du Martroi just at the corner of an old wall which has now been pulled down. It was at this point that the turnstile, from which the street took its name, was situated. The turnstile was not destroyed till the year 1823, when the city of Paris had a ball-room constructed upon the site of a little garden attached to the Hôtel de Ville, on the occasion of the entertainment given in honor of the Duc d'Angoulême, on his return from Spain. The widest part of the Rue du Tourniquet was where it debouched into the Rou de la Tixeranderie, and even at that point it was not five feet wide; so that in rainy weather black streams soon began to wash the feet of the old houses which lined the street, bearing with them the refuse deposited near the kerbstone by each household. The dust-carts being unable to pass through this gorge, its inhabitants looked to the storms to cleanse their ever-muddy street. And how, indeed, should it have been otherwise than muddy? When the summer sun was darting its perpendicular rays upon Paris, a sheet of gold, incisive as the blade of a sabre, would for a moment illuminate the darkness of the street, but had no power to dry up the persistent moisture which crept from the ground-floor to the first storey of those black and silent houses.

The inhabitants lighted their lamps at five o'clock in the afternoon in the month of June.   In winter they were kept burning all day.   Even up to the present time, if any bold pedestrian wants to go from the Marais to the quays, starting from
the end of the Rue du Chaume, and following the Rues de
l'Homme-Armé, des Billettes, and des Deux-Portes, which lead
to the Rue Tourniquet St. Jean, he will fancy he has been
walking under archways.   Much as the chronicles have vaunt-
ed the splendors of old Paris, almost all its streets resembled
this damp and sombre maze—in which the antiquary may still
find some historic peculiarities to admire.   Thus, so long as
the house which was situated at the corner of the Rue du
Tourniquet and the Rue de la Tixeranderie existed, the
observer might there behold the traces of two large iron rings
fixed into the wall, and being a remnant of those chains which
the constable used, in by-gone days, to stretch across the street
for the safety of the public.   In the construction of this house,
which was remarkable for its antiquity, there had been displayed such precautions as attested the insalubrity of these
ancient dwellings; for to render the ground-floor more wholesome, the vaults of the cellar had been raised some feet above
the soil, and one had to mount three steps in order to enter
the house.   The door-way described a complete arch, the key-
stone of which was adorned with a woman's head, and with
some time-worn arabesques.   In that part of the ground-floor
which looked upon, and received its light from, the Rue du
Tourniquet, there were three windows, the sills of which were
about a man's height from the ground.   These windows were
protected by thick iron bars, placed wide apart and terminating
in a round projection, like that which finishes off the gratings
of bakers' shops.   If any inquisitive passer-by cast his eyes into
the two rooms of which this apartment consisted, it was impossible for him to see anything in them during the day-time; for
in order to discover in the second room two beds with green
serge hangings, placed close together under the wood-work of

an old alcove, the July sun was needed. But towards evening about three o'clock, when once the candle was lighted, there might be seen through the window of the first room, an old woman seated on a stool at the corner of a fireplace, and engaged in coaxing a chafing-dish, on which one of those ragoûts, such as porteresses are skilful in concocting, was simmering. A few cooking utensils and household implements might be seen in the clear-obscure hanging on the wall. About this hour an old table placed upon an X-shaped stand, but with no cloth upon it, was spread with a few pewter covers and the dish which the old woman had cooked. In this room, which was both a kitchen and a drawing-room, there were three miserable chairs. Above the fireplace was a broken mirror, a tinderbox, three glasses, some matches, and a large white pot very much chipped. Yet there was something pleasing about the whole aspect of the room. Floor, utensils, fireplace, and all partook of the air of order and economy which reigned in that chill and dark abode. The pale and wrinkled face of the old woman was in keeping with the obscurity of the street, and the dinginess of the house. Had you seen her asleep in her chair, you would have said that she was attached to the house, just as a snail is attached to its brown shell. The face of the old dame, which in spite of its assumed good nature, wore a mischievous look, was surmounted by a round flat cap made of tulle, beneath which her white hair could easily be seen. Her large grey eyes were as calm as the street itself, and the numerous furrows of her countenance might be compared to the crevices in the walls. Whether she had been born in poverty, or had lapsed from former splendor, she seemed to have been long resigned to her dull existence. From sunrise until evening, the old woman would sit in the second room, in front of the last window, and facing a young girl; except when she was engaged in the preparation of a meal, or when with a basket on her arm she sallied forth in search of provisions. With this exception she spent the whole day in the other room before the

Q

last window, seated opposite to the girl. At all hours of the
day those who passed that way could see this young workwoman
sitting in an old red-velvet arm-chair, her head bending over
her embroidery frame, hard at work. Meanwhile her mother,
with a green tambour upon her knees, was making tulle; but
her fingers worked the bobbins with painful effort; her sight
had grown weak, for on her sexagenary nose she wore a pair of
those old-fashioned spectacles, which keep their place at the
end of the nostril by dint of compression   At night these two
industrious creatures would place between them a lamp, whose
l ght, passing through two globes filled with water, would enable
the one to see the finest threads, furnished by the bobbins of
her tambour, and the other to follow the most delicate designs
traced upon the stuff which she was embroidering. The bend
in the iron bars had enabled the girl to place upon the window-
sill, a wooden box filled with earth, and containing some sweet
peas, some nasturtiums, a poor little honey-suckle, and some
convolvuluses, whose fragile stalks crept round the bars. The
pallor of the flowers which sprang from these stunted plants
harmonized with all the surroundings, and gave a sad and
touching aspect to the picture presented by the window, whose
embrasure formed a good frame to the faces of the two women.
A chance-glimpse of this interior fixed in the mind of the most
egotistical passer-by, a complete image of the life led by the
needlewomen of Paris; for needlewomen pure and simple, the
embroiderer seemed to be. Few persons reached the turnstile
without asking themselves how a young girl living in such a
cellar contrived to preserve her fresh complexion. If a student
passed through the street on his way to the Quartier Latin, his
lively imagination would compare that obscure and vegetable
existence to that of the ivy, which drapes the cold wall, or of
those peasants who are born to toil and die unknown to the
world which they have fed. The man of independent means,
after having cast a landlord's eye upon the house, would say to
himself, " What will become of these two women if embroidery

should go out of fashion?" Among the persons who were compelled to pass through the street at certain fixed hours, in order to reach their office at the Hôtel de Ville or the Palais, there might perhaps be found some charitable soul Perhaps some widower, or some Adonis of forty, by dint of sounding the recesses of that melancholy existence, had begun to found upon the poverty of the mother and daughter, hopes of achieving an inexpensive triumph over the heart of the innocent little needlewoman, whose plump and agile hands, fresh-looking neck, and white skin (for which latter charm she was no doubt indebted to her abode in that sunless street) excited his admiration. Perhaps some worthy civil servant, with a salary of 1200 francs, daily witnessing the young girl's industry, and respecting the purity of her morals, was waiting for some promotion in order to join one obscure existence to another obscure existence, one life of incessant toil to another life of incessant toil, and ready to offer at least the support of a manly arm and a love peaceful, but as colorless as the flowers in the window. The dull grey eyes of the mother kindled with vague hopes. In the morning, after the most humble of breakfasts, she would go back to her tambour as an excuse, rather than from necessity, for she would lay her spectacles upon a little work-table of red wood, as old as herself, and from half-past eight till about ten, pass in review the habitual passengers, catching their glances, making remarks upon their gait, dress, and features, and seeming to be offering them her daughter for sale; so eagerly did her tell-tale eyes with oglings worthy of the side-scenes of the theatre seek to establish sympathetic feelings between herself and the pedestrians

It was easy to see that this review was a spectacle to *her*; perhaps her only pleasure. The daughter rarely raised her head. Modesty, or, it might be, the painful consciousness of her penury, seemed to chain her eyes to the embroidery frame; so that she only showed her anxious face to the passengers when her mother uttered some exclamation of surprise.

The civil-service clerk with a new coat on, or the regular ass-
senger appearing with   lady on his arm, might then catch
sight of the somewhat *retroussé* nose of the needlewoman, her
small rosy mouth and grey eyes, that, in spite of her exhausting toil, sparkled with life.   Her laborious vigils told no tales,
except in a circle more or less white, traced beneath either eye,
upon the fresh skin of her cheeks.   The poor child seemed to
have been born into the world for love and gaiety.   Love had
painted above her eyelids two perfect arches, and had given her
so thick a forest of chestnut-colored hair, that she might have
hidden herself behind it, as under a pavilion impenetrable to
a lover's eye.   And gaiety had given life to her mobile nostrils,
had planted two dimples in her unwasted cheeks, and taught
her quickly to forget her trials.   Gaiety, that flower of hope,
had lent her strength to look without a shudder upon the arid
path of life.

The hair of the young girl was always carefully combed.
She, like all the needle-girls of Paris, deemed her toilette complete when she had smoothed her hair, and shaped into two
crescents the little tufts which played on either temple, and
contrasted with the white skin.   So gracefully did the hair
spring from her forehead, and so charming an idea of her
youth and beauty did the line of *bistre*, clearly traced upon her
neck, impart, that the observer who saw her bending over her
work without allowing the noise to induce her to raise her
head would accuse her of coquetry.   Promises so seductive
excited the curiosity of many a young man, who would look
round in the hope of seeing that modest countenance—but to
no purpose.

"Caroline, we have another *habitué* now, better than any of
the old ones."

These words, uttered in a low tone by the mother, one
morning in the month of August, 1815, had overcome the
young needlewoman's indifference.   She looked into the street,
but looked in vain.   The stranger was already at a distance.

"Which way did he go?"

"He is sure to pass by again at four o'clock. I shall see him coming, and will touch your foot to give you notice. I am sure that he will go by again, for he has gone through our street for the last three days. But he is unpunctual. The first day he went by at six o'clock, the day before yesterday at four, and yesterday at three. I remember to have seen him formerly, from time to time. He must be some clerk at the Prefecture, who has changed his quarters in the Marais. Well," she added after a glance into the street, "our gentleman in the maroon coat has taken to a wig; how it has changed him."

It would seem that the gentleman in the maroon coat was the last of the regulars—the one who closed the daily procession; since the old mother resumed her spectacles and took up her work again with a sigh

As she did so, she cast at her daughter so singular a glance, that Lavater himself would have been puzzled to analyze it. It was a combination of admiration, gratitude, a touch of hope for a better future, and pride in having so pretty a daughter.

In the evening, at about four o'clock, the old woman touched Caroline's foot; she looked up in time to see the new actor, whose periodical passage was to give fresh life to the scene. This man was tall, slim, and pale; he was dressed in black, and was about forty years of age. There was something solemn in his gait and bearing. When his hazel and penetrating eye encountered the dull glance of the old woman, it made her tremble; she credited him with a gift or habit of reading what was passing in people's breasts. His address must be as freezing as the air of the street. Was the somewhat green and earthy hue of that terrible face the result of excessive toil or of delicate health? This was a problem to which the old mother found twenty different solutions. But the next day, Caroline, and only Caroline, discovered on that brow—which was so prone to knit—the traces of protracted mental suffering. On the

slightly hollow cheeks of the stranger might be seen the mark
of that seal which sorrow sets upon its subjects, as if it would
leave them the consolation of being able to recognize each other
with a fraternal eye, and unite their strength in resistance. At
first, the eye of the young girl brightened, from innocent curiosity
simply ; but as the stranger receded in the distance, looking like
the last mourner in a funeral procession, her look was one of
gentle sympathy Between the great heat of the weather and
his own absence of mind, the stranger had not replaced his
hat as he passed through the close, unwholesome street, so that
Caroline had an opportunity of observing the appearance of
sternness which the stranger's hair, rising brush-like from his
forehead, gave to the features. The vivid, but not agreeable
impression produced on Caroline's mind by the aspect of this
man, was different from any that had been created by any
other of the *habitués* Now, for the first time, she felt compassion for some one, other than her mother and herself. To
the queer conjectures which supplied food to the irritating
loquacity of her mother, she made no answer ; but kept passing
her long needle up and down through the tight-stretched tulle.
She was sorry she had seen so little of the stranger, and waited
for the next day ere passing a definite sentence upon him.
Never before had any of the frequenters of the street caused
her such a number of reflections. As a rule the suppositions
of the mother, who hoped to find in every passer-by a protector for her daughter, were greeted only with a mournful smile.
If such ideas, thus imprudently suggested, aroused no evil
thoughts in Caroline's heart, her indifference must be imputed
to that incessant and, alas, indispensable toil which was devouring the forces of her precious youth, and must infallibly,
in the long-run, trouble the clearness of her eyes, and steal
from her pure cheeks the delicate color with which they
.were still tinged. For about two whole months *the black gentleman*--such was his nickname--was very capricious in his
proceedings. He did not always pass through the Rue du

Tourniquet; the old woman often saw him in the evening,
without having seen him in the morning; he did not return at
fixed times like the other civil servants, who were as good as
a clock to Madame Crochard. In short, but for that first
encounter of glances, from which the old woman had imbibed
a kind of dread, the eye of the stranger had never seemed to
take the slightest notice of the picturesque group presented
by the two female gnomes. Two large gates and the dark
shop of a dealer in old iron were, with the exception of some
grated windows which lighted the staircases of some neighboring houses, the only openings into the Rue du Tourniquet, at
the period of which we are speaking; so that the slender
curiosity of the passer could not be laid to the score of dangerous rivalries. Madame Crochard was necessarily tantalized
to see her *black gentleman* always lost in serious thought, keeping his eyes fixed upon the ground, or looking straight before
him as if he would read the future in the fog of the Rue du
Tourniquet. Nevertheless, one morning towards the end of
September, the playful head of Caroline Crochard stood out
so clearly against the dim back-ground of her room, and looked
so fresh amid the tardy flowers, and the withered foliage en-
twined about the window bars, while the everyday scene pre
sented such contrasts of light and shadow, of red and white,
so happily combined with the muslin which the dainty little
workwoman was looping up, and with the red and brown tints
of the armchairs, that the stranger looked very attentively at the
living picture. It must be admitted that the old mother, weary
of the indifference of her *black gentleman*, had adopted the
plan of making such a clicking with her bobbins, that the sad and
careworn passer was perhaps compelled by the unwonted noise
to look at her abode. The stranger only exchanged with
Caroline one glance, a glance rapid it is true, but long enough
to bring their minds into contact, and to inspire them with
the presentiment that they would think of one another. When,
at four o'clock in the afternoon, the stranger returned, Caroline

distinguished the sound of his footsteps upon the echoing pavement, and there was a kind of premeditation in the looks which they exchanged. The eyes of the passenger were beaming with a benevolent expression, and Caroline blushed, while the face of the old mother assumed a satisfied air. Reckoning from that memorable morning, with very few exceptions, not unnoticed by the two women, *the black gentleman* passed through the Rue du Tourniquet twice a day. From the irregularity of his hour for returning, they came to the conclusion that he was not so soon released from his duties, nor so strictly punctual as a subaltern clerk. During the first three winter months Caroline and the stranger saw each other thus, during the time he took to traverse the piece of pavement stretching from the door past the three windows of the house. From day to day this rapid interview assumed a character of benevolent intimacy, and ended by becoming almost brotherly. Caroline and the stranger appeared from the first to understand each other, and finally, by dint of examining each other's faces, they gained a profound knowledge of them. This passing glance soon became, as it were, a visit which the stranger owed to Caroline. If *the black gentleman* happened to pass without greeting her with the half-formed smile upon his eloquent mouth, or the friendly glance of his brown eyes, there was something wanting in her day. She was like those old men to whom the reading of the newspaper has become so great a pleasure, that the morning after a grand festivity, they go away quite disconcerted, asking as much through inadvertence as impatience, for the sheet which helps them to fill for the moment the void of their existence. But these fugitive interviews possessed, both for Caroline and the stranger, all the interest of a familiar chat between two friends. The young girl was no more able to conceal from the intelligent eye of her silent friend her sadness, uneasiness, or anxiety, than he could hide from Caroline his preoccupation.

"He had some trouble yesterday," was a thought which

often sprang up in the heart of the needlewoman, when she beheld the changed features of *the black gentleman.* "Oh, he must have been hard at work," was another exclamation, which certain slight alterations, known to Caroline, would call forth. The stranger, on his part, could tell when the young girl had been working on Sunday, in order to finish the dress in the pattern of which he took an interest. When rent day approached he saw the pretty face clouded with anxiety, and could tell when Caroline had sat up late ; but he had especially remarked how the sad thoughts which disfigured the gay and delicate features of the young face disappeared, as their acquaintance ripened. When winter came to wither the stems and leaves of the window-garden, and the casement was closed, the stranger noticed, with a smile of harmless mischief, the extra-ordinary cleanness of the glass, to the height of Caroline's head. In the scanty fire, and certain patches of red which heightened the color of the two women, he saw the indigence of the household ; but if painful compassion could be read in his eyes, Caroline met it with assumed gaiety. The feelings, however, which had budded in their hearts had remained buried there. No.event happened to reveal to either the strength or extent of the other's feelings. They did not know even the sound of each other's voices. The two dumb friends avoided involving themselves in a closer union—as if it were a misfortune. Each of them seemed to dread inflict-ing on the other a misery more weighty than that which they took pleasure in sharing. Was it the modesty of friendship which checked them at that point? Was it that selfish apprehen-sion, or that atrocious distrust which separates all the inhabi-tants of a populous city? Was it that the silent voice of conscience gave them warning of the approaching danger? It would be impossible to explain the sentiment which made them half enemies, half friends, half indifferent and half attached, as much united by instinct, as separated in fact. Perhaps they wanted to preserve their illusion. At times, one

would come to the conclusion that the stranger feared he
might hear some coarse language from those fresh lips, which
were as pure as a flower, and that Caroline did not deem
herself good enough for that mysterious being, whose mien
and bearing spoke of wealth and power.   As for Madame
Crochard, that tender mother, almost discontented with the indecision of Caroline, looked sullenly at her *black gentleman*, at
whom she had formerly cast smiling glances that were almost
servile.   Never had she so bitterly complained to her daughter
of being compelled to do the cooking at her time of life ;
never had her rheumatism and her catarrh extorted from her
so many groans ; and lastly, she had not been able to make as
many ells of tulle that winter as Caroline had till then counted
on.   Such being the situation of affairs, and it being now the
end of December, the time when bread is always dearest,
and when the scarcity of grain, which made the year 1816 so
hard for poor people, was beginning to be felt, the stranger
noticed upon the face of the young girl, whose very name was
unknown to him, the fearful traces of some secret thought, not
to be dissipated by his benevolent smile.   Soon afterwards he
could read in Caroline's eyes the wan effects of nightwork.
On one of the last nights of that month, the stranger returned
towards one o'clock a.m. through the Rue du Tourniquet St.
Jean.   The night was so silent that long before reaching
Caroline's house he could hear the querulous voice of the old
mother, the more mournful tones of the young sempstress
mingling shrilly with the whistling snowstorm.   He tried to
creep up slowly, and at the risk of being arrested, ensconced
himself beneath the window, to listen to the mother and
daughter, while he watched them through the largest of the
holes which gashed the curtains of yellowish muslin, and made
them look like large cabbage-leaves gnawed into holes by
caterpillars.   The inquisitive passenger saw a stamped document upon the table, which stood between the two frames and
supported the lamp with its two water-globes.   He saw at

once that it was a summons. Madame Crochard was crying,
and Caroline's voice had a guttural sound, which marred the
natural sweetness and gentleness of its tones.

"Why distress yourself so, mother? Monsieur Molineux
will not sell us up, or turn us out before I have finished this
dress. Two nights more and I shall take it to Madame
Roguin's."

"And what if she makes you wait as she always does, and
will the price of the dress pay the baker as well?"

The spectator of this scene was so much in the habit of
reading faces that he saw, at least so he fancied, as much
affectation in the mother's sorrow, as genuineness in that of
the daughter. • He suddenly disappeared, but returned a short
time afterwards. On looking through the slit in the muslin, he
saw that the mother was in bed, while the young girl, with her
head bent over her frame, was working with indefatigable
assiduity; on the table close to the summons lay a piece of
bread, cut in the form of a triangle, and placed there, no
doubt, for the young girl to eat during the night, while remind-
ing her of the recompense of her courage. The stranger,
trembling with pity and sorrow, threw his purse through a
broken pane to the very feet of the young girl. Then, without
staying to enjoy her surprise, he decamped with beating heart
and burning cheek. The next day the sad and unsociable
stranger assumed a preoccupied air as he passed by; but he
could not evade the gratitude of Caroline, who had thrown the
window open, and was amusing herself by digging up with a
knife the soil in the snow-covered box—a pretext whose ingenious clumsiness showed her benefactor that this time she
did not wish to see him *through* the glass. The sempstress,
with her eyes full of tears, bowed to the stranger, as if to say,
"I can only pay you with my heart." But *the black gentleman*
looked as if he did not at all understand this expression of
genuine gratitude. As he repassed in the evening, Caroline,
who was engaged in repasting a sheet of paper over the broken

pane, displayed the enamel of her gleaming teeth in a smile that was full of promises. Thenceforth *the black gentleman* sought another thoroughfare, and was seen no more in the Rue du Tourniquet. One Saturday morning, in the early part of the ensuing May, Caroline espied between the two black rows of houses a small bit of blue sky, and while watering out of a tumbler the root of her honey-suckle, said to her mother,—

"Mamma, we must go for a walk at Montmorency to-morrow." The joyous phrase had scarcely passed her lips when *the black gentleman* went by, sadder and more dejected than ever. The modest but kindly glance which Caroline cast at him might well be taken for an invitation. Accordingly when, on the following day, Madame Crochard, dressed in a merino robe of reddish brown, a silk bonnet, and an imitation Cashmere shawl with large stripes, presented herself at the corner of the Rue du Faubourg St. Denis and the Rue d'Enghien, for the purpose of choosing a *coucou*, she found her stranger standing there, like a man who is waiting for his wife. A smile of pleasure chased the furrows from the stranger's face when he saw Caroline. Her little feet were cased in pure puce-colored prunello. Her white dress, the sport of a wind that would have been treacherous to an ill-made woman, displayed her attractive figure. Her face, shaded by a rice-straw hat, lined with rose-colored silk, was lighted up, as it were, with a ray from heaven. Her large puce-colored sash set off to great advantage a very slender waist. Her hair parted into two bands of bistre over her snowy forehead, gave her an air of candor which there was nothing in the rest of her features to counteract. Joy seemed to make Caroline's heart as light as the straw of her hat; but when she caught sight of *the black gentleman*, there was kindled in her breast a hope, which at once eclipsed her dress and beauty. It was perhaps this sudden revelation of the joy occasioned by his presence, that determined him to be the travelling companion of the little needlewoman ; for at first he seemed undecided. He hired a cabriolet with a decent horse, to go to Saint-Leu-Taverny, and offered Madame Crochard and her daughter a place in it. The mother accepted the offer without waiting for it to be repeated; but as soon as the cabriolet had reached the road to St. Denis, she took it into her head to have some scruples, and uttered timidly polite fears that the presence of the two women might cause their companion some inconvenience.

"Perhaps you wished to go to St. Denis alone, sir," said she with affected good nature. But she soon began to complain about the heat, and especially about her cold, which had not, so she said, allowed her to close her eyes the whole night through. So, suiting the action to the word, she seemed to be fast asleep, almost ere the carriage had reached St. Denis. Some of her snores seemed to *the black gentleman* to be extremely suspicious, and as he looked at the old woman, he frowned with an air of singular distrust.

"Oh, she is asleep," said Caroline artlessly, "she did not cease coughing the whole night through. She must be very tired."

The only response of her companion was a subtle smile which seemed to say to the young girl, "you innocent creature, you don't know your mother." Nevertheless, when the carriage was bowling along the road in the long avenue of poplars which leads to Eaubonne, *the black gentleman* in spite of his suspiciousness, came to the conclusion that Madame Crochard was really asleep. Perhaps, also, he did not care to pursue his investigations into the genuineness of the slumber, any further. Whether the beauty of the sky, the pure country air, and the intoxicating perfumes of the first shoots of the poplar-tree, and of the flowers of the willow, and the white thorn, had caused his heart to unfold itself as nature was unfolding herself; whether longer self-restraint was becoming irksome to him, or Caroline's sparkling eyes reflected the disquiet of his own, *the black gentleman* began a conversation with his young companion, that was as vague as the undulating movements of the tree

swaying in the breeze, as rambling as the wandering flight of
the butterfly in the blue sky, as illogical as the melodious murmur of the fields, though filled like that with a mysterious love.
At this season of the year the country trembles like a bride
who has just donned her wedding-dress, and bids the coldest
heart rejoice. Quitting the dark streets of the Marais for the
first time since the last autumn, and plunged into the midst of
the harmonious and picturesque vale of Montmorency ; passing
through it in the morning with its boundless expanse before
the eye ; turning from that to eyes which also speak of infinity
by expressing love, who would not melt ? what lips would keep
a secret ? The stranger found Caroline gay rather than witty,
affectionate rather than well informed ; but, if her laugh was
giddy, her language showed that her feelings were genuine.
As the young girl replied to the skilful questionings of her companion, with that lavish outpouring of the heart which is
characteristic of the lower classes, who disdain the reticence of
the denizens of the world, the face of *the black gentleman* grew
animated, and seemed to gain new life. His countenance
gradually lost the sadness which had contracted his features,
then, tint by tint, assumed an air of youth and beauty, which
made Caroline quite proud and happy. The pretty embroiderer guessed that her protector had been so long weaned
from tenderness and love, that he had ceased to believe in
womanly devotion. At length an unexpected sally of Caroline's
light tongue removed the last veil which had concealed the
real youthfulness and native character of the stranger's face.
He seemed to bid an eternal farewell to the ideas that had
troubled him, and began to display the vivacity which underlay his solemn face. The chit-chat became by imperceptible
degrees, so intimate, that when the carriage stopped at the first
houses in the straggling village of Saint-Leu, Caroline had
begun to call the stranger "Monsieur Roger." Then for the
first time the old lady woke up.

"Caroline, she must have heard all we have been saying," whispered Roger to the young girl suspiciously.

Caroline's answer was a charming smile of incredulity which scattered the dark cloud that fear of some scheme on the part of the mother had brought to the brow of the suspicious man. Without expressing any surprise, Madame Crochard approved of everything, and followed her daughter and Monsieur Roger into the park of Saint-Leu, whither the two young people had agreed to go, to see the laughing prairies and perfumed groves, which the taste of Queen Hortense has made so celebrated.

"My God, how beautiful it is!" said Caroline, as, mounted on the top of the green slope, whence rises the forest of Montmorency, she saw at her feet the vast valley unfolding its sinuosities sown with villages, the blue horizon of its hills, its steeples, fields, and prairies, while the whisper of the vale, like the murmur of the sea, stole to her ear and died. The three travellers skirted the banks of an artificial stream, and reached the Swiss valley, whose cottage more than once received Queen Hortense and Napoleon.

When Caroline had seated herself with religious respect upon the moss-grown bench on which kings and princesses and the emperor had rested, Madame Crochard manifested a desire to gain a nearer view of a suspension bridge joining two rocks, which was to be seen in the distance, and directed her steps towards that rustic curiosity, leaving her child under the care of Monsieur Roger, but telling him that she would keep an eye upon them.

"And do you mean to tell me, my poor little creature," cried Roger, "that you have never sighed for wealth and the enjoyments of luxury? Don't you sometimes wish to wear the handsome dresses which you embroider?"

"I should not be telling you the truth, Monsieur Roger, if I said that I never think of the happiness which the rich enjoy. Oh, yes, I often think, especially when I am going to sleep, of the pleasure I should find in seeing my poor mother not obliged at her time of life to go through all kinds of weather to fetch our little necessaries. I should like to have a char-woman to take her her coffee, well sweetened with white sugar, in the morning before she gets up. She loves novel reading, poor old soul; well, I would rather see her wearing her eyes out over her favorite reading, than doing nothing but moving her bobbins from morning till night. She would want a little good wine too. In short, I should like to see her happy, she is so good."

"She has shown you her goodness then?"

"Oh, yes," replied the young girl in a low voice. Then, after a brief interval of silence, during which the two young people looked at Madame Crochard, who, having reached the middle of the rustic bridge, was skaking her finger at·them, Caroline continued,—

"Oh, yes, she has proved it to me. What care she took of me when I was little! She sold her last bits of plate in order to apprentice me to the old maid who taught me embroider-ing. And then, my poor father; what trouble she took to make his last moments pass comfortably!" As this thought crossed her mind the young girl shuddered and covered her face with her two hands. "Ah, bah, let us never think of bygone evils," said she, trying to resume a cheerful look. She colored when she saw Roger was affected by her words; but did not dare to look at him.

"What was your father, then?" he asked.

"My father was an opera-dancer before the revolution," said she, in the most natural manner possible, "and my mother was a chorus singer. My father, who used to marshall the troops at the theatre, was accidentally present at the taking of the Bastile. He was recognized by some of the assailants, who asked him if he who commanded sham assaults on the stage, could not lead a real attack well. My father who was a brave man, accepted their proposal, headed the insurgents, and was rewarded with the grade of captain in the army of the Sambre et Meuse, where he behaved so well as to gain rapid promotion; he became a colonel; but he was so severely wounded at Lutzen, that he returned to Paris only to die, after a year's illness. The Bourbons came back, my mother could get no pension, and we sank back into such deep poverty, that we were compelled to work for a living. For some time past the good soul has been ailing, and I have never seen her so little resigned; she complains, and I can understand it; she has tasted the sweets of a happy existence. As for me, who cannot regret pleasures which I have never known, I only ask of Heaven one thing."

"What is that?" asked Roger quickly: (he seemed pensive.)

"That women may always wear embroidered tulle, so that work may never fall short."

The frankness of these confessions secured the young man's interest; he looked at Madame Crochard with a less hostile eye, as with tardy steps she returned to them.

"Well, my children, have you had a good chat?" she inquired, with a half-indulgent, half-bantering air. "When one thinks, Monsieur Roger, that *le petit caporal* has sat where you are now sitting," she resumed, after a moment's silence. "Poor man," she added, "my husband loved him, that he did. Ah! Crochard did well to die, for he could not have endured to know that he is where *they* have put him."

Roger put his finger to his lips, and the good woman nodded her head, and said gravely, "Enough, I'll keep a close mouth and a still tongue. But," added she, opening the folds of her dress and displaying a cross with its red riband, fastened round her neck by a bit of black silk, "*they* won't prevent me from wearing what *the other* gave to my poor Crochard, and I will certainly have it buried with me. . . ."

On hearing these words, which would at that time be deemed seditious, Roger interrupted the old mother by rising abruptly, and they returned to the village through the alleys of the park.

R

The young man left them for a few moments, to go and order
something to eat at the best eating-house in Taverny; he then
returned for the two women, and took them to the house
through the forest paths. The dinner was gay. Roger was
no longer the ill-omened shadow that used formerly to pass
through the Rue du Tourniquet; rather than *the black gentleman*, he now resembled a confident youth, ready to swim with
the current of existence, like those two heedless and industrious women, who might perhaps be wanting bread to-morrow.
He seemed to be under the influence of youthful joys, his smile
was caressing and childlike. When towards five o'clock
sundry glasses of champagne brought the dinner to an end,
Roger was the first to suggest that they should join the village
ball beneath the chestnut-trees, where he and Caroline danced
together. There was a meaning in the pressure of their
hands, their beating hearts were inspired by the same hope;
and beneath the blue sky, in the red horizontal rays of the
setting sun, their looks shone with such radiance as to dim
the light of heaven. What strange power in an idea and a
desire! Nothing seemed impossible to these two beings. In
these magic moments, when pleasure casts its glamor even on
the future, the heart foretells nothing but delight. That bright
day had already created, for these two beings, memories with
which nothing in their past existence could compare. .Is,
then, the spring more grateful than the stream, desire more
enchanting than enjoyment, hope more attractive than possession?

"Ah, then, the day is ended!"

This exclamation escaped the stranger's lips, when the dance
was over. Caroline, seeing that a slight touch of sadness was
stealing back to his face, looked at him with an air of compassion.

"Why should you not be as happy in Paris as here?" said
she. "Is happiness to be found only at Saint-Leu? It
seems to me that I cannot be unhappy anywhere now!"

Roger trembled when he heard these words, the offspring of that sweet self abandonment which ever leads women farther than they would go, just as prudery often makes them seem more cruel than they really are.

For the first time, since that glance which had been in some sort the commencement of their friendship, Caroline and Roger harbored the same thought. If they did not give expression to it, they felt it at the same time, through the medium of a mutual impression, which resembled the warmth of a grateful fire, consoling them for the chill of winter. Then, as if they dreaded their mutual silence, they walked to the place where the carriage was waiting for them. But before they got into it, they took each other's hands like brother and sister, and ran on in front of Madame Crochard, down a dark avenue. When they had lost sight of the white tulle bonnet which, peeping through the foliage, showed them where the old woman was, Roger cried with troubled voice and beating heart, "Caroline?" The young girl, recognizing the passion that breathed in that interrogation, stepped back a pace or two, confused; still she held out her hand, which was ardently kissed, then quickly withdrawn, for rising on tip-toe, Caroline had caught sight of her mother. Madame Crochard pretended that she saw nothing; as if, in memory of her former calling, she was only called upon to figure there in an *aparté.*

The love affair of these two young people was carried no further in the Rue du Tourniquet. If you would find Caroine and Roger now, you must transport yourself to the centre of Modern Paris, to those new-built houses which seem to have been constructed expressly for young couples to pass their honeymoon in them. Paint and paper, like the pair, are new; the decorations like the love, are in their first bloom. Everything is in harmony with young impressions and effervescent desire. There stood in the middle of the Rue Taitbout, a house whose freestone was still white, and the columns of its door and vestibule free from stains, while its walls shone with

that coquettish style of painting which our first relations with
England had rendered fashionable. On the second floor of
this house the architect had arranged a little dwelling, as if he
had guesed what its destination would be. A neat and simple
anteroom, lined breast-high with stucco, communicated with a
drawing-room and a small dining-room. Beyond the drawing-
room was a pretty bedchamber, and adjoining that, a bath-
room. The chimney-pieces were furnished throughout with
tall mirrors in tasteful frames. The doors were ornamented
with refined arabesques, and the cornices were of the purest
style. An amateur would have recognized there, better than
elsewhere, that knowledge of distinction and ornament which
is characteristic of our modern architects. Caroline had occupied these apartments for about a month. They had been
furnished by one of those upholsterers who follow the directions of the artist. A succinct description of the most important room will suffice to give an idea of the marvels which this
little abode presented to the eyes of Caroline when Roger
installed her in it.

Hangings of grey material enlivened by borders of green
silk, adorned the walls of her bedroom. The chairs, covered
with light kerseymere, were of the slight and graceful form
prescribed by the latest caprices of fashion. A commode of
some indigenous wood inlaid with brown lines guarded the
treasures of the wardrobe. There was a writing-table of similar description for the inditement of billets-doux on perfumed
paper. The bed, with its antique drapery, could not fail to
inspire voluptuous ideas, by the softness of its elegantly
arranged muslins. Its curtains of grey silk, with their green
tassels, were also drawn so as to exclude the light. The bronze
timepiece represented Cupid crowning Psyche; and lastly a
carpet with gothic designs upon a reddish ground brought out
in full relief the accessories of this abode of pleasure. In
front of a Psyche stood a little toilet-table, and seated before

it was the ex-embroiderer, growing impatient over the science of Plaisir, a celebrated hair-dresser.

"Do you expect to finish my head to-day?" said she.

"Madame's hair is so long and thick," replied Plaisir.

Caroline could not help smiling. The flattery of the hair-dresser had no doubt awakened in her heart a recollection of the enthusiastic praise which her friend bestowed upon the beauty of the tresses which he so strongly admired.

When the hairdresser had gone, the lady's maid came to hold a council with Caroline as to the toilette which would please Roger best. It was then the beginning of September, 1816, and the weather was cold, so that choice was made of a dress of green grenadine, trimmed with chinchilla. As soon as her toilette was complete, Caroline rushed to the drawing-room, and opened a window leading to the elegant balcony which ornamented the front of the house.

There she stood with folded arms, in a charming posture, not in order to attract the admiration or the passengers, and see them turning their heads to look at her, but that she might command the boulevard at the end of the Rue Taitbout. This prospect, which one might compare to the slit made by actors in the curtain of a theatre, enabled Caroline to catch sight of a multitude of elegant carriages, and a number of people sweeping on with the rapidity of Chinese shadows.

The whilom sempstress of the Rue de Tourniquet not knowing whether Roger would come on foot or in a carriage, scrutinized in turn the pedestrians and the tilburies, those light vehicles imported into France by the English. Mingled expressions of mutiny and love chased each other over her youthful features, when, after watching for a quarter of an hour, neither her piercing eye nor her heart warned her of the approach of him whom she was expecting. What contempt, what utter disregard for all the beings who were bustling about like ants beneath her feet, might be read upon that beautiful face. Her grey eyes danced and sparkled with mischief. Absorbed in her passion she avoided homage with as much care as the very proudest take to reap it during their walk in Paris. Little indeed did she reck whether the impression made by her cream-white complexion, or by the little foot jutting out from the balcony, or the tantalizing picture of her lively eyes and daintily retroussé nose, would on the morrow be erased from the memory of the admiring passenger, or not. She saw but one face, she had but one idea, when the spotted head of a certain dark bay horse showed itself beyond the line of houses.

Caroline trembled, and stood on tiptoe to try to recognize the white reins and the color of the tilbury. It was he. Roger turns the street corner, catches sight of the balcony and whips his horse, the horse darts forward to the bronze door, that he knows as well as his master knows it. The door of the apartment was opened in advance by the lady's maid, who had heard her mistress's joyful exclamation. Roger rushes to the drawing-room, presses Caroline in his arms, and kisses her with that outburst of feeling which always accompanies the meeting of two lovers who meet rarely. He leads her, or rather, though locked in each other's arms, they walk with one accord, to that charming, sequestered, and scented chamber. They sit down upon a sofa before the fire, and gaze at each other for a moment in silence, expressing their happiness by ardent pressure of each other's hands and communicating their thoughts in one long look.

"Yes, it is he," she at length exclaimed, "yes, it is you. Do you know that it is three long days—a century, since I saw you. But what is the matter? has anything annoyed you?"

"My poor Caroline!"

"There now, 'my poor Caroline,' indeed!"

"No, don't laugh, my angel, we cannot go to Feydeau's this evening."

Caroline began to pout a little, but soon looked bright again.

"I am a stupid.   How can I think about the theatre when I am looking at you?   Is not seeing you the only spectacle I care for?" said she, passing her fingers through Roger's hair.

"I am obliged to go to the attorney-general's; we have a difficult matter on hand.   He met me in the great hall, and as I shall have to speak, he asked me to go and dine with him; but, my darling, you can go to Feydeau's with your mother; I will join you there if the conference is soon over."

"What, go to the theatre without *you!*" cried she, with an expression of astonishment; "enjoy a pleasure which *you* do not share   O my Roger, you do not deserve to be kissed," she added, springing to his neck with a movement that was at once unaffected and voluptuous.

"Caroline, I must go back and dress myself.   The Marais is some distance off, and I have still some business to get through."

"Take care, sir, what you are saying, there," said Caroline, interrupting him.   "My mother told me that when men begin to talk to us about their business, they have ceased to love us."

"Caroline, have I not come to see you?   Haven't I stolen this hour from my inexorable—"

"Hush," said she, placing a finger on Roger's mouth; "hush, don't you see that I am only in fun."

They had now gone back to the drawing-room.   There Roger caught sight of a piece of furniture which the cabinet-maker had brought that very morning; the old rosewood frame, which had fed Caroline and her mother when they were living in the Rue du Tourniquet St. Jean, had been refurbished, and a tulle dress of rich design was already stretched upon it.

"Well, my dear friend, this evening I will work.   While I embroider, I shall believe myself back again, in those old days when you used to pass me without speaking, but not without looking at me; those days when the recollection of your looks kept me awake at night.   O my dear frame, the best piece of furniture in my drawing-room, although it is not a gift from

you : you don't know ;" she said, sitting down on the knees of
Roger, who unable to restrain his emotions, had sunk into an
armchair. "Listen to me now ; I intend to give what I make
by my embroidery to the poor. You have made me rich
How I love that pretty little estate at Bellefeuille, not so much
for what it is, as because you gave it me. But tell me, Roger,
I should like to call myself Caroline de Bellefeuille, can I ?   Is
it legal, or would it be winked at ?"

Seeing Roger's slight gesture of assent, which was inspired
by his hatred of the name of Crochard, Caroline gave a light
skip and clapped her hands.

"It seems to me," she cried, "that I shall be much more
your own like that. As a rule a girl renounces her own name,
and takes that of her husband." A troublesome thought which
she at once dismissed, brought the color to her cheeks. She
took Roger's hand and led him to the open piano. "Listen,"
said she, "I know my sonta like an angel, now ;" and her
fingers had begun to wander over the ivory keys, when she
felt herself seized by the waist and borne aloft.

"Caroline, I ought to be far away from here."

"You want to go ?   Well, then, away with you," said she,
pouting ; but she smiled when she looked at the timepiece, and
joyously exclaimed, at all events I shall have kept you a quarter of an hour beyond your time."

"Farewell, *Mademoiselle de Bellefeuille*," said he, with the
gentle irony of love.

She snatched a kiss and accompanied her Roger to the
door ; when she had lost the sound of his footsteps on the
stairs, she ran to the balcony, to watch him getting into his
tilbury, and taking the reins into his hands, to catch his last
look, hear the crack of his whip and the rattling of the wheels
upon the pavement ; to follow with her eyes the gallant horse,
its master's hat, the gold lace on the groom's, and still to gaze
long after the dark angle of the street had hid the vision from
her sight.

Five years after the installation of Caroline de Bellefeuille, in the pretty house in the Rue Taitbout, there took place another of those domestic scenes which draw still more closely the bonds of affection between two beings who love one another.

"In the middle of the blue drawing room, in front of the window that opened on to the balcony, a little boy, four-and-a-half years old, was making a most infernal noise, as he whipped his rocking-horse, the leg-sustaining curves of which were not moving fast enough to suit his fancy. His pretty little head, covered with light hair, that fell down upon his embroidered collar in a thousand curls, assumed an angelic smile when his mother called on him from the armchair in which she was plunged,—

"Not so much noise, Charles; you will wake your little sister."

Thereupon, the inquisitive child dismounted briskly from his horse, stole to his mother on tiptoe as if he dreaded the noise of his feet upon the carpet, placed a finger between his teeth, and, assuming one of those childish attitudes which derive their principal charm from being so entirely natural, raised the veil of white muslin which covered the fresh face of a little girl, who was sleeping on her mother's knee.

"Eugéne is asleep, then?" said he, quite astonished. "Why should she be asleep when we are awake?" he added, opening his large black liquid eyes.

"God only knows why," replied Caroline, smiling.

The mother and child gazed at the little girl, who had been baptized that very morning. Caroline, who was now twenty-four years old, was in the full bloom of that beauty which unclouded happiness and continuous enjoyment had developed. In Caroline, the woman was complete. Only too glad to fall in with the wishes of her dear Roger, she had acquired the accomplishments which she lacked. She played the piano tolerably well, and sang agreeably. She was ignorant of the usages of society, which would have rejected her, and she

would not have frequented, even if she would have been
welcomed into it; for the woman who is happy does not care
about society.   She had not learned those drawing-room
manners, nor that drawing-room style of conversation, which is
so full of words and void of ideas.   But by way of counterpoise, she laboriously acquired that knowledge which is indispensable to a mother whose whole ambition is to bring up her
children well.   Her only pleasures were to be always with her
boy, to give him, from the cradle, those perpetual lessons which
imbue the hearts of the young with a taste for the true and
the beautiful, to preserve him from every evil influence, and to
fulfil alike the troublesome functions of the nurse, and the
sweet obligations of the mother.

This discreet and gentle creature had, from the very first, so
cheerfully made up her mind to keep strictly within the
charmed circle in which all her happiness was bound up, that
after six years of the most affectionate intimacy, she still knew
her friend only by the name of Roger.   The engraving of the
picture of Psyche coming with her lamp to look at Cupid in
spite of his prohibition, hung in Caroline's bedroom, and
reminded her of the conditions of her happiness.   Not once
during those six years had any misplaced ambition on her part
worried the heart of Roger, which was a real treasure of goodness.   She never wanted dresses or diamonds; nor did her
vanity induce her to accept the offer of a carriage, which was
twenty times repeated.   To stand on the balcony and wait for
Roger, to go with him to the theatre, or in fine weather to take a
walk with him through the environs of Paris, to expect him, to
see him, and look forward to seeing him again—such was the
story of her uneventful, but love-abounding life.

While she lulled to sleep the little child of a few months old
that was lying on her knee she took pleasure in recalling the
memories of bygone days.   She dwelt more particularly on the
month of September, the period at which Roger took her to
Bellefeuille to enjoy those fine days, which seem to belong to

every season in turn. At that time of year nature is as prodigal of flowers as of fruit; the evenings are warm, the mornings mild, and the melancholy of autumn often gives way to the brilliance of summer. During the earlier portion of their union, Caroline had imputed the many proofs of an equable temperament and gentle disposition which Roger had given her, to the rarity of their meetings, and to their mode of life, which precluded them from being, like husband and wife, always together. She now remembered with delight how, tormented with idle fears, she had watched him with fear and trembling during their first visit to the little estate in the Gatinais. Vain espionage of love! Each of those happy months passed like a dream, amid perpetual happiness. There was always a smile of affection upon the lips of that excellent being,—a smile that seemed like the reflection of her own. As these scenes passed too vividly before her, her eyes grew moist with tears, she thought she was not affectionate enough, and fancied she could see in the misfortune of her equivocal position, a sort of tax, levied by destiny, upon her love. And then an invincible curiosity led her to ponder over the accidents of existence, which could induce a man so affectionate as Roger, to confine himself to a clandestine and illicit happiness. She forged a thousand romances, simply for the purpose of sparing herself the admission of the true reason, long guessed but reluctantly believed by her.

She rose, with her baby still sleeping in her arms, and went into the dining-room, to superintend the preparations for dinner.

It was the 6th of May, 1822, the anniversary of the trip to Saint-Leu which had been decisive of her destiny; so that every year, as that day came round, it was kept as a festival of the heart. Caroline selected the table-linen, and ordered the arrangement of the dessert. After gladly devoting to these details the minute attentions which fascinated Roger, she placed the little girl in her pretty cradle, went to her post on the balcony, **and soon** descried the cabriolet which her friend, **now** arrived at full maturity, had adopted, instead of the tilbury of earlier days.   After having sustained a first discharge of kisses from Caroline and the little rogue who called him papa, Roger went to the cradle, watched, for a time, the slumbers of his daughter, kissed her little forehead, then drawing from his coat pocket a long **document** variegated with black lines, he said,—

"Caroline, this is Mademoiselle Eugénie de Bellefeuille's portion."

The mother gratefully accepted the dotal deed, which was the title to a certain sum in the public funds.

"Why three thousand francs a year for Eugénie, while you have given Charles only fifteen hundred?"

"Charles, will be a man, my angel," replied Roger. "Fifteen hundred francs will be enough for him. With that income a man of energy is above want. If your son should be an ordinary man, I don't wish him to have the means of committing follies. If he is ambitious, the narrowness of his means will inspire him with a taste for work. Eugénie is a woman, and must not be portionless."

The father now began to play with Charles, whose unrestrained caresses showed the independence and freedom of his bringing-up. There was no timidity on the part of the lad towards his father, to interfere with the charm which rewards the performance of the duties of paternity. The gaiety of the little family was both gentle and genuine. In the evening a magic lantern displayed upon a white cloth its illusions and mysterious pictures, to the great surprise of Charles. More than once the ecstatic joy of the innocent little fellow, drew wild shouts of laughter from Caroline and Roger. When, later in the evening, the little boy was in bed, the little girl awoke demanding nourishment. Seated by the fire in that chamber of peace and pleasure, Roger gave himself up to the enjoyment of watching, by the light of a lamp, the soothing picture presented by the child, as it hung on Caroline's breast, and by Caroline herself, white and fresh as a new-blown lily, with her hair falling down in a thousand brown curls, and almost hiding her neck. *All the charms of the young mother stood out clearly in the lamplight, which surrounded her, her dress, and the child, with manifold and picturesque effects, produced by the combination of light and shade. The calm and silent features of the young woman seemed to Roger a hundred times sweeter than they had ever been. Tender was the look with which he gazed at the curved and coral lips which had never uttered a disagreeable word. The same thought gleamed in the eyes of Caroline, who watched Roger furtively, either to enjoy the effect she produced on him, or to forecast the future of the evening.

Her unknown friend, who understood the coquetry of that subtle look, said with affected sadness, " I must be off now; I have a stiff bit of work to finish, and am expected at home. Duty before everything; isn't that right, my darling?"

Caroline scrutinized him sadly, but at the same time softly, then with that resignation which disguises none of the sorrows of a sacrifice, she said, "Adieu, go away. If you stayed another hour, I should not be able to part with you so easily."

" My angel," answered Roger, smiling, " I have three days' leave of absence, and am supposed to be now twenty leagues away from Paris."

One morning, a few days after this anniversary of the 6th of May, Mademoiselle de Bellefeuille, fearing she might be too late, rushed off to a house in the Rue St. Louis, in the Marais, to which she generally paid a visit once a week. A messenger had come to inform her that her mother, Madame Crochard, was sinking under a complication of sufferings, caused by her catarrh and rheumatism. While the driver of the hackney coach, stimulated by Caroline's urgent request, backed by the promise of an ample gratuity, was lashing his horses to their utmost speed, the timorous old dames whom the Widow

Crochard had gathered around her by way of society in her
last days, introduced a priest into the neat and comfortable
second-floor apartments, occupied by the whilom ballet-dancer.
Madame Crochard's servant did not know that the pretty girl
at whose house her mistress often dined, was that mistress's
own daughter; and she was one of the first to beg that a confessor might be called in, hoping that that ecclesiastic might
be as serviceable to her as to her mistress. Between two
games of boston or while strolling in the Turkish garden, the
old women with whom the Widow Crochard gossiped every
day, had succeeded in awakening in the frozen bosom of their
friend, some scruples about her past life, some ideas about the
future, some fears of hell, and certain hopes of pardon founded
on a sincere repentance. On this solemn morning, these three
old women from the Rue St. François, and the Vieille-Rue-du-
Temple, had established themselves in the *salon* in which
Madame Crochard entertained them every Tuesday. They
took it in turns to leave their armchairs, to go and sit at the
head of the sick-bed to keep the poor old woman company,
and buoy her up with those vain hopes with which we soothe
the dying. However, when the crisis seemed to them to be
close at hand, and the doctor, who had been called in on the
preceding evening, gave no hopes of the widow, the three
dames took counsel together, as to whether it was necessary to
summon Mademoiselle de Bellefeuille. Françoise having given
her opinion on the matter, it was determined that a commis-
sionaire should go to the Rue Taitbout, and tell the news to
the young relative, whose influence seemed to the four women
so formidable; but they hoped that the Auvergnat's summons
would not bring the young woman, who had so large a share in
Madame Crochard's affection, till all was over. The widow,
who clearly had an income of a thousand crowns, would not
have been so carefully nursed by that trio of females, but for
the fact that none of those good friends, nor Françoise, knew
of any expectant relative. The opulence of Mademoiselle de

Bellefeuille, whom Madame Crochard, following the customs of the old Opera, strictly abstained from calling by the sweet name of daughter, almost justified the plot of the four women, to share among them the fortune of their dying friend.

Shortly afterwards, the particular sibyl who was keeping guard over the patient, popped her palsied head into the room in which her anxious coadjutors were sitting, and said, " It is time to send for Monsieur l'Abbé Fontanon.   Two hours hence she will have neither head nor hand to write a single word."

Thereupon the toothless old servant started off and returned with a man dressed in a black coat.   This priest had a vulgar face, and his contracted forehead showed a narrow mind; while his large pendant cheeks and double chin betokened selfish prosperity.   His powdered hair softened the aspect of his features, until he raised his small brown prominent eyes, which would not have seemed out of place beneath the eye brows of a Tartar.

" Monsieur l'Abbé," said Françoise, " I thank you for your advice; but you may be sure that I have taken the utmost care of the dear woman."

The servant, she of the lagging foot and mourning face, was silent when she saw that the door of the apartments was open, and that the most insinuating of the three dowagers had stationed herself upon the landing, in order to be the first to speak to the confessor.   After the clergyman had endured with complaisance a triple broadside of honied and sanctimonious talk from the friends of the widow, he took a seat by Madame Crochard's pillow.   Common decency and a certain sense of shame, compelled the three dames and old Françoise to remain in the *salon*, where they assumed for each other's benefit, airs of grief such as only those wrinkled faces could produce in such perfection.

" Ah, isn't it sad?" cried Françoise.   "This is the fourth mistress, now, that I shall have the pain of burying.   The first left me an annuity of a hundred francs; the second fifty crowns, and the third a thousand **crowns**. After thirty years in **service,** that is all I possess." **Thereupon the** servant exercised her privilege of coming **and going, to** ensconce herself in a little closet, where **she** could overhear what **the priest said.**

"It gives me pleasure," Fontanon was saying, "to find that you have such pious sentiments, my daughter; you have upon you a sacred relic . . . ."

Madame Crochard made a vague movement, which seemed to indicate that her mind was wandering, for she pointed to the imperial cross of the Legion of Honor. The priest when he caught s'ght of the Emperor's head started back one step, but, immediately afterwards, again drew near to his penitent, who held some conversation with him in so low a tone that for some moments Françoise heard nothing.

"A curse upon me!" suddenly ejaculated the old woman, "don't forsake me. What, Monsieur l'Abbé, you believe that I shall have to answer for my daughter's soul?"

The priest replied in too low a tone, and the partition was too thick, for Françoise to hear his answer.

"Alas," cried the widow, shedding tears, "the wretch has left me nothing of what I can dispose. When he took my poor Caroline, he separated us, and only gave me a life annuity of 3000 francs, the capital of which belongs to my daughter."

"Madame has a daughter, and has only an annuity," cried Françoise, rushing into the *salon.*

The three old women looked at each other in profound amazement. One of them, whose nose and chin almost joined each other, and seemed thereby to confer upon her the palm of hypocrisy and cunning, winked, and so soon as Françoise's back was turned, made a sign to her two friends, as much as to say, "She is a knowing creature; she has already had three legacies."

So the three old women made up their minds to stay. But the clergyman soon reappeared, and when he had said one word to them, the witches hobbled down the stairs together after him, leaving Françoise alone with her mistress. It was all very well for Madame Crochard, whose sufferings were becoming more and more intense, to ring for her servant now; Françoise contented herself with calling out "Coming, coming directly."

Cupboard-doors and wardrobe-doors were opening and shutting, as if Françoise were looking for some lottery-ticket that had been mislaid. Just as this crisis was at its climax, Mademoiselle de Bellefeuille reached her mother's bedside, to lavish on her sweet words of comfort.

"Oh, my poor mother, what a criminal I am! you are in pain, and I knew nothing of it; my heart did not tell it me.. But here I am. . . ."

"Caroline."

"What, mother?"

"They brought a priest to me."

"They should have fetched a doctor," said Mademoiselle de Bellefeuille. "A doctor, Françoise! How is it that these women did not send for a doctor?"

"They brought me a priest," continued the old woman with a sigh.

"How she suffers! and no sedative—nothing, on the table!'

The mother made a vague sign, which Caroline's penetrating eye understood, for she kept silence, that her mother might speak.

"They brought me a priest—under pretence of getting me to confess. Caroline, beware," groaned the whilom ballet girl, making a final effort; "the priest extracted from me the name of your benefactor."

"But who could have told it you, my poor mother?"

In the attempt to assume a knowing look, the old woman died. If Mademoiselle de Bellefeuille could have observed her mother's face she would have seen what no one will ever see—Death smiling.

In order to understand the interest which underlies the

s

introduction to this scene, we must for a moment forget the
actors in it, and listen to the recital of certain anterior events,
the last of which is closely connected with the death of Madame
Crochard.   The two parts will then form one story, which, in
obedience to a law peculiar to life in Paris, divides itself into
two distinct series of events.

Towards the end of November, 1805, a young advocate,
about twenty-six years of age, was descending, at about three
o'clock, a.m., the grand staircase of the hotel inhabited by the
arch-chancellor of the empire.   When he reached the court,
dressed as he was in ball-room attire, a fine sleet was falling.
He could not restrain an expression of disgust—not, however,
entirely devoid of that gaiety which rarely forsakes a French-
man,—when, on peering through the railings of the hotel, he
could neither discover any hackney-coach nor hear the sound
of horses' hoofs, or the hoarse voices of the Parisian hackney
coachmen.   The silence was broken only by the impatient
feet of the horses of the grand judge (whom the young man
had left at the card-table of M. Cambacérès) as they pawed the
pavement of the court of the hotel which was dimly lighted by
the carriage-lamps.

All at once the young man received a friendly slap on the
shoulder, and turning round recognized and saluted the grand
judge, who just as his footman was letting down the carriage-
steps, guessed the young man's difficulty.

" In the night all cats are grey," said he gaily.   " The grand
judge will not compromise himself if he gives a lift to an advocate—especially when that advocate is the nephew of an old
colleague who was one of the luminaries of the grand State
Council which gave the Code Napoléon to France."   At a gesture
of the supreme chief of the imperial judges, the pedestrian
stepped into the carriage.

" Where do you live ?" inquired the minister of the advocate,
before the footman, who was waiting for directions, closed the
door.

"Quai des Augustins, mouseigneur." The horses started off and the young man found himself alone with the minister, whom both before and after Cambacérès' sumptuous dinner, he had endeavored to accost, but in vain; for the grand judge had visibly avoided him throughout the evening.

"Well, Monsieur *de* Granville you are in a fair road—"

"So long as I am by the side of your Excellency."

"I am not joking," said the minister. "You were admitted to the bar two years ago, and your conduct of the defence in the Simeuse and D'Hauteserre affair has given you a high position."

"I thought until now, that my devotion to those unfortunate *émigrés* had done me harm."

"You are very young," said the minister gravely; then after a pause he continued, "you created a very favorable impression on the High Chancellor this evening. Join the magistracy of the *parquet;* we are in want of men. The nephew of a man in whom Cambacérès and I take so lively an interest must not remain an advocate for want of patronage. Your uncle helped us to weather some very stormy times, and such services as those are not to be forgotten."

Here the minister paused for a moment.

"In a short time," continued he, "I shall have three places vacant at the tribunal of first instance, and at the court imperial of Paris; come and see me then, and choose whichever of them you prefer. Till then work on, but don't present yourself at my audiences; for, in the first place, I am overwhelmed with business; and in the second, your competitors might guess your object, and injure you in the eyes of the Emperor. Cambacérès and I, in not speaking to you this evening, have saved you from the perils which beset a favorite."

As the minister concluded, the carriage stopped at the Quai des Augustins; the young advocate thanked his generous protector with great emotion for the *two* seats which he had given him, and began to thunder at his door; for the north-east wind was whistling about the calves of his legs with great severity. The bolt of the door was at length withdrawn by the old porter. As the advocate passed the lodge, the porter called to him in a hoarse voice, " Monsieur Granville, there is a letter for you." The young man took it, and, in spite of the cold, tried to read the address by the feeble light of a lamp, whose wick was well-nigh burnt out. " It is from my father," said he, taking his candle, which the porter had at last succeeded in lighting. Then he went quickly up to his apartments, and read the following letter :—

" Take the express, and if you can get here quickly, your fortune is made. Mademoiselle Angélique Bontems has lost her sister ; so she is now an only daughter, and we know she does not hate you. Now, Madame Bontems has it in her power to leave her nearly 40,000 francs a year, besides the marriage portion which she will give her. I have smoothed the way. Our friends will be astonished to see members of the old nobility intermarrying with the Bontems family. Bontems, the father, a red republican of the deepest dye, picked up a number of the national estates at a very cheap price. But, in the first place, it was church property, and will therefore never be restored ; secondly, since you have already stooped to the position of an advocate, I do not see why we should recoil from another concession to existing ideas. The girl will have 300,000 francs ; I will give you 100,000 ; your mother's property must be worth 150,000 crowns, or thereabouts. Thus, then, my dear son, I see you in a position if you choose to join the magistracy, to become a senator, just like any one else. My brother-in-law, the Councillor of State, will not give you a helping hand towards *that*, of course; but, as he is a bachelor, his fortune will come to you some day, so that if you should not get a senatorship upon your own merits, you will succeed to his. Then you will be perched high enough to see how events are likely to turn out. Adieu. I embrace you."

Thus, then, young De Granville went to bed, framing a

thousand projects, each brighter than the last. Under the powerful patronage of the Grand Judge, and of his maternal uncle, one of the compilers of the code, he was about to make a start in an enviable position in the first court in the empire, and would be a member of that *parquet* whence Napoléon selected the chief functionaries of his empire. Then, ready to his hand, there presented itself a fortune large enough to help him to maintain his rank, as he could not have done on his meagre income of 5,000 francs, derived from an estate which had once formed part of his mother's property. That happiness might be added to his ambitious dreams, he conjured up the artless face of Mademoiselle Angélique Bontems, the playmate of his childhood. So long as he had not arrived at years of discretion, his father and mother had not opposed his intimacy with the pretty daughter of their country neighbor; but when, during the brief visits which his vacations enabled him to pay to Bayeux, his parents, who were bigots in the matter of nobility, perceived his liking for the young girl, they forbade him to think about her. So that during the last ten years Granville had only been able to catch momentary glimpses of her whom he used to call his *little wife.* During these moments stolen from the active surveillance of their families, they had been barely able to exchange a few vague words in passing each other at church or in the street. Their happiest days were those when they were brought together by one of those rural fêtes which in Normandy are called *assemblies,* and looked at one another furtively and from afar. During his last holiday Granville had seen Angélique twice; and the downcast look and melancholy attitude of his *little wife* led him to believe that she was being subjected to some secret tyranny.

By seven o'clock the next morning the young advocate was at the coach-office in the Rue Notre-Dame des-Victoires, and was lucky enough to find room in the vehicle which started for Caen at that hour.

Deep was the emotion with which the sucking advocate

caught sight once more of the steeples of Bayeux cathedral.
As yet, none of his aspirations had been defeated, so that his
heart expanded under the influence of the beautiful feelings
which animate the young. After the protracted congratulatory
banquet prepared for him by his father and some of his friends,
was over, the impatient youth was conducted to a certain house
situated in the Rue Teinture, and well known to him. His
heart beat violently as his father—who at Bayeux was still
called as Comte de Granville—knocked so loudly at the
carriage-gates, that the green paint fell from them in scales. It
was about four o'clock in the afternoon. A young maid-
servant, with a white cotton cap upon her head, greeted the
two gentlemen with a little courtesy, and told them, in answer
to their inquiries, that the two ladies would soon be back from
vespers. The count and his son entered a low-pitched hall,
which was used as a drawing-room, and looked like a convent
parlor. A ceiling of polished walnut-wood gave a gloomy
aspect to the room, round which some tapestry—covered chairs,
and antique armchairs were symmetrically ranged. The only
ornament of the stone chimney-piece was a mirror of greenish
glass, from either side of which projected the tortuous branches
of a pair of those old candelabra such as were manufactured at
the epoch of the Peace of Utrecht. Against the wainscot,
and opposite to the chimney-piece, young Granville noticed an
enormous crucifix of ebony and ivory, surrounded by consecrated box-wood. Although the room had three windows,
looking into a country garden, whose symmetrical squares
were bordered with long lines of box, so little daylight entered
the room, that it was difficult to distinguish three ecclesiasti-
cal pictures, which were the work of some skilful brush, and
had doubtless been purchased, during the Revolution, by old
Bontems, who, in his capacity of leader of the district, never
forgot his own interests. From the carefully polished floor, to
the curtains, with their square green pattern, everything shone
with a monastic neatness. The heart of the young man in-

voluntarily shrank within him, in that still retreat, which formed the home of Angélique. His continual habit of frequenting the brilliant drawing-rooms of Paris, and the vortex of gaiety in which he lived, had readily effaced from the memory of Granville the sombre and peaceful life, led by the denizens of the provinces. The contrast was so sudden, that it caused him an internal shudder. To quit one of the assemblies of Cambacérès, where existence was on so grand a scale, where large minded men abounded, and where the glory of the emperor was reflected, and fall suddenly into a circle of petty ideas, was like being transported from Italy to Greenland. "To live here, is not to live at all," he said to himself, as he looked at the methodistical *salon*. The old count, who observed his son's astonishment, led him to a window, through which a little daylight was struggling, and while the servant lighted the old wax candles, tried to dissipate the clouds which the aspect of the room had piled on Granville's brow.

"Listen to me, my boy," said the count; "old Bontems' widow is furiously sanctimonious. When the devil grew old—you know the saying. . I see that the aspect of the room rather sets your teeth on edge. Well, the truth is this. The old woman is besieged by the priests; they have persuaded her that it is never too late to win heaven; and to make sure of St. Peter and his keys, she buys them. She goes to mass every day, hears all the services, communicates every Sunday that God gives us, and amuses herself by restoring chapels. She has presented to the cathedral so many ornaments, aubes, and copes, she has covered the dais with so many plumes, that, at the procession of the last Fête Dieu, there was as great a crowd to see the magnificent dresses of the priests, and the newly-gilded cups and plates, as there ever was at an execution. So that this house is a regular Holy Land. It was I who prevented the old madwoman from presenting these three pictures to the church; look you, a Dominichino, a

Correggio, and an André del Sarto, which are worth a lot of money."

"But about Angélique ?" said the young man sharply.

"If you don't marry her, Angélique is lost," said the count. "Our good apostles have advised her to live and die a virgin and a martyr. It took me an infinite amount of trouble to rouse her little heart by talking about you; that was as soon as I saw that she was an only daughter. But you see at a glance that, as soon as you are married, you will carry her off to Paris. There, what with marriage, dissipation, theatres, and the torrent of Parisian life, she will soon forget confessionals, fasts, hair shirts, and masses, which are meat and drink to these creatures."

"But won't the 50,000 francs per annum, the spoils of the Church, go back to the . .?"

"There we are !" said the count, with a look of subtlety. "In consideration of the marriage—for the vanity of Madame Bontems was not a little tickled at the notion of engrafting the Bontems on the genealogical tree of the Granvilles—the aforesaid mother gives the *corpus* of her fortune to her daughter, reserving to herself only a life interest. You will have the prettiest girl in Bayeux, a little gossip who will cause you no anxiety, because she will be a woman of principle. She has been *mortified*, as they term it in their jargon, by prayer and fasting, and," added the count in a low voice, "by her mother."

A gentle rap at the door stopped the flow of the count's eloquence; for he thought he saw the two ladies coming in. But it was a busy-looking little page who entered. Overawed at the sight of the two gentlemen, he beckoned to the maid-servant, who went up to him. The lad wore a waistcoat of blue cloth with little flaps which hung about his thighs, and blue and white striped trowsers; his hair was cropped all round; his face looked like that of a chorister; so strongly did it savor of that forced sanctimoniousness which all the inhabitants of a methodistical household acquire.

"Mademoiselle Gatienne, do you know where the books for the Service of the Virgin are? The ladies of the Congregation of the Sacred Heart are going to have a procession in the church this evening."

Gatienne went to look for the books.

"Will it last much longer, my little militia man?" asked the count.

"Oh, half an hour, sir, at the utmost."

"Let us go and look at it, there are some pretty women to be seen," said the father to the son. "Besides, a visit to the cathedral can't do us any harm."

The young advocate followed his father with an air of irresolution.

"What is the matter?" said the count.

"The matter is, father,—the matter is,—that I am right."

"Right? Why you have said nothing yet."

"True, but it has occurred to me that you have saved 10,000 francs a year from the wreck of your former fortune; you will leave them to me at as distant a date as possible, I hope. But if you give me 100,000 francs to make a stupid marriage, you will allow me to ask you for 50,000 of them to avert a calamity, and enjoy, while preserving my bachelorhood, a fortune equal to that which your Demoiselle Bontems would bring me."

"Are you mad?"

"No, father. The fact is this. The grand judge promised me on the day before yesterday a place in the *parquet* of Paris. Now 50,000 francs added to what I have, and to the salary attached to my office, will yield me an income of 12,000. I shall then, assuredly, have opportunities for making my fortune, a thousand times preferable to those afforded by a marriage as bankrupt in happiness as it is rich in money."

"It is easy to see," said the father, smiling, "that *you* didn't

live under the old régime ; are we men ever shackled by having a wife, think you ?"

"But, father, in the present age marriage has become . . ."

"Ah, then," said the **count**, interrupting **his son**, "**all** that
my old companions in emigration **tell** me, is really true? The
revolution **has** bequeathed to us manners **devoid of gaiety**,
and **infected** our young men with equivocal principles ? **You
are** going, just like my Jacobin brother-in-law, to preach to me
about the nation, public morality, and disinterestedness. O
my God, but for the emperor's sisters, what *would* become of
us ?"

They were under the roof of the cathedral as these last
words fell **from the lips of the still lusty old man,** who was
always called by the peasants on his estate, "Le Seigneur de
Granville." Heedless of the sanctity of the spot he hummed as
he dipped his fingers into the holy water, an air from the opera,
"Rose et Colas ;" and while conducting his son along the **side**
aisles of the nave, he stopped at each pillar to take a look **at the**
body of the church, with its rows of heads ranged in line, like
soldiers on parade. The appropriate service of the Sacred
Heart was on **the point of** beginning. The ladies belonging
to that society being placed **near** the choir, the count and his
son made their way to that part of the nave, and stood with
their backs against one of the darkest pillars, whence they
could perceive the entire group of heads, which had the appear-
ance of a prairie enamelled with flowers. Suddenly, from a
spot not **more than two paces** from young **Granville, a** voice
which seemed **too** sweet to belong to a human **being,** rang out
clear as the notes of the first nightingale that sings to welcome
the return of spring. Though accompanied by a thousand
female voices and the organ, **this voice** acted on the nerves as
if they had been attacked by the over-rich and vivid tones of
the harmonica. The Parisian turned round and saw a young
woman, **whose face** was, in consequence of the bending of the
head, completely buried beneath a large hat of white material.

He came to the conclusion that it could only be from her that this clear melody proceeded. He fancied he recognized Angélique, in spite of the pelisse of brown merino in which the girl was wrapped, and he nudged his father's arm.

"Yes, it is she," said the count, after looking in the direction indicated by his son. The old seigneur pointed to the pale face of an old woman, whose eyes, deeply bordered with dark circles, had already descried the strangers, though her deceptive glance had not appeared to quit the prayer-book in her hand. Angélique looked up towards the altar, as if to inhale the penetrating perfumes of the incense, whose clouds floated to the spot where the two women were stationed. Then by the weird mysterious light spread through the vast and sombre building by the tapers which were burning on the altar, by the lamp that depended from the centre of the nave, and by sundry wax candles that were fixed against the pillars of the cathedral, the youthful advocate caught sight of a countenance which completely overthrew his resolutions.

Under a white mohair hat he saw a set of features of wonderful regularity, to which the black satin strings of the hat, meeting in a bow beneath the dimpled chin, formed a perfect oval frame. Hair of a pale gold color was parted into two bands, over a narrow but pretty little forehead, and fell upon the cheeks like the shadow of foliage upon a tuft of flowers. The two eyebrows were traced with that regularity which one admires in beautiful Chinese faces. There was a rare firmness in the outlines of the almost aquiline nose, and the two lips resembled two rosy lines traced *con amore* by a delicate hand. In the expression of the pale blue eyes there was much candor. If Granville observed in this face a sort of taciturn rigidity, he might well ascribe it to the devotional feelings, by which Angélique was at that moment inspired. The sacred words of prayer passed through two rows of pearls, and the cold air condensed the breath into a cloud, as it were, of incense. The young man could not resist the temptation to lean forward and

inhale the divine breath. **This** movement attracted the attention of the young girl, and **the steady** gaze which had been
fixed upon the altar was **now turned upon Granville,** in whom,
though the dim light prevented **her from** seeing him distinctly,
she recognized the companion of **her** childhood. A souvenir
more **powerful** than the spirit of prayer **gave an** unnatural
brightness to her face ; she blushed. **The** advocate, trembled
with **joy at** beholding the hopes of the life to come vanquished
by the hopes **of love ; the** glory of the sanctuary eclipsed by
the memories of earth. **But his** triumph was of brief **duration.**
Angélique **dropped her veil over her** face, assumed a calm
appearance, **and resumed** her singing, without betraying in her
voice **the slightest** emotion. Meanwhile **he found** himself
under the influence of a single **desire, and all** his prudential
ideas vanished. When the service **was over, his** impatience
had become so great, that instead of allowing the two ladies to
go **home alone, he went** straight up to his *little wife* and
accosted her. A recognition, **timid** on both sides, **took place**
beneath the church **porch, in the presence of** the faithful.
Madame Bontems trembled with **pride as she** took the arm of
the Comte de Granville, who, being **compelled to offer it in
the presence of so many persons, bore his son no good will for
his indecent impetuosity.**

During the fortnight **which elapsed** between **the** official presentation of the young Vicomte de Granville as the intended
husband of Mademoiselle Bontems and the **day** fixed for the
solemn **ceremony,** he assiduously **paid** his respects to Angélique
in the sombre **parlor, and** grew **accustomed to it. The object**
of his long visits **was** to study the disposition of Angélique, for
his prudence had luckily been **aroused on the** morrow of their
first interview. He always found his future wife seated before
a little table of Saint Lucia wood, employed in marking the
linen of her trousseau. Angélique never introduced the subject **of religion.** If the young advocate began to toy with the
rich rosary which was kept in a small green velvet bag, or

smiled at the relic which always accompanies that implement
of devotion, Angélique with a beseeching look, would gently
take the rosary from his hands, and, without saying a single
word, replace it in the bag, and put it away.   If Granville in a
spirit of mischief sometimes ventured to declaim against certain religious practices, the pretty Normandy girl listened and
encountered him with a smile of conviction, "You must
believe nothing, or believe all that the Church teaches," was
her reply.   "Would you like to have an irreligious girl for the
mother of your children?   No.   Where is the man who would
dare to judge between God and unbelievers?   Well, then,
how can I find fault with that which the Church receives?"
Angélique seemed to be inspired with such pathetic charity,
the young advocate observed such touching looks directed to
himself, that he was sometimes tempted to embrace the religious views of his intended bride.   Her profound belief that
she was walking in the right path, awakened in the heart
of the young aspirant to the magistracy, doubts, by which
he endeavored to profit.   Granville now committed the enormous blunder of mistaking the charm of desire for that of love.
Angélique was so glad to reconcile the dictates of the heart,
with the dictates of duty, by yielding to an attachment formed
in early childhood, that the deluded advocate could not discover which of the two voices was the stronger.   Are not all
young men disposed to rely upon the promises of a pretty face,
to infer that where there is beauty of feature, there is beauty
of heart?   An indefinable feeling impels them to believe that
moral and physical perfection always accompany each other.
If religion had forbidden Angélique to allow free play to her
feelings, they would have withered in her bosom as quickly as
a plant would wither, if sprinkled with some deadly acid.
Could a man who loved and was beloved discover the existence of such well-concealed fanaticism?

Such is the history of young Granville, during this fortnight
which he galloped through, as we gallop through a book, when

we want to know how it ends. Angélique, when carfully
studied, seemed to be the gentlest of women ; he experienced,
to his surprise, a feeling of gratitude to Madame Bontems,
who, by imbuing her daughter so strongly with religious sentiments, had in some sort prepared her for life's cares and
troubles.

On the day appointed for the signing of the fatal contract,
Madame Bontems extorted from her son-in-law a solemn oath
that he would not interfere with the religious practices of her
daughter, that he would give her entire liberty of conscience,
would allow her to communicate, to go to church, and to confession, as often as she felt inclined, and would never thwart
her in the choice of a confessor. At that solemn moment,
Angélique looked at her future husband with an air of such
ardour and purity, that he did not hesitate to take the required
oath. A faint smile played on the lips of the Abbé Fontanon,
the spiritual director of the household. Mademoiselle Bontems, by a slight movement of the head, promised her friend
not to abuse the liberty accorded. As for the old count, he
simply hummed in an undertone, the air, " *Va-t'em voir s'ils
viennent.*"

After some days spent over the *retours de noces*, which figure
so conspicuously in provincial life, Granville and his wife
returned to Paris. There the young advocate received the
nomination to the post of advocate-general to the Imperial
Court of the Seine. In looking about for a dwelling, Angélique, using the influence which all women possess during the
honeymoon, prevailed upon Granville to take a spacious set of
rooms on the ground floor of an hotel situated at the corner of
the Vieille-Rue-du-Temple and the Rue Neuve Saint-François.
Now the principal motive of this choice was that the house was
close to the Rue d'Orléans, in which there was a church, and
within a short distance of a little chapel in the Rue Saint-Louis.

" It is the duty of a good housekeeper to lay in a good stock
of provisions," was her husband's laughing remark. Angélique,

with great justice, pointed out to him that the district of the
Marais lies near to the Palais de Justice, and that the magistrates whom they had just been visiting, lived in that district.
Attached to the house there was a large garden which to a
young couple enhanced the value of the position; their children, *if heaven should send them any*, might run about in the
garden. The court of the hotel was spacious, and the stabling
was good. The advocate-general wanted to live in an hotel in
the Chaussée-d'Antin, where all is fresh and lively, where the
fashions are to be seen in all their novelty, and whence the
boulevards, strewn with people of fashion, the theatres, and
places of amusement, are more easily accessible. But he was
forced to give way to the coaxing of the young wife, who was
asking her first favor; and thus, in order to please her, he
buried himself in the Marais. As Granville's duties were new
to him, he was obliged to devote a very large amount of time to
them; so his first care was to furnish a study, and set up his
library. He hastened to install himself in a room that was
soon encumbered with briefs, and left his young wife to super-
vise the fitting up of the other apartments. He was all the
more ready to involve Angélique in the bustle of making the
first household purchases which give rise to so many pleasures
and memories, in the hearts of young wives, because he was
ashamed of paying his bride less attention than the laws of the
honeymoon ordain. As soon as he was familiarized with his
work, the advocate-general allowed his wife to drag him from
his study, and show him the general effect of the furnishing
and decoration, which he had yet as seen only in detail. If there
be any truth in the adage, that one may form an estimate of
a woman's character from the appearance of her house-door,
her rooms should be a still more faithful index to her mind.
Whether or not, Angélique had inscribed her own character
upon a world of things, of which she had had the ordering, the
young magistrate was surprised at the stiffness and chill
solemnity which reigned throughout his rooms; he sought in

vain for grace and harmony ; there was nothing to rejoice the
sight. The spirit of rectitude and politeness which was stamped upon the parlor at Bayeux, was here repeated. It breathed
from the large round hollow ceiling, adorned with those arabesques, whose long curling lines are in such execrable taste. In
his desire to exculpate his wife, the young man retraced his
steps and renewed his examination of the long and lofty anteroom, which served as a vestibule to the other rooms. The
color which his wife had ordered the painter to lay upon the
wainscoat, was too gloomy, and the dark green velvet with
which the seats were covered, added to the sombre aspect of
this apartment, which, however unimportant, always gives an
idea of the whole house, just as a man's intellect is judged of
from his opening phrases. An anteroom is a kind of preface,
which should announce everything, but promise nothing. The
young magistrate asked himself whether it was possible that his
wife would have selected the lamp in the antique case, which
hung in the centre of that bare hall, with its pavements of black
and white marble, and its paper representing a stone wall, with
here and there a line of green moss. A highly ornamented but
old-fashioned barometer hung in the middle of one of the walls,
as if to make its nakedness more conspicuous. When all this
met his eye, the young man looked at his wife, and saw that
she was so well satisfied with the red fringe of the muslin curtains, with the barometer, and the decorous statue which
adorned the large gothic stove, that he lacked the barbarous
courage to destroy such strong illusions. Instead of condemn-
ing his wife, he condemned himself; he accused himself of
having neglected his first duty, the duty which summoned him
to guide the first steps in Paris, of a young girl brought up at
Bayeux. From this specimen, every one may judge of the
manner in which the other rooms were decorated. What could
be expected from a young woman who took fright at the naked
legs of a caryatid, who keenly repulsed a candelabrum, a candlestick, or a piece of furniture, if it were ornamented with an

Egyptian torso in a state of nudity? At that epoch the school
of the painter David, was just reaching the apogee of its glory.
Everything throughout the length and breadth of France felt
the influence of the accuracy of his drawing, and of his love
for the antique, which made his painting a sort of colored
sculpture. Not one of the creations of the luxury of the empire gained the rights of citizenship with Madame de Granville.
The vast square *salon* of her dwelling retained the faded white
and gold with which it was decorated in the days of Louis
Quinze, the lozenge-shaped gratings and intolerable festoons
due to the sterile fecundity of the painters of that period. If
there had only been harmony of detail, if modern mahogany
had assumed the tortured shapes brought into fashion by the
corrupt taste of Boucher, Angélique's home would simply have
afforded the amusing contrast of a pair of young folks living in
the nineteenth century, as if they had belonged to the eigh-
teenth; but a crowd of things in it, produced ridiculous
antitheses. Consoles, time-pieces, and flambeaux, all were redolent of those warlike attributes which imperial victories
rendered so dear to Paris. The Greek helmets, the Roman
cross-swords, and the bucklers, due to military enthusiasm,
which at that period were employed in the decoration of the
most peaceful articles of furniture, did not exactly harmonize
with the delicate and labyrinthine arabesques, in which Madame de Pompadour delighted. Sanctimoniousness induces a
certain wearisome humility, which by no means excludes pride.
Either through modesty or from inclination, Madame de Granville seemed to have a horror of soft, light colors; perhaps
also she thought that purple and brown were suitable to the
dignity of a magistrate. But how should a young girl, accustomed to a life of austerity, have had any notion of those
voluptuous couches which inspire naughty ideas, those elegant,
perfidious boudoirs, in which sin is rough-sketched? The poor
magistrate was quite disheartened. The tone of approbation
in which he endorsed the praises which his wife bestowed upon

T

herself, showed her that he was not pleased with anything.
Thereupon she exhibited so much chagrin that the loving Granville took her profound regret to be a proof of love, not a
manifestation of wounded self-esteem. How could a young
girl, suddenly snatched away from commonplace country notions, and ignorant of the vanities and refinement of Parisian
life, do better? The magistrate preferred to believe that his
wife had been controlled in her choice by the contractor, rather
than admit the truth ; if he had not been so much in love, he
would have felt that the shopkeepers, so quick in detecting the
wishes of their customers, so far from controlling his wife's
taste, had thanked heaven for sending them a tasteless little
Puritan, to help them to get rid of their old-fashioned stock.
He therefore began to console his pretty Normandy bride.

"Happiness, my dear Angélique, does not depend on the
greater or less elegance of a piece of furniture, but on the
gentleness, complaisance, and affection of a wife."

"But it is my *duty* to love you, and never will the accomplishment of a duty give me so much pleasure," said Angélique
gently. Nature has endowed women with so great a desire to
please and to be loved, that even in the case of a young
Puritan, ideas about a future state and eternal salvation must
give way to the first delights of matrimony. Accordingly,
from the month of April, when their marriage took place,
until the beginning of winter, the husband and wife lived
together in perfect harmony. Love and labor have the merit
of rendering a man tolerably indifferent to mere externals.
Granville, being obliged to pass half the day at the Palais de
Justice, and to debate weighty matters involving the lives and
the fortunes of men, was less able than another to notice certain
home affairs. If on Friday there was nothing but fish for
dinner, and he asked in vain for a dish of meat, his wife,
whom the Gospel prohibited from lying, nevertheless contrived
by means of little tricks permitted in the interests of religion,
to ascribe to her own heedlessness or the emptiness of the

markets what was really premeditated ; she would often justify herself at the expense of the cook, and sometimes went so far as to scold him. At that epoch, young magistrates did not, as in these times, observe fast days, ember week, and the eves of saints' days ; so that Granville did not at first notice the periodicity of the Lenten dinners ; especially as his wife, with perfidious care rendered them very appetizing by means of teal, moor-hens, patties, or fish, whose amphibious flesh or the seasoning deceived the taste. Thus the magistrate, without being aware of it lived very orthodoxly, and secured his salvation incognito. On weekdays he did not know whether his wife went to mass or not, but on Sundays, with very natural complaisance, he accompanied her to church to make up, as it were, for her occasionally sacrificing vespers on his account. Thus he could not at first discover the rigor of his wife's religious practices. Places of amusement being insupportable in summer-time on account of the heat, Granville was even deprived of the pretext of a successful hit for taking his wife to the play ; so that the serious question of the theatre was not raised. In short, during the first days of a marriage to which the beauty of the young girl has formed the principal inducement, 'tis very difficult for a man to be exacting in the matter of amusements. Youth is gluttonous rather than dainty, and moreover mere possession is a charm. How can a man recognize coldness, dignity, or reserve on the part of a woman when he endows her with his own enthusiasm, when the flame which inspires him is reflected in her ? A man must reach a certain stage of conjugal tranquility in order to discern that a Puritan waits for love with folded arms.

Granville, therefore, believed himself happy enough, until the occurrence of a fatal event, which arose to influence his married life. In the month of November, 1808, the canon of Bayeux Cathedral, who formerly directed the consciences of Madame Bontems and her daughter, came to Paris, attracted thither by an ambition to obtain a cure of souls in the capital, a post which he probably coveted as a stepping-stone to a bishopric. On resuming his old dominion over his sheep, he shuddered to find her already so much changed by the air of Paris, and longed to bring her back into his frigid fold. The ex-canon, a man of about thirty-eight, introduced into the midst of the Parisian clergy—a body so tolerent and enlightened—the harsh provincial asceticism and inflexible bigotry whose multiplied exigencies are so many bonds for timorous souls. Madame de Granville repented and returned to her Jansenism. It would be tedious to recount with exactitude the incidents which gradually and imperceptibly introduced unhappiness into the bosom of this household; it will perhaps be sufficient to relate the principle facts, without attempting to arrange them in strict chronological order. The first misunderstanding, however, between this young couple, was striking enough. Madame Granville did not refuse to accompany her husband to grave re-unions, dinner-parties, concerts, or to the assemblies of magistrates, placed above her husband in the judicial hierarchy; but she contrived for some time to feign a headache whenever it was a question of going to a ball. One day Granville, weary of these pretended illnesses, destroyed the note of invitation to a ball at the house of one of the Councillors of State, and surprising his wife with a verbal invitation one evening when there was not the least suspicion of ill-health, he produced her in the midst of a wonderful fête.

The dejected look which his wife wore on their return home offended Granville, and he said to her, " My dear, your position as a wife, the rank which you hold in the world, and the fortune which you enjoy, impose upon you certain obligations which no divine law can abrogate. Are you not the glory of your husband? You ought therefore to go with me to balls, and appear there in proper trim."

" Why, my friend, what was there so much amiss about my toilette? "

" I am not speaking of your dress, but of your manner, my

dear. When a young man comes up and addresses you, you grow so serious that a wag might conclude your virtue extremely fragile. You seem to fear that a smile might compromise you. You really looked this evening, as if you were invoking God's forgiveness for the sins that were being committed all round you. The world, my dear angel, is not a convent. But since you *have* mentioned your toilette, I will confess to you that it is also your duty to follow the fashions and customs of the world."

"Would you then have me display my figure like those brazen-faced women who wear such low dresses that unchaste eyes can see their naked shoulders? . . ."

"There is a difference, my dear," said the substitute, "between exposing the whole breast, and dressing the upper part of the body gracefully; you have a triple row of tulle-ruches which envelope you from neck to chin. It looks as if you had besought your dressmaker to deprive your shoulders and the outlines of your bosom, of all grace, as earnestly as a coquette entreats hers so to make her dresses as to bring out all the secrets of her figure. Your bosom is buried beneath folds so numerous, that everybody was laughing at your affectation of coyness. I should cause you pain were I to repeat the absurd things that were said about you."

"Those who are pleased with such obscenities will not have to bear the burthen of our sins," answered the young wife drily.

"You didn't dance, did you?" asked Granville.

"I will never dance," she replied.

"What if I tell you that you ought to dance," resumed the magistrate sharply; "yes, you ought to follow the fashion, put flowers in your hair, and wear diamonds. Consider, my dear, that rich people, and we *are* rich, are obliged to support luxury in the state. Is it not better to encourage manufactures than to scatter one's money about in almsgiving, through the hands of the clergy?"

"You speak as a statesman," said Angélique.

"And you as a priest," retorted Granville sharply.

The discussion grew very bitter. Madame Granville in her replies, which were always gentle, and uttered in a voice that was as clear as a church-bell, exhibited an obstinacy that betrayed the influence of the priest. When in claiming the rights which Granville's promise had given her, she said that her confessor had specially forbidden her to go to balls, the magistrate tried to prove to her that the priest exceeded the requirements of the Church. This odious theological dispute was renewed with much more violence and acrimony on both sides, when Granville wanted to take his wife to the play. At length the magistrate, with the sole object of overcoming the pernicious influence exercised over his wife, by the ex-canon, placed the quarrel on such a footing that Madame de Granville accepted her husband's challenge, to write to the Court of Rome for information as to whether a woman could, without imperilling her mortal soul, wear low dresses, and go to balls and theatres, to please her husband. The response of the venerable Pius VII. was not long delayed. It boldly condemned the resistance of the wife, and censured the confessor. The letter, which was a regular catechism of matrimony, seemed, as it were, dictated by the gentle voice of Fénelon, breathing throughout his elegance and mildness. "A woman is well placed wherever she goes with her husband." "If she commits sin by his order, she will not one day have to answer for it."

These two passages of the pope's homily led Madame de Granville and her confessor to accuse the holy father of irreligion. But before the brief arrived, the substitute noticed the strict observance of *maigre* days imposed upon him by his wife, and ordered his servants to serve meat throughout the year. Notwithstanding the displeasure which this order caused his wife, Granville, who cared little or nothing for feasts or fasts, adhered to it with manly firmness.

The weakest creature that can think, is wounded in its tenderest point when performing at the instigation of a will other than its own, something which it would have done of its own accord. Of all tyrannies that is the most odious which perpetually robs the heart of its thoughts and actions. It is abdication without having reigned. The word which it would have been most sweet to utter, the sentiment which it would have been most sweet to express, when we believe them to be commanded, die upon the lips. The young magistrate soon gave up receiving his friends, and ceased to entertain them. His house seemed to be in mourning. A house whose mistress is a Puritan has an aspect peculiar to itself. The servants, who are constantly subjected to the surveillance of the wife, are chosen from among the class of so-called pious persons who have faces which are *sui generis*. Just as the most jovial lad who joins the police force will acquire the look of a policeman; even so, people who adopt Puritan habits contract a uniform cast of countenance. The habit of looking upon the ground, of maintaining an attitude of compunction, invest them with a livery of hypocrisy, which rogues can don with marvellous facility. Then again, the Puritans form a kind of republic, they all know each other; the servants whom they recommend to one another form a distinct race, which is carefully preserved by them; just as lovers of horse-flesh only admit to their stable, horses whose pedigrees are beyond dispute. The more those who are termed irreligious examine the house of a Puritan, the more clearly do they perceive that everything which it contains is stamped with a certain indefinable want of grace; there is the same appearance of avarice and mystery that stamps the house of the usurer, the same incense-perfumed dampness that chills the air of the chapel. This sordid regularity, this poverty of ideas everywhere portrayed, can be expressed by one word only—*bigotry*. In these sinister and unbending households bigotry is imprinted upon the furniture, the engravings, the pictures; the talk is bigoted, the silence is

bigoted, the faces are bigoted. **The** transformation of men
and things through bigotry **is an** inexplicable mystery, but the
fact is there. Every one **may have noticed** that bigots do not
walk, do not **sit** down, do not **talk as men of** the world walk,
sit down, **and talk.** In the house **of the bigot** there is constraint; **people do not** laugh; there is stiffness and formality
in everything, **from the** cap of the mistress of the house, to **her**
pincushion; **there are** no frank looks; people move about
like ghosts; the lady **of the** house **seems to be seated** on a
throne of ice.

One morning poor Granville remarked with sadness and with
sorrow, all the symptoms of bigotry in his house. There are
in the world certain **circles where the** same effects exist, though
they are **not produced by the same causes.** Boredom traces
around their miserable haunts, a wall of brass, which includes
all the **horrors of the desert, and the infinity of** emptiness.
Under such conditions **a** household is not **a tomb; it** is worse,
it is a convent. **Placed in the** centre of this glacial sphere, the
magistrate considered **his wife** dispassionately; he observed,
with acute pain, the **narrow ideas** betrayed by the manner in
which the hair was **planted on the low** and somewhat sunken
brow; he noticed in the too perfect regularity of the features an
immobility and stiffness which soon rendered the affected
gentleness by which he had been seduced, quite odious to him.
He **felt that some day,** on the arrival of some misfortune, those
thin lips **might say to him,** " It is for your good, my friend."
The face **of Madame Granville** assumed a pallid hue and serious
expression fatal **to the** cheerfulness of those **who came** near
her. Was it **to the** ascetic habits of a puritanism which is no
more piety than avarice **is economy,** that this change was due?
Was **it** the result of the sterility natural to the bigoted mind?
It would be difficult to **determine.** Beauty without expression
is perhaps an imposture.

The imperturbable smile which the young woman wore upon
her countenance when she looked at Granville seemed with

her to be a Jesuitical formula of happiness, whereby she believed that she satisfied all the exigencies of marriage; her
charity inflicted wounds, her passionless beauty seemed a mon-
strosity to those who knew her, and the gentlest of her words
caused irritation! She obeyed not feeling, but duty. There
are some female defects which may yield to the stern lessons
of experience, or to the teaching of a husband; but nothing
can overcome the tyranny of false ideas of religion. An eter-
nity of happiness to be won, weighed in the balance against a
worldly pleasure, triumphs over everything, and makes everything endurable. Is not this the very apotheosis of egotism,
the ego beyond the tomb? The pope, accordingly, was condemned at the tribunal of the infallible canon and the young
Puritan. Not to be in the wrong is one of those feelings which
supplant all other feelings in these despotic minds. For a
long time past there had been a secret conflict between the
ideas of the husband and those of the wife, and the young
magistrate soon grew weary of a strife which was destined to
have no end. Where is the man, where is the despotism,
which can overcome a face of affectionate hypocrisy and cate-
gorical remonstrances opposed to the slightest wishes? How
can one deal with a woman who makes use of one's passion as
a shield for her own insensibility, who seems resolved to remain
mildly inexorable, joyfully prepares herself to play the part of
a victim, and looks upon her husband as an instrument in the
hands of God, as a scourge whereby to escape the scourges of
purgatory? What colors can one employ to give an idea of
those women who, by carrying beyond all bounds the sweetest
precepts of that religion which St. John summed up in the
words "Love one another," make virtue itself detestable?

Was there in some milliner's shop a particular hat doomed
to hang on hand or to be despatched to the Isles, Granville
was sure to see his wife adorned with it. Was there manufactured some material of peculiarly untasteful design, she muffled
herself up in it. These poor Puritans are terrible in their style

of dress. Want of taste is a defect inseparable from mistaken
piety.

Thus, then, in that intimate home-life to which the most
perfect freedom is essential, Granville found himself alone; he
went into society alone, he went to balls and theatres alone.
In his own home, there was nothing sympathetic about him.
A large crucifix, placed between his wife's bed and his own,
stood there as a symbol of his destiny; for does it not represent a divinity put to death, a man-God killed in all the beauty
of life and youth. The ivory of that cross was not so cold as
Angélique, crucifying her husband in the name of virtue. It
was between those two beds that unhappiness was born. This
young wife could see nothing but duty in the pleasures of
marriage. There, between these two beds, on a certain Ash
Wednesday, arose the keeping of the fast—a pale and livid
spectre, who, in curt tones, ordained a complete Lent; nor did
Granville on this occasion deem it fitting to write to the Pope,
to obtain the opinion of the Consistory as to the mode of
observing Lent, Ember Week, and the vigils of the Festivals.
The unhappiness of the young magistrate was complete; he
could not even complain; he had a pretty, virtuous young
wife, devoted to her duties, in fact, the model of every virtue.
Every year she presented him with a child, which she herself
suckled, and educated in the best principles. The charitable
Angélique was promoted to the rank of angel. The old women,
who composed the society in the midst of which she lived (for
at that epoch young women had not yet taken it into their heads
to launch out into extreme Puritanism, as a matter of fashion),
all admired the devotion of Madame de Granville, and regarded her, if not as a virgin, at least as a martyr. They blamed,
not the scruples of the wife, but the procreative barbarity of
the husband. Granville, meanwhile, overwhelmed with work,
cut off from pleasure, and weary of the haunts of society, in
which he wandered solitary, fell imperceptibly, as he approached
thirty-two, into the most frightful atrophy. Life was hateful to

him. Having too keen a sense of the obligations imposed upon him by his station, to set the example of an irregular life, he tried to relieve his mind by labor, and therefore engaged in a great work upon the law. But he did not long enjoy that monastic tranquility on which he reckoned. When the celestial Angélique saw that he forsook the gaieties of the world, and took with a kind of regularity to working at home, she essayed to make a convert of him. She was really grieved to know that her husband's principles were barely Christian; she sometimes wept, when she reflected that, if her husband should die, he would perish in final impenitence, and that she could not hope to snatch him from the everlasting flames of hell. Granville, therefore, became the target of those petty notions, those empty arguments and narrow thoughts whereby his wife, who fancied she had gained one victory over him, endeavored to obtain another, by bringing him within the pale of the Church. That was the final blow. What could be more distressing than those silent contests, in which the obstinacy of the Puritan tried to subdue the dialectics of the magistrate? What more fearful to describe, than those acrimonious cavils which, to impassioned minds, are worse than the point of the dagger?

Granville deserted the house, in which everything had become insupportable to him; his children, bowed down beneath their mother's frigid tyranny, did not venture to go with their father to the play, nor could Granville procure them any diversion, without drawing down upon them the chastisement of their terrible mother. This man, so full of affection, was forced into an indifference, into an egotism, worse than death. He, however, saved his sons from the infernal regions of home, by sending them to school while quite young, and keeping the reins of management in his own hands. He rarely interfered between the mother and her daughters, but he resolved to procure husbands for them, so soon as they should attain a marriageable age. Had he tried to assume the high hand,

there was nothing to justify him ; his wife, supported by a formidable phalanx of dowagers, would have secured his condem-
nation by the whole earth. Granville's only resource, then,
was to live in complete isolation, but, bowed as he was beneath
the tyranny of misfortune, he was disgusted with his own
features, withered by misery, and worn by toil. And to crown
all, his relations and intercourse with women of the world
taught him that it was vain to expect consolation from them.
Of such consolation, moreover, he was afraid.

The didactic history of this melancholy household did not,
during the fifteen years which had elapsed between 1806 and
1821, present any scene worth reporting. Madame de Granville, from the time when she lost her husband's heart, remained
exactly the same as she had been during the days when she
called herself happy. She fasted for nine days at a time, in
order to pray to God, and His saints, to enlighten her as to
the faults which displeased her husband, and to teach her the
means of bringing back the wandering sheep; but the more
fervently she prayed, the more persistently did Granville absent
himself from home. For about five years past, the advocate-
general, who, in consequence of the Restoration, obtained high
functions in the magistracy, had taken refuge in the entresol
of his hotel, to avoid living with the Countess of Granville.
Hence, every morning, a scene took place, which, if we are
to believe the scandal of society, occurs in several
households, where it is produced by certain incompati-
bilities of temper, by maladies, moral or physical, or by
caprices, which involve many an union in the misfortunes
recorded in this story. At about eight o'clock in the
morning, a lady's maid, bearing a strong resemblance to a
nun, came to ring at the door of the Comte de Granville's
rooms. After being admitted into the *salon,* which formed an
anteroom to the magistrate's study, she repeated to the *valet-
de-chambre,* always in the same tone of voice, the message of
the day before. " Madame wishes to know whether Monsieur

le Comte has passed a good night, and whether she will have
the pleasure of breakfasting with him."

"Monsieur," replied the valet, after having gone and spoken
to his master, "Monsieur presents his compliments to Madame
la Comtesse, and begs her to accept his excuses; important
business compels him to go to the Palais."

An instant afterwards, the lady's maid again presented herself, and inquired, on madame's behalf, whether she would
have the pleasure of seeing Monsieur le Comte, before his
departure.

"He is gone," replied the valet; whereas it would often
happen that his cabriolet was still in the court.

This ambassadorial dialogue became a quotidian ceremony.
Granville's valet, who was a favorite with his master, and had
caused more than one quarrel in the establishment, on account
of his impiety, and the laxity of his morals, would sometimes,
as a matter of form, go into the study, where his master was
not, and then return, to make the customary answer.

The afflicted wife always watched for her husband's return,
and stationed herself upon the *perron*, in order that as he passed
she might be in the way, and meet him like a *Remorse*. The
teasing triviality which is the essence of monastic tyranny, was
at the root of that of Madame de Granville, who, though only
thirty-five, looked forty. When, constrained by decorum,
Granville addressed his wife, or remained at home to dine,
pleased to inflict upon him her pressence, her bitter-sweet
discourse, and the intolerable boredom of her society of bigots,
she would seize the opportunity of putting him in the wrong
before her servants, and her charitable friends.

Just about this time, the presidency of one of the Courts
Royal was offered to Granville, who was at this time in high
favor with the king; but he begged the minister to be allowed
to remain in Paris. This refusal of promotion, the motives of
which was known only to the Keeper of the Seals, suggested the
oddest conjectures to the intimate friends, and to the confessor

of the countess. Granville, who had 100,000 francs a year,
belonged to one of the best families in Normandy; his nomination to the presidency was a step towards the peerage. Why
this lack of ambition? Why had the great law-work been cast
aside? Whence this dissipation, which, for nearly six years,
had made him a stranger in his own house, to his family, to
his labors, to all that ought to have been dear to him? The
countess's confessor, who, for the obtaining of the bishopric,
counted as much upon the suffrages of the houses in which he
reigned, as upon the services he rendered to a religious society,
of which he was one of the main supporters, was disappointed at
Granville's refusal and endeavored to calumniate him by various
suppositions. If Monsieur le Comte had so much dislike to
the provinces, it might be that he was afraid of the necessity
he would be placed in, of leading a regular life. Forced to set
an example of good morals, he would live with the countess,
from whom nothing but an illicit passion could divide him.
Would a woman so pure as Madame de Grenville ever recognize the irregularities of her husband's mode of life? The
worthy friends of the countess turned these hypotheses into
truths; and unfortunately they were not mere hypotheses.
Madame de Granville was thunderstruck. Not knowing anything of the morals of the great world, ignorant of love and its
follies, Angélique was so far from thinking that marriage could
involve any incidents different from those which had alienated
Granville's heart, that she believed him incapable of faults,
which, in the eyes of every woman, are crimes. When the
count had withdrawn his attentions from her, she imagined
that the calm, which he seemed to enjoy was natural; and now
that, after she had given him all the affection which it was in
her power to bestow on any man, all the illusions—which up to
that moment, she had cherished—were wholly dispelled by the
conjectures of her confessor, she undertook her husband's
defence, but without being able to get rid of the suspicions
which had been so cunningly instilled into her mind. These

apprehensions caused such ravages in her weak head, that she fell ill, and was attacked by a slow fever. These events took place during the Lent of 1822; she would not consent to abate her austerities, and so gradually sank into a consumptive condition, which excited grave anxiety for her life. The unconcerned air of Granville killed her. Such care and attention as the magistrate did bestow upon her, resembled that which a nephew constrains himself to show to a rich old uncle. Although the countess had renounced her system of teasing and remonstration, and endeavored to greet her husband with gentle words, the bitterness of the Puritan pierced the disguise, and one word would often destroy the work of a whole week. Towards the end of the month of May, the gentle breath of spring, and a diet more nutritious than Lenten fare, restored some strength to Madame de Grenville. One morning, on her return from mass, she went into her little garden, and sat down upon a stone bench, where the caressing warmth of the sun reminded her of the first days of her married life. She was taking a bird's-eye view of the whole of her life, in order to discover in what respect she had failed in her duties as a wife and a mother, when the Abbé Fontanon appeared before her in a state of agitation difficult to be described.

"Have you met with any misfortune, father?" she inquired, with daughterly anxiety.

"Ah!" replied the Normandy priest, "I would that all the misfortunes with which the hand of God afflicts you, were allotted to me; but my estimable friend, there are trials to which we must learn to submit."

"Is it possible that greater chastisement can be in store for me than that with which Providence overwhelms me by employing my husband as the instrument of its wrath?"

"Prepare yourself, my daughter, for chastisement even greater than that which we and your pious friends formerly supposed."

"I ought then to thank God," replied the countess, "for

deigning to employ you as the messenger of His will; thus placing, as He ever does, the treasures of His mercy beside the scourge of His wrath, as formerly, in banishing Hagar, He opened up for her a fountain in the wilderness."

"He has proportioned your troubles to the strength of your resignation and the weight of your sins."

"Speak, I am prepared to hear all." With these words the countess raised her eyes to heaven and added, "Speak, Monsieur de Fontanon."

"For the last seven years monsieur has been guilty of the sin of adultery with a concubine by whom he has had two children; and he has squandered on that adulterous household more than 500,000 francs, which should of a right belong to his legitimate family."

"I must see it with my own eyes," said the countess.

"Take care how you do that," said the abbé. "You must forgive and wait in prayer, my daughter, until God shall enlighten your husband, unless you resort to the remedies which human laws provide."

The long conversation which thereupon ensued between the Abbé Fontanon and his penitent produced a violent change in the countess. Having dismissed him, she appeared before her servants with a face that had almost a color in it. She ordered the horses to be put into the carriage; countermanded her order, changed her mind twenty times in the course of an hour; but at length, as if she had arrived at some important resolution, she set out at about three o'clock, leaving the household astonished at so sudden a change.

"Is your master coming back to dinner?" she inquired of the *valet-de-chambre*, to whom she never spoke.

"No, madame."

"Did you take him to the *Palais* this morning?"

"Yes, madame."

"Is not to-day Monday?"

"Yes, madame."

"Then there is business at the *Palais* on Monday now?"

"May the devil take you !" cried the valet as he saw his mistress drive off, with orders to the coachman to drive to the Rue Taitbout.

Mademoiselle de Bellefeuille was weeping. Roger close beside her had one of her hands in his. He was silent and gazed first at little Charles, who, not understanding his mother's grief, looked on without speaking, while she wept ; then at the cradle in which Eugénie was sleeping, and then at the face of Caroline, whose tears resembled an April shower.

"Well, yes, my angel," said Roger, after a long silence, "that is the great secret, I am married. But some day, I hope, we shall make one family. My wife has been in a desperate state of health since last March. I do not wish for her death, but if it please God to take her to Him, I believe she will be more happy in Paradise, than in the midst of a world to the pains and pleasures of which she is equally indifferent."

"How I hate that woman ! How could she render you unhappy ? However, it is to your unhappiness that I owe my felicity."

And her tears suddenly dried.

"Caroline, let us live in hope," said Roger, snatching a kiss. "Don't be frightened at what this abbé may have said to you. Although my wife's confessor is, on account of his influence over the congregation, a formidable man, if he should seek to disturb our happiness I should know what to do. . . ."

"Why, what would you do?"

"We would go to Italy, I would fly. . . ."

A cry from the neighboring drawing-room made Roger shudder, and Mademoiselle de Bellefeuille tremble. They rushed into the drawing-room, and there found the countess in a swoon. When Madame de Granville recovered consciousness, she sighed profoundly on finding herself between the count and her rival, whom she repulsed with an involuntary gesture full of contempt.

U

Mademoiselle de Bellefeuille rose to leave the room.

"You are in your own house, madame; I beg you to remain," said Granville, taking hold of Caroline's arm.

The magistrate raised his dying wife, carried her to the carriage, and took a seat by her side.

"Who has induced you to wish for my death—to desert me?" asked the countess in a feeble voice, while she looked at her husband with as much anger as pain. "Was I not young? You thought me beautiful. What have you to reproach me with? Have I deceived you? Have I not been a virtuous and prudent wife? My heart has treasured no image but yours, I have listened to no other voice than yours. In what duty have I fallen short? What have I refused you?"

"*Happiness*," said the count firmly.

"You know, madame, that there are two ways of serving God. Certain Christians imagine that by going into a church at fixed hours to say Paternosters, hearing mass there regularly, and refraining from all sin, they will gain heaven. Such persons, madame, go to hell. They have not loved God for His own sake, they have not worshipped Him as He would be worshipped, they have made no sacrifice for Him; although in outward seeming gentle, they are harsh to their neighbor; they see the rule, the letter, but not the spirit. *That* is how you have acted towards your earthly spouse, you have sacrificed my happiness to your salvation; when I approached you with my heart full of joy, I found you on your knees; when you should have lightened my labors, you were weeping; you have entirely failed to minister to my pleasures."

"And if they were criminal," cried the countess passionately, "was I bound to lose my soul in order to please you?"

"That would have been a sacrifice which another more loving than you has had the courage to make for me," said Granville coldly.

"O my God," cried Madame de Granville, weeping. "Thou hearest him. Was he worthy of the prayers I uttered, and the austerities I underwent in order to redeem his faults as well as my own? What is the use of virtue?"

"To gain heaven, my dear. One cannot be at the same time the wife of a man and of Jesus Christ; that would be bigamy. Women must choose between a husband and a convent. You, with an eye to the future, have divested your heart of all love, of all the devotion which God ordained that you should have for me; and for the world you have no feeling but hatred."

"Have I not loved you, then?"

"No, madame."

"What, then, is love?" asked the countess involuntarily.

"Love, my dear?" replied Granville, with a kind of ironical surprise. "You are not in a condition to understand it. The cold sky of Normandy cannot be that of Spain. Doubtless the question of climates is the secret of our unhappiness. To yield to the caprices of a lover, to divine them, to find pleasure even in pain, to sacrifice for his sake the opinion of the world, self-esteem, even religion itself, and to regard these offerings as mere grains of incense, burned in honor of the idol—that is love."

"Yes, the love of opera girls," said the countess, horrified. "Such fiery passion cannot last, and must soon leave us nothing but coals and ashes, sorrow or despair. A wife, sir, ought, in my opinion, to offer you a true affection, an even warmth of feeling—"

"You talk of warmth, as negroes talk of ice," said the count, with a sardonic smile. "Consider, the most humble Easter daisy is more seductive than the proudest and most brilliant of the roses which in the spring-time attract us with their penetrating perfumes and vivid colors. Moreover" added he, "I do you justice; you have kept so strictly within the line of duty laid down by the law, that in order to show you in what respect you have failed in relation to me, it would be necessary for me to enter into details which would offend your dignity, and to teach you certain things which would seem to you to be the subversion of all morality."

"You dare to talk of morality, when you have just left a house in which you have squandered the fortune of your children—in a place of debauchery!"

"Madame, there I stop you," said the count coolly, interrupting his wife. "If Mademoiselle de Bellefeuille is rich, she is not rich at any one's expense. My uncle was the master of his fortune, he had several heirs, but in his lifetime, and out of pure friendship for her whom he regarded as his niece, he gave her the estate of Bellefeuille. As for the rest, I owe it to his liberality."

"That conduct is worthy of such a Jacobin," said the countess.

"Madame, you forget that your father was one of those Jacobins whom you, as a wife, condemn with so little charity," said the count severely. "Citizen Bontems was signing death-warrants, while my uncle was rendering only services to France."

Madame de Granville was silent, but as the recollection of what she had just seen aroused that jealousy which nothing can extinguish in the heart of a woman, she said in a low voice, as if speaking to herself, "Is it possible thus to destroy one's own soul, and that of others?"

"Ah, madame," resumed the count, fatigued with this conversation, "perhaps it is you who will some day have to answer for all this." (At this phrase the countess trembled.) "In the eyes of the indulgent Judge who will weigh our offences, you will doubtless be excused on account of the good faith with which you have wrought my misery. I do not hate *you;* I do hate the persons who have perverted your head and your heart. You have prayed for me, just as Mademoiselle de Bellefeuille has given me her heart, and poured out on me the treasures of her love. You should have been in turn, my mistress and a saint praying at the foot of the altar. Do me the justice to admit that I am neither wicked nor depraved. My morals are pure. Alas, at the end of seven years of suffering, the want of happiness has led me by imperceptible degrees to love another woman than you, and to create another family than mine. Don't suppose, however, that I stand alone; there are in this city thousands of husbands who have all been led by divers causes to this double life."

"Great God," cried the countess, "how heavy is my cross become. If the husband whom, in Thine anger, Thou hast imposed upon me, cannot find happiness here below save by my death, recall me to Thy bosom."

"Had you always been actuated by such admirable sentiments, and such self-sacrifice, we should still have been happy," said the count coldly.

"Ah, well," said Angélique, bursting into a flood of tears, "forgive me, if I have committed faults. Yes, sir, I am ready to obey you in all things, feeling sure that you will ask only what is just and natural. I will be henceforth all that you would wish a wife to be."

"Madame, if your object be to lead me to say that I no longer love you, I shall have the ruthless courage to enlighten you. Can I command my heart? Can I in one instant efface the memory of fifteen years of misery? *I have ceased to love.* Those words enshroud a mystery as deep as that contained in the words *I love.* Esteem, consideration, regard, may be won, may be lost, and be regained; but as for love, if I lectured myself for a thousand years, I could not cause it to grow again, especially for a woman who has tried to make herself old."

"Ah, Monsieur le Comte, I most sincerely hope that those words may not some day be uttered to you in that tone, and with that accent, by her whom you love."

"Will you put on a dress *à la Grecque,* and come to the opera with me this evening?"

The shudder which this question at once caused the countess was an unspoken reply.

————————

In the early part of the month of December, 1833, a man whose snow-white hair and the general appearance of whose face seemed to show that grief rather than years had aged him, was passing at midnight through the Rue de Gaillon. When he had got as far as a mean-looking house two storeys high, he stopped to look at one of the attic windows which at regular intervals pierced the middle of the roof. This humble window, some of whose panes had been replaced by paper, was very dimly illuminated. The passenger was looking at the flickering light with the indefinable curiosity of the Parisian idler, when a young man suddenly came out of the house. As the pale rays of the street lamp fell upon the face of the inquisitive loiterer, it will not seem surprising that, though it was in the night-time, the young man advanced towards the passenger with the hesitation which a Parisian displays when he fears he may be mistaken in supposing that he is meeting an acquaintance.

"What," cried he, "you, Monsieur le President, alone and on foot at this hour, and so far from the Rue St. Lazre ? Allow me to have the honor of offering you my arm. The pavement this morning is so slippery, that if we do not support one another " (this he said in order not to offend the old man's self-esteem) "it will be very difficult to avoid a fall."

"But my dear sir, unhappily for me, I am as yet only fifty-five years of age," replied the Comte de Granville. " A doctor so celebrated as you are, ought to know that at that time of life a man retains all his strength ?"

"Then you must have a little love affair on hand ; you are not, I fancy, in the habit of going about Paris on foot. When a man has such splendid horses as yours . . . ."

" Why, unless I go out in the evening," interrupted the Comte de Granville, " I generally return from the Palais Royal or from the Strangers' Club on foot."

" Having large sums of money, about you, no doubt," said the doctor. " Isn't that inviting the assassin's dagger ?"

" I am not afraid of *them*," said the Comte de Granville with careless sadness.

" But at all events it is wrong to stand still," resumed the doctor, dragging the magistrate towards the boulevard. " I shall soon begin to think that you want to rob me of your last illness, and to die by another hand than mine."

" Ah, you have caught me playing the spy," replied the count. " Whether I pass on foot or in a carriage, and whatever the hour of night may be, I have for some time past seen the shadow of a person,—who seems to be working with heroic courage—cast upon the window of the third storey of the house which you have just left." Here the count frowned as if he had felt a sudden pang. " I have begun to take as much interest in that attic, as a citizen of Paris can possibly feel in the completion of the Palais Royal."

" Well," cried Horace quickly, interrupting the count, " I can tell you . . . ."

" Tell me nothing," replied Granville, cutting the doctor short, " I would not give a single centime to learn whether the shadow that trembles on those tattered curtains, be that of a man or that of a woman, and whether the occupant of the garret be happy or miserable. If it surprised me to see no one working there to-night, and if I stopped, it was simply for the pleasure of forming conjectures as numerous and silly as idlers form at sight of a building suddenly abandoned. For the last nine years my young—" Here the count hesitated to employ some expression ; then with a gesture continued— " No, I will not call you my friend, I hate everything which resembles a sentiment. In the last nine years, then, I have ceased to wonder at the pleasure which old men find in culti

vating flowers and planting trees. The events of life have
taught me no longer to put any faith in human affections, and
I grew old in a few days. I want to sever myself from everything, save unreasoning animals, plants, and the mere externals
of life. I attach more importance to the movements of Tagli-
oni than to all human sentiments put together. I hate life;
I hate the world in which I find myself alone. Nothing,
nothing," added the count with an expression which made the
young man shudder, "no, *nothing* moves, *nothing* interests
me."

"But you have children ?"

"My children!" he resumed in a peculiarly bitter tone.
"Well, as to my children, there is the eldest of my daughters,
is she not Comtesse de Vaudenesse? As for the second, her
sister's marriage will be the means of securing her a good match.
As for my two sons, have they not met with very great success?
The vicomte, after being attorney-general at Limoges, has been
made first president at Orleans, and my younger son is here as
the king's attorney. My children have cares, anxieties, and
business of their own. If one among them had entirely devoted herself or himself to me, and tried to fill with affection the
void which I feel *there*," said he striking his bosom; "well,
that child's life would have been a failure, would have been
sacrificed to me. And after all, to what purpose? To embellish my few remaining years. Would he have succeeded?
Should I not perhaps have looked upon his generous attentions
as a debt? But, doctor" (here the old man began to smile
with profound irony), "doctor, it is not for nothing that we
teach our children arithmetic; they know how to calculate.
Perhaps at this very moment my children are on the look out
for my fortune."

"Oh, Monsieur le Comte, how could such an idea occur to
you who are so good, so obliging and so humane? Truly if I
were not myself a living proof of that benevolence which you
conceive in all its breadth and beauty. . . ."

"For my pleasure," quickly interposed the count. I pray for a sensation as I would to-morrow give a heap of gold for the most puerile illusion which would stir my heart. I help my fellow creatures, just as I gamble—for my own sake. Thus, I do not count upon the gratitude of any one. I could without a sign of grief see you yourself die, and I require you to feel towards me as I feel towards you. Ah, young man, the events of life have passed over my heart as the lava of Vesuvius over Herculaneum; the city exists, but it is dead."

"Those who have reduced to such a state of insensibility, a heart so warm and susceptible as yours was, are highly culpable."

"Don't add another word," said the count with a feeling of horror.

"You have a disease which you should allow me to cure," said Bianchon, in a voice of deep emotion.

"Do you know any remedy for death?" cried the count impatiently.

"Well, Monsieur le Comte, I undertake to reanimate the heart which you think so dead."

"Are you equal to Talma?" asked the chief president ironically.

"No, Monsieur le Comte, but nature is as superior to Talma as Talma is to me. Listen; the denizen of the garret in which you take an interest is a woman of thirty; with her, love reaches fanaticism. The object of her worship is a young man with a handsome face, but endowed by some wicked fairy with every possible vice. The youth is a gambler, and I do not know which he likes best, women or wine; he has been guilty, to my certain knowledge, of actions which ought to bring him under the notice of the correctional police. Well, this unfortunate woman has sacrificed for his sake a very prosperous existence, a man who adored her and by whom she has children. But what is the matter, Monsieur le Comte?"

"Nothing—go on."

"She has allowed him to squander a complete fortune, she would give him the world, I believe, if she had it; she works day and night, and she has often without one murmur seen the monster she adores rob her of the money which was intended to pay for the clothes which her children lacked, and even the morrow's food. Three days ago she sold her hair—the most beautiful hair I ever saw; he came in before she had time to hide the piece of gold; he asked her for it, and—for a smile— for a kiss—she surrendered what would have secured them food and tranquility for a fortnight. Is it not at once horrible and sublime? But work is beginning to hollow her cheeks. The cries of her children have rent her heart; she has fallen ill, she now lies moaning on a truckle bed. This evening she had nothing to eat, and her children were too weak to cry; they were quiet when I went in."

Horace Bianchon stopped. The Comte de Granville had, as if in spite of himself, plunged his hand into his waistcoat-pocket.

"I understand, my young friend, how she manages still to exist, if she is under your care."

"Ah, poor creature!" cried the doctor, "*who* would not render her aid? I wish I were richer, for I hope to cure her of her love."

The count, who, unobserved by the doctor, had put his hand into his pocket, now withdrew it full of notes which he appeared to have been searching for there.

"But," replied he, "how can you expect me to sympathize with suffering, the pleasures of which would seem to me to be cheaply purchased with my whole fortune. This woman feels; she lives. Would not Louis Quinze have given his whole realm to have risen from his coffin, and have three years of youth and life? Is not that the history of millions of dead folks, of millions of invalids, of millions of old men?"

"Poor Caroline!" cried the doctor.

When he heard that name, the Comte de Granville trembled,

and seized the arm of the doctor, who felt as if he were in the grasp of the iron lips of a vice.

" Is her name Caroline Crochard ? " asked the president in a voice that betokened deep emotion.

" You know her, then ? " asked the doctor in astonishment.

" And the wretch's name is Solvet. Ah, you have kept your word," cried the first president; "you have excited in my heart the most terrible sensation which it will experience till it turns to dust. This emotion is yet another gift of hell, and I always know how to pay such debts."

At this moment the count and the doctor had reached the corner of the Rue de la Chaussée d'Antin. One of those children of the night who go about with a wicker basket on their backs, and a hook in their hands, and were therefore during the revolutionary epoch wittily called, "members of the committee of researches," was standing near the post before which the president had just stopped. The rag-gatherer had an old face worthy of those which Charlet has immortalized in his caricatures of the scavenger school.

" Do you often find thousand franc notes ? " inquired the count.

" Sometimes, master."

" And do you give them up ? "

" That depends upon the reward that is offered."

" There, my man," said the count, presenting the rag-gatherer with a thousand franc note. " Take that," said he, " but bear in mind that I give it you on condition that you spend it in the public-house, that you get drunk there, fight, beat your wife, and knock your friends' eyes out. That will make work for the watchmen, the surgeons, the apothecaries, perhaps for the gendarmes, the king's attorneys, the judges, and the jailers. Stick to that programme, or the devil will sooner or later have it out with you."

To do justice to this nocturnal scene a man would need the

pencils of Charlet and Callot, and the brushes of Teniers and Rembrandt.

"Now my account with hell is settled, and I have had some pleasure for my money," said the count, in a deep voice, as he pointed out to the astounded doctor the indescribable face of the gaping rag-gatherer.

"As for Caroline Crochard, she may die in all the horrors of hunger and thirst, with the heart-rending cries of her children in her ears, and in her heart the full conviction of the baseness of the man she loves. I would not give one farthing to hinder her from suffering, and for the single reason that you have given her help, I hope that I may never see you more—"

Leaving Bianchon more motionless than a statue, the count disappeared in the direction of the Rue St. Lazare, with all the speed of youth. He very soon reached the door of the little hotel which he occupied. Somewhat to his surprise, a carriage was waiting at the door.

"Monsieur le Procureur du roi came here an hour since to speak to you, sir, and is waiting in your bed-room," said the valet to his master.

Granville motioned his servant away.

"What important motive compels you to infringe the order I gave my children not to come to my house unless I send for them?" said the old man, as he entered the room where his son was.

"Father," replied the young man, in a trembling voice, and with a respectful air, "I venture to hope that you will forgive me when you have heard me."

"That is a very proper answer," said the count. "Sit down. But whether I walk about or remain seated, take no notice of me."

"Father," resumed the baron, "this afternoon at four o'clock, a young man who was arrested in the house of one of my friends, from whom he had stolen a considerable sum, referred us to you. He says he is your son."

"What is his name?" said the count, trembling.

"Charles Crochard."

"Enough," said the father, with a gesture of command.

Thereupon Granville began to pace up and down the room amid profound silence, which his son was careful not to interrupt.

"My son" (these words were uttered in a voice so gentle and so paternal, that the young man trembled with emotion), "Charles Crochard has told you the truth. I am glad you came this evening, my good Eugène," added the old man. "Here is a considerable sum of money," said he, producing a pile of bank-notes; "you will employ it in this matter as you think best. I trust to you and approve beforehand of all your arrangements, whether for the present or the future. Eugène, my dear boy, come and embrace me; this is perhaps the last time we shall see each other. To-morrow I shall ask the king for leave of absence, and shall start for Italy. If a father is not bound to account to his children for his life, he is bound to bequeath them the experience fate has sold him; is it not a part of the inheritance? When you marry," resumed the count, with an involuntary shudder, "do not lightly enter into that solemn engagement, the most important of all those which society forces upon us. Remember to study for a long time the disposition of the woman with whom you are about to associate yourself; but consult me; I should like to form my own opinion about her. The want of union between husband and wife, no matter whence it springs, brings dreadful misery in its train; we are, sooner or later, punished for not obeying the laws of society. I will write to you from Florence upon this subject. A father, especially if he has the honor of being president of a supreme court, ought not to have to blush before his son. Good-bye."

THE END.

www.ingramcontent.com/pod-product-compliance
Lightning Source LLC
Chambersburg PA
CBHW030923050726
47498CB00003BA/878